RASHAD

RASHAD

VIKES, MIKES, AND SOMETHING ON THE BACKSIDE

AHMAD RASHAD

WITH PETER BODO

VIKING

VIKING
Published by the Penguin Group
Viking Penguin Inc., 40 West 23rd Street,
New York, New York 10010, U.S.A.
Penguin Books Ltd, 27 Wrights Lane,
London W8 5TZ, England
Penguin Books Australia Ltd, Ringwood,
Victoria, Australia
Penguin Books Canada Ltd, 2801 John Street,
Markham, Ontario, Canada L3R 1B4
Penguin Books (N.Z.) Ltd, 182–190 Wairau Road,
Auckland 10, New Zealand

Penguin Books Ltd, Registered Offices:
Harmondsworth, Middlesex, England

First published in 1988 by Viking Penguin Inc.
Published simultaneously in Canada

1 3 5 7 9 10 8 6 4 2

All photographs, unless otherwise credited, are from
the author's collection.

Library of Congress Cataloging in Publication Data
Rashad, Ahmad
Rashad: Vikes, mikes, and something on the backside.
1. Rashad, Ahmad.   2. Football players—United
States—Biography.   I. Bodo, Peter.   II. Title.
GV939.R36A3   1988   796.33'2'0924   [B]   88-40103
ISBN 0-670-82301-5

Printed in the United States of America by
Arcata Graphics, Fairfield, Pennsylvania
Set in Primer
Designed by Victoria Hartman

To a strong lady whose inner peace gave me confidence when I had none, who gave me the strength to survive, and who also showed me that with these attributes there is joy and peace in life—my mother, Condola Moore

—A. R.

For Crocker Nevin, the longest-suffering Jets fan of them all

—P. B.

CONTENTS

RASHAD

1

THE SHIP IS SAILING

I've spent most of my life working on Sunday mornings, and I'm not even a man of the cloth. That's what I was thinking as I drove down the Henry Hudson Parkway from my home in Mount Vernon, on my way to the NBC studio in Rockefeller Center, at nine in the morning. Every Sunday morning during the National Football League season we broadcast our show, "NFL Live," from New York. It's a wraparound show, meaning we're in the studio all day, watching games and providing scores, updates, and commentary to the network and various affiliates around the country. It's a job that any football freak might envy, but just try watching eight monitors showing eight different games simultaneously. You might love it, or it just might flip you out.

The Palisades reared up out of the Hudson, on the New Jersey side, still green. But that's a relative value when you come from the Pacific Northwest. I grew up in Tacoma, Washington, and in that part of the country, green is a deep, dark, damp color. Eastern green doesn't have the same punch. There was nobody on the road; the speedometer edged up to 90 mph. I drive to work every Sunday morning. I've always loved cars, and the trip gives me a chance to blow some carbon out of my engine and the cobwebs out of my brain.

The sky was bright blue. It was late October 1987 in New York, and except for the balmy temperature, it might have been a typical football morning in Minnesota, where I spent my seven best years playing for the Vikings. I loved Minnesota and still keep my house there. Fate is funny—when I was traded to the Vikings by Seattle, I probably couldn't have found the state if I had a map in front of my nose.

The night before home games in Minnesota, I used to go to bed praying that the temperature would be at least 20 degrees Fahrenheit at kickoff. Our head coach, Bud Grant, wouldn't allow us to wear long johns, and we were into the Ice Age part of the season before they passed out the turtlenecks. It almost made me happy now to be heading for eight hours of climate control.

Last night, I laid out the shirt and tie I would wear. But in the morning, it was still different from walking into the locker room and seeing my jersey hanging there, all nice and clean, ready to go, with my helmet on the wooden stool in front of my cubicle.

I can change my mind and pick a different tie on the morning of a broadcast, although I wouldn't think of wearing the same pair of socks like I did for five or six years at Minnesota. I wore a brand-new pair of undersocks and new shoes for every game with the Vikings, but I wore the same pair of outer socks, until they had so many holes that they just about fell off my feet.

The big difference these days is that after getting dressed for work, I go downstairs and have breakfast with my wife, Phylicia, and my daughter, Condola Phylea, who's nine months old. Phylicia puts in long days at work, playing the role of Clare Huxtable, Bill Cosby's wife, on "The Cosby Show." But she still likes to get up early on Sunday mornings to fix breakfast for the three of us.

Breakfast isn't just some quick toast-and-coffee deal either, with Mama wandering around in a robe, slamming stuff down.

Phylicia makes eggs and grits, smoked turkey, our favorite exotic teas. It's a real major-league breakfast. The ritual is a highlight of our week, a chance for a busy family to spend some time together.

Phylicia and I never talk football on Sunday mornings. But if this were still my playing days, the team would be holed up in the Registry Hotel in Minneapolis before a home game. I'd go down for breakfast after a shower, in my sweats. Week in, week out, season after season, I sat at the same table, in the same chair, for the team meal on game mornings. It wasn't Phylicia but Bud Grant, a fanatic for routine, presiding over our meal. Every Sunday, we had steak, scrambled eggs, and a roll with some honey and a pat of butter—not three, not two, but *one* pat of butter.

I sat at a veterans' table with a bunch of the Viking elite: Carl Eller, Jim Marshall, Alan Page, and Bobby Bryant among them. We'd spend most of breakfast joking around. If we were playing the Chicago Bears, the defensive linemen would bear the brunt. "Oh, man," one of us would say, "Walter Payton's gonna run all over your ass today." If we were playing the Oakland Raiders, I might be the target, because they had real fine cornerbacks in Willie Brown and Skip Thomas and Lester Hayes.

The humor got silly, but silly was funny. Invariably, somebody would make a joke about how cold it was. That was Alan Page's cue to ask us if we'd heard the weather forecast. We knew our lines; we'd answer "No." Then Alan would say, "The forecast is, hot today, but chili tamale." In my first year with the Vikings, the atmosphere threw me. Here were all these legendary guys I'd read about, the Purple People Eaters, telling the goofiest jokes and laughing like little kids.

Finally, Alan Page would dip an index finger into his water glass and rub it around the rim to make an annoying squeak. That was the signal for Bud Grant to give his speech so we could leave the room. Bud liked to eat like he did everything else—slowly. And he wasn't fiery, or even very verbal. Most of the time, Bud just reminded us that we had a game to play in three hours, and that he didn't want any of us to get to the stadium before 11 a.m.

In the next hour or two, we'd go room hopping, on social calls. Some of the guys, at one point or another, stopped at the room of one of the veterans. There, each player would pick up the Bible and appear to read some Scripture. Then he'd close the Good Book.

I thought the ritual was a touching tribute to the God-fearing, Christian character of the Vikings. Then one day my curiosity got the better of me. I picked up that Bible and found a cavity in the Good Book filled with "bennies," or "beans"—Benzedrine, the powerful amphetamine that was the stimulant of choice in those days.

I liked to get to the stadium early on game days. I was never a fanatical football player, but in a very quiet way I was a perfectionist. One of the ways to recognize the type is that he—or she—appears oblivious to criticism. Sometimes the perfectionist comes off as arrogant, or indifferent to the rules others try to impose on him. It's only because nobody is harder on the perfectionist than he is on himself. If he ignores the rules of others, it's only because he has a strong sense of personal standards. The perfectionist might forget that he's supposed to wear a beanie with a propeller on top to a team meeting, but he doesn't get caught holding to kill a crucial drive, either. And he never forgets that he has to do everything in his power to ensure the conditions that make him perform best.

So I would sneak out and get to the stadium early, and I'm going to make a confession that I hope Bud Grant won't hold against me: I used to get there early just so I could sneak a pair of long johns on under my uniform.

Past the George Washington Bridge, I hit the West Side Highway. (Thanks, Mayor Koch, for repaving that road in 1986.) I pushed the accelerator and the needle edged toward triple digits. What the hell—there was nobody else on the road, and my Porsche was made to run. I considered it my reward for being up and at 'em so early.

Columbia University flew by, then all of Morningside Heights and Riverside Park. I was doing 130, and the car was rock steady. The skyline of midtown Manhattan rose like a defensive line— the famous Seven Blocks of Granite, or, in this case, concrete and steel. I broke 140 and backed off, afraid I might overshoot my exit and end up landing on Staten Island. I caught the West Fifty-seventh Street exit and parked in a garage at Rockefeller Center. The car was warm as a baked potato, and the engine ticked softly as I walked away from the Porsche and straightened up my tie.

I was the first member of the cast in Studio 6-A, just like I'd always been the first in the locker room. There are no pictures of quarterbacks or defensive ends in the halls leading to the studio—it's Johnny Carson, not Harry Carson, along with David Letterman, Frank Sinatra, Steve Allen, and some tributes to old shows like Kay Kyser's "Kollege of Musical Knowledge" and "Juvenile Jury" with Jack Barry.

By the time the rest of the cast and crew drifted in, I'd written out most of the comments I was going to make when the show went to my weekly feature. The big story of the week was the end of the strike, and my feature was about the Washington Redskins, whose "replacement" team had won all three of their games. None of the Realskins, the Washington regulars, had crossed the picket line during the strike, so they weren't plagued by any problems of resentment or disunity when the strike was settled. They were sitting pretty with a 4–1 record.

I had mixed feelings about the strike in general, sentiments that were related to my most fundamental feelings about the game of pro football. If anything good came out of the failed strike, it was this: the regular players had to realize that they were dispensable. The game always went on, with or without you. It was fall; people wanted to see football. The replacement teams didn't have weird logos on their helmets and play in May, like they had in the defunct United States Football League. Striking players might have found it hard to swallow; but in football, the beat goes on.

It's a hard, cruel lesson to learn when all your life coaches drill into you the importance of laying life and limb on the line for the team, when you've basked in the adulation of fans and press, when you've had all of the girls, and all of the people pointing at you and whispering when you walked through some shopping mall. All of that amounts to a king-sized inoculation against the realities of life.

For a football player, those realities can be brutal. That's why it's so important—and so damned hard—to realize that you're just playing a game. Almost every coach in football has a hidden agenda, to convince you that football is your life. But the smartest and luckiest guys are the ones who realize all along that football is just *part* of their lives.

Football may be the most thrilling, agonizing, inspiring, and demanding job you'll ever have, but it has to be part of a larger picture unless your sole ambition is to go into coaching when your playing days are done. One of the toughest realizations for a football player to accept is that his future is in his own hands. It's easy to fumble when you don't know what you're holding.

I was never the type to take the football home and sleep with it just because the coach told me to do it. Back when I played Midget League football, coaches would tell us to run at a certain hole, but I always ran for the daylight instead. I often caught heat about that, because most coaches want you to be putty in their hands, so they can mold their own vision of the game out of you. You're under pressure to hit that hole because if you don't, you're somehow less of a man. Coaches get so caught up in that mentality that they sometimes lose sight of the basic goal, which is to score a touchdown, to win a game. I've seen it happen a thousand times, even at the professional level.

The best description I've ever heard of the situation for most football players was a simple phrase used by Jerry Burns, the current head coach at Minnesota. Burnsie was the offensive coordinator when I was with the Vikings, and he always used to say: "The ship is sailing. It doesn't matter who you are—if you miss the boat, it goes without you." It's hard to believe that when you're rushing at a one-hundred-yards-per-game clip or throwing two touchdown passes per game. But it applies to every single person on a team.

The proof is in the pudding when a guy gets cut. One day he's there, and the next his locker is empty, or there's a new guy sticking his shaving cream, Mars bars, and Ben Gay on the shelf. It's eerie—if you're cut on Monday, you don't even show up in the game films on Tuesday. I mean, you're gone *the very next day.*

The reality of the situation is just as brutal for the stars as it is for the journeymen, even though the stars usually have more money to soften the blow. When Fran Tarkenton injured his ankle pretty badly one year, he was history as soon as they put the cast on his leg. His name never came up again until he was healthy. The ship sailed.

During the strike, you heard the word "career" bandied around a lot. It's a crazy word to describe the NFL player, because the average player lasts for under four years. I was lucky, a bunch of other guys are lucky; but for the typical pro prospect, the truth is tough to swallow: pro football is not a career. It is a temporary income opportunity.

I was a Viking during the last major strike in 1982, and I found myself in a delicate situation—namely, I was having a great time. In addition to playing football, I was a vice-president of public relations for Jeno's, a pizza company that was doing $250 million a year in business, and I was working for WCCO, a local Minnesota television station. I was only taking about $75,000 per year out of my football salary, which was up around $200,000. I was pretty well set up. During the strike, I went out and bought a brand-new Ferrari.

When I hear the word "strike," I think of coal miners fighting to improve income opportunities in a career that lasts some twenty or thirty years. But for an NFL player, every paycheck lost is irreplaceable income, and the vast majority of the guys will never be eligible for that kind of money again.

It was also a mistake to make free agency such a big issue, when the players could have focused on guaranteed contracts.

Free agency may give the best players greater financial opportunities and control over where they live and play, but guaranteed contracts are a step toward greater basic security.

But the most important thing is for a player to have options, not to turn himself over body and soul to the game of football. I'd always noticed the old-timers hobbling away and I would think, "Wow, I remember watching that guy, he was a star. And now here he is, hanging on by a hair, fighting for his job, fighting for his life."

The smartest guys in football are like those second-string linemen who used to sit around the Minnesota locker room studying their med school textbooks before big games. They were in a world of their own, so much so that the regulars hardly even bothered with them. Those guys had direction, they had purpose. Other guys would be punching lockers or just sitting there working up a hate, and these big beefy guys with faces like cherubs would be working up a good score on some midterm.

There's a big advantage to having options: the coaches tend to know your situation, and they treat you differently. You're not putty in their hands anymore. Doing something besides playing the game gives you leverage—if you play well enough.

The only guys who ever really want to quit football are the disenchanted players, or the ones who are frustrated by journeyman status or crippling injury. To quit football is to quit on the kid in you—that's how you feel. The game continues something that most players began to do, to live for, from a very early age. When you can't play anymore, you're letting go of an activity and a way of life that nothing will ever replace. Your reaction to that stark truth sets the tone for the rest of your life.

I didn't find it too tough to quit football, mostly because I'd always maintained other interests and seen the handwriting on the wall from a pretty early age. The prospect of change didn't scare me; it got me excited. That was partly because of my background.

As a kid growing up in the projects of Tacoma, Washington, I spent a lot of time in neighborhoods that weren't my own. I enjoyed mixing with all different kinds of people. And from about the ages of six to twelve, I had a skin disease that the best doctors couldn't cure or even diagnose. That turned me inward and taught me some harsh truths about self-reliance—along with some comforting truths about the joy and beauty you can find within yourself.

My disease and my early training in the Pentecostal Church helped foster a sense of spirituality in me. I played collegiate ball at Oregon in the late 1960s, when the headlines were filled with news of Vietnam, flower children, Black Panthers, Richard Nixon, the guru Maharaji, LSD, and riots in Newark, Watts, and Detroit. Everybody, it seemed, was dancing in the streets or setting them on fire. Every American institution was under attack, and football was no exception. If you were at all sensitive, you did a lot of soul searching during those years.

My own inner quest resulted in my conversion to Islam, and changing my name from Bobby Moore to Ahmad Rashad. I was in my second year as a professional at the time, playing for the St. Louis Cardinals—a franchise with a reputation for conservatism and bigotry. I bucked the system and challenged the Cardinal mentality, and it almost broke me. I could just as easily have quit football when the Cardinals finally traded me to Buffalo. But those two years in St. Louis were vital to my education in the limitations of football as a profession.

I sense that some people see me as a "celebrity," a retired football player who's living off his name. Oh yeah, Rashad—that guy who married the famous actress and got himself a nice cozy little seat to the left of Bob Costas on the "NFL Live" show. The rap doesn't get to me emotionally as much as it does professionally. Few people know that I'd been in broadcasting for years before I joined NBC, that I quit football as a career move when I was lucky enough to have the major networks bidding for my services.

Sometimes you come to a decision slowly, hardly even aware

that your mind is working over some problem until one day the
last piece fits into place and you come to a realization about
yourself or your work. At other times, it all happens in a flash.
My decision to leave football for broadcasting was partly slow
realization, partly thunderbolt.

During the fifth week of the '82 season, I announced my
retirement. Two weeks later, in a game against the Detroit Lions,
my decision was sealed for good by a couple of defensive backs.
The Lions always played rough football, but we pretty much
had their number. That time the game was close. In the second
half, I was called on to run a simple down-and-in pattern, where
I cut across the middle.

I was wide open as I made my cut; every fiber in my body
was screaming, "Throw the ball, throw it now." But our quarterback, Tommy Kramer, didn't throw it right away; he held it
a little too long. By the time he let the pass go, traffic was getting
heavy around me, and every fiber in my body was screaming,
"*Don't* throw it, don't throw the ball."

The pass was thrown too high, and it was sailing with no zip
on it. Everybody and his brother was going to have time to get
under it. The message flashed through my mind—"Don't go for
the ball, don't risk it." In the back of my mind I knew I was
quitting soon, and I was a little skittish. For all of my ups and
downs through eleven years in the NFL, I'd been lucky about
one thing: I'd never suffered a serious injury. Staying healthy
was a major priority for me in that last year.

But the football player in me took over. I thought, "Shit, I'm
going to climb the ladder for this one—I'm going to make a great
catch on these mothers." So up I went, and as soon as I touched
the ball, James Hunter hit me flat out in the chest. Then, *oomph!*
Alvin Hall speared me from behind—got me right in the small
of my back.

Everything went blank.

When I came around, I couldn't feel anything in my legs or
my toes. "Oh, man," I thought. "I'm paralyzed for life. I'll never
walk again."

There I was, a four-time All-Pro and a Super Bowl veteran who thought he could do it all just one more time. It's a story as old as the hills. I was vain. I was arrogant. And it was going to cost me the rest of my life. Out of the corner of my eye, I saw Hunter and Hall dancing and high-fiving and all that. I knew that too was part of the game.

Ultimately, they took me to this X-ray room behind one end zone. The doctor laid me out to take his pictures, and I heard this great roar from the stadium. The Lions must've scored. I opened my eyes and the doctor wasn't around. He'd snuck over to the door leading to the field and was craning his neck, trying to get a glimpse of the field. I guess the Hippocratic oath this guy took had some fine print about NFL Sundays.

The X-rays confirmed that I had broken some bones in my back. I was really hurting, and I made the doctor give me some painkillers. The game was close, almost over. All the staff was stacked up by the door, jockeying for the best view. The Vikings had a game to win out there. The ship was sailing, and I realized that I wasn't aboard.

Like most players, I always saw myself going out in a burst of glory, making five or six touchdown catches without hardly getting a grass stain on my uniform. It's always the other guys who hobble out.

The painkillers I'd been given hit me, and I pulled myself off the examination table and slowly headed for the Viking locker room. I don't think anybody noticed.

Suddenly, the level of commitment that the major networks were asking of me as a broadcaster became appealing. I was becoming more and more of a broadcaster by the minute. By the time I reached the locker room, my thoughts were far from the fate that the mighty Vikings were wrestling with on the field of the Silverdome.

Their ship was sailing one way, mine another.

By the time cast and crew arrived and we went through some of the fundamentals for the broadcast, it was about 11:30 a.m.

Jimmy Cefalo, who had a good career at Penn State and with the Miami Dolphins, was with us for the show. We were sitting around throwing the bull in the closest thing you'll find to a locker room on a studio set—the makeup room. The irony wasn't lost on me.

In Minnesota, the only guy who was in the locker room when I arrived was our equipment manager, Stubby Eason. Talk about a guy from Central Casting—Stubby was an old guy with a wooden leg, and he'd told me about thirty different stories about how he'd lost that pin in the Second World War. He had a low, gravelly voice, and the most sophisticated he got was to mumble, "God damn it now, just go out and kick somebody's ass."

Stubby held my gum during games. I was a gum addict, going through at least six packs of gum per game, so Stubby's pockets were always bulging. I'd spit the juice on my hands while the gum was sugary and sticky—that was my version of stickum. So we had this routine where I'd always be going, "Stubby, where's Stubby? Hey, Stubby, I need some gum." And Stubby would come hobbling over, muttering and cursing like an old sailor about the other team.

I often miss the sense of control I had in football, especially in my later years. In football, I used to feel that in order for us to win, I would have to do something, make a big play. That was just fine with me, because I always wanted the ball in a critical situation. I wasn't afraid to fail, because there was one thing worse than that—being afraid to try.

I was the catalyst in the locker room. I was always a loose guy, so I enjoyed working on certain individuals, or on certain moods, like a conductor trying to get the right sound out of an orchestra. But a football team probably is even more tightly knit than an orchestra. The fact that you live together during training camp and on the road is one part of it. Another part is the shared pain and injury. Those things build empathy and sympathy, no matter how well or badly the basic personalities mesh. The closeness you find in a locker room is unlike anything else I've ever experienced. I'll probably never know it again, and I'll miss it forever.

You could talk to teammates like you would never talk to other guys at an office. Locker-room talk is full of posturing and bragging. It might sound like so much macho baloney, but then Greek must sound like so much yapping if you've never spoken that language. The thing is, football has its own language, and if you don't speak it you're in trouble.

We had a backup quarterback at St. Louis called Gary Cuozzo. He was a nice, clean-cut guy with a nice, clean-cut mouth—he just wouldn't curse. In the huddle in the middle of a tight game he'd say something like, "Okay, guys, we're going to take that moneymaking ball and ram it down their barking throats." A couple of guys would exchange glances or mutter, "What the fuck is he talking about?" The feeling was like, I don't want to get down into the trenches with this guy. He isn't one of us, he doesn't even talk our language.

I was working a game in Minnesota a few years ago for NBC, so I spent a lot of time in the locker room. Then I had to step out and deliver this live television segment, talking about the game. After we did the spot, backup quarterback Steve Dils came over to me and said, "I've never seen anybody who can talk jive and locker-room stuff one minute and then step out and use normal English on a moment's notice. It's like you're bilingual."

The differences between football and television don't end there, either. It's funny to see these big tough guys who've played in the NFL walking around wearing makeup. Maybe the guys who used to put black grease under their eyes to help cut down on the glare of the sun deal with it better, but I doubt it.

Whenever I watch a studio show, I'm amazed by how bright and warm and cozy the place looks. Seeing it on TV, you get the impression that the studio is a glamorous place, on a par with some trendy restaurant or plush corporate office. But when you push back the twin metal doors leading into Studio 6-A, you find something very different.

It's almost always freezing in Studio 6-A. The David Letterman show is shot in the same studio, so his stage sets are all there, pushed back in the darkness. The false windows and rinky-dink skyline used behind Letterman are shoved up against the far wall, where they don't fool anybody. The drum kit looms in one corner like a Disney castle. A few portable walls, some of them containing monitors, are pushed together to form the backdrop for the "NFL Live" show. The long, angular desk where we sit is on a rolling platform covered with bright red carpet. If you peeked behind the desk, you'd see all of these makeshift stands and tables made out of raw wood. And miles of wires, all coiled up and plugged into different consoles and boxes with blinking lights.

The real mark of a studio is the overhead lighting. The entire ceiling of Studio 6-A is covered with those show-biz lights that look like satellites. They can be aimed any which way, moved on tracks, tilted to all different angles. Some of them have red bulbs to give the lighting a warm tone. The key to appealing television is lighting. With good lighting, you can get away with almost anything.

I'm used to the conditions now, but the unreality of it all is still striking. When you spend a few hours on a set, you feel cut off from the rest of the world. The air gets stale and smoky. You get wired on coffee; your eyes are strained by the sharp contrast between the darkness and the bright lights tightly focused on the set. Eventually, you lose your sense of location. You become an astronaut of the airwaves. The person with the strongest sense of *your* reality is some guy sitting in front of the tube in Dayton, Ohio. It's a lot different from being outside on a fall Sunday morning, when you can see your breath and smell the wood smoke—or when you get rammed into the turf for a loss, and your helmet fills up with the smell of grass and damp earth.

We were getting ready to roll. Bob Costas, center stage, was moving his shoulders like a football player whose pads don't fit quite right. Cefalo and I were in our places, to the right and left of Bob respectively, arguing about some details for our upcoming Rotisserie League draft.

There's an awful lot of dead time with a wraparound show like ours. It can be a killer for an athlete, who's used to a more intense drill, bringing total concentration to his job over very limited periods of time. Basically, we do our major half-hour "NFL Live" show at 12:30 p.m. EST, which leads us into the kickoff of the East Coast games. Then we sit back and watch any of six or eight games on the monitors, until halftime of the early games, when we do updates, highlights, and some commentary. Then there's a wrap-up show after the early games, right before the four o'clock games start. Usually, we wrap things up with a halftime show for the late games. That's four substantial segments, along with updates delivered like news bulletins as they end.

Bob Costas is the main man; he runs the show. Physically, he's not very big—you sense that he's always made his way with his quick wit. He's neat and precise, always ready for a little verbal sparring. With some people in show business, you can sense that they're always "on," meaning that they have a persona—they work on how they behave and act, on and off camera. I find traces of that in Bob. He's also a catalog of fifties and sixties pop music, including famous television theme songs. He's a real child of the media. If you put a stethoscope to his heart you'd probably hear jingles from famous commercials.

The success of David Letterman has had a far-reaching influence at NBC. It's eerie—all over the building, people are trying to imitate his smart-alecky collegiate humor. It's like a cult, the Letterman Believers. For a while last season, I felt that Costas was under the Letterman influence too. But his particular brand of humor doesn't sit well with pro football players. It's too much like the wit you'd get from a kid who sits in the stands during football games, making fun of the tackle who was a little too fat and slow, or of the gangly defensive back who tripped over his own feet.

Athletes resent that kind of humor because that same wiseguy kid wouldn't ever put himself on the line by trying to make the team. The crux of it is that it's not participant humor but observer humor, and there's no room for that kind of detachment in pro sports. Few things in life are as direct as the sports experience.

The emphasis is on doing the job and doing it *now*. The unspoken rule is that if you haven't done it, don't criticize it. And nothing you say about another guy is all that funny unless you say it to his face—sometimes *in* his face.

That's why rookies can't stick the needle to veteran players; that's why so many athletes don't like sports writers. In football, you develop this attitude that can come off as pure arrogance when you take it beyond the locker-room door. You deny credibility to anyone who isn't your peer, who hasn't been through the same experience as you. And it's the immediacy of that experience that makes it so different from anything else you'll ever do. When you have a big ego, you've got to back it up. And you can't do it with office memos—you've got to do it in broad daylight, head to head. That's why a player just doesn't accept the criticism of someone who hasn't tried to do the job.

Last year, I had a little talk about barbed humor with Costas. I told him that there are only so many lines you can cross when you haven't played the game. You can't cut a guy up with a few quips and keep the respect of the players. You might get a laugh from your fans, you might get every interview you want to do because you're a powerful media figure; but the players are secretly going to lose respect for you and write you off as worthless.

I've worked with Costas long enough to appreciate just how good he is at his job. And he's been around sports enough to understand the banter. In fact, I've developed a relationship with Bob that's like the best ones I've had with some teammates. We bullshit, laugh a lot, and generally keep each other in check. I think that comes across on the show—we look like we're having a good time, and it's hard to fake that. The best thing that happened to my career was Bob's joining the show. He's a real professional—a perfectionist.

We get a little craziness going sometimes, playing off each other, having fun. One morning before the show I gave him this menacing look and said, "Last week when we went to a commercial you were pointing at me, talking. Well, my boys called me. They said it looked to them like you were lecturing me."

"Oh no," Costas said, a little defensively. "That wasn't it . . ."

"You know what I started to do? I started to lean over, I was going to slap you right out of that chair."

Costas looked at me. He smiled. "You realize that if you'd done that, I'd never dish off to you again. Remember, I'm the man who controls when you go on the air. Make that *if* you go on the air."

We both laughed. It was almost like being back in a locker room again.

Every week during the season, I go to a different NFL city to shoot a feature for the upcoming show. It's the most satisfying part of my job, because I pretty much get to produce the piece any way I want and I work with some great guys in Cary Glotzer, Rick Diamond, and Bucky Gunts.

I've got the advantage of being young enough and familiar enough to most players to be accepted by them in a way that members of the media at large aren't. While I was in Washington shooting a recent feature, Redskin cornerback Darrell Green had the tough assignment of covering the Jets' veteran wideout, Wesley Walker. Darrell was looking for advice. He asked me if I'd been around when Walker broke in, "way back" in the late 1970s.

"Oh, sure," I said. "But you've got to remember, it was a different game back then. We wore leather helmets and the goal posts were made out of two-by-fours nailed together."

I was impressed by Washington's overall attitude, and "attitude" means something different in pro football than in college ball or even in a classroom. The game isn't very complicated: it comes down to passing, blocking, running, and kicking and believing that you can win. Teams simply do not win without that confidence. No amount of talent, no training techniques or tactical adjustments change that.

Washington had no wounds to heal because of the strike, and only one of their successful replacement players, tight end Craig

McEwen, made the regular team. The Jets, on the other hand, had experienced some internal strife. Freeman McNeil had to be coaxed into respecting the picket line after declaring that he wouldn't strike. Mark Gastineau had been spat on when he crossed the line; and two of New York's outstanding linemen, Joe Klecko and Marty Lyons, announced that they were going back to work before the strike was officially settled. Everybody wondered how those differences would affect the game.

The show went off fine, although I got restless once or twice just sitting there. The time I actually spend on the air can be measured in seconds, which often leaves me feeling unsatisfied. It's not a matter of getting my face on camera more but one of having enough time to do justice to whatever issue is in question. One of the challenges of television is putting enough meat on the bone for an audience that wants action, not talking heads or panel discussions.

We wrapped the "Live" show and watched the Redskins get off to a lousy start against the Jets. Both teams looked rusty, and they made plenty of errors through the first half of play, which closed with the Jets ahead. It's easy for an announcer to get flip when there's a comedy of errors going on on the field. But I leave that stuff to the guys who specialize in it. Sometimes, former players doing commentary are accused of not being "entertaining." It isn't because they take football as a life-or-death matter but because they're coming at the game from a different perspective. For a career broadcaster, the game is often a stage— an opportunity for him to show off.

You have a problem when the announcer thinks he's bigger than the game he's covering. No telecast is great because of the announcer; it's memorable because of the quality of the game. Former players are more aware of that than some announcers. A dull game isn't an opportunity for commentary; it's just a lousy football game. Broadcasters sometimes make the same mistake that some players do—they assume that people are watching a game solely because of them, individually. I hope I never make that mistake.

My halftime comment was that the Redskins' offense looked rusty: their defense was keeping them in the game. I predicted that Washington would loosen up and generate more offense in the second half. After those pearls of wisdom, we all got back to the serious business of fleshing out our Rotisserie League.

It works like this: six or seven people each put up fifty bucks to buy "franchises" in the Rotisserie League. Then you hold a draft, with each owner picking two quarterbacks, four running backs, two wide receivers, and two tight ends from the actual NFL rosters. Everybody also gets a kicker and a special teams unit from an NFL club. The scoring performance of the players in the regular NFL games earns points for their owners in the Rotisserie League. The owner who amasses the most points at season's end gets all of the seed money.

A couple of the girls on the technical side had pooled their resources to buy a team, and they were assembling a great one with the help of the NFL stat book. And Cefalo, choosing right ahead of me, drafted two players I wanted, Dan Marino and Curt Warner.

Lunch at the studio is a "catered brown-bag" affair, set up in the hallway outside Studio 6-A. I blasted a tuna melt sandwich in the microwave and took it back to our studio desk. Bob Pergament, a reporter from Buffalo, where I'd played for two years, was interviewing Costas. When he was finished, we began to reminisce about my years there.

I'd had a great time up in Buffalo, but Pergament seemed leery, as if I were just setting him up for some incredible put-down of the city. People from places like Cleveland, Indianapolis, or Buffalo get defensive about their cities. They're eager to tell you what a great ballet or orchestra or theater they have, as if that would make them the equal of the major cities. Maybe I've still got a lot of Tacoma in me, but after living in Los Angeles and for the past five years in New York, I still think those smaller cities can offer a much better quality of life. And what's more important than that?

Smaller cities are good for pro athletes, especially when yours is the only game in town. The people in Buffalo loved their Bills. In Minneapolis, if you're a Viking, you're a god. The warmth you find in those cities makes up for the climate. Besides, Buffalo isn't the Arctic, either geographically or meteorologically.

I'm kind of an expert on cold weather, and all I can say is that 10 degrees isn't much different from 15, and that's about the difference between Manhattan and Buffalo on a winter's day. Buffalo and Minneapolis weathermen always used to talk about a day being "a warm 17," but to me there was no such thing. "A warm 17"—that's like calling somebody "an honest crook."

In Buffalo, I was reunited with two good friends, O. J. Simpson and Reggie McKenzie—the Juice and the leader of the Electric Company, the great offensive line that helped O.J. become the first NFL back to rush for over two thousand yards in one season. As it turned out, I needed O.J.'s counsel during my very first practice with the Bills.

Buffalo had a little skinny guy called Dwight Harrison, who was a tough, hard-nosed defensive back. I almost got into a fistfight with him on the first day of training camp. When we got back to the locker room after practice, O.J. waved me over.

"Do you know who Dwight is?" he asked me.

I shook my head.

"He was with Denver, and he had some problem with Lyle Alzado. So one day he showed up at practice with a gun—he was going to shoot Lyle. So they traded him to us."

"Oh." I gulped. I went over to Dwight and began to rap with him. "Dwight, my man—we gotta get along, buddy. We're going to do it here in Buffalo. Cool out, man. I'll tell you something— I don't like that Alzado dude much either."

Buffalo also had a great coach, Lou Saban. But the best thing about Buffalo was that the Bills were a winning team. That has a big impact on your general outlook.

The Redskins and the Jets continued to play like two out-of-shape boxers, throwing wild punches at each other. Washington crept to within two in the fourth period, 16–14, on a two-yard touchdown pass.

The bull in the studio was flying around pretty thick by then, as Pergament and I went on about various players who'd played for the Bills. Certain superstars stand out, certain guys become identified with the teams they play for in a lasting way; but the number of guys who come and go in pro football is staggering. It provides irrefutable proof that your basic everyday football player is an interchangeable part. "Replacement" became a catchword this season, but it's the working concept every day in the NFL.

Pergament said he was concerned about the free-agency issue. Like other sports writers from the less imposing NFL cities, he felt that nobody good would ever go to play in Buffalo if he had a choice. He thought that the income opportunities in "major markets" would knock a lot of the owners out of the bidding game.

I didn't agree with him. For one thing, there just isn't enough room in the major cities for all the potential stars. There's enough talent to go around. More important, players rarely reject the idea of playing in any city because it's too small. A lot of the players don't especially want to live or stake their futures in big cities. When a guy says he doesn't want to play in, say, Green Bay or Indianapolis, he's almost always talking not about the city but about the franchise and the state of the team.

Players want to go to winning teams with stable programs. When I was traded to Minnesota after spending training camp in Seattle in 1976, I didn't think about how many nightclubs, car dealerships, or cable television stations Minneapolis had, and I didn't think about how many balls I might drop because of the cold weather. I thought about the Viking tradition, I thought about playing with Jim Marshall, Fran Tarkenton, Alan Page, and Carl Eller.

That was enough to get me on the first plane out.

The early games were ending, like a row of falling dominos. Ali Haji-Sheikh kicked a twenty-eight-yard field goal in the last minute of play to give the Redskins a 17–16 win over the Jets. The studio was becoming hectic as the updates grew more and more frequent. Down in Philadelphia, head coach Buddy Ryan pulled a controversial move. He had a game against Dallas all wrapped up, with seconds to go, when his quarterback Randall Cunningham threw a fifty-yard bomb that resulted in a pass interference call against Dallas. On the next play, the Eagles took the ball in to run up the score. Ryan was exacting revenge, because during a replacement game a few weeks earlier, Tom Landry had played Cowboy veterans Randy White and Tony Dorsett against replacement Eagles even when the Cowboys had a good lead.

I couldn't get all worked up against Ryan, like some people did. In fact, I'd always felt that the taboo against running up the score was hypocritical at best: you're basically punishing your own guys because you want to make the other coach look better, or you're more worried about their guys than yours. When I was in high school, we played a team called Centralia. We once beat them by about 60–0, and I had four touchdowns and lots of rushing yards. Basically, it was like running windsprints. But I still got upset when the coach put the second string in, because I wanted as many touchdowns as I could get. It's natural.

Another studio Sunday began to wind down after the late games got under way at about four p.m. Crew people were bunched up backstage on the set, talking. Cefalo and I got to talking about injuries. The most painful ones are broken or cracked ribs. You can hardly move without feeling pain; your whole upper body is tender. I gave him one last chance to trade Curt Warner for Mark Duper, but he didn't go for it. One of my co-commissioners in the Rotisserie League came in with a neatly typed set of league rules and rosters.

We did a halftime discussion for the late game, and that pretty much wrapped up the day except for a few more updates during the late games. It was almost seven p.m. when I went to work in the makeup room, using a cotton ball and cleanser on my face. Soon my cheeks were covered with brown foam. Costas was trying on somebody's hat, a black felt job like a riverboat gambler might have worn. He was singing the theme song to the old TV show "Bat Masterson."

My postgame routine in Minnesota was different. I would always take my time in the shower, and I'd invariably be the last player to leave, just as I'd always been the first to arrive. Stubby always had a bottle of scotch stashed in one of the equipment bags; the two of us would sit there and have a few pops in the deserted locker room. Then I'd walk down to the stadium manager's office, deep in the bowels of the place. His people—ushers, first-aid personnel, security guards—would be sitting around, drinking beer. I'd have a few with them. Usually, I took a couple of beers and put them in my bag. I did that every week, win or lose.

When I'd finally leave Metropolitan Stadium, there would still be some diehard fans in the parking lot, waiting to catch a glimpse of their heroes. Often, the sky would be gray and the weather blustery and cold. It was really a downer, because all the action was over. When I got home, I'd have nothing to do, so I'd often pick up the phone and call friends on the West Coast.

As I left Rockefeller Center and Studio 6-A, I was happy to be going home to my wife and daughter. I decided to drive carefully on the way home.

2

PLAY BREAKERS AND BONE CRUSHERS

Almost everybody's been a center at some time or other. It's a fact of life—like having to take out the trash or doing homework on a Sunday night. Let's face it—not too many kids dream of growing up to be Dwight Stephenson or Mike Webster.

When kids try out for youth football leagues, they all want to be quarterbacks or wide receivers or running backs; they all want to be football heroes. But it's a fact of life: somebody's got to play center. A lot of the kids who get elected to play center show up for two or three practices, go through the motions, and do a slow fade.

Football players get sorted out and put into bins at a pretty early age. It's part of the football mentality. Unfortunately, many kids who probably could have a good experience right up through the high school level are turned off to the game. I was made to play tackle for my first Midget League team, and I was crushed. As a kid, I wanted to throw, catch, or run with the ball. So I had my father telephone the coach to tell him that I wanted to play a position where I could touch the ball. Eventually, I got to play backup quarterback.

I believed—no, I *knew*—that I was a better player than the

starter; but then Little League football is often full of Little League politics controlled by personal and neighborhood loyalties. Learning that was a valuable part of my education, because it taught me that the judgments of a coach aren't always accurate or even honest, his motivations aren't always pure. I still wonder what would have happened if my dad had refused to pick up the phone or had told me just to shut up and do as I was told. I know I wouldn't have ended up playing on the line in the NFL. Sometimes, I don't even understand the guys who *do* play on the line in the NFL.

But one thing is for sure: those big guys up front aren't just butting heads and mauling any piece of moving flesh they can get their hands on. Offensive linemen, particularly centers, have to play with a lot of intelligence and finesse. John Madden is an eloquent spokesman for the breed. Linemen have been his "guys" ever since he played offensive guard for the Philadelphia Eagles in 1959. When he talks about offensive linemen, Madden likes to throw around the barnyard analogies. He says good centers look like they should be carrying calves on their shoulders. He once said that his great right guard for the Oakland Raiders, George Buehler, was a "275-pound silo."

That's the Madden persona. You get the feeling that he should be from someplace like Red Dirt, Kansas; instead of taking trains (Madden refuses to fly), he ought to be riding around the country on a John Deere combine. He's a sentimentalist who likes that elemental struggle in the trenches. He isn't happy unless some guy's got blood running down his arm, a big chunk of turf stuck on his face guard, and a torn jersey hanging out of his pants— preferably with a hunk of flesh hanging out in the breeze. No wonder Madden was awed by the offensive line of the Washington Redskins when they won Super Bowl XVII—the collective nickname of that line was "the Hogs." But I still find myself asking the fundamental question: what's the fun of football if you never touch the ball?

To most people, the guys slugging it out on the line of scrimmage are indistinguishable from each other. But the style and mentality of offensive and defensive linemen are very different. Defensive linemen play with greater abandon, letting all of their aggression and hostility hang out. When I was traded to the Vikings in '76, three of their legendary defensive linemen were still active. Gary Larsen had retired, but Carl Eller, Alan Page, and Jim Marshall were still playing devastating football. I enjoyed watching them work.

The objective for defensive linemen is to stop the ball carrier or to sack the quarterback before he has time to complete a pass. Those clear and simple goals don't weigh too heavily on them or curb their style in any way. Defensive linemen pursue their ends with all kinds of spontaneous moves, coming from inside or outside, spinning off blockers, throwing blocking halfbacks out of the way or running over them. They're the hunters, the invaders, the play breakers and bone crushers. They're on an eternal rampage.

The job of the offensive linemen is much more complex, so their aggression is carefully marshaled and controlled. On running plays, their moves are carefully orchestrated. To open holes in the line or to execute a sweep calls for precise timing and coordinated movement. Offensive linemen clear the way for ball carriers, like some giant human snowplow made of five or six simple moving parts, or they drop back to protect the quarterback against the onslaught of the defensive pass rush. They are like the corps of engineers or the palace guard—they have to be eternally vigilant.

Don't get me wrong: offensive linemen don't wear halos (I don't think they make halos big enough), and they don't spend all their time sacrificing life and limb for running backs and quarterbacks. Some of them are downright ornery. The Vikings had a guy, Tim Irwin, who was as aggressive as any defensive player. In our training camp in Mankato, Minnesota, in 1982, he squared off against defensive tackle Duck White. Football fights are great slapstick: you're wearing so many pads that about the only harm you can inflict is a broken finger—on yourself, for trying to punch out a guy wearing a helmet.

A few hours after that fight took place, someone wrote on the blackboard in our dining hall: THE THRILLER IN MANKATO, DUCK (RIGHT HAND) WHITE VS. TIM (MOUNTAIN MAN) IRWIN. I played the role of Don King, stopping just short of sticking my finger in an electrical socket to get the hair right. I touted Irwin as the Great White Hope. Somebody dimmed the lights, and when they came back bright again, Duck came strutting into the room, carrying his arms in front of him just like Larry Holmes. That's training-camp humor for you.

Just a few weeks later, before we broke camp, Mountain Man Irwin got into another fight. He went at it with our big defensive end, Doug Martin, and actually got some punches in between Doug's face-mask bars. Martin got one punch in to the stomach and a nice kick. After practice on the day they fought, Irwin and Martin went fishing together. I'll say it again: I don't understand linemen.

Offensive linemen often seem to be on a different wavelength, or they hear music to which the rest of us are deaf. Their jobs are clearly defined, relatively cut-and-dried. Maybe that's why so many of them are brooders, guys who channel their emotions and instincts very carefully and strictly. If one of them misses a block, the whole offensive play comes to a crashing halt. On defense, one man can make the big play; on offense, one man can ruin it. That tremendous difference is reflected in the personalities of the players.

Offensive linemen range from graduate students who spend their free moments in the locker room boning up on their studies to guys who make extra money in the off-season raising pit bull terriers, hugging and smothering their pups with affection. One of the strangest dudes on the Vikings was Ron Yary, a guy who always seemed all wound up and unbelievably tense for a bona fide All-Pro.

Yary was one of the most intense guys I've been around in my life. Before a game, I would be joking around with Joe Senser or ribbing somebody in the locker room. Yary sat on his stool right next to me, staring straight ahead. Suddenly I would hear this wheezing voice that sounded like it was out of some Frankenstein movie. It was Yary, trying to speak. "Come on, Ahmad," he'd say. When he was really psyched up, he'd squeeze out an extra phrase, like, "Let's go, man."

In '76, my first year with the Vikings, we had a big game against the Detroit Lions. Just minutes before game time, Wally Hilgenberg paid a visit to the most popular sanctuary in the stadium, the john. He came back out and said to linebacker Jeff Siemon, "You'll never guess what I saw."

A couple of guys turned around. Hilgenberg continued. "Yary's standing in the john, in full uniform and cleats, having a shave."

So much for the soul searching that goes on before a big game.

Centers are different from the guards and tackles who make up the rest of the offensive line. The center is like the sun— every play revolves around him. The position is second only to that of the quarterback in terms of importance, because without a good snap on the right count, no play goes anywhere. When a team doesn't trust the center, it becomes fidgety, prone to jump offsides, disorganized and tentative. Pretty soon the whole rhythm of the offense is shot, and the defense washes over it like a tidal wave.

No kid under the age of sixteen likes to play center, and few men over the age of twenty have the skill, courage, and temperament the position demands. The word "quarterback" doesn't have any meaning outside of a football context. But "center" has a clear, independent meaning that defines the importance of the man in the position.

At the start of each and every play, the center is saddled with a unique handicap. Every other lineman can come up out of his stance with both arms up to attack or to protect himself from his opposite number. The center has to snap the ball before he can do anything else, and as soon as he moves his ball hand, the defense can pounce. It's a little like letting the other guy land the first punch in a fight, play after play.

Ultimately, the center tries to get the snap off precisely and to get his free hand up to ward off the nose tackle or middle linebacker before he can take advantage of the center's weak side. The center needs nerves of steel to wait out the count of the quarterback, and a cool head to remember the count in the first place. That's no mean feat, as any player will tell you. You'd be amazed at how often players are so concerned with their specific assignment on any given play that they just plain forget the snap count. Any other player who forgets the count can sometimes take a cue from his teammates or watch for the snap. But the center needs the memory of an elephant. If he forgets the snap count, the result is often disastrous.

The emergence of black quarterbacks in the NFL generated a lot of talk in 1987. But I found it just as significant that during one game, Redskin quarterback Doug Williams lined up over a black center, Raleigh McKenzie. Go down the lists of all-time centers and see how many black ones you find. Until very recently, the assumption was that black players lacked the intelligence and mental discipline required of a good center.

Dwight Stephenson of the Miami Dolphins, a perennial All-Pro center, finally put that rap to rest. I got to know Dwight during one of the Superstars competitions. He's as humble, soft-spoken, and personable as he is tough. In the Dolphins' film room Dwight provides major entertainment. Some of the licks he lays on opposing players are run back three and four times to a howling audience of Dolphins.

The Dolphins were the only team to beat the Bears in 1985, the year Chicago stormed through the schedule and playoffs to win the Super Bowl. Playing with his left arm strapped to his side to protect a separated shoulder, Stephenson still manhandled the Bears' 325-pound tackle, William "the Refrigerator" Perry. Watching films of that game before Cleveland met Miami in the playoffs, the Browns' noseguard, Bob Golic, remarked, "Dwight just took Perry on about four of five plays and just threw him to the ground. I asked myself why I was watching. The only thing I could learn from it was how to bounce."

Mick Tingelhoff, the Viking center who holds the NFL record for most games started in a career, was a teammate of mine. I don't know how centers attain such longevity, unless they just get beat on so much that they grow indifferent to the punishment. Mick and I used to go out after practice and drink scotch— you wouldn't catch a veteran like Mick messing around with beer or one of those fancy pink mixed drinks with an umbrella sticking out of it.

Sometimes we'd go over to Fran Tarkenton's house on Monday evenings and the three of us would sip scotch and discuss Sunday's game. We developed a pretty good rapport, considering the different worlds we inhabited on the playing field. I was always curious about other types of players, and I enjoyed the camaraderie you can develop among so many disparate personalities. Among other things, it improves the morale of the team when you have some sense of community.

During one important game on a rainy day in Tampa, I made a great catch on a third-and-long situation. The pass was a little high, but I climbed the rope and caught it, taking a hard shot as my punishment. As I lay there, Mick sprinted down the field. He was the first guy who arrived to check on me. For the rest of that game, Mick kept shaking his head in the huddle and muttering, "That was a great catch, that was one of the biggest catches you ever made." You don't forget incidents like that.

But Mick, who was six foot two and only about 240 pounds, was the last of a breed: the small, mobile center. The type has become extinct because of the 3–4 defense used by most teams these days, in which there are only three down linemen, including the noseguard, who plays right over the center. The trend began in the early 1970s, with the granddaddy of noseguards, Kansas City's Curley Culp.

By putting Culp, the Chiefs' biggest, toughest defensive lineman, directly over the center, the defense could penetrate at the most vulnerable point of the offense. The handicap of having to snap the ball before he can fire out or drop back to protect the quarterback was just too great. In the classic 4–3 defense, nobody played directly over the center. Usually, the center's job was to block the middle linebacker. As tough as that assignment could be, the center at least had time to snap the ball and get his balance because the middle linebacker started the play behind the line of scrimmage.

The development of the noseguard was an evolutionary step that has to impress any of those grumpy old-timers who won't believe that today's players are superior to those of yesteryear. It's a shame that the first, surprised victims of the revolution were the Vikings, in the 1970 Super Bowl.

Playing from the noseguard position, Culp manhandled Tingelhoff and the Chiefs won the Super Bowl, 23–7, over the Vikings. It's just another twist of irony for my poor Vikes that in their first Super Bowl appearance, they would be point men for the ambush set by the 3–4 defense.

But don't get the impression that playing against the 4–3 defense was a cakewalk, either. When I was with the Cardinals, we played the Bears about four times one year—twice during training camp, once in preseason, and once during the regular season. Their middle linebacker is my choice for the greatest player in NFL history, Dick Butkus. He liked to move in and play right over the center, getting a jump on the offense just like a noseguard.

After our first three meetings with the Bears, our first-string center was so tired of being beaten up by Butkus that he flat out refused to play against him again. The backup center was so nervous before the fourth game that he could barely walk or talk. I watched him closely in the locker room, wondering how he was dealing with the imminent ass kicking he was about to receive.

One of the fun things about sports is the personal confrontation, the resolution of that old question "Who's better, you or me?" Usually, the calibers are close enough so that either man has a chance to prevail. But sometimes a guy just knows there's no way on earth that he's going to win that individual struggle. That's a frightening truth to face in a sport like swimming or tennis: imagine how much worse it is in a game of heavy contact, like boxing or football.

All you can really do when it's obvious that you're going to get your ass kicked but good is avoid sweating or crying—at least until you get into the thick of the game, when everybody else might be busy enough with his own battle not to notice too much. I watched our center go through all the emotions, fighting to keep his self-control, right through the warm-ups. But when the game started, I could see that he was resigned to being Butkus's rag doll.

For the next sixty minutes, this guy lived in a state of shock. Butkus pounded him so hard that by the second quarter, he began snapping the ball whenever he wanted. Our quarterback would call a play "on two," and our center would turn right around, run out of the huddle, and line up. As soon as the quarterback put his hands down, the center snapped the ball and fell to the ground like a guy during an air raid. He wasn't embarrassed about it, either. And when it looked like somebody in the huddle might say something, he snapped: "If any of you fuckers want to snap, be my guest."

Of course, there were no takers.

3

BONUS BABY

Phylicia and I were married in Harlem, at the beautiful Church of the Master. As I slipped the ring onto her finger, a strange memory flashed through my mind. As a boy on the brink of my teens, when I was just learning about girls and rings and going steady, I had these mysterious bumps on most of my joints. I'd had them since I was about six years old, and they kept me from being able to even put on a ring.

Once, out of curiosity, I tried forcing a ring on and caused one of the protuberances to break and bleed. I had to wait two days before I could get the ring off again. I remembered thinking that I'd never get a girlfriend, never mind a pretty one or a smart one. The bumps were the bane of my life. They swelled and hurt and caused me all sorts of physical, emotional, and social discomfort.

But in another way they could have been diamonds stuck under my skin. I learned how to look beyond appearances, to seek beauty within things. I spent a lot of time alone, learning at an early age something that would comfort me through the years: life goes on, it goes on no matter what unexpected problems you encounter. You can't dote or dwell on hardships. The key to happiness lies in expanding your horizons, in searching for new things to understand or to do, because learning is something everybody can do. You don't have to be a great athlete to learn; you don't have to be a schoolroom whiz or a beauty queen.

One of the first things I learned was to enjoy my own company. Sometimes I would wander down to Wapato Park in Tacoma and just lose myself for the day among the strangers. I would eat up the world with my eyes, or I would take along books to read. Little kids don't understand pain and sorrow like adults do, but when they're faced with hardship they have a remarkable ability to adapt. It's an early form of maturity. And it helps a ton to have supportive parents, like I did.

I was born in Portland in 1949, the last of six kids born to O. C. and Condola Moore. My dad used to say that O.C. stood for anything you wanted—Oscar Charles, Oliver Carl. It didn't make no never mind to him. I always thought Mom had a beautiful name, but American blacks weren't as conscious of their roots back then. I remember my brother Dennis telling me that some of his friends thought Condola was some kind of African name, as if that meant it was bad.

Doc Moore, my paternal grandfather, was a local legend back in Mississippi. He was a very tough guy who owned a store, lent people money, and carried a gun. He became the first guy in his town to own a brand-new Model T. Dad was one of nine kids, and a bit of a dandy. He used to show up at dances driving the Model T. Before he would dance with a girl, O. C. Moore put a handkerchief on the shoulder of his crisp suit so it wouldn't get smudged by makeup on those hot Mississippi nights.

I can't remember ever seeing my father in a pair of sneakers. Even after he retired, he would get up in the morning and put on a nice suit and a tie. He had that old southern dignity, and a work ethic to match, holding as many as four jobs at once. He was at various times a grader for a lumber company and a railroad worker, but his main occupation was barbering. He cut hair at Fort Lewis, a big military base near Tacoma. We moved there from Portland when I was five.

My athletic gifts probably came from a cousin in Mississippi,

Bill Moore. He was one of the toughest guys in the state. When I asked far-flung relatives about him, their eyes would get wide and they'd say something that sounded like it was right out of some old movie: "Oh, that Bill Moore, he could sure knock the cover off a baseball!"

I know for sure that I didn't get my love of sports from Dad. We played catch exactly once in my life, when I was about thirteen, and the only reason for that was because my sister Claire was taking a baseball class. So one day Dad announced to me and Claire that he was going to show us how to play. He took us out back. You know how catch goes—it's a nice slow game. You savor the sound of the ball hitting the pocket of the mitt . . . you take your sweet old time throwing it back . . . you might look at the ball for a moment . . . you might start into this long, exaggerated windup. Catch is a ritual, just like stropping a razor or warming up before a tennis match.

But not for old O. C. Moore. He threw the ball funny, with a fast, jerky motion. And after he caught it, instead of taking his time he would just fire that sucker right back as soon as he could pick it out of his glove. It was a "Beat the Clock" version of catch, the weirdest game I ever played. But it was typical of Dad, because he believed that the key to life was in doing as many things as possible, as fast as possible.

Dad never believed I was going to make it as an athlete because I had this leisurely, slow way about me, especially when it came to getting up after being tackled. Most of the time, I was just trying to conserve energy. Some of it was my personal style. O.C. didn't like that much. He would tell me, "Son, you've got to pop right up off the ground and run back to that huddle. You've really got to hustle out there if you want to make it."

I relate more strongly to another tenet of my father's basic philosophy, which was that the more a man could do, the better off he was. He encouraged us to be well-rounded. Even if we weren't going to be barbers, it wasn't bad having the license. My brother Dennis listened to him and now he's a millionaire, retired and living in Beverly Hills. Dennis made his money in real estate, but it all started with haircuts he gave his buddies at cut rates on weekends.

Dad cut hair and he also had the shoeshine concession at Fort Lewis. There was a donut shop out there, too. The owner used to give Dad day-old donuts to bring home for us. I sometimes went out to work with Dad, and even as a little kid I had a very weird feeling about him shining shoes. I didn't like it at all.

When the National Guard descended on the base, my brother Dennis and a couple of cousins would go out and shine shoes for a few days, picking up a quick fifty or sixty bucks a day. As in any business, you had to be accommodating to get good tips. But I still hated to see my dad saying "Yes, sir" and "No, sir" to these nineteen- and twenty-year-old servicemen. These guys would talk to him and treat him like a boy even though he was fifty years old and working double time to support a family. I felt the biting injustice in that situation.

I shined shoes one summer, when I was about twelve. I worked hard, but I refused to do the extra things that so many of the other guys did. They would sit around in the back and talk about the technique for getting big tips—how you might want to call a younger guy "boss" or "sir." They could laugh about it later. It was nothing more meaningful than a con game for getting bigger tips. But I still wouldn't play along.

I had a special relationship with my mom, like so many youngest children do. She was a big, beautiful, loving woman who worked as a domestic. It was just a job to her, but I resented the position—especially when I got older and understood the social implications. Mom worked for an eye doctor whom she really liked. But I saw how little she was earning, and it just didn't sit right with me.

The best thing about Mom's job was that through the years she learned about my athletic exploits from her employers. Otherwise, she might never have known. She was a devoutly religious woman who considered sports a frivolity. So even when Dr. Smith congratulated her after I won the high hurdles at a track meet, it was almost like she was more impressed by the fact that Dr. Smith had noticed than by the fact that I'd accomplished something.

Mom worked awfully hard. It seems that when she wasn't out working, she was either with me or lying in bed. She was always exhausted. When I got involved in sports and began to come home later and later in the day, she would be fast asleep when I got home. But she always left me dinner, and often it was my favorite meal: cheeseburgers. As a kid, I could eat cheeseburgers three times a day, seven days a week, and for snacks in between, too. The other thing I loved was chocolate cake. Once when I was playing for Buffalo, I called one of my sisters and asked her to make me a nice cherry cake. Word got back to Mom, and she was on the phone in no time. "So my choc'late cake isn't good enough for you anymore," she said. "Since when did you take such a fancy to cherry cake?"

When I wanted something that was beyond our means, Mom would go and buy it on layaway, paying it off over the next two years. One of the proudest moments of my life occurred in second grade, when Mom was named room mother. I was the only black kid in the class, but it was my mom who was in charge of bringing in some cupcakes and stuff for the class. Mom was Superwoman in my eyes. Often, she would drive Dad to work, drop the other kids at school, and then take me to this ice-cream stand for a cone. It was a daily ritual that I loved—and one that became very important to me when the bumps first appeared.

To this day, I don't know where those bumps came from. Nor did the hundreds of doctors who examined me, tested me, poked me, pulled me, cut me, burned me, and turned me over, under, sideways and down, trying to determine the nature of the bumps. One day, I just noticed them, like raisins on my skin. When they began to swell and hurt some, we began to seek medical help.

One dermatologist saw me free of charge, but I'm convinced he did that so he could experiment on me. I can't count how many pills and drugs I took, elixirs that made me sick to my stomach. The side effects included headaches, a runny nose, and a bunch of stomach disorders. Some of the drugs made the bumps swell and burst, which was scary.

This doctor was like some mad scientist—at least that's how I remember him. He would always smooth-talk my mom, and then when he got me into his examination room alone, he'd turn rough. He would take biopsies all the time. I had one of those bumps on my nose once and the doctor shot me up with some kind of Novocain. Then he took an electric device and went to work on the bump. I saw a little wisp of smoke going up before my eyes and I smelled my skin burning. I tried to kick him in the crotch; I did anything I could to get away. Some of those visits got me so upset that I would spend the rest of the day crying.

Even the doctors at Fort Lewis got into the act. That summer when I shined shoes with my dad, I had bumps on my ears. Noticing them, a military doctor decided to take me to the infirmary to cut one of them off. He never asked my father for permission; he never asked me. He just told me that he'd be back at three, to take me away so he could do some testing.

I didn't dare tell my dad. I sat there shining shoes until about two-forty-five, and then for the next few hours I hid in various places along the base road. I was way down at the other end of the base until about eight, when I started to make my way back so that I could meet Dad when he got off at eleven. We always took the bus home, and I remember worrying that this lieutenant doctor was going to jump on me by surprise and drag me off.

But the most brutal of those experiences occurred when Mom and I went up to Vancouver, to a hospital that was holding a major freak show of strange diseases. A whole bunch of us with different problems sat in various rooms, as an endless parade of doctors from all over the world came through, examining us. There was no real contact, just a lot of pawing and squeezing and peering. The only break occurred when they gave each of us a sandwich and a carton of milk for lunch.

It was a cold, frightening experience, followed by a long bus ride home in the night. I could see in the reflection of the lights dancing on the window that Mom was crying. I told her we wouldn't ever do anything like that again. If the bumps didn't go away, so what. We still had each other.

Religion was another major influence in my youth. My parents belonged to a fundamentalist denomination, the Pentecostal Church. I was raised on fire and brimstone, which was a strange experience. But it also made me think and make important decisions about spiritual matters. As a young adult I was predisposed to believe, to seek a religion that expressed my convictions. When I eventually found Islam, I felt like I had met a belief that I already had within me without even knowing it.

I'm convinced that man has a spiritual dimension. It's something everybody can find within himself if he wants, or bothers, to look. Phylicia finds that some of her spiritual needs are fulfilled by meditation. Others turn to traditional worship. The nature of your beliefs probably isn't as important as the simple fact that you're paying attention to your inner being.

Sometimes my family went to church two, three, or even four days a week, and in the summer there were two-week marathon "reunion" meetings. I envied my Catholic friends who went to church for one measly hour on Sunday morning. Man, I was stuck in church all day every Sunday, and then again after dinner from seven-thirty until almost eleven. That lasted until ninth grade.

In the Pentecostal faith, you didn't do anything on Sunday except try to get yourself saved. You didn't play sports. You didn't wear lipstick. You didn't listen to the radio. And you didn't play Monopoly, because handling dice was forbidden. Girls weren't allowed to wear slacks, and red was considered the devil's color. About all you could do was go to church, a place that became a main source of fear because of all the strange things that went on there.

Pentecostals believe in the Old Testament and in the power of miracles. During a service, somebody right next to you might jump up and begin speaking in tongues. When you were really saved, you would start shouting too. Once a lady next to me leaped up and hit me upside the head. I learned to stake out my seat from that experience, near people who weren't likely to carry on too much.

It was weird to go back the very next day to a predominantly white, Catholic neighborhood and way of life. Everybody in the Pentecostal Church is called brother or sister, so all these kids in the neighborhood thought I was some super Catholic kid who was friends with all of these nuns, because I would refer to friends of the family as Sister Edwards or Sister Jones. When I tried to explain to my friends what I'd seen on Sunday—demons being cast out of people, testimonies, and all that—that got pretty heavy.

My mother often went to revival meetings, where they trafficked in miracles. She once took me to see a famous faith healer, a minister, A. A. Allen, hoping that he might work a miracle and rid me of the bumps. I knew that one of the rules for faith healing was that you had to believe in its power in order to be healed. I couldn't discuss this with the kids at school, because it was totally foreign to them. I had an urge to be objective about the faith, but I was just a kid. Plus you had to believe in miracles to get a miracle, so on the day I went to see Reverend Allen, I told a friend at school the same thing that I'd been telling myself, over and over: that I was going to get rid of the bumps on my ears and arms that night. Tomorrow at school, they would be all gone.

That night we lined up in Reverend Allen's tent, waiting for our turn to be healed. He would mumble some prayers over these sick people and reach toward them, saying, "And now you shall be healed." Sometimes he didn't even have to touch the person; just putting his hand near the man or woman created this whiplash effect. People were knocked out by his power. Cripples would just straighten up and walk right out. Or Reverend Allen would pull some guy right out of his wheelchair and the man would walk off.

I walked up to Reverend Allen, petrified. I was only about ten years old. My basic reverence told me I had to believe, but when the Reverend Allen spoke his mumbo jumbo and passed his hands over me, nothing happened. I didn't have to touch my ears to know the bumps were still there; I could tell that by my mother's lack of reaction. That Allen guy could cure polio, I guess, but he couldn't beat the bumps on a little boy's ears.

Reverend Allen had another franchise going. He had this great big cloth that he would pray over, and if you sent him five bucks he would cut a piece and send it to you. If you needed a miracle, you'd just pin that piece of cloth to your clothes, on a sleeve or a pocket. There was a time when I had pieces of cloth pinned all over me—I must have looked like some kind of doll with the stuffing coming out. When guys in the locker room asked about it, I tried to smooth over it real quickly, and change the subject.

Then there was the olive oil. Preachers who really had a line to God had only to pray over a couple of bottles of olive oil and they would become sacred, assuming miraculous properties. My mother made me anoint myself with the oil. I must have done that right through high school and college.

Mom had a religious friend, Sister Scott, who lived on a farm someplace outside of Tacoma. Her cure for my bumps was some kind of weird elixir that smelled just awful—I mean, it smelled like manure. Mom made me put it on, and I walked out of the house every day stinking of the stuff. It was too much. I would walk out and wipe it off as soon as I got out of the house. At the low point of my childhood, I was made of rags, smelled like a barnyard, and sprinkled with dressing like some crazy salad.

Kids can be cruel, so the bumps left me with some unusual problems—like when we were told to line up for recess two by two, nobody wanted to hold my hand. The kids in the neighborhood always talked about the bumps, teasing me, warning me not to touch them, getting on me with nicknames like "Raisin Ears." Even my sister Mary got into the act, calling me "Bumpy."

I never got into fights. I was very good about holding back my feelings and not letting the hurt show. But sometimes when I got home, I'd shut my door and cry for a couple of hours. It seemed that Mom was always there, dying a little with me. She would often come in and we'd get to talking. Eventually, she would make me feel better.

Maintaining the front took a lot of energy, but I had plenty of that. In fact, I had so much energy to expend that I needed an additional outlet. I found it at the local Boys Club, where for some reason nobody bothered about the bumps. The place became my haven. It was about three miles from my home, but I was happy to walk the distance.

I remember lots of long walks home from the Boys Club in the rainy Tacoma evenings. Sometimes I'd see Jim McKuen, the football coach of the Boys Club team, driving by after practice with a carload of kids. That bothered me a little. The kids on the team were mostly Catholic boys from a school called Visitation. They all lived in the same neighborhood, in the opposite direction from the projects where my family lived. We were worlds apart in some ways, but on the field we were equals. And they always gave me the chance to prove that at the Boys Club.

The Boys Club was a melting pot of neighborhoods, a place that welcomed anybody with no questions asked, and the variety of activities attracted a cross section of kids. It was for gym rats and budding pool sharks and kids who had noplace else to go. Among other things, you could use the wood shop, jump on the trampolines, swim, play basketball, shoot pool, or play Ping-Pong. It was a different society there—how you did in school, or how you got on with your family or the kids in your neighborhood, didn't matter at all. Nobody knew, nobody cared.

There was camaraderie too, the kind that develops at any club. The egalitarian nature of the place was really neat. Your place in the eyes of the other kids depended on your athletic and social skills. That fostered pride and loyalty to the place.

I began to make a reputation for myself on those Boys Club teams, and I enjoyed the environment so much that I got a job in the place, passing out billiard cues. I even went to the Boys Club summer camp for two years. I tried the Boy Scouts too, but it was too militaristic for me. I didn't like dealing with all those badges and ranks and uniforms.

School, home, and the Boys Club formed a triangle on the map, so I was forever trying to recruit friends from my neighborhood to go down to the club with me. I talked this one buddy of mine into joining the football team with me. During the second or third practice, Coach McKuen made us run laps. This kid stopped at the far end of the field, which was right by the bus stop, hopped on a bus, and went home. I watched him go, thinking, "Well, I've got nobody to walk home with anymore."

I played the most embarrassing game of my life on behalf of the Boys Club basketball team, at the McNeil Island Penitentiary. I was a starting forward, a very good shooter and an intimidating rebounder. I'd never been near a penitentiary before, so I was surprised to see that most of the guys at McNeil Island were black. They took to me right away because I was the only black kid on either team—I was the instant star.

But there was this little problem of my bumps. I could hide them pretty well in a helmet and all those pads you wear in football, but a basketball uniform is like a bikini. I had a bad case of the bumps on my elbows and wrists at the time, so I ran up and down the court with my hands covering different parts of my arms, trying to hide the bumps.

The inmates were cheering for me—I still remember them yelling, "Hey, number thirteen, loosen up! Come on, thirteen, loosen up." But I never loosened up—I was too busy hiding my bumps. Those were the times when I'd get home and just burst into tears, thinking the torture would never stop. In pictures from my adolescence, you can pick me out without even looking for my face. I'm the kid with his hands in his pockets, hiding his bumps.

Sports were a big escape for me. I was sick of going places with my mom and hearing some lady say, "Why, you're such a nice-looking little boy, but what's that on your ears?" I quickly grew wary of meeting new people. I went to school with Band-Aids stuffed in my pockets. I couldn't wear jeans because they were too abrasive. That hurt, because jeans were in style.

Sometimes I'd come home after some kind of a game, and I'd be all cut up and nicked. The bumps would be acting up because of the physical punishment, but I liked sports enough to put up with it. Naturally, my mom was worried that I would aggravate my condition or hurt myself, so she tolerated my involvement without really supporting it. At a time when typical parents were getting a big kick out of their kids' early athletic exploits, my folks knew only concern.

I guess I always wanted to be a professional athlete, but I was never single-minded about it. I wanted to be a broadcaster when I listened to Mel Allen, the voice of the Yankees, doing his "Gillette Cavalcade of Sports" show. I saw *Jack and the Beanstalk* and wanted to be an actor. I decided I was going to be in the Air Force Band after I saw and heard them play "The Flight of the Bumblebee." That inspired me to take music lessons until about the eighth grade, when I got sick of lugging around the saxophone.

My family lived in government projects that were cheap but pretty well maintained. It was a mixed neighborhood, but I attended predominantly white schools. The worst thing about the projects was the rate of transience among the armed forces families. But the turnover also taught me to deal with new people and not to rely too much on a single group of friends. When new kids moved in, the first thing we wondered about was whether or not they could play sports. That was the most convenient yardstick.

As a kid, I didn't really have a peer group in the classic sense. I was very curious about others, and my friends included juvenile delinquents, athletes, nerds. The jive kids in the neighborhood had processed hair and wore slick clothes. I was very straight-looking. I had short hair and I wore nice slacks and sportshirts. But I could hang around with the tough guys, partly because of my brother Dennis. He was a smooth dude, smart and streetwise.

"Don't mess with Bobby—he's Dennis Moore's brother," the homeboys would say. "Dennis can roll a seven with his eyes closed."

My mother was mortified when she heard things like that.

She would throw away dice whenever she found them in the house, and she would pray for us to be delivered from temptations like gambling and liquor. But out in the street, it was always the same: "Hey, Bobby—how's your brother Dennis? Man, that Dennis can roll a seven with his eyes closed."

I roamed around a lot as a kid, and I developed a minor reputation. Tacoma had an array of neighborhoods and a handful of high schools. If you lived in my neighborhood, Lincoln Heights, you tended not to go to Eastside—they would kick your ass over there. Because of my brother and my athletic ability, that law of the street didn't apply to me. I'd go hang out with the Catholic boys at the Boys Club or play basketball with guys in the inner city.

During the summer, a group of us in the neighborhood developed a schedule that we followed like clockwork. On Monday, we played basketball. That was the day the girls showed up, which introduced an element of danger, because anytime there were girls around somebody would get beat up. The presence of a couple of cute girls always had some bizarre effects. Guys who couldn't jump would all of a sudden be trying to dunk the ball. If you faked out a guy big time, he could take it and look like a fool or try to kick your ass to make *you* look like the fool. So it wasn't enough to be a good player if any of the guys you were playing against were bigger and stronger. You had to know *when* to be good.

On Tuesday, we played touch football with live blocking. But if the girls showed up, we began to play tackle. Wednesday was basketball day again, but the girls didn't usually come around, so the games were safer. Those games were the hub of our social activity. During the course of the day, anybody who was somebody came by the court. People would be hawking hot tapes, televisions and clothes, and pot and wine.

The ticket to being recognized as a bad dude was scoring thirty points while drinking wine out of a brown bag on every break. The mentality was like "Anybody can score thirty, but Sloane can do it *high*." Bob Sloane was the original B-boy, a kid who could talk shit and score thirty and orchestrate the activities on Thursday, which was Pill Day. The street dudes would get high after basketball on Thursday and cruise until Sunday. On Monday, they'd be back at the courts, because the girls were coming around again. . . .

Because I was a good athlete, I always played with older kids. It was funny how some of these bad dudes would take an almost paternal interest in me. If they were going to get high, they'd invariably say, "You'd better go home now, Bobby. We're gettin' ready to do some drugs."

"Okay," I'd answer. "I'll see you guys tomorrow."

I had a boyhood friend, Gary Carr, whose mother was also a Pentecostal. But he was lucky, he didn't have to attend church with her. Jerry would watch the football game on Sunday and then report on everything that had happened while I'd been sitting in church.

Those were the years when the American Football League was independent of the NFL. I was an AFL fan, because they had wild offensive games that ended with scores like 57–49— you could mistake them for halftime basketball scores. Paul Lowe of the San Diego Chargers was one of my big-time heroes, along with Lance Alworth, Raymond Berry, and Galloping Willie Galimore. I adopted Galimore's number, 28, and kept it through my career.

I couldn't watch football on Sundays, but athletics did figure into the church program. The church always occupied a major place in black society, particularly in the South or with those people who left the South to seek opportunity up North. Social and religious life were deeply intertwined in a way that no longer seems to happen. Although a Pentecostal service lasted all day, after the collection we were allowed to go outside. We would always go down to some nearby alley, take our shoes off, and race.

The competition was casual but fierce—imagine the pent-up energy in a bunch of kids who'd been sitting in church all morning on a warm spring day. Believers from all over attended services, so we would organize competitions to see if the kids from Tacoma were faster than the ones from Seattle. And the girls in their pretty dresses stood by on the sidelines, checking it out.

I was standing in front of church with a friend one day just before services resumed. Suddenly a relative of his appeared at the door. She ordered him to get into the church right away, and then she turned on me with a scary, intense glare. Her words haunted me for a long time, and I still remember them clearly. "And you, Bobby—I had a dream that nothing good is going to come of you. You're out there chasing that ball all day like a dog chasing a bone. You'll never amount to anything."

Her outburst shocked me. Adults in the church policed the kids, making them spit out chewing gum or telling them to stop talking, but my mother was very protective of me. Time and again she would tell the adults to see her if they had a complaint about me. I was unaccustomed to the kind of attack this sister made on me. It cut me deeply, and I never forgot her for it.

By the time I was in the ninth grade, my athletic skills were highly developed. Having to spend all day Sunday in church was a real roadblock against what I most wanted to do. But for all her religious devotion, my mother put my well-being and happiness in the forefront of her life. She yielded, and I was allowed to play sports instead of passing Sundays in church.

I became a popular kid, partly because I made a point of knowing everybody. And I was interested in all kinds of things besides sports. I had a friend who used to go to catechism class on the weekend and talk about it at school. I became so curious that I went along with him one day, making me probably the only kid in history ever to voluntarily go to a catechism class on Saturday morning, when all those cartoon shows were on TV.

Much later, I would have to take two buses to get to high school, changing in the center of town. It was my choice to go to a better school, while most of my neighborhood friends went to local Lincoln High. The bus stop in town was where all the prostitutes used to work, so I got to know them on a first-name basis. They nicknamed me "Bonus Baby," and they kept an eye on me, making sure I got on that bus instead of hanging around and getting into trouble. I had guardian angels like that, all over the place. I always felt looked after and protected.

The armed forces tend to level people out socially, and they bring together all kinds of people from different backgrounds. Racism was not a big issue around Tacoma, not as far as I knew. Whatever problems occurred were imported from places where prejudice was a way of life. I remember as if it were yesterday watching civil rights marches telecast from Alabama, and incidents like Lester Maddox throwing a bucket of lye in a pool because black people had gone wading in it. Those events were incomprehensible to me, and I was too hell-bent on what I was doing to be deterred by racial fears.

When I was in seventh grade, this kid LeRoy McDowell moved to Tacoma from Tennessee. He turned up at my predominantly white school, and I felt good about that—here was another black kid. I thought maybe we could hang out a little bit.

One of the first days of school, we were walking down the hall together and I said, "Hey, LeRoy, look over there—look at that girl. She's great-looking, isn't she?" But LeRoy didn't bat an eyelash. I thought maybe he didn't hear me, so I went on, "You'd better check her out now, man. She's somethin' else." But he still wouldn't look. "LeRoy," I said. "She's right in front of us. Will you take a look at her?" But LeRoy kept his eyes riveted to his shoes.

After the girl went by, I asked LeRoy what was wrong with him—why hadn't he looked at the girl? He told me he didn't want to do any "reckless eyeballing." I'd never heard that expression before. I laughed out loud and asked him what the heck it meant. He told me that a black guy wasn't supposed to look at white girls in the first place. If you did, you couldn't look directly at them. That constituted reckless eyeballing.

I thought his paranoia was funny. From that day on, whenever I was walking with LeRoy and we saw a pretty girl, I made an effort to point her out, to try to make him look at her. He never loosened up. His reaction was always the same: *boom*—his head went down like he'd been hit over the head with Lester Maddox's ax handle.

By junior high school, I'd dealt with the bumps. I'd learned to find things to be happy about, even when I had the option to be serious and unhappy. I still remember one of the happiest days of my youth, a moment that I've shared with very few people, and certainly nobody at that time.

I was almost a teenager, but there I was sitting in a doctor's office once again. He shot me full of Novocain and went to work cutting bumps off my ears. I fought back, and it became like a major-league brawl. By the time I left his office I was exhausted, and wearing a huge bandage on my head.

On my way home, I ran into a neighbor, Josie Horton. She asked what had happened, and I told her a miserable lie. I claimed I just had a headache. But when the bandage was removed a few days later, the bumps were gone. The ones on the rest of my body quickly flattened out and eventually disappeared. They vanished as mysteriously as they'd arrived, and they never troubled me again.

But I never forgot those nights before the bumps disappeared, when I'd wake up for a moment and see Mom kneeling by the side of my bed, praying.

Sometimes, the combined demands of family life and broadcasting turn me into a civilized version of the Road Warrior. Here's an example.

During one swing I found myself driving up the West Coast from Los Angeles to Santa Barbara. I reached over to get something out of my briefcase and came up with a handful of—well, let's say "intimate apparel." I'm happy to report that it was my *wife's* intimate apparel, just some things Phylicia had left behind in the hotel room in Los Angeles where we'd spent the previous night. She had an early flight out to New York, so she just got up, grabbed whatever was at hand, and left. Dutiful husband that I am, I collected her things. It's the best way yet I've found to fill a briefcase.

I really missed Phylicia when I saw those things, and I missed our baby, Phylea. I've spent most of my life on the road in one way or another: playing in one city but living in another, just moving around as my career dictated. I've been in New York for five years now—it's the longest I've lived anywhere since my childhood.

The "NFL Live" show keeps me traveling during the season; and then there are other projects, like the one that had me traveling to Santa Barbara to do some promotional photographs. At the end of the summer, I co-hosted a pilot called "The Family Show." The idea was to create an upbeat show about unique families. You hear a lot these days about how the family unit is an endangered entity, but this show is a celebration of the traditional family and its values.

Instead of preaching at people, the producers went for the light touch. But the show has the potential to convey the message that the family can be a powerful unit. If you pull together and fight hard and love each other, you can hold your lives together through some pretty trying times. That's a good message.

If the show is bought by a network, I'll have to spend thirty-nine weeks a year in Los Angeles. Phylicia's committed to "The Cosby Show" back in New York, which makes me wonder what might happen to my other, private "family show." I don't want to be away from my wife and daughter for two or three weeks at a time. I have three children by previous marriages, and I pretty much missed the experience of seeing them grow up. I don't want the same thing to happen with my infant daughter, Phylea.

Experience has taught me that being apart can really keep things interesting and lively, but if you cross a certain line it isn't exciting anymore. You just drift apart; the emotional gaps just get bigger between you. Being together every day is impossible for us, and it takes a toll. Doing something together every other day is great, but being apart for three or four days at a time is bad. Some people get a kick out of seeing how Phylicia and I operate. We'll turn to each other and say, "Okay, what's your schedule? . . . Tuesday I've got this, Thursday you've got that . . . so let's do this dinner thing on Wednesday when we're both free."

Still, I need to branch out and do more than my football features. It seems that the more things I have going, the better and calmer I am at each of them. So there I was, with a briefcase full of ladies' underwear, heading for Santa Barbara after a madhouse week that would make even the Flying Dutchman look like a homebody.

It all started out at six in the morning on the previous Thursday, when I caught a plane from New York to Kansas City to tape a feature on the Nigerian running back, Christian Okoye. I wanted to be back on Friday night to see my wife and child, because I had a speaking engagement in Toledo on Saturday.

I had a reservation in first class, but the flight to Kansas City was oversold. With a little fast talking, I finally got a seat. We got into Kansas City at about nine in the morning. The hotel was fully booked, and they wouldn't give me a room until one p.m. All they could do was hold my bags. Gee, thanks. I had been hoping to rest and organize my thoughts for the taping, but all I could do was sit in the lobby until check-in time.

I realized a long time ago that I'm no John Madden. You'll never catch me taking a train when I go on the road, or in any other way extending my travel time. Madden's been one of the greatest things to happen to pro football in the last few decades. He's a great communicator and a natural entertainer, with the accent on "natural." His great asset is force of personality, which is something that can't be imitated successfully.

Even if he weren't afraid of flying, those long train rides would suit Madden, because he's like a folksy guy from the old days, a real storyteller. He's the kind of a guy who will sit in a hotel lobby and wait for somebody to come along so they can talk. On a train, he's got those guys captured; he probably keeps them up all night, talking, playing cards, whatever. The train is a perfect way for Madden to travel.

I finally got checked in and we shot the interview with Okoye. I did a double take when I saw him, because he's like an Earl Campbell with a mild Nigerian accent. Okoye stands six foot three and weighs just over 250 pounds, and he was playing only his fourth year of organized football. Okoye leg-presses seven hundred pounds and bench-presses four hundred—and he runs the forty-yard dash in 4.4 seconds. Those are Campbell-style stats.

Okoye holds the African record for the discus throw. He was persuaded to try American football while he was at Azusa Pacific University, and he ended up in the NFL. Like most everybody else, I used to wonder what "Azusa" means. It stands for the school's goal to serve as the melting pot of universities: A to Z in the USA. I guess they've accomplished that by producing Okoye for the NFL.

The flight back to New York that evening was oversold, too. I was bumped out of first class, but at least I made the flight. We were approaching La Guardia when violent thunderstorms broke and forced us to divert to Philadelphia. It was eleven at night, and after going through all that trouble to get back to my family, I was looking at spending the night in Philly.

The pilot couldn't give us a departure time for New York, so I decided to get off the plane to check out the options. I called the rental-car agencies, thinking I might drive the NBC crew and myself up to New York, but there were no cars available. I decided to take a room in Philadelphia, so I could fly right out to Toledo in the morning. But there was some big celebration of the Constitution, and all the hotels were booked.

It was almost midnight when I called Phylicia, who was in the middle of taping "The Cosby Show," and explained my predicament. She got Bill on the phone. "Relax," he told me, "I'll give you the number for my house in Philly and somebody will take care of you. They'll pick you up, give you a nice bed, fix you breakfast in the morning, and get you to the airport."

Bill's generosity was comforting, but there was no answer at his number in Philadelphia. On top of that, I heard the announcement that our plane was ready to leave for New York. I figured that the plane would still have to sit on the runway for a few hours, but I took a chance, my only shot at getting home. By the time I walked in the door, it was after two a.m., and there was nobody to see but my own tired face in the bathroom mirror.

I was booked on a noon flight to Detroit the next day, so I had to settle for a quick breakfast with Phylicia and Phylea. There was another man heading for Detroit that morning—Pope John Paul II. Just my luck. The scene at the airport ticket counter was something right out of a disaster movie, with heavy security and tons of people fighting to get onto my flight. Here we go again, I thought. I was unprepared for this speech I had to give, and I was due back in New York the next morning to do a voice-over for the "NFL Live" show. I was already exhausted; the last thing I wanted to do was fight my way through the Pope's retinue just to get to Detroit.

I'd told the people in Toledo to send a car to Detroit for me, thinking I'd rest up and prepare my speech during the ride. When you do an engagement like this, your hosts assume that you've spent a few days boning up, preparing for the affair, because it's so important to them. If you're tired, or indifferent, or unprepared, you'd better know how to put on a game face. And I needed a game face, because the function was a Martin Luther King Scholarship awards dinner, with about eight hundred people in attendance.

Once we got rolling, I began to plan my speech for the mid-western crowd. I'd talk about the Lions, a team I had plenty of stories about, because they were rivals of the Vikings.

We once showed up half an hour late for a televised game against the Lions at the Silverdome after getting tied up in a horrendous traffic jam. Bud Grant didn't like to get to a stadium too early—he had an army officer's sense of timetable, and he felt that the team would lose its edge if it had too much time to kill in the locker room before a game. He liked to arrive at a stadium one hour before kickoff, so the Viking buses left the Northfield Inn at eleven-forty-five, allowing fifteen minutes for the ride to the Silverdome.

The tie-up was so bad that at twelve-twenty-five, general manager Mike Lynn got out of one of the buses and ordered the driver to continue on the grassy median, a strategy that failed— at twelve-thirty, we were still stuck in traffic. Football players love it when things go wrong and for a change nobody can blame them for it. They pull out all the needles and wisecracks. "Hey, Mike," Fran Tarkenton called out, "We need another pregame meal or these guys are going to starve."

The driver spotted a cop standing before a barricade at an access road. He pulled back his window, hoping to convince the cop to let us through.

"Hey, I've got the Vikings," the driver shouted out.

"Oh yeah?" the cop called back. "I've got the Lions and three."

The entire bus howled.

The game finally started, twenty-five minutes late. That night my mother called me and told me how embarrassed she was for us, being late and all. That was Mom. If I made five TD catches and we won in the last minute, that was business as usual. Being late, now *that* was a trauma.

That cop was crazy to take the Lions against the Vikings. We had Detroit bamboozled, convinced that they couldn't beat us. They would be up by seven or ten with eight minutes to go and pretty soon they were walking off the field, after having lost by two, muttering: "Damn those Vikings. They ain't shit, they're just the luckiest team in the league."

It wasn't luck as much as confidence, but a lot of the time they go hand in hand. Look at all those times Bjorn Borg, who won the Wimbledon men's singles tennis title five straight times, was a point or two from elimination. It was never the other guy's shot that took a funny bounce or hit the net and fell over. It's never the defensive, tentative guy who gets lucky. You *do* make your own luck, and confident teams or individuals make good luck, not bad.

We beat Detroit, 10–9. Gutsy guy, that cop.

But my own luck turned bad in the Motor City, which was the second reason why I'll never forget Detroit. My career ended in the Silverdome, giving me a jolt I'll never forget as either a physical or a psychological experience.

And then there was a guy who moved to Tacoma from Detroit, James Murray, or as we called him, "Pimp James." The nickname was inspired not by his profession but by the way he walked. Of course, nobody dared to call him Pimp James to his face. Murray was a local celebrity during my boyhood. All my friends in later life loved to hear Pimp James stories, especially Kareem Abdul-Jabbar. Somehow this big, shy, fantastically successful guy loved to hear about Murray, who stood five foot six and never made it very far out of the ghetto. He was the original A–Number One B-boy, a bad, bad, bad dude. It got to the point where anytime Kareem and I had some minor hassle he would look at me and say, "Don't worry, man, I'll just call Pimp James."

In Detroit, Murray had led a gang called Ali Baba and the Forty Thieves. He would produce these letters from girls back home, these soppy hero-worshiping pages smelling of perfume which all began, "Dear Ali." I once saw James shoot a stick out of the hand of a kid who was standing in a crowd. James would walk by the window at school and if you looked out he might show you a gun and signal with the barrel. That meant you had to leave class because he wanted to see you.

I was a little kid when James first moved to the neighborhood, so he never bothered with me much. But one time he beat up my best friend, my best friend's older brother, and my best friend's dad, all within an hour. He wasn't the kind of guy you could keep out of a touch football game if he decided to play, and he took particular relish in hitting with his fists, elbowing, and clotheslining the poor guys who ended up on the other team. He was the kind of guy who would play tackle in the park without equipment, in leather street shoes and a nice pair of slacks, without thinking twice.

James's home was right by the bus stop. He would often sit by the window while a group of us kids formed up outside. Then some days he'd come out and march everybody into his house at gunpoint. He would keep us hostage until about noon, when we would finally make it to school, trying to think up some excuse for why we were half a day late.

The Vikings used to love to hear Pimp James stories, too.

Flying to Detroit one year, I had the whole team in the back of the plane, gobbling up the legend of Pimp James. When we arrived at the hotel, we barely had time to check in and shower before we were due at a team meeting. I was just changing when my phone rang and a gravelly voice on the other end said, "Yo, big mo', this is James Murray."

"James—" I was stunned. I hadn't seen Pimp James since ninth grade. "Where are you, man?"

Murray was down in the lobby, with a nephew he wanted me to meet. I was going to beg off, explaining that I had a team meeting to attend. But then I remembered those times when he took us hostage on school days. What the heck, I figured, the only difference between then and now was that this time, I'd get fined no matter what excuse I produced. But I was making pretty good money. I told Murray I'd be right down.

But my most important memory of Detroit is the happiest of them all. The Silverdome was the place where I proposed to my wife on national television, before the kickoff of the 1985 Thanksgiving Day game between the Lions and the New York Jets.

To this day, I'm amazed at how much publicity that gesture generated when it was nothing more than that—a romantic gesture intended to impress the woman I loved. But I'm probably better known for that proposal than I am for the "Miracle Catch" I made against the Browns in the last seconds of the game that gave us the divisional title in 1980. I guess not everybody can relate to making a great catch in a big football game, but the whole world relates to romance.

I've paid a price for that gesture, too. A lot of people think, "Oh, Ahmad Rashad—wasn't he that guy who proposed to his wife on TV?" It's the handle on me; it defines me as a celebrity, no matter what I did with my life before or after. To some people, I'm just going to be "that guy" who got a lot of publicity for proposing on television.

At the time I proposed, Phylicia and I had been seeing each other in a very low-key, quiet way for a few months. We'd gotten into the habit of Sunday-evening dinners at Elaine's, the cozy restaurant on Manhattan's Upper East Side. The owner, Elaine Kaufman, has had tons of famous patrons over the years, from Woody Allen to Evonne Goolagong to Andy Warhol. Famous people like the privacy they find at Elaine's—she protects her brood from the press and the curiosity seekers.

Phylicia and I conducted a very proper courtship over fried calamari at Elaine's. Then she would drive all the way home to her mother's house in Westchester. Very few people besides our mutual friend Bill Cosby and Elaine knew we were a couple. We wanted it that way. My wife and I have a strong sense of privacy, and she's a master of propriety.

Phylicia's a real lady. I was lucky to meet her at a time when I was ready to appreciate her qualities. In the past, I'd met and been in awe of proper women. I'd lived a freewheeling life that didn't have much room for rituals like an extensive courtship. But Phylicia appealed to me right away. The test came when I cussed, just to see if I could get away with it. Not only did I get away with it, but I found out that she let go with a few choice words now and then, too. Ultimately, Phylicia taught me that a lady could be everything. She could cook, cuss, and carry her end of a conversation about any subject in five languages. After all, Phylicia graduated magna cum laude.

I could see that our relationship was heading toward a proposal, and I didn't want to mess it up. I guess every guy has a romantic streak: being able to make a great gesture is part of being cool. But if you're going to make a gesture, you'd better do it right. If you're going to get a girl a corsage, you'd better make it a nice one instead of a bunch of dandelions or something.

So one evening over dinner early in that Thanksgiving week, I asked Phylicia what she'd say if I asked her to marry me. I wanted to feel her out, because we'd both been married before. We'd both learned our lessons. Lesson Number One for us was: there's no reason at all to be married unless you love somebody so much you can't bear to be apart.

Besides, we weren't under any economic pressure to get mar-

ried. We were both busy and independent. In some ways, it was
an ideal situation in which *not* to get married. But I was crazy
about her, so rational arguments went flying out the window. I
found myself testing the water. Naturally, Phylicia saw right
through my gambit, and she wasn't buying any half-effort. Her
answer was simple: "I can't tell you what my answer would be
because you haven't asked me."

I figured the door wasn't all the way shut; there was a little
light leaking through the crack. So I let the subject drop and
filed away her answer. On the plane to Detroit a few days later,
I thought about my options. I knew that she was going to be in
the Macy's Thanksgiving Day Parade, which NBC was also covering. People at the network would always know exactly where
she was, so she could hear my proposal and give an answer, too.
When I got to the hotel, I called Cosby to fly my plan by him.
But I got the answering service and left him a message, saying
it was urgent.

My friend Bobby Reese, the Jets' trainer, was waiting for me
in the hotel bar that evening. He'd put me through rehabilitation
when I'd hurt my knee while I was playing in Buffalo, and we'd
become good friends. I told Bobby I planned to propose to Phylicia at halftime, and he was very skeptical. It took me about
fifteen beers to convince him that it was a cool thing to do. In
fact, after those fifteen bruisers, he was more convinced than
I was.

When I got up to my room, I found two dozen long-stem roses
waiting for me. They were from Phylicia. That's what I mean
about her being a lady, and still doing things her own way. So
I did something I hadn't done before and haven't done since. I
actually rehearsed what I planned to say in front of a mirror,
curious about how stupid I was going to look.

Before I went to sleep, I called our producer, John Filippelli.
I told him I wanted to clear some time to do something a little
different on the air the next day—propose to Phylicia. John had
met a girl I was going out with a while back, and I hadn't told
him about Phylicia. "Why her?" he asked. "You don't even
know her."

John called our executive producer, Mike Weisman, who gave the okay to clear the extra time. Before game time the next morning, I stood nervously on the floor of the Silverdome. I would introduce my feature, and then they would cut back to me for a live tag. After that, I was on my own. The game stuff went off without a hitch, and when the time came for the proposal I just went on automatic pilot. To this day I still don't know exactly what I said. But at the end I felt relieved, and I thought, "Well, I did it. This girl could make me the most embarrassed man in America, but at least it's over now."

I was invited to watch the game from the box of a friend, Jets president Jim Kensil. They have a live feed to the monitors in most of those boxes, but they don't get audio. So Kensil and company didn't know what I'd done, and when I told them they didn't believe me. I'd asked Phylicia to give me an answer by halftime. By then, Kensil had my confidence pretty well shot. He'd been ribbing me mercilessly. He claimed that when they went to find Phylicia, she was off somewhere with CBS commentator Irv Cross.

At halftime, I took care of my football stuff with a small monitor at my feet so I could see what was happening in the studio. I heard the director in my earpiece: "Ahmad, we've found Phylicia. We've got her right here. She's got an answer for you." At that very moment, the monitor went blank.

I could still hear them in the studio in New York, and I knew that my picture was up on the big screen at the studio, and in most homes. Suddenly, the audio went dead, too.

Dick Enberg was standing nearby. He was all wired up, connected to the studio. He was hunched over, listening. Then he started laughing.

"What if she just said no?" I wondered. My options for a reaction seemed pretty limited. There I was on national television, on Thanksgiving Day, which is second only to Super Bowl day in sheer numbers of viewers.

My mind flashed back to my very first experience in broadcasting, when I messed up a sportscast so badly that the news anchorman on the show turned away in disgust and pretended not to know me. When I get very nervous, I break a sweat. We're talking about golf balls here, busting out on my forehead and temples. I felt those suckers popping, and I found some tissue and wiped my face. This all happened in a few seconds that went by like years, while I was cut off from the studio.

I found out later that Bob Costas ad-libbed from the studio—something he does better than anybody else in the business. Seeing me all worked up, he said, "You *ought* to be sweating, pal."

I'd gotten a fleck of tissue caught on my face, so home viewers saw Dick Enberg's hand suddenly appear on the screen as he wiped the particle away. As it turned out, Phylicia had appeared on screen very briefly, given an answer, and then the studio cut away to something else. I was about the only person in the country who *didn't* know what she had said.

That night, I flew back to New York with the Jets. They had lost, 31–20, leaving head coach Joe Walton in a funk. He was watching this little portable television in his lap. I saw my picture pop up on the "Entertainment Tonight" show and heard the whole story for the first time.

I finally saw and heard Phylicia. She's not one to clap her hands or jump around or go hysterical like somebody on a game show; she's too dignified for that. She looked the camera straight in the eye and spoke just one word. Thank God it was "Yes."

The banquet went off smoothly right up to the awards segment. At that point, the mayor of Toledo stood up to introduce me. She went on about what an excellent role model I was, how I was an upstanding citizen and a great credit to my family. She gave this whole spiel, winding up to a great big climax as she said something like "Now it's my great pleasure to give this award to—uh . . . Ashad Ahnmad . . ."

She blew it. I forget exactly what she called me, but it was some weird twist on my name. But I took it in stride. I made my speech, deciding at the last moment that it wasn't exactly the right occasion for telling stories about Pimp James.

My hosts took me out for a nightcap after the banquet, so it was late by the time I got to sleep. Bright and early the next morning, I arrived at La Guardia and went straight to the studio to do a voice-over for a piece about the NFL draft. Because of my schedule the previous week, I was depending heavily on the producer of the piece to make sure that the copy was clean and the segment was free of errors; but sure enough, we stumbled on an inaccuracy. There were a few testy moments over that, an implication that I hadn't done my homework. But we got it ironed out and wrapped the piece.

I got home to Westchester in time to turn on the television and catch Phylicia on "The Cosby Show." It seemed like ages since I'd seen her, and I was feeling pretty sentimental after my speech in Toledo. But she was already en route to Los Angeles, so I had to settle for watching the show—something I've done in various hotel rooms all over the country. When we're apart, Phylicia and I try to talk every night, but there's one place where I know I can catch her for sure: on NBC at 8:00 p.m. on any Thursday night. Me and two hundred million other people.

Watching Phylicia, I missed her so much that I booked an early flight to Los Angeles for my meeting with the producers of "The Family Show." In just about eighteen hours we were together. We spent Monday night at the Westwood Marquis with our daughter, and on Tuesday morning she was gone. I had nothing left but a case full of briefs that would make a lawyer's eyes pop right out of his head.

But the beat goes on, from September through January. A week after the strike was settled, I found myself heading out to Chicago to do a feature on Jim McMahon. He'd been out of the Bears' lineup since late November of 1986, when Green Bay's defensive end Charles Martin ended Jim's season with a savage, late hit. Jim had surgery for a torn rotator cuff in his shoulder, and he was out of action right through the replacement games. Some people, including Bears coach Mike Ditka, weren't sure that Jim would ever come back. In six years with the Bears, he'd missed a total of twenty games because of injury.

But Jim got the call in the first regular game after the strike, against Tampa Bay. Replacing Mike Tomczak at the start of the second half with the Bears behind, 23–14, Jim led his team to a 27–26 win, passing for one touchdown and running for another in the final six minutes. One Chicago newspaper called it a "McMiracle"—fast-food heroics from a guy who endorses a chain of drive-through taco restaurants.

Going out to do the piece, I was skeptical; I wasn't sure what to think of McMahon. It was hard to measure his sincerity from television—he seemed to work hard at appearing ultracool. He wore dark shades during interviews; his taco commercials looked like videos straight from MTV. Then there was the headband controversy: in 1986, NFL commissioner Peter Rozelle had prohibited Jim from wearing a headband that read "Adidas," so the next week the quarterback wore one that read "Rozelle."

I suspected that Jim was just a media event: a brassy, irreverent, self-centered guy who knew how to get the attention of the camera. Guys like Jim and Brian Bosworth were the end product of a long transition that began during my career. In the 1970s, football opened up, went liberal, became much more tolerant than ever before of the individual and his needs—and idiosyncrasies.

When I was a rookie, growing your hair out—whether it was a natural Afro or long blond locks—was considered a heavy statement. The veterans who had crew cuts would give you the evil eye or question your willingness to die for good old St. Louis, or wherever. Like most American institutions, football was under fire during the early 1970s, and sweeping changes took place.

I spent time at a Bears practice, and then Jim and I sat around for a few hours at his restaurant, just talking, before we rolled an inch of film. My skepticism was laid to rest quickly. I'd misjudged Jim, just like I'd been misjudged at times by veterans from another generation. For one thing, Jim's teammates love him. That counts for a lot, because you can fool a lot of people, but it's impossible to hoodwink the guys who line up alongside you in duress.

Jim knows where his bread is buttered. He has a close relationship with his offensive line, something like the bond O. J. Simpson had with the Electric Company in Buffalo. Jim and his line go out for dinner every Thursday night, a little affair they call the Thursday Night Follies.

The other Bears told me that Jim's an enthusiastic, communicative leader. He gets all excited in the huddle when he thinks the Bears can pull off a big play; he thanks linemen when they execute well. I played with Fran Tarkenton, a guy who used to draw plays with his finger in the turf like any kid in a pickup game. I know the value of that enthusiasm. Leadership like that makes you a players' guy, rather than a coach's guy or a media guy.

A lot of great players are perfectionists, so they're often misunderstood. A guy like Jim demands that you perform at the same level he's on—sure, that's pressure, but it also shows tremendous respect for *your* talent. And he's the first to acknowledge that talent when it's been put to use. Nobody critiques a perfectionist more thoroughly or accurately than he does himself. That's how I was, that's how Jim is. Just look at John McEnroe, whose frustration in the quest of perfection has caused him—and various opponents and officials—so much grief in pro tennis. Half the time that McEnroe blows his cork, it's triggered by his own shortcomings. You rarely see him explode when he's playing really well. His problems almost always begin with his failure to live up to his own standards.

You can't ever judge a quarterback just by the quality of the spiral he throws; you judge him primarily by whether or not he can win. Dave Kreig of the Seattle Seahawks has been rated as high as number four in quarterback efficiency, and the statistics for his career to this point bear comparison with anybody else's. But people whisper about Kreig's consistency; they whisper about his leadership qualities. Over the past few years, the Seahawks have shown great promise, but in the late season in the crunch, they've gone flat or come up short. The quarterback gets painted with the same brush that critics use on the rest of the team. Often, he gets the first coat.

At one point in my conversation with Jim, I had this gut reaction: if I had a team, this is the guy I'd want as my quarterback. This guy is a winner all the way. If you've got adequate talent, the key to winning is to make the team feel that it can win. Jim was the kind of guy who instilled that feeling. He made a valuable point, talking about the game against Tampa Bay. "Tampa was up by twenty-some points, but you could see in their faces that they were weirded out to be ahead. You could see they didn't believe they ought to be ahead, because we were the Bears and we'd won the Super Bowl."

That's how the Lions and a lot of other teams used to look at us Vikings. Their expressions, their body language—all of it conveyed a lack of conviction. They figured they'd play pretty hard but eventually they'd lose. They were willing to accept it. One of the hardest jobs a coach has is to turn that attitude around. And it's one of the main reasons coaches lose their jobs. It doesn't have a whole lot to do with X's and O's all the time.

But Jim's talents go far beyond the intangibles. What impressed me most about him was how well he knows the game and how opportunistically he exploits the weaknesses of a defense. In a word, Jim's a throwback. These days, football is full of big, tall, pretty-boy quarterbacks who get the play delivered from the sidelines and throw the ball according to plan. Discussing what went wrong with a certain play the next day in the newspapers, you'll often find a quarterback saying, "I don't know, I didn't call the play." The Jets' coach, Joe Walton, was under fire just recently because of the plays he calls. Talk about taking the game away from the players!

But the philosophy of bringing plays in from the sidelines is part of the increasing complexity of the game. It was beginning to develop while I was still a Viking, after Fran Tarkenton retired. When Bud Grant sent in a play for Fran, the poor messenger was just as likely to get chased off the field. But Tommy Kramer had big shoes to fill when Fran retired, and the staff thought it would make things easier if they called the plays for Tommy. So the play would come in, and Tommy would in effect rubber-stamp it. We'd break huddle and line up, and guys would be mumbling all up and down the line: "Hey, man, this play ain't going to work. This is some bullshit here."

Jim's a throwback. He isn't very tall, and he sure isn't very pretty. He doesn't have great speed, and his passes often have a little waddle in the air. Jim is from the same mold as Fran Tarkenton and Billy Kilmer. As Johnny Unitas once said, "A quarterback hasn't arrived until he can tell the coach to go to hell." Jim measures up to that standard. He calls audibles, which means that when he comes up to take the snap, he checks out the defensive alignment. If he sees something he can exploit, he'll cancel the original play and bark out the signals for one he likes better. At the start of a game, Ditka still calls the plays. But as the flow develops, he gives Jim more and more latitude to run the show from the field.

The key to taking advantage of a defense is knowing how to read one, which calls for a good football mind and reliable instincts. Mike Ditka knows that. By the end of the Tampa Bay game, Jim was calling all his own plays. But it took Jim a long time to get that vote of confidence, partly because he's not a student of the game in the classic sense of the phrase. He claims he never learned anything from game films; even in his college days, he hated to watch them. That's no small deal, because game films are a sacred cow in the game.

Jim's celebrated "communication" problems with Ditka were caused partially by his indifference to game films. Watching game films, McMahon would start looking for his buddies, to see how they were doing. He'd sit there like a fan before his television. If a friend of his took a good lick, he'd laugh. Ditka just couldn't understand how McMahon knew his job without extensive film study. But in time, Ditka realized that Jim wasn't being lazy, or rebellious. He's just an instinctive, hands-on player. Like I said, he's a throwback to a different time that was tighter in some ways and a lot looser in others. Talking to him, I became a McFan.

4

THAT *IS* DICK BUTKUS OVER THERE

Scott Studwell. Now there's a football-player name. Scott Studwell, linebacker. It's got a ring to it, you've got to admit. Scott Studwell, football hero. He was part of my generation, but the veteran Purple People Eaters liked him, and that was a great endorsement. He fit the great Viking mold: he was a hard-drinking, hard-nosed, hard-assed guy—and a good friend.

Scott was also a very handsome guy, with muscles on top of muscles. During training camp, we used to go over to a disco called the Albatross, which was right across the street from our facility. The Albatross was known to the girls of southern Minnesota and the plains of Iowa as a place where they might go and land a Vike. You can imagine how the guys locked up all day in training camp felt about that. Once Scott and I were watching the action, just feeling kind of mellow and not really looking for anything, when a waitress came over with a note from a beautiful girl across the way. It simply said, "Dear Scott, I would love to have your baby."

Another time, we sat at a table watching all of the rookies and free agents on the dance floor. The kids from big urban centers, especially Southern California, liked to get down and show off

all of the hot new dance steps to the hicks in Minnesota. Scott
had knocked back a few drinks, and I guess he felt inspired. He
looked at me real seriously and announced, "Ahmad, now I'm
going to get up and dance like fuckin' F.E."

"F.E.?"

"Yep," he said. "Fred Estaire."

That was Scott Studwell, linebacker.

It was a little unusual for a wide receiver to be buddies with
a linebacker. That's because linebackers are different. I never
even pretended to understand them, and Scott was a classic
linebacker: he would be bleeding and his jersey would be hanging out of his pants before the game even started. Like most of
his breed, Scott was a real player, a guy who played tough and
played hurt and just played some more instead of talking about
it. The attitude comes with the territory, and linebackers cover
a lot of territory.

Unlike linemen, linebackers at least get to touch the ball once
in a while when they force a fumble or make an interception.
But their take on the game is still different from that of wide
receivers or halfbacks. Basically, linebackers love to run and hit;
and the faster they run and the harder they hit, the happier they
are. Collisions at speed—that's what it's all about for them.
They're the big cats on the plain: cornerbacks might be a step
faster, nose tackles might be a little stronger, but nobody is a
better all-around predator. When he walks by, a linebacker
would just as soon give you a shot as shake hands—and that's
if he likes you. I'll give you an example.

I always used to watch linebackers warm up before games.
They work themselves up to the right pitch by banging each
other on the pads or smashing their heads together. I always
wondered about that psyching process—how high could you get,
whipping yourself into a frenzy. Well, before one game a few
years ago I decided I was going to let it all hang out in a way
that's never been my style. It was a big game, the band was
playing adrenaline music, the fans were already whooping.

I ran over to where the linebackers were going through their ritual and rushed up to Scott, yelling, "Come on, baby, gimme a shot." Scott hit me so hard in the shoulders that my feet went numb. I staggered away and never made the mistake of mixing it up with the linebackers again. It was bad enough to have the other team's 'backers hit me—I didn't need it from my own guys.

But in terms of how they do their job, linebackers do have some things in common with players in the offensive finesse positions. Linebackers have to range far and wide, reading the offensive patterns, just like a receiver ranges over a lot of territory and reads defenses. To play either position well, you need great instincts. A linebacker needs to do more than cover his immediate territory, just like a wideout must be able to adjust on a pass route.

Through the course of a game, the linebacker will be called upon to take a turn at almost every defensive job that exists: he has to stop the run, cover receivers, sack quarterbacks, and tackle guys in the open field. They never talk about linebackers being versatile, because versatility is the essence of the job.

The 3–4 defense, which uses a pair of outside and a pair of inside 'backers behind a three-man defensive front, puts a real premium on good linebacking. The position is having a golden age now: it's glamorous, just like being a bull terrier is glamorous since the beer commercials featuring Spuds MacKenzie became a hit. There's a bumper crop of linebackers out there today. Maybe it's a natural result of the four-linebacker defense, but have you noticed how 'backers now seem to come in pairs, like Fredd Young and Brian Bosworth, Lawrence Taylor and Carl Banks, Shane Conlon and Cornelius Bennett?

Young may be the most underrated of that bunch. He's been in the Pro Bowl for the last two years, and after just four years in the league he's taken over as Seattle's defensive leader. That's on a team that also has strong safety Kenny Easley, the AFC defensive player of the year in 1983. Easley's gotten banged up over the last two years, and Young just stepped up and became a leader even though he was only twenty-five.

Easley has a great attitude, admitting that Fredd's become

the Seahawks' defensive big-play guy. Easley's always been
known for his toughness, for how hard he hits. Young is the
same type of player, having made his mark originally on special
teams service. But when Easley talks about Young, he hardly
mentions his teammate's power and aggression. He talks about
Young's football "intelligence." That's what you have when you
learn to identify and evaluate your football "instincts." And Easley talks about leadership.

One of the main ingredients in leadership is consistency. It's
as true in football as it is in politics and corporate finance. Every
athlete in the NFL has big-play potential in his bones and muscle
fibers. The great players and the leaders are the ones who can
harness and unleash that potential like a dam producing hy-
droelectricity rather than a dam bursting in a storm. It takes
intelligence, and it also takes motivation; it takes ambition, and
it takes a desire to win that's stronger than a fear of failure. And
it takes a little bit of the kid that ought to live in every football
player, the kid who's fantasized a thousand times that it's fourth
and long, with ten seconds on the clock, and the team is behind
by six . . .

The guys who lead on the field have all kinds of different
qualities and ways of influencing play. But one thing they always
have in common is that when a big moment comes down the
pike, they want the play to come their way. At important times,
an ordinary player might think, "Shit, I hope they don't run at
me this time." A leader thinks, "Run at me, I'm going to stop
you," or "Throw it to me, I'm gonna catch it."

I was always willing to take the chance of making a big play,
because to me, nothing could be worse than being left out of
the key play or moment of a game. It's just a matter of holding
your destiny in your own hands, even when your hands are
sweating. And you're that much better off when you realize that
the destiny you're dealing with is nothing more serious than
winning or losing one of the thirty-some football games that take
place every Sunday, for months, year after year.

Still, you can't underestimate the physical qualities that go into the making of a great player. The Seattle coaches like Fredd Young because he's explosive. It sounds like a cliché, but that capacity to explode is a subtle, real quality that's different from having just power or speed or a nice combination of both. Rusty Tillman, the special teams and assistant linebacker coach for Seattle, puts it this way: "Young has that burst, that special coiled-up-and-ready-to-explode quality that all great players possess."

Two or three times in your career as a player, you spend an entire game looking for one guy. It doesn't matter where you are or who has the ball, you're always conscious of his position. It's the ultimate compliment to a defensive player. Only two linebackers really made me feel that way: Willie Lanier, who was with the Chiefs when I joined the Cardinals, and Dick Butkus.

I was lucky Dick Butkus had retired from the Bears by the time I got to the Vikings, because they were divisional rivals. I knew from my first experience with Butkus that I didn't want to spend my career trying to run away from him.

Fresh out of Oregon and drafted in the first round by the Cardinals, I played on the 1972 College All-Star team which met NFL teams in scrimmages and the annual exhibition game. I wasn't a big hit with the coaches, Bob Devaney and Tom Osborne of Nebraska. They ran the operation like Marine boot camp, and I didn't think that level of scrutiny was appropriate to the situation—not with my rookie year in the NFL looming ahead.

Anyway, Reggie McKenzie was my partner on the All-Star team by then. On the bus ride to the Chicago training facility where we would play the Bears, everybody was afraid. Butkus was the main reason, but the rest of the Bears were a rough-ass bunch, too. Of course, nobody said anything, but you could tell by the mood. The guys who usually talked a lot of shit were quiet all of a sudden. You didn't hear a peep out of them.

The Bears let us get on the practice field first. It was a hundred degrees out there—you could *smell* the heat. When the tension had built to a pitch, the Bears suddenly came running out of one end of the complex. They ran down to their end of the field in a neat line, in those plain uniforms that send the message: real men don't wear pastels, or helmets with little pictures of horses or birds on them.

Naturally, we all were afraid to look over at them. I leaned over to Reggie and whispered: "Reg, man. There's Butkus. Don't look now, man, but he's about forty yards down over there."

Reggie's eyes got real big inside his helmet, and after he nonchalantly checked out the scene, he said, "God damn, that *is* Dick Butkus, right over there. Number 51. He's in this scrimmage."

Early in the game, I ran a counter-reverse play. I tucked in the ball and ran parallel with scrimmage, trying to get outside. Out of the corner of my eye, I saw Butkus, well off the play but coming on strong, bowling people over and picking up a head of steam. I was dipping and bobbing, making some moves on the outside linebackers and cornerbacks. I was about to break loose, but I knew Butkus was gaining ground. At the last moment I just stopped dead in my tracks and broke the play back the other way, and Butkus ran by me like a runaway truck. I gained forty yards, and it turned out to be our biggest play of the game.

After that gainer, Butkus was looking at me a lot. Bobby Moore, huh? His eyes were burning inside that bird cage he wore for a helmet. But he never said anything to me, and I sure didn't dare talk to him. I went on to have a pretty good day, catching three or four passes. I felt good, because I thought Devaney and Osborne were trying to make me feel that I couldn't play, and there I was, kicking the Bears' asses.

Late in the game, I had to jump up to catch a little "out" ball thrown to the sideline. This Bear, Charlie Ford, tackled me out of bounds. It was a cheap shot, and I came up swinging— shocking the hell out of Ford and the rest of the Bears. These guys didn't expect college players to retaliate. My stock with the Bears, who always appreciated tough, aggressive play, rose. I don't know what Devaney and Osborne were thinking, but my performance in the game spoke for me.

A great linebacker needs football intelligence and the physical characteristics of a big cat, but general intelligence helps too. That's one of the reasons I think Brian Bosworth is going to develop into a great linebacker. However you feel about the contract negotiations that got him a ten-year deal for eleven million bucks, however you feel about his aggressive self-promotion, or whatever you think about his haircuts, Bosworth has shown that he's a tremendously aware guy.

A lot of young athletes just want to get out and play the game; they don't want to be hassled by or even responsible about things like money. But people who are aware tend to be tuned in to everything around them, all the time. There are some great players who seem to do it all on raw instinct, but they're exceptions who succeed almost in spite of themselves. An aware guy is mentally sharp. There's less chance that he's going to be beaten by mental weaknesses or lapses; he's only going to be beaten by a bigger, stronger, faster football player who also has a good football mind.

There are plenty of smart guys playing football today, and there are going to be more of them all the time. I learned in my career that dumb guys didn't win unless there were smart guys around them. And most of the big winners are smart guys. It's because they're aware, and they don't shut their awareness off on the field, at home, or even at the negotiating table.

Look at how many of the guys who decided they were going to take an aggressive role in contract negotiations are winners. I'm not saying that to pump bad blood through the front offices of the league but because the rap management tries to lay on players who fight for more money is that they're spoiled, or somehow not concentrating on football. The average guy out there in television land sees how much pros make and he's seduced by the argument. After all, he doesn't want to know from contracts; he just wants to see great football on Sundays.

But look at the facts. Fran Tarkenton became a human business conglomerate and a Hall of Fame quarterback as a natural, parallel progression. People hated John Elway when he refused to play in Baltimore; they said he was cocky, selfish, and mercenary. People sure don't hate John Elway now—except maybe in Cleveland. Maybe the best example of the aware, opportunistic athlete of the 1970s and '80s was a guy who's got a lot of linebacker in his personality and a little linebacker in his past, Reggie Jackson.

Sports Illustrated dubbed Reggie a "superduperstar." Reggie hit four home runs on four consecutive swings in the World Series of 1977, three of them in the final game. Reggie was called "Mr. October." One of his more famous quotes, given while he was still in Oakland, was that if he ever played in New York, he'd have a candy bar named after him. And that's exactly what happened.

Reggie did things that real people just don't do. As big as he was in New York, he was twenty times bigger in terms of his achievements. He did things that turned Manhattan Island into Fantasy Island. Nobody hits three homers on three swings in a single game in the World Series; it just doesn't happen. Somebody forgot to tell that to Reggie.

But to me, Reggie played a major role in making athletes smarter, less gullible guys. He was in the right place in the right time when big money came into baseball with the free-agency rulings, and he took advantage of that. Of course, few fans knew that he had successful business ventures going long before that. Reggie sent the message that he was a successful guy, not just a great athlete. That's a rule every potential pro should have tacked up inside his brain: don't settle for being a great player; be a successful guy, too. There's no contradiction there.

I first met Reggie when he was working as a broadcaster for ABC at the annual Superstars competition in 1979, shortly after I was named MVP in my first Pro Bowl game. I stayed at his place when I was in New York sometimes; and later, he liked to visit me when the California Angels came in to play the Twins.

Once, Reggie paid a surprise visit to our training camp at

Mankato, Minnesota. As soon as the photographers saw him, they posed him centering for punts, things like that. He grumbled about all the fuss, but then he always does. The only thing that would have made him feel worse is if nobody had recognized him or treated him like a celebrity. You can pretty much define a star as a person who wants it both ways—the adulation and the privacy, the recognition and the anonymity.

Later on, Reggie got tired standing around watching us practice; he lay down on the sideline with a football for a pillow. Bud Grant caught my eye and nodded. I swallowed hard and went over. "Hey, Reggie, listen. Sorry, man, but nobody lies down. It's Bud's rule. Nobody even sits."

Reggie gave me this incredulous look through his tinted glasses, like I had to be kidding.

I told him that I was serious, mentioned that the other day an owner had come out to visit and even he wasn't allowed to sit down.

"That's okay," Reggie said softly. "I make more than any owner."

I had this prickly sensation on my neck and took a good hard look at him, trying to see if he was just putting me on. He slowly got to his feet, grinning.

Over the years Reggie came to be perceived as a tough-minded mercenary. That was partly because of the novelty of free agency and the penchant George Steinbrenner had for throwing money at the problems of his organization. Reggie just happened to be one of the first guys to benefit from the windfall, and he learned to play the money game as well as anybody. The notorious New York press had a field day with all the juicy stuff about money and big egos—after all, that's the stuff New York is made of in the first place.

Baseball is the worst of sports when it comes to the public's perception of a player through the press. Because a team plays almost every day, the writers who cover the beat fall under the illusion that they really know the players, when nothing could be further from the truth. You'll hear a writer say, "Hey, I've got a pretty good relationship with Reggie. Hell, I see him around the batting cage every day." Let me tell you, you could see Reggie around the batters' cage every day for the next fifteen years and, unless he chooses otherwise, still not know a thing about him except how he swings and how he zings his teammates.

Not only would you not know him; chances are pretty good that you don't really care to know him—all you really want is a spicy quote. That's all right; it's part of the job for both athlete and journalist. But it should never be confused with real knowledge of a man or a real relationship with him. The day-after-day exposure just lulls some writers into making assumptions.

Reggie is a complex, dynamic individual. But lately, it isn't just the high-profile guys who are demanding and getting their due. Even the linebackers are getting into it now; they're not as prone to sacrificing their own well-being to conform to the front office or the public stereotype of an athlete who's so rugged and tough that he couldn't care less about money.

Last year, linebacker Cornelius Bennett held out in contract negotiations with the Indianapolis Colts, got traded to Buffalo, and immediately helped the Bills become a contender. Wilber Marshall, Chicago's All-Pro linebacker, struck a blow for free agency when he played out his option with the Bears and signed with the Redskins at the end of the 1987 season. There's no doubt about it: linebackers today are bigger, faster, stronger—and smarter.

5

THE SNOWY MOUNTAINS
OF MIAMI

tudio 6-A is a clean, well-lighted place—a cozy place that's sometimes like a locker room but almost never like a field. On a field, during a game, on any given play, you've got just one chance to do what's expected of you. Do it now and do it right—that's the mentality in football. Joe Senser, a close friend from my Viking days, summed it up when he complained that in his first two years with the club, Coach Grant spoke just four words to him: "Catch the fucking football."

We're under similar pressure on the show when we do a live segment, but in television "live" isn't always live. We tape most of the show beforehand, and elements like my weekly feature are dropped into the appropriate slot. Then at airtime we take our places on the set, ready to go truly "live" in the event that the tape breaks or some other disaster occurs. In the event of some major news story breaking, we can go live from the studio. If there's a pressing need to go to a stadium and hook up for an interview, we can do that.

Most of the halftime shows and the updates are live, because they're going out to different cities at different times. We sometimes have a brief live dialogue, but nothing too extensive, because in television, time has the value of diamonds, and it gives

you the power of an oil baron. Time is an almost tangible com-
modity that, like most precious things, you get in tiny amounts.
Two minutes of welding to a guy working in a garage is nothing;
two minutes of airtime for a reporter or analyst is a windfall.

The "talent" on any given show usually fights tooth and nail
for airtime. Grown men and women have at each other over 120
seconds of exposure to the camera. Time is so carefully measured and doled out that you're left with little breathing room.
Worst of all, you don't have nearly as much direct control over
the size of your own role as you do in football, where performance
is judged by much simpler, more obvious standards: catch the
fucking football. Do it, and we'll throw it your way again.

The differences between my football and broadcasting careers
sometimes add up to trouble in Studio 6-A, like they did during
a halftime commentary last season. Frank DeFord, the respected
writer for *Sports Illustrated*, is a regular contributor to our show
with a halftime feature. That too is taped, and we just feed it
into our live format. One week, Frank did his piece on some
problems experienced by black players on the Green Bay
Packers.

Green Bay is a pretty small city that doesn't offer too much
in the way of popular black culture. Some guys on the team felt
exiled, out of touch with things they knew. It's a long, cold winter
in Green Bay, which creates cabin fever. The black guys in
Green Bay complain that they can't even find a barber who
knows how to give them a good haircut.

Costas had introduced and framed the piece in a serious tone,
and Frank's analysis was scrupulous social criticism wrapped
inside a sports feature. When Frank finished, Costas turned to
me and said, "Ahmad, as a black man, how do you feel about
that Green Bay situation?"

I said that the real problem was that the Packers were a losing
team. If they were winning, everybody would be earning more
money and the guys could afford to chip in and fly in a barber
to cut their hair.

As a former player, I'll stand by that analysis, because if I learned one thing in the NFL, it's that winning teams don't have excuses or invent side issues to blame for their performances. It doesn't matter what color you are—the bottom line is that when you're doing the job right, everybody is happy. I learned that when I was a purple Viking, from some of the greatest black and white competitors who ever played the game.

But under the circumstances, my remarks could have been interpreted as very flippant, and they undermined the earnest tone of the piece, which meant that either Frank or I would end up looking silly in most people's eyes. In short, I'd misread the nature of the piece, and I was damned lucky we weren't on live. I decided to do it over.

Unfortunately, our producer, John Filippelli, resisted me. Flip's a good guy and a friend, but for some reason he got upset when I asked to do the take over. He snapped at me, saying something like, "Who do you think you are—Bob Costas?"

I told Flip I'd never confused myself with Costas, but that I still wanted to do the piece again. He answered that it was impossible and made some lame excuse about the piece being all wrapped up and sent out into the electronic heartland of TV already. Meanwhile, the director's voice in my earpiece was saying that we had plenty of time to reshoot the segment.

I couldn't really let the matter rest. Racial problems are loaded issues, capable of polarizing people even in the most harmless context. This was one of those situations in which the piece would go out and some TV critic or sports writer would take it the wrong way. He might make a few phone calls to prominent politicians or civic leaders and *bam!*—suddenly I'm embroiled in a huge controversy, with people who know nothing about me or the issue questioning my "sensitivity," all because I got a little sloppy on the job and didn't bother to do it over.

Costas supported my position. He knows the commentary axiom: as soon as you think that nobody really cares what you say, someone takes offense and begins to raise hell. It's happened a thousand times. But I still resent having to take a grave attitude on all racial issues, just like I always resented having to look mean and serious on the day of a big football game, simply because some coaches thought that was the only way to appear. Besides, people don't always realize that because of the high degree of integration and the obvious emphasis on performance above all else, athletes are sometimes the most relaxed about racial problems. They may be naive to some bitter truths lurking out there in the "real" world, where things aren't quite as cut and dried as in football. But the truth of the matter is that most guys in the "real" world, white or black, will never know the kind of camaraderie that's bred on a football team, will never know the quality of friendship that can exist between teammates of different color. It happens because of the proximity, the shared struggle, pain, and joy, and the great leveling effect of performance.

But that doesn't mean that I'm any less perturbed by racism—just as I wasn't any less serious about winning football games. I don't want to be the Voice of Black America because through all of my life I wanted to have my own voice. And in cases like the Green Bay episode, that's the voice of a concerned American. That's why I found myself insisting on doing the piece over.

"Racism" is a big word. It's a *very* big word, and one that I don't like to throw around very often. When you use any word too much, it loses its power and nobody takes it very seriously anymore, even if people pay lip service to it. At the same time I know that racism exists, and it's often hiding right there in our daily lives like a cancer.

During the last U.S. Open tennis tournament, Chris Evert was upset by a black player from Houston, Lori McNeil. In the semifinals, McNeil had to play the world's number-one woman, Steffi Graf. The announcers called Lori a great athlete, but they never really discussed her strokes. It sounded as if Lori were just a person who could run real fast. Is that all it takes to get to the semifinals of one of the two biggest tennis tournaments, in a sport where technique is crucial?

Bryant Gumbel, who's moved on from sports to become the host of the "Today" show, once shared with me some observations about racial thinking. He said that racial distinctions are made constantly during athletic events. If you close your eyes and listen, you can tell whether a commentator is discussing a white or a black athlete. When he says that somebody is a "natural," so fluid and graceful, you know he's talking about a black performer. When you hear that this other guy's a hard worker, or that he comes to play every day on the strength of guts and intelligence, you know that the player in question is white. Just open your eyes.

Bjorn Borg was one of the greatest athletes ever, yet commentators always talked about his concentration and nerves. Sure, Borg was a great mental competitor, but if he were black, the media probably would have focused on his fantastic speed or his remarkable reflexes. People—black and white—look where their eyes are directed. The people who do the directing really have to be on their toes. Dwight Stephenson works as hard as any player in football, and he's intelligent. How often do you hear that?

When a white player has an abundance of natural talent, he's often called a "genius." That's been the case with John McEnroe. But I always laugh when I hear the word "genius" applied to athletes. To me, a genius is a person whose work lifts the spirit of mankind or dramatically improves life on this earth—a Picasso, a Jonas Salk, a Louis Armstrong. Bill Parcells, the New York Giants coach, is not a genius. It doesn't take a genius to play or coach football, but it takes a real idiot to call a Michael Jordan or a John Elway a genius.

Lori McNeil is shortchanged when she is called a great natural talent. And it's insulting when Chris Evert doesn't get credit for being a fantastic athlete. People who aren't great athletes don't get into pro sports, period. Calling McNeil a great athlete isn't really saying very much at all. Sure, there are degrees, but an Evert is just an inch away from a McNeil in athletic ability, and fifteen miles distant from most recreational tennis players.

Doug Williams, the Washington Redskins quarterback, has also been the victim of prejudiced thinking. As a receiver, I always had trouble with the argument that a quarterback throws too hard, which is the rap against Williams. There are just two questions to ask about a quarterback's passing ability: does he throw it to the right place, and does it arrive on time? Saying a quarterback throws too hard is like saying a running back runs too fast, or that a boxer punches too hard. The guys at the other end of the spectrum throw so weakly that the ball never gets where it's going on time. Those guys never get any further than intramural college football.

This receiver always wanted the ball to arrive as soon as possible. The faster the ball got to me, the more of a jump I had on the defensive back for the rest of the play. When the ball got to me fast, the chance that I would get clobbered as soon as it touched my hands went down dramatically. The faster the ball got to me, the better the chance I had to break the play for a long gain.

Granted, you don't throw a ninety-mile-per-hour strike at a halfback on a little flare-out pattern, but that's a mistake of judgment, like a running back outrunning his blocking. Before Doug Williams jumped to the short-lived United States Football League, he led the Tampa Bay Buccaneers into the playoffs. His credentials as a legitimate NFL quarterback are above question.

Watching games, I've seen receivers drop passes that prompted commentators to say that Williams throws too hard. Then I'd change channels, and when John Elway threw the ball at 300 mph, the guys in the booth talked about his great arm. I'm not trying to compare Williams and Elway. I just want to point out that they have two of the best arms in the NFL, and how hard each of them throws is not the major issue in their success as quarterbacks.

Arthur Ashe, a man who's deeply involved in social and racial issues, used to tell me that he resented always being called "the first black Wimbledon champion." Sometimes, he just wanted to hear somebody call him "the Wimbledon champion." Qualifications, whether they're racial, ethnic, or any other kind, take a little of the edge off. Muhammad Ali hit the absolute peak of sports when people began just calling him "Champ." I'll take that any day—just plain "Champ."

We've come to a stage where the racial scorekeeping sometimes accomplishes the wrong thing for all the right reasons. During the '87 season I had a call from a *USA Today* reporter. I was on the road, so I didn't have a chance to return it. The next day in the paper, I saw an item pointing out that for the first time the producer, director, and color analyst on a football telecast would all be black.

I guess that's what *USA Today* wanted to contact me about. But what was so newsworthy about a black producer and director working together? Did it mean that somebody not good enough was getting a chance? Was it really earth-shattering news that blacks could hold those positions? I guess someone put out the information hoping to generate some publicity. But in my eyes, it was a nonstory.

So we all know that racial issues exist; there's a little bit of Green Bay everywhere. Airing out and addressing those things is a part of living in a free, open society. Ultimately, Filippelli came to see my argument and he let me make a more appropriate comment on Frank's piece.

Looking back, I've got to say that catching the football was never a problem for me. I'm amazed at the impact such a minor faculty had on my life. I guess that's what some people would call "fate"—the influence of forces we don't choose or can't control. Fate, in different forms and shapes, has a tremendous role in your success, or your failure.

Getting stuck playing behind the coach's son even though you're potentially a pint-sized O. J. Simpson is one simple example. At the pro level, most fans assume that the draft is a handy way to sort out the talent, a kind of final ranking of players based on the judgment of scouts, head coaches, and general managers—the football people. But many factors go into draft selections, and fate is unkind to plenty of guys.

The draft is the machine that produces the parts for the NFL, and the owners spend a lot of time justifying its performance. But sometimes a team won't cut a number-one draft choice, because it's a confession that somebody in the system made a huge error, and the result is a big cover-up: the guy will hang in for a couple of years, and if he's lucky, he'll get traded to another team, where he can prolong his career for another year or two.

Sometimes the choice comes down to having to cut a high draft choice or a guy who you took in the ninth round but who's really shown that he can play. Well, if you cut the guy you took in the second round—the one who got a fat signing bonus—it makes news and raises eyebrows. And unless the ninth-round pick is a one-in-a-million sleeper, nobody's going to praise your creativity in finding him when you've just cut Mr. Franchise from Major University. People may turn to football to escape from realities like politics and economics, but the reality of football involves politics and economics.

Late in my career with the Vikings, I was sitting around at O. J. Simpson's house in L.A. on the night before the draft. We figured out that if some people made the right moves to shore up their teams, Marcus Allen might still be available by the time Minnesota got to pick. We'd read the cues perfectly. When the Vikings' turn came, Allen was still available, and the front office went right for—Darrin Nelson. I'd been ready to call Marcus on the phone. I was going to scare him with some stories about life with all of those deer-hunter dudes and walleye fishermen in the sticks of Minnesota before I told him the truth about the place. Instead, I was pissed off, wondering, "Who's Darrin Nelson?"

Darrin's a nice guy, and he's become an exciting running back who really came into his own in '87, especially in the postseason playoffs. The Vikings reasoned that they were looking for the best available runner for the artificial turf of the Metrodome, which means smaller, thicker guys who cut well on the carpet; but I thought they just went for a guy who wouldn't cost them a lot of money. And that's mostly what got me mad. That's fate, too.

A Moore family gathering for my parents' thirty-fifth anniversary. That's me in my first double-breasted suit.

That Championship Season: South End Boys Club (Tacoma). Guess which one I am.

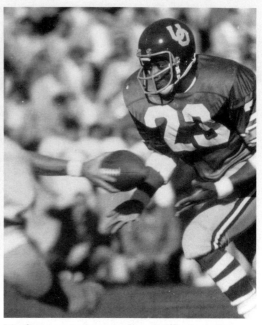

Brothers from another planet? Ed Marinaro and I at the Playboy mansion in 1971. (Photo courtesy *Playboy*)

My first appearance in *Sports Illustrated*, as a Heisman Trophy candidate my senior year at Oregon. It was also Dan Fouts's first appearance (that's his hand). (George Long, *Sports Illustrated*)

Monday Night Football opener, 1974—a time to shine. Here I am beating the Raiders' Hall-of-Famer Willie Brown for a game-winning touchdown.

Leaping was my forte—and also my downfall, as Jim Marsalis tore up my knee with this hit. (Bob Bukaty, *Courier Express*)

Fran Tarkenton inscribed this: "To Ahmad, Thanks for making me a decent quarterback." If it weren't for Fran, I'd still be taking pictures with Marinaro at the Playboy Club.

I was a great lead blocker. Hey, Chuck, this way! (Fred Anderson/NFL Photos)

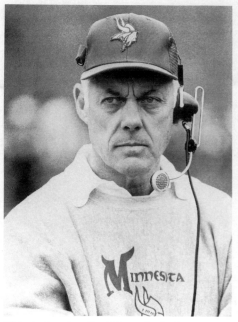

This is the way Bud Grant looked when we were winning. It's also the way he looked when we were losing. As a matter of fact, this was the way he looked all the time. (Billy Robin McFarlend/NFL Photos)

My favorite corner of the world. (Fred Anderson/NFL Photos)

My Super Bowl highlight—interviewing boyhood hero Raymond Berry, 1986. My Super Bowl lowlight? Losing to the Raiders in 1976. (Thomas J. Croke)

Interviewing Jim McMahon, 1987—my kind of quarterback, all he does is win.

Three Men and No Baby, in Hawaii, 1988.

Bill Cosby, putting the finishing touches on his role as Cupid.

My biggest moment. (LEFT TO RIGHT) Mike Paulucci, O. J. Simpson, me, Bill Cosby, Phylicia, Debbie Allen, and the Reverend Eugene Calendar.

Find the adult in this picture. With Ahmad Jr. and Billy Bowles.

My daughters Keva, at eighteen (ABOVE), and Maiysha, at thirteen (BELOW).

With Phylicia and me, our daughter, Condola Phylea, at fifteen months.

You can't do it all by yourself. Sometimes, even if you could do it all by yourself, other people won't let you. You can't just will yourself to be something. And you shouldn't put yourself under extra pressure by trying to be something you're not. Time will usually tell what you're best suited for. I wasn't meant to play "The Flight of the Bumblebee" with the Air Force Band; I was meant to catch a football. Right from the start, it was as if all I had to do was put out my hand and *whap!*—the football just stuck to it.

My first experience in football was orchestrated by my brother Dennis, who would be my inspiration as I progressed from high school through college and into the NFL. He was a sports fanatic—he knew the nicknames of all the players, and he could imitate all of the famous announcers of the day. He loved schools whose names could be shortened to a few letters, so he was always going on about LSU or SMU or TCU or whatever.

My childhood friend Ronnie Bender lived nearby, in an area full of small houses with little yards and narrow strips of lawn between them. Dennis and I would go over there to play this game: Dennis would throw me the ball, pretending it was a kickoff, and I'd run it back, trying to get by him on that narrow strip. Meanwhile, he would do a running commentary that got me all excited: "And Bobby Moore has the ball on the twenty . . . he makes a move and gets to the twenty-seven . . . he sheds a tackle . . . holy cow, he's at the fifty! He cuts for the sideline—can anybody catch him now? . . ."

Then, *boom!* The lights would go out. After stringing me along, at the last second Dennis would trip me or reach out and push me off balance just before I got by him and crossed our imaginary goal line. I would go down in a heap, and half the time I was just about to burst out crying when he picked me up, got the grass and dirt out of my ears, and gave me this pep talk about what a great run it was, before sending me down to start the game all over. I developed all of my moves on that small strip of lawn, trying to dodge Dennis or Ronnie.

I also participated in every Junior Olympics track meet that was held nearby, from about fifth grade through high school.

They gave out ribbons at those meets, and I collected my fair share. I kept them all in a little box, and I'd take them out and look at them on special occasions. I also tacked a few up to the wall.

The only sport that got my father excited at all was baseball, so I tried organized baseball for a brief time. I gave up on it because of the curve ball—not because I couldn't hit it, but because the other kids couldn't throw it. You know how in the pros, the pitchers throw the ball and it's heading right for the batter's head until it breaks and goes over the plate? Well, it was the same in Little League, but 90 percent of the time the curve didn't break.

Once I was in the on-deck circle when the kid at the plate got beaned pretty badly. When I stepped up to the plate, I struck out on three swings, eager to get away from there before I got hit too. Baseball may be less dangerous physically, but when I was a kid, batting seemed about the same to me as standing there while somebody threw rocks at you. At least in football you had a running chance—you could put the moves on somebody and elude the tackle. Ironically, I was attracted to football because it seemed less dangerous.

I tried to explain that to my father, but O. C. Moore wasn't buying any of it. He thought baseball was the sport smart kids played. When I did tell Dad that football was my chosen sport, he said that was the dumbest move I could make. In his eyes, sports was another career opportunity. Among all the sports, football carried the greatest risks and promised the least amount of longevity and security. Telling him that football was my first love was like saying that I wanted to be a barber on a battleship—it wasn't the barbering he was against but the battleship.

I told Dad that I had a plan. I was going to play football intelligently, as cautiously as I could without undermining my performance. I stuck to that philosophy, and it brought me some grief over the years. Just about the worst thing you can be called in football is "chickenshit." It's right up there with "quitter" as an insult, a motivational tool, an epithet that can break your spirit. The football ethic is built on a foundation of physical courage and manly virtues like bearing pain without complaint. Coaches ingrain the philosophy in their players, and they manipulate it to achieve their ends.

Tell a guy that he's dumb or ugly, and he'll just hang his head; he may even smile and take some pride in the insult. There's a kind of reverse snobbery in football, with a lot of guys taking pride in their image as cavemen. But call him chickenshit and chances are that he'll run the length of the field on a broken leg to clear his name—either that or tear your head off your shoulders.

But I was just as committed to surviving football as I was to playing it, so I was immune to that mentality. Over the years I've had coaches who implied that I was chicken, but I always thought I saw through their ploy. One of the less appealing aspects of coaching is that you ask guys to make sacrifices that, if you were in their shoes, you might not make yourself. Asking guys to play when they're hurt, asking them to perform recklessly, goading them to violence or unsportsmanlike conduct— most coaches have resorted to some or all of those tactics under stress, and the lousier the coach, the more inclined he is to do it. But I decided that I wasn't going to jeopardize my career or my health to live up to some frustrated coach's loaded notions about courage. I always felt secure enough about my abilities to ignore those kinds of challenges.

My talent became obvious as I entered my early teens. Saturday became the most important day of my life, because I'd go down to this park in Seattle where a group of high-school and college football players staged a big game. Charley Mitchell, a great NFL runner who'd attended the University of Washington, was a relative of mine, so I was plugged into this tradition, this grapevine of elite athletes, without even really being aware of it.

I was almost always picked early because of my good hands and speed, so I learned early on how to deal with older guys. By the end of ninth grade, I faced a really hard decision. I was in a bind that a lot of talented black people in every field face. I had to choose between security and opportunity—between a familiar environment and a new, challenging one. It isn't an easy choice for a young, happy-go-lucky kid who doesn't really know too much about the way the world works.

A lot of the kids in my neighborhood, including my brothers and sisters, went to Lincoln High School; but because of the busing rule, you could attend any of four high schools in Tacoma. So I had to consider Mt. Tahoma High School, which had an excellent football program.

It takes great guidance, determination, and maturity to break into a new environment when you're a kid. It's an experience that most people underestimate, because few people, rich or poor, go through it. Other kids faced the choice before, and plenty more will in the future. You can stay in the neighborhood and maybe go on to become a local legend, or you can grab the chance to see what the wide world has to offer.

You won't necessarily end up as a pimp or junkie if you stay at home. You may wind up with a good, secure job, a wonderful family, the whole deal. But there's the danger that you might outgrow your environment. And if you end up feeling trapped and passed over, you can ruin the rest of your life with regrets. Growth is the key issue.

But venturing out is risky business, too. Some people don't adjust to a new environment very well at all. There's the obvious pressure to perform. The rewards that you're promised suddenly look like they're within arm's reach, and you've got to be very mature not to grab at them, to take what you can when it's there for the taking. There are lots of easy ways to throw it all away.

Athletes are especially vulnerable. They're promised so much, fawned over, coddled, and made to feel so superior. I was lucky: I came from a family with solid values; my social experience was fairly extensive; and I had a natural curiosity about the world and what it had to offer. Some other guys lacked one or more of those advantages.

The best athlete I ever knew in my life was a guy who came

to Tacoma from Mississippi, Bob Sloane. He was the dude who could score thirty on the playground while drinking cheap wine. Bob was five or six years older than me, but he went to my church. I would sit next to him and he'd tell me stories. He was a supremely cool guy.

Bob Sloane was remarkably talented. If he went out for baseball, he made the all-state team. The next year, he might dig track; he'd end up winning the state half-mile title. About the only thing he couldn't do was find a sport he couldn't master. Basketball was Bob Sloane's ticket out of Tacoma—he averaged close to forty points a game in high school—and he ended up going to a junior college in Montana. It was a few years until I saw him again.

Even Kareem Abdul-Jabbar had heard the Sloane legend. Sloane's school once opened a doubleheader for UCLA, and the Bruins' staff was just blown away by Sloane's talent—so much so that they were still talking about him during Kareem's era. Sloane played just one year of college ball. He got into a car wreck and tried to score big on the insurance settlement; but when that failed, he drifted out of school and disappeared into the Seattle underworld.

One of our favorite teenage pastimes was walking through Chinatown in Seattle, checking out the lively street scene. On one of those adventures, I spotted this guy standing in front of a restaurant, wearing some outrageous Superfly suit, his hair all laid back. When I realized it was Sloane, I looked away quickly and hurried along. I was puzzled and confused; I just didn't know enough to figure it all out.

Over the next few years, I was able to piece together some of the elements in the sad and wasteful history of Bob Sloane. I heard horror stories on recruiting trips to some of the same schools that he'd visited years before: he'd put Tacoma on the map of lots of people's minds for good. Sloane would get caught stealing things from the bookstore or from dorm rooms; he would start a card game and clean out all these fresh-faced kids who thought he was just another naive recruit.

Sloane drifted into pimping and dope. It must have been the

logical step for a guy who was always looking for the quick, unearned buck. That was the consensus on Bob Sloane: that more than anything else, he wanted to reap the rewards that most people only get after they've put in years of hard work. He didn't burn inside to play basketball—maybe it just came too easily to him. He didn't have that work ethic in which the process of getting to the top is the real kick. He wanted the rewards right away: he wanted flashy cars and girls. He wanted a life-style more than a life.

I would see Bob Sloane one more time in my life. After my first year in the NFL with the Cardinals, I was walking through a mall in Tacoma when a broken-down bum came up to me. I almost did a double-take when I recognized Sloane. He told me that his little brother had been shot, and he wanted to borrow money to buy a suit for the funeral. The story sounded suspicious, but I couldn't resist him. I gave him a hundred bucks and wished him good luck. Two years later I heard that Bob Sloane had died of kidney failure caused by drug abuse.

But there are always smart, levelheaded people around, and part of the trick of growing up right is learning whose advice to take. Even the guys who would start messing around with pills and other drugs after we played basketball looked after me. They took care of me when I was with them, and they made me go home when they were about to do some bad stuff. One of them, Phelon Cole, used to set me straight. "Look at these guys," he would say. "They've been around for ten years and they ain't going nowhere for the next ten, or the ten after that. Is that the kind of life you want?"

Phelon was killed in Vietnam, but his message stayed with me. I decided that I was going to attend Mt. Tahoma High School, instead of Lincoln. And I was going to play football.

Blockbuster in Studio 6-A: Eric Dickerson was traded by the Los Angeles Rams to the Indianapolis Colts for *eight* players (counting future draft picks as bodies). Dickerson reportedly signs for $5.3 million over four years.

What was I saying about the rewards waiting at the end of the dedicated athlete's rainbow, the pro leagues? Nobody would doubt that such a contract is worth waiting for; but then Dickerson is a player worth waiting for if you're the Colts, needing just a few more horses to become a legitimate playoff team.

The Dickerson deal was a classic, a megadeal that dwarfed all the other deals of the past twenty-five years. It involved the largest number of players since '59, when Los Angeles sent the rights to nine players to the Chicago Cardinals for the Dickerson of that day, Ollie Matson. The engineer of that deal was the aggressive young general manager of the Rams, Pete Rozelle. By the end of the '87 season, the Dickerson deal would look like the deal of the century for everybody concerned.

Trades are an experience unique to pro sports. They can make or break a franchise, destroy or revive any number of careers. They can be as welcome as ice out in the north country, or hit a player like a death sentence. I was traded three times, and two of those times the deal saved my career and gave me motivation to keep playing football. At the other end of the spectrum lies a guy like Reggie Jackson. When he was traded from the Oakland A's to the Orioles, he was shocked. He'd broken in with the A's; they were like family to him. When Reggie was traded, he felt disowned.

Dickerson, on the other hand, wanted out. He had been through a long period of discontent with the Rams because the club refused to meet his salary demands, with both parties feuding and renegotiating since the middle of 1985. At the time of the trade, Dickerson was making $682,000—well below what he thought he deserved. He said that as the top running back in the league, he was entitled to "quarterback money." Dickerson haggled until, he said, he felt like a stallion whose spirit was broken.

Dickerson sulked, and the Rams lost. On October 25, 1987, he took himself out of a game against the Cleveland Browns, claiming he had aggravated a sore muscle in his thigh. The Rams lost that game, too. Three days later the Rams' head coach,

John Robinson, put Dickerson on the inactive list, announcing that Dickerson was "physically and mentally unable to play"— and the Rams lost even more games, getting off to their worst start in ages.

Then, almost overnight, Dickerson was heading for a fresh start with an old friend, his coach at Southern Methodist University, Ron Meyer. Under Meyer, the Colts have been transformed from perennial losers to a club on the upswing, tied for first place in the AFC East when the Dickerson deal was finalized. The club was willing to meet Dickerson's salary demands, which brought about a major adjustment in Dickerson's attitude toward football.

This is the kind of story Costas loves, because it's got elements of a news story, elements of a high finance story, and national scope as a sports story. It's tailor-made for a show like "NFL Live," because it gives Costas a shot at working like an anchorman, a role I think he likes. But he did something that disappointed me during his live interview with Dickerson. The previous summer Charles White, Dickerson's backup at Los Angeles, had relapsed into cocaine abuse. White had enrolled in a rehab program as a result, and things were pretty quiet after that. But right out of the blue, Bob asked Dickerson about White's drug problem—a surprise question that was sensationalistic and inappropriate to the story at hand.

Some people think that Dickerson burned a lot of bridges with his attitude and behavior, but all that stuff tends to fall into the past the moment you get traded. It's like being born again. Think about it: you're being traded, like a piece of furniture at a swap meet. Sometimes, it really is that simple.

The idea is bizarre to begin with. Imagine if trades were a part of everyday life outside of sports. You might come home one afternoon to find that your loving wife has traded you to a woman up the block, for her husband, her tennis racket, and an undisclosed sum of cash. Imagine some guy with a problem child on the phone with another parent: "Hello, Jack? . . . Say, Jack, that little girl of yours, Lisa—I hear she's got some musical

talent. How would you feel about trading Lisa for our Tommy?
. . . Yeah, he's a year older, five. Loves sports. He eats a lot, but
he ain't fussy. . . . Okay, okay, okay, I'll tell you what—I'll throw
in an electric drill and that shoe tree of Betty's that your wife
likes so much. . . ."

The very notion of trades would be repugnant if it weren't for
the fact that they're designed to make everybody happier—at
least they look that way on paper. When the object of the trade
is a big talent, the entire franchise gets a big boost. The message
from a new team is always the same vote of confidence: "Come
on, help make us a winner."

Football offers a pretty pure product of the competitive urge.
But when you play with one club for a long time and become
an "untouchable," you may grow complacent. If your relationships aren't good, you may get bitter. If the team goes into
decline, a veteran may give up hope. And there's always the
discontent brought on by money hassles. A trade always shakes
the tree and everybody sitting in it.

Just look at how many people besides Dickerson, Meyer, and
the rest of the Colts benefitted from the deal. The Colts had not
been able to sign their top draft choice, linebacker Cornelius
Bennett. As part of the package, the Colts traded the rights to
negotiate with Bennett to the Buffalo Bills. Those parties came
to terms, and the Bills became a hot young club led by two rookie
linebackers with Hall of Fame potential: Bennett and Shane
Conlon.

After Dickerson left the Rams, Robinson made Charles White
his big gun in the backfield. In his first start, against St. Louis,
White gained over a hundred yards and the Rams finally won
a game. Charles had won the Heisman Trophy in 1979, but he'd
had trouble fitting in with the pro club that drafted him, the
Browns. Robinson, who'd been White's coach at USC, picked
him up on waivers after the 1984 season, even though Charles
had developed a problem with drugs. Playing in Dickerson's
shadow, White did little. But when Dickerson sat out two games
in 1985 as part of his prolonged contract hassles, Charles scored

two touchdowns and gained over 220 yards. He would win the
NFL rushing title in '87, leading a dramatic Ram turnaround
that almost won them a playoff berth.

It seemed like everybody on earth was happy with the Dickerson deal, except for some critics who questioned the star's
ethics. Their argument goes like this: Dickerson had signed a
contract and then violated his end of the bargain by holding out
for forty-six days in the fall of '85. Part of the settlement after
that action was Dickerson's written agreement not to demand
to renegotiate until the contract expired. The hagglings that led
to Dickerson's trade in '87 violated that agreement—he'd held
out and demanded to renegotiate the same contract twice.

It's hard to refute the reasoning behind the analysis, but I still
side with Dickerson. Just the fact that these situations occur
proves that football is unlike any other business. Football puts
tremendous restrictions on the freedom of its "employees," the
players. NFL players can't seek the best deal with their employer
of choice. They are even prevented from working and living in
the city of their choice by the system based on the draft. So
when a situation grows unacceptable to a player, he doesn't have
the ordinary options. He can't say "Take this job and shove it"—
not unless he wants to quit the game altogether. So his only
recourse is to violate an agreement in which he's never been an
equal partner in the first place.

Sure, the $682,000 the Rams were paying Dickerson is hardly
slave wages; sure, their final offer of $975,000 is huge money—
Dickerson and everybody else in the world knows that. But here's
another thing about owners: they often underestimate the pride
of a player, especially a great player. The key to understanding
Dickerson's position was his comment on the Rams' final offer:
"I know that almost a million dollars a year is a lot of money,
but not for what I do. I feel like I gave them so much and that
they weren't willing to thank me for it."

I believe you have to be a man of your word, but in football
you don't enter into an agreement on an equal footing in the
first place. A football player should be able to get his fair market

value like any other individual. Besides, Dickerson isn't driving the Colts into bankruptcy but conceivably taking them to the Super Bowl. Dickerson could have made twice the amount he did in Los Angeles without violating the league salary structure. There isn't a better running back in football. Eric Dickerson is worth a million bucks—easily.

At Mt. Tahoma High School, I played on an unforgettable basketball team. In my freshman year, the Thunderbirds' varsity went something like 26–1. John Moseid, the coach, started me as a sophomore. He was an inspirational coach, a former small-college All-American in basketball. We had a pretty good team, but Coach Moseid took the basketball coaching job at a local junior college at the end of my sophomore year.

Our new coach was Milt Theno, and the program fell apart. We lost game after game. It got to be so discouraging that once I almost forgot to show up for a game, and it takes a lot to make a high-school kid do that.

Theno was a science teacher—physics, I believe. We nicknamed him Bear, as in Bear Bryant, not because of his brilliance as a coach but because he was always asleep, like a bear in hibernation. I'll always believe that the first law of physics is that when a basketball team is up by ten points, it's bound to give up ten points to create a balance in nature. That was a reflection of the coaching philosophy of Milt the Bear Theno.

Let's say we were down by ten points and made a run at the other team. Okay, so we tied the score. Then Coach Theno would take out the first string. His philosophy was that after catching them, we probably were real tired. He sent in the second string and presto, in a few minutes we'd be down ten again. He figured that was okay—his well-rested first team would always be able to catch them again.

It was that kind of deal. Need I say more?

Luckily, our football and basketball teams at Mt. Tahoma were like yin and yang. We were a football powerhouse, with a great coach in Joe Stortini, half a dozen kids who would win athletic scholarships, and a great local tradition. Dave Williams, who was chosen second in the NFL draft, was a Tacoma native. His friend Donnie Moore, another great running back, dated a sister of mine, so I got to visit Dave a few times up at the University of Washington campus. He gave me some cleats and loomed as my role model.

As a high-school sophomore, I was ready for varsity football even though I was on the light side at 150 pounds. I was the second-string end behind a guy named Dennis Smith. I scored touchdowns whenever I got in, but Coach Stortini wouldn't move me up. I did start in the defensive backfield, and I ended up making the all-city team as a defensive back. I also made the second offensive team despite playing behind Smith. Still, I might have decided to concentrate on basketball if I hadn't gained thirty pounds between my sophomore and junior years. As a sophomore, I'd been a starting forward and also won the state high-jump championships; but even at 180, I could run the forty in under four and a half seconds. I played flanker in my junior year and running back as a senior, alongside another outstanding player, Richard Harr. They called us the Touchdown Twins. What else could a kid want out of life?

I don't know how many yards I gained or touchdowns I scored; I was too busy just having fun, being a kid, to keep track of the figures. I was on a roll, literally growing by leaps and bounds. I reached the highest weight of my life during the spring of my senior year at Mt. Tahoma, when I hit 230 pounds. I still high-jumped six-eight. If I weighed less, I might still be in the air.

I was still pretty sensitive, especially to criticism. I sometimes felt that Coach Stortini sold me short. He would say that I was good, but not as good as Dave Williams had been. When a recruiter from Notre Dame watched us work out and talked to us one day, Coach Stortini said that Don Falk could catch as well as I could and ran just as fast. That wasn't true, but I don't hold that against Stortini now. I can see that he was just trying to get Don a good scholarship, too.

It also hurt me when he said that if I tried harder, I'd be a better player. Stortini knew football, but just like my dad he was fooled by my fluid style and easy lope. I'd be out there trying my ass off, but it just never looked that way. I wasn't trying to be cool; I wasn't nonchalant—that was just my style.

My family was supportive without going overboard. My father worked hard, but sometimes he'd get away and show up for the second half of my football games. He'd be easy to spot, down near the end zone: he'd be all by himself, one of the few black people in the crowd, dressed in a suit and wearing a nice felt hat.

In my first two years of high school, I was a regular Joe College type—the other kids even called me "Collegiate." I had a short haircut and dressed in sharp Ivy League clothes—madras shirts, penny loafers, oatmeal jeans. I had only one brush with delinquency, and the instigator was a guy who would go on to have a great baseball career with the Dodgers, Ron Cey.

Ron's father owned a gas station in Tacoma and sponsored a Boys Club team. I was two years younger than Ron, so our high-school careers overlapped, but the funny thing is that we've only seen each other two or three times since then. We've told the same stories to mutual friends and always send regards, but our paths just never cross.

When I was a sophomore, Ron and a few of his friends took me out with them on a little beer-drinking party. They got me good and drunk; then, not knowing what to do with me, they dumped me out of the car in front of my house. O. C. Moore was not the sort of man who would tolerate that, but I was violently sick all night, and Dad figured that was punishment enough. My brothers and sisters really got pissed—they thought I was getting off easy.

Considering the social upheaval and turmoil that the next few years would bring, and the change in attitudes that resulted from them, my fling with beer seems awfully innocent. During 1964, the year I started high school, Dr. Martin Luther King won the Nobel Peace Prize and the number of American casualties in Vietnam broke one hundred. The Beatles and the

Supremes had their first number-one hits with, respectively, "I Want to Hold Your Hand" and "Where Did Our Love Go?" Jim Bunning pitched the first perfect game in the National League since 1880. Jim Brown ran for 114 yards, and flanker Gary Collins caught three touchdown passes as the Cleveland Browns stunned the Baltimore Colts in the NFL championship game, 27–0.

But things were changing fast—dazzlingly fast. During my last year in high school, Dr. King and Robert F. Kennedy were assassinated. Eldridge Cleaver published *Soul on Ice*. Tommie Smith and John Carlos were expelled from the Olympics for giving the black-power salute during the medals ceremony. At Cornell University, an Ivy League school, armed black militant students staged a protest. The Vietcong launched the Tet Offensive. The Beatles' "White Album" knocked Jimi Hendrix's "Electric Ladyland" off the top of the charts. Stamps went up to six cents each; Denny McLain won thirty-one games for the Detroit Tigers; and the Oakland Raiders beat the New York Jets in the famous "Heidi" game. Bill Cosby launched a show, "Of Black America."

They were some four years, and the stress was reflected everywhere. I underwent a big change myself in my junior year, 1966–67. That's when the social issues of the day really penetrated my personal protective shell. Even in Tacoma, people were waking up to the issues smoldering and burning throughout America. Suddenly, it wasn't just funny when a black kid talked about "reckless eyeballing." You just couldn't be happy-go-lucky anymore, unless you had your head stuck in the sand. And I was just starting to pull my head out. I began to outgrow my environment.

The way you dressed in high school was just about the strongest statement you could make about your nature and your goals—whether you were a rebel in a black leather jacket and sharkskin slacks, a sharp guy with processed hair, or a good student in a button-down oxford shirt. In short order, I got rid of the collegiate haircut and grew an Afro, a small "natural."

Bill Cosby became my hero, and I went and bought a pair of wire-rim glasses just like the ones he wore.

I also started to get heat because I had these flirtations with white girls, and some people just couldn't abide that. One of my high-school coaches once pulled me over after he saw me talking with a girl in the hallway. He told me how much he liked me, and he also told me how the one thing he just couldn't stand was the sight of a black guy dating a white girl.

Of course, we aren't talking just bigotry but full-blown hypocrisy too. I could play football for Mt. Tahoma High, but the taboo against dating white girls put us blacks in a crazy social position. In a sense, black kids were almost like mercenaries. This other black guy, Richard Harr, and I would sit around mulling over the slim pickings we faced. A Filipino family with a few girls moved into town during my junior year, and they became the hot ticket for us. Everything was all right for a while, but then their father developed a weird attitude, too.

My reaction was to rebel, to send the message that I'd do whatever I damn well pleased. I had impressive credentials in my peer group. All of my friends had pretty girlfriends; why couldn't I? My pride wouldn't let me retreat, so I kept up these flirtations with a couple of girls. But it was strictly a school relationship—come three o'clock, I'd take those two buses and go home to a different world.

I did beat the system a few times. I had a friend from about seventh grade on named Rod, a handsome white kid who played quarterback for the Thunderbirds. In our senior year, Rod started going out with this very pretty black girl, and I was going out with a white girl. None of the parents approved of either of these relationships, so Rod and I worked out a system. I would borrow the family car and pick up his girl, and Rod would go get mine. We'd meet at a local diner that was a big school hangout, and switch girls. Then we'd ride back and forth on the strip a hundred times, or park on top of the hill overlooking the airport and watch the planes take off and land. When time came to go home, we just met up and switched girls again. Everybody went to sleep happy.

I did find a beautiful black girl to take to the prom. Her name was Lelia Cornwell. Her mother was a schoolteacher and her father was an army big shot. She went to Franklin Pierce High School, which was predominantly white, like mine, so we had that experience in common. At the time, "tough" meant what "cool" or "def" means today, and we were one of the toughest couples in town: the star athlete and the prom queen.

I achieved a lot in sports, and I had a ton of fun in school; but there was stress, too—pressure I didn't really understand. Toward the end of my high-school career, I became a little paranoid as the result of a meeting I had with my teachers and people from the guidance department; even the principal was there. We sat at this big table and they went down the line, person by person, telling me what was wrong with me.

The consensus was that I'd changed. They said my hair was funny. I wasn't the shy, polite kid they'd known a few years earlier; I was growing cocky. They compared me with this other black kid in the school, a kid I considered an Uncle Tom character. They wondered why I couldn't be more like him.

George Nordi, a teacher who also was the line coach of the football team, was an ally of mine. He was genuinely interested in me, and he became the most important influence on me through high school. He was forever on me about getting good grades so I could attend any college I chose. Mr. Nordi was at that meeting, too. I'll never forget that when it came time for him to deliver his criticism, he just looked up and said, "I pass."

After the big powwow about me at school, Mr. Nordi hauled me over and said, "Don't you worry about what they said. Don't let it get you down. Just keep working, because you'll be out of here soon and you'll have all different kinds of things to deal with—new and exciting things."

It was a foregone conclusion that I'd be going away somewhere to college, and by the time I had to decide on a school I knew I'd never live in Tacoma again. Athletically, I'd outgrown just about everybody except the basketball junkies who lived for their games and gambling and drugs. But I wasn't into robbing grocery stores or shooting at other guys, so there was nothing left for me at either end of the spectrum in Tacoma. I didn't like the two options of struggling to be accepted on the one hand and turning self-destructive on the other.

I knew I had to get out, and the recruiting trips I took as a senior clearly showed me the ticket. The recruiting trip is one more step up the ladder toward fame and wealth, and those steps get more and more slippery unless you've got your head screwed on straight. You grow up watching people like O. J. Simpson, Joe Namath, or Walter Payton; you wear their numbers, you fantasize that you're duplicating their exploits. And if you're good enough, one day the telephone rings and your mom says, "It's for you, Bobby. Somebody named Sayers."

That was just how it happened. I was sitting in the living room with some friends—I was really lucky they were there, or else they never would have believed it—when Mom announced that Gale Sayers was on the phone.

"Sure," I said.

I picked up the phone and this man started talking to me about what a great school Kansas was, and how the running-back coach there could really develop my potential. I don't remember much else, because I was in awe holding that phone, knowing that at the other end of the connection, Gale Sayers was holding a phone too. I put my hand over the mouthpiece, looked at my friends, and, pointing at the receiver, I kept silently mouthing the words "It's Gale Sayers—*Gale Sayers.*"

When I met him years later, I told him the story and asked if he'd really been the one who called. He laughed and said yes.

You were really made to feel like a king on a recruiting trip. As you drove into town, the billboards in front of the motels all had some message like WELCOME TACOMA'S BOBBY MOORE. Then you might go off to meet some alumnus who lived in a great big house and he took you out to the best steak house in town. Of course, there was the campus tour and visits to all the athletic facilities and frat houses. And there was spending money. A recruit needed spending money, even though everything was free in the first place. Sometimes you got a lot of spending money, as much as five hundred bucks, and when you left town the recruiters forgot to ask for the money you hadn't spent.

Most of the time, guys who played at the school took you out. They introduced you to girls, and if you wanted some action, you just used the line that you were a junior-college student thinking about transferring to the university. It was part of the deal. As a high-school recruit, you weren't trafficking in the great ideas of civilization on these university trips: the great issues were money, girls, promises of stardom, and flashy clothes.

Some school stars became almost professional recruits. You'd meet a kid from Los Angeles or Dallas on one of these trips and he'd tell you, "I ain't coming to this school, but I knew I'd get three hundred bucks for making the trip." A few weeks later you might run into the same kid, and you might even plan to visit some other school together in the weeks to come. Some guys would lie about how many schools they'd visited and what they got, and you never sat back and marveled at any of it because there were always other guys getting—or claiming to get—more.

I was impressed by Notre Dame. Coach Ara Parseghian promised I'd get to carry the ball twenty-five times a game, and he listed all of the TV and radio stations that broadcast the Fighting Irish games. It was an awesome number, because of Notre Dame's national following. But there was snow on the ground when I went to South Bend, and I didn't like that at all.

I had an even colder experience in Montana. I had no intention of going to Montana, but I told them I'd visit if they also invited four or five of my teammates. So we all went to Helena. The staff there tried to pressure me into signing a letter of intent—an official commitment to attend—right on the spot. I was also told that though there were no girls at Helena, if I had a girlfriend from home she could come along to school with me on an academic scholarship. Of course, the Montana campus was loaded with tall, blue-eyed, blond-haired cowgirls, but the recruiters were just using poetic license. Translation: If you want female company, bring a black girl with you from home. But overall the trip was a success—a few of my teammates landed scholarships.

Smart recruiters knew how to cover their bases. If they found out that your parents liked Nat King Cole, they'd come to your house with armloads of his records, sometimes even trying to pass it off as coincidence. A lot of them figured out what you wanted to hear and then told you that whether it was true or not: if a guy from Florida heard you liked to ski, he'd be telling you about all the snowy mountains just outside Miami.

The local war for my services was pretty intense in the Pacific Northwest. Jim Sweeney, a friendly guy who coached at Washington State University, got to know my mother almost as well as I did. He gave Mom a picture of his own family and told her to put it someplace where we could look at it, like it was our own family. He gave her a record of the Washington State fight song and told her to play it every morning when I got out of bed.

The coach at Oregon State had the inside track with my parents because he was a religious man. He would call up and say things like "You know now, Mrs. Moore, I been praying for you and your Bobby too." That was all Mom needed to hear. Next thing, she was saying how nice it might be if I went to school in Corvallis.

Sweeney finally got me to visit Washington State. I'd asked him to introduce me to some offensive linemen because I wanted to see their size. He later told a newspaperman that he'd rounded up the bartenders from the three taverns in Pullman and claimed I rejected them for being too "fat." So much for Washington. (I did keep the record of their fight song.)

The University of Oregon came into the picture through a cousin, Elliot Lewis. He was a very good high-school athlete, and he liked the free, open atmosphere in Eugene. My visit was a huge success: I fit right in from the start. The athletic facility was impressive, with a great big basketball gym. I met some neat people, and the football staff was a rare blend of talented, flexible, understanding individuals.

Bruce Snyder was the man who recruited me, and he's since gone on to become the head coach at the University of California. Oregon may have had the most talented coaching staff ever in college football. John Robinson, who would have all that success at USC and with the Los Angeles Rams, was an assistant. The freshman coach was George Siefert, who's now defensive co-ordinator of the San Francisco Forty-Niners. Gunther Cunningham went on to the Chargers, and John Marshall also ultimately moved on to the NFL. The head coach was Jerry Frei, a wonderful, open-minded man who now scouts for the Denver Broncos.

I'd love to say that I chose Oregon because I carefully evaluated all of the factors. But it's hard for a kid to make that kind of decision. In fact, during recruiting I'd met this guy Bill Etter from across the state. He was a quarterback, and we decided we were going to be on the same team. We both narrowed our choices down to Notre Dame or Oregon. On the night before we had to sign our letters of intent, I called Bill and asked where he was going. He said, "Oregon."

"Great," I said, "I've been leaning toward Oregon too."

The next day, I read in the newspaper that Bill Etter, my future quarterback, had signed to attend Notre Dame. I'd already committed to Oregon. I would end up having to play not with Bill Etter but some guy called Dan Fouts.

6

NAKED ON AN ISLAND

t was the talkers who always got me.

For no reason I can figure out, defensive backs do more talking than anybody else on a football team. They talk jive; they talk shit; they talk hurt—or they talk all of it at once, like "Okay, mo'fuck, your career's over 'cause I'm gonna fuck you up. You hear? You're finished. You can't go anywhere on me anyway, 'cause I'll burn your ass, mo'fuck."

Monologues like that weren't just the specialty of these lean, fast, sinewy cornerbacks (who all seem to come from schools with names like Northeast Texas L & M), either. Talking shit is an attempt to intimidate, just like taking a cheap shot at a guy early in a game. The dirtiest player I ever went up against was a defensive back who played for the Bears, Doug Plank. His specialty was spearing people—you know, diving helmet-first at a guy's back or kidneys, sometimes after the whistle. Plank played alongside Gary Fencik, a Yale graduate with all kinds of degrees but whose specialty was degrees of pain. Fencik just rocked you when he hit; you could tell he took special joy in the experience. He wasn't dirty like Plank, but between the two of them you didn't want to know from the Bears.

The relationship, if that's the right word, between a receiver and a cornerback gets pretty personal. Most of the time it's a one-on-one deal, and you go up against each other for whole games, season after season. Everybody tries to intimidate you differently. They'll glare at you, spit on you, or talk. Some receivers talk back, but I was never that type. Usually I tried to stay far enough away not to hear what a guy was saying in the first place. And I took pride in playing well enough that the guys would get so absorbed by the job at hand that they forgot to talk.

Besides, I considered it an insult when some of these guys talked to me. I was a class receiver; I had a good reputation and got along great with all kinds of people. If I had to lay down the law to some cornerback who thought he was the supreme homeboy, I just said in a very businesslike tone, "Hey—fuck you."

Kenny Johnson, who was with the Falcons, used to talk shit to me all the time, even though I'd have big days against him. He said, "I'll be on you all day, Rashad. You ain't goin' nowhere without my permission."

Once I asked Johnson if he ever bothered to look up at the scoreboard, because we were winning in a coast and I'd already caught eight or nine balls off the guy. Even that wasn't enough to make him shut his mouth, but that's the way it is with the talkers.

Guys try to intimidate you with talk and by acting crazy—like they're liable to do anything at any moment, oblivious to the consequences. Every player does that at one time or another. The easiest way to send the message that you'll do anything was to flagrantly clip a guy—just hit him in the back of the knees in broad daylight. That would usually scare him and make him think twice about messing with you.

On the other hand, you can get a tremendous kick out of cornerbacks when they're your own homeboys. The Vikings had a good one in Nate Allen, who came to the team the same year I did. Early in that season of 1976, we blocked a punt by the New York Giants. Nate picked up the ball and ran twenty-eight yards for a touchdown to give us a 10–0 lead.

The real shocker was that Nate spiked the football after he scored, which was something that no Viking who played for Bud Grant was supposed to do—ever. Bud later said he didn't see the gesture, but it was pretty clear to the rest of us that we had a loose cannon in Allen, and his quotes to the press after the game proved it. "Call me Nate the Trashman," he said. "I pick up blocked punts, rolling footballs, hand-me-downs, anything they don't want to nail down or paint or kick in the end zone. I'm not particular. All I am is available."

Nate was an individualist, a tough guy who lived by his own standards and seemed to have a different radio station playing in his head than the rest of us. He was a great blocker of punts and field goals, and he was the most valuable player the Vikings had in the first few games of that '76 season, a Super Bowl year.

One day a bunch of us were in the trainer's room when Nate walked in, toting this big old board that he must have picked up at some construction site. Nate was a wild dresser, a flamboyant guy who tried to be at the cutting edge of fashion. He was looking to beat up on his roommate because he thought the guy had stolen the belt from one of his jumpsuits.

It was too funny; we all cracked up. But that only got Nate really sore, and he decided he was going to beat up on one of us. That shut us up fast. We solemnly promised Nate that we'd help him find his belt. That's a cornerback—don't ever get caught fooling around with his jumpsuit.

When I joined the NFL, there were very few rules about pass coverage. In fact, there were so few rules compared with today that I wonder how we managed to play the game without getting killed before our rookie seasons were over. In '78, the league owners decided to bring more offense into the game. One of the rule changes they came up with was the "bump-and-run" concept, which drastically changed the way defensive backs played the game.

Previously, almost all coverage was man-to-man, a battle of strength, speed, and wits similar to the matchups you had at the line of scrimmage between the interior linemen. Man-to-man was really nothing more than bump-and-run all the way down the field. If you were a receiver, it was a mugging: everybody took his shot at you. I remember getting hit by three people on the same play: one guy hit me in the knees with a roll block (which is outlawed now too); another guy chopped me; the third guy went for my head with a forearm. I was harassed all the way down the field.

In '78, the rules were changed to allow contact only for the first five yards downfield from scrimmage, but that contact could be continuous over that area. In one of his books, John Madden reveals why his cornerback Lester Hayes wore so much stickum: Hayes wasn't nearly as interested in holding on to the ball as he was in holding on to the wide receiver for that vital five yards. He was basically trying to paste himself to the receiver. His hands looked like two brushes out of glue pots. I enjoyed playing against Lester, but I hated to get that sticky stuff on me. I would never shake his hand after a game.

Dan Marino threw forty-eight touchdown passes in '84—a number so big that the league decided that the rule changes may have tied the hands of the defensive backs too tightly. They changed the rule again, allowing defensive backs to collide with the receiver—provided the defenders were looking back at the ball. The decision eliminated a lot of cheap pass-interference calls. The rope was a little looser on the cornerbacks' wrists.

Maybe that's why so many cornerbacks are skittish, brooding, intense guys. If linebackers are the big cats of the game, cornerbacks are the cheetahs—smaller, lither, faster versions of a similar creature. Now imagine if the cheetah had to wear manacles and drag a short piece of chain around with him. No wonder these cornerbacks are a little schizy, a little paranoid. They wear their pads like chips on their shoulders.

The cornerback and the wide receiver are mirror images of each other in the same way that the defensive and offensive units of any team are two sides of the same coin. Offensive players in almost any position are learners, guys who know the value of timing, memorize plays, concentrate on execution, work with whatever finesse is at their disposal. Ideally, they're the cool, reflective, rational types. Defensive guys run on passion. Mayhem appeals to them. Some of them don't even want to know about plays; they're big old guys who just like to knock shit over.

But the best defensive players have an offensive mind-set. They develop their finesse and hone their moves. Cornerback is an "intelligence" position that can't be mastered with let-it-all-hang-out aggression. Basically, a cornerback is in a reactive position. He doesn't hunt down a guy the way a linebacker does, nor does he just charge at his target like a defensive end lighting out after a quarterback. He depends on the receiver for his cues. He tries to force the receiver to go one way or another, but the offensive player always has one huge advantage: he knows where he's going in the first place.

Getting beat on a pass play in front of the whole stadium is about tops in public humiliation, although even the most persecuted cornerback has to admit that nothing's quite up there with playing wide receiver and having an easy pass bounce off your chest in the end zone. The thing is, all cornerbacks get beat, while receivers who drop easy passes just get cut.

The best cornerbacks I went against were Mel Renfro, Jimmy Johnson, Mike Haynes, and maybe the best tandem that ever played together, the Oakland Raiders' Willie Brown and Skip Thomas. Madden relates how Thomas used to complain to him about the cornerback's job. "Coach," he would say, "I'm naked out there. Naked on an island." That's the kind of pressure a cornerback feels, and the image Thomas used to express himself is interesting too. Naked on an island. That's a guy in the jungle, an antisocial guy, a guy who has to live by his instincts, beyond the law.

Willie Brown made it into the Hall of Fame in his first year of eligibility. He was always partial to man-to-man coverage, even after the bump-and-run rule was written. It wasn't just pride. Willie believed that if you played man-to-man, you had that many more people—mostly linebackers—free to blitz and otherwise terrorize the quarterback. And Willie was smart enough to know that the best way to shut down a passing attack is to get to the passer.

On the other hand, I've never gone against a cornerback who could shut me down in a man-to-man scheme. Sure, I was fast; but there were guys who were faster and didn't catch as many balls. I was big, so guys couldn't push me around; but then anybody who's seen me block will tell you I'm not designed to overpower anybody at anything—my blocking was an impersonation of a guy rushing after a taxicab on a crowded Manhattan street. But I could beat any cornerback I ever went against.

My moves and my ability to run sharp, precise pass routes that took advantage of any individual weakness or seam in a zone were probably my biggest assets. But the greatest advantage I had was that I knew where I was going. It's amazing how many receivers never take full advantage of that edge. When you become conscious of all it means, you should beat any cornerback. It's simply too great a factor—you're running without those manacles on your ankles.

A top receiver should be virtually unstoppable by a man-to-man defense. Most coaches agree with that, which is why you see so many zone defenses, double coverages, and nickel-back alignments—when there are five instead of the usual four defensive backs on the field. A lot of these prevent defenses, which are designed to give up a short gain but "prevent" the big play, were devised as a reaction to the bump-and-run rule changes.

The irony of the situation is that though the rule changes were supposed to open up the game, in some cases they just shut it down. The mentality that makes you play a zone or a prevent defense is conservative, defensive in the broad sense of the word: the defense is there like a big net, and the receivers are like fish trying to swim through it. That's a far cry from the exciting man-to-man battles that used to characterize the receiving game.

Still, nobody's yet come up with a scheme that fully eliminates the individual battle between cornerback and wideout. And as long as there's an Al Davis and a Raider team somewhere in California, there will be great cornerbacks. Those guys are Davis's pet projects. Brown and Thomas were a tough act to follow, but Lester Hayes and Mike Haynes stepped right in and became the NFL's top pairing.

I've always had the greatest respect for Al Davis, both as a football mind and as a tough, smart, fair individual. It's common knowledge that he's a rebel, a guy with antiestablishment instincts in maybe the second most exclusive club in America, the owners of NFL franchises (the U.S. Senate is often called the most exclusive men's club). Davis dresses in black and his team wears black and silver—not your usual healthy sporting colors. The logo on the side of the Raiders' helmet is a picture of a pirate-type guy with a patch over his eye, and the team lives up to the image.

The Raiders have welcomed and rehabilitated lots of guys who were considered malcontents or misfits, from Warren Wells to John Matuszak. In their glory years in the 1970s, the Raiders were the Wild Bunch in pads and helmets. That's a real hothouse environment for defensive backs, who've become the perfect symbol of the Raiders' spirit.

It isn't just image, either. Davis believes as a matter of coaching philosophy that the cornerbacks are the foundation of the entire defense. His coaches, especially Madden, haven't always agreed. But the Raiders are first and foremost Al Davis's team— never make any mistake about that. His fingerprints are all over the team. Al Davis always made sure he had premium defensive backs like Brown, Thomas, Hayes, Haynes, George Atkinson, and Jack Tatum.

The safeties are almost a hybrid between linebackers and cornerbacks. The strong safety is so named because he lines up opposite the "strong" side of the offense, the side with the tight end. When the tight end is used as a receiver, he's the strong safety's responsibility. When the offense runs the ball, the strong safety is at the line of scrimmage, mixing it up with the trenchmen.

The free safety has been called the center fielder of a football team. He roams throughout the pass coverage, helping out. He may come up on a safety blitz, just as in soccer the best sweepers sometimes penetrate and score goals. The prime responsibility of the free safety is to help prevent the long completion, the theory being that from his "deep" position in the field he ought to reach either sideline while a pass is in the air.

The free safety is the guy the wide receiver has to beat after he's done his job of beating the cornerback. He's also the guy who sometimes gets in the choicest lick on a receiver, because he's barreling upfield or across field to help out as the passing play unfolds. He can't always bail out the cornerback who's been beaten, but he sure can make the receiver pay for catching the ball.

The receiver is never more vulnerable to a bad injury than when he gets blind-sided by a free safety just seconds after hauling in a pass. That's why a general awareness of the flow of play—call it football "intelligence"—can really prolong a receiver's career.

I absorbed only three or four shots in my career that rattled my teeth or put serious thoughts about a change of jobs into my mind. One of those shots was laid on by Cliff Harris, a tough Cowboy safety who thrived on contact and took special joy in trying to behead receivers.

Thanks to Harris, there was one game against the Cowboys where I never made it past the first play. He got a shot in to my chin and the lights went out. I was tap-dancing down that old boxers' boulevard, Queer Street: I could hear my teammates' voices on full reverb, calling out, "Come on, Champ. Get up, Champ," and I vaguely remember their laughter echoing in that big, deserted ballroom in my head.

The lights came back on slowly. The next thing I remembered sharply was the usual hospital stuff: the TV on the steel arm poking from the wall, the pale green walls, the empty wastebasket. It turned out that I wasn't badly hurt, meaning there was no permanent brain or spinal damage.

When I went back to practice the next Wednesday, I realized

that the voices I'd heard while lying on the field weren't hallucinations. There was a big sign hanging in front of my locker: WELCOME BACK, KNOCKOUT RASHAD. While I was gone, the guys had decorated my locker with all kinds of ribbons, cards, and boxing paraphernalia, including a pair of Everlast gloves. For the next few weeks, I was dubbed "Champ." In the middle of practice, some guy would walk by, holding up his hand: "Hey, Champ, how many fingers I got up?"

Harris was bad, but the dirty Bear Doug Plank was by far the worst. We used to joke and laugh about it: Plank's famous late hits were cheap ammo if you wanted to needle a guy who was in a position to go against him. But it wouldn't have been very funny if he'd put some guy in a wheelchair. Plank was so bad that Bud Grant used to let the linemen release after a play passed the line of scrimmage just so they could head downfield and try to protect our guys from the dirty Bear.

Often as not, Plank's victim was one of his own teammates. He was so indiscriminately aggressive most of the time that he'd close his eyes, put his head down, dive—and spear one of his own guys. You kept hearing Bears going, "God damn it, Plank, open up your eyes! You nailed my ass."

Rickey Young came to the Vikings from San Diego in '78. He was only six foot two and 195, but it was all heart. Coming from the AFC, Rickey didn't know about Plank. But Chicago was a conference rival of ours, so Rickey found out about the dirty Bear soon enough.

In one game, Rickey was trailing a play or something, just slowing up as the action ended nearby, when for no reason Plank hit him—just hauled off and cracked him upside the head with a forearm. Rickey's knees buckled. As he went down, he mumbled something about a "dirty motherf——." I couldn't keep from laughing; it was like one of those cartoon scenes when a piano falls on the head of an innocent bystander and irons him out.

So when Rickey got up he was pissed at me too, for laughing. He was really seeing red. For the rest of the game, he was looking to get back at Plank, chasing him all over the field. The whistle would blow, and Rickey would still be running around trying to catch up with Plank. I never saw him more exhausted after a game than after that one, but he did finally get in one good lick long after the whistle. That's the ideal time to retaliate—and if you don't, everybody in the league is going to take his cheap shot at you.

The next week in the film room, Rickey looked like a guy out of a Marx Brothers movie. That's the worst thing about messing up, getting knocked cold, doing anything stupid on the field—it's all down on film for everybody to see and laugh about a few days later.

When the film came to the point where Rickey finally nailed Plank, the entire room burst out laughing. Bud Grant just cleared his throat and said, "There's no need for that kind of thing, Rickey."

Somehow, anybody who hadn't known that Bud himself had been a wide receiver knew it then.

7

CAN MAN SURVIVE?

"**S**o get this. Larry Davis said this. Honest!" Bob Costas was all excited; his voice rose an octave. Bob Trumpy and I looked at each other. Costas mimicked a slow, deep drawl. "You know, there's only two dudes I really want to meet. One of them is Michael Jackson, and the other is . . . Bob Costas, the sportscaster dude."

We all burst out laughing. The idea that Davis, the crack addict who went on a killing spree that launched one of the greatest manhunts in the history of New York City, wanted to meet Bob Costas, was bizarre to say the least. I leaned back in one of the three barber chairs in the brightly lit makeup room for Studio 6-A and said, "He probably ain't even so sure about Michael Jackson."

"Honest to God! That's what he said." Bob grinned. " 'That sportscaster dude, Costas.' "

It's fun to have a former player like Trumpy in the studio. You start telling war stories and before you know it, a bunch of guys who never played are sitting around listening. That's when you realize that maybe there is something special about the football experience. Maybe it wasn't the most important thing you ever did; maybe it didn't contribute to the advancement of civilization; maybe you walked away with nothing but a couple of game balls and a bum knee. But the bonding that occurred leaves you with an aura.

Some people are fascinated by the atmosphere of the locker room—mostly people who didn't have a lot of exposure to it. When there's an old athlete around, the vibes become loose and natural. Some guys like the cool, tough image projected by many athletes, and they want to be kids again, talking shit: "Yo', man, underneath this suit and tie I'm a bad-ass mother. I was too slow to play sports, but hey, I seen all kinds of heavy shit in international marketing. It's a war out there, too, bro. I'm hip to where you're coming from."

Costas pulls off the attitude because the makeup room *is* his locker room and the set *is* his field. In Studio 6-A, he's the All-Pro, so we really are equals. Some other guys in different situations just go overboard. It's especially true with white guys and black athletes. I've had yuppie guys come up to me babbling jive that even *I* don't understand. There's a pretty well-known football commentator and journalist who thinks he's so hip to black culture that he throws around the word "nigger."

The guy probably isn't a racist; I think he just wants to be cool. Some blacks call each other "nigger" as an expression of ridicule, even though they would fight some white guy for saying the same thing. So this white sports writer has decided he's a homeboy, which is already phony. He's so cool he can use an ugly, loaded word like that without shame—almost as if it proved that he's not a racist. I guess that's like being so honest that you feel entitled to steal. No matter how you cut it or whose mouth it comes out of, "nigger" is an ugly word. What difference does it make if you use it to show self-hatred or hatred of others?

Whenever old football players get together, sooner or later they talk about injuries. It's just like fishermen talking about the one that got away. Injuries are the ultimate reality for a pro athlete—they throw a shadow over your days, loom in the background as a reminder of how quickly the fun and exhilaration can turn to pain or even tragedy. Football is like the army in that you know that a third of your men are going to become casualties. You just hope it isn't you that gets hit. Football is not just a job, it's an adventure—until it comes time to get killed.

"I remember playing an exhibition against your Vikings once," Trumpy said. "You had this guy Ted Brown—a defensive back. He dislocated his hip on a kickoff return. I was on the sidelines, and I watched the other guys bouncing off the pile, waving to the sidelines. Then I saw this leg sticking out and up at a crazy angle. It gave me chills. The doc just ran out there, stuck his foot in Brown's crotch, and yanked on the leg. It popped right back into the joint."

It was the dislocated fingers that made me wince. I'd see these guys coming to the sidelines, holding their hands, their fingers pointing every which way like pins in a cushion. The doctor would just grab them and *pop, pop, pop*, set them back in place.

Trumpy told a story about Charlie Joiner. One time he caught a ball between his index and middle fingers and split his hand wide open. It wasn't a cut but a sloppy tear. Charlie came to the sidelines and there was all this meat hanging out of his hand. It took something like two hundred stitches to sew him up.

That was why in training camp I always let the hard passes go for about a week. Meanwhile, all of these rookies and free agents who were trying to impress the coaching staff would get split hands. Some players were unbelievably tough. They came out of games with lips, noses, cheeks split wide open. The doc sewed them up right there on the bench and the players went back in to finish the game.

But rib injuries are the worst, even when they aren't too serious. When you have cracked or fractured ribs, you can't take a single breath without feeling sharp pain. It's the most immobilizing injury of them all.

You might get the impression from this that football is a very violent game. In fact, we had a critic on the show a few weeks ago, an academic guy who was always talking about violence in football. I didn't want to get involved with that segment or lend it credibility in any way. I take exception when people characterize football as a violent sport. Football is probably the most physical of games, but that doesn't make it violent. Football contains a high risk of injury, but then so does hang gliding, and nobody calls that violent. There are violent football players, sure—just like there are violent mailmen and violent lawyers.

Football is a game of orchestrated collisions, all with a higher purpose: to move the ball downfield or to stop it from being advanced. You can't play football without hitting; if you don't like that premise, you should learn to play golf or something. Every player on the football field has made a conscious choice to accept the risk of injury.

You use your physical powers to the ultimate degree in football. I've heard people say that rugby or Australian rules football is "tougher" than football, because the guys don't wear pads or helmets. But that's bull, as I learned from trying those sports. The players are much more inhibited. The fact that you've got pads and a helmet allows you to play football with abandon, a reckless feeling of invincibility that doesn't exist in a sport like rugby.

Football players laugh about injuries because they don't want to be intimidated by them. The worse the injury, the funnier it is to your teammates as long as you're not dead. A broken rib, a shot in the head that knocks you silly, a hit that knocks the wind out of you—those are all hilarious. When a knee goes, the laughter dies. Everybody begins thinking that it can happen to him, too.

There's this unwritten rule about not faking injuries, or not making any more of a deal out of them than is necessary. Playing against Tampa Bay once, I got hit in the leg so hard that it knocked the wind out of me. I didn't know what was wrong. I was scared. Our Viking trainer Fred Zamberletti came out and asked if I was okay. That got me sore. I said, "If I was okay I'd be standing up. Sure I'm okay, I just got my leg broke."

When Fred determined that I was okay except for my wind, he said loud enough for everybody standing around to hear:

"You mean you walked my ass all the way out here just because you got the wind knocked out of you?"

I was so mad at Fred that I could have killed him—if I could have stood up. But that's the ethic in football. One good way to tell how big a star you are in football is by how many guys come out on the field when you get hurt. A rookie or special-teams guy might not merit anyone more important than some assistant trainer from Mankato College. A star might get the head trainer, but even then he doesn't necessarily get the nicest bedside manner.

After the Detroit game in which I busted my back, I flew back to Minnesota with the Vikings. I was pretty much knocked out by painkillers and drinks, but I still managed to have a few words with my buddy Joe Senser. "See that, Joe? Don't tell me I ain't no star, man. I had everybody out there when I went down. Did you see that? I even had Bud out there."

I had a fresh football story for Trumpy too, having just come back from a few days in San Diego. I went to do a feature on the Chargers, who were burning up the AFC during the first half of the season.

Dan Fouts made me feel at home in San Diego. I was standing in the offensive huddle during practice when a public-relations guy from the Chargers asked me to move to the sidelines. My old buddy Fouts looked at the guy and barked, "Fuck off."

We went out for Mexican food after practice, and who turned out to be in the same bar but Joe Kapp, the quarterback for the Vikings' 1969 Super Bowl team, before Fran Tarkenton came back to Minnesota. Kapp was a fiery guy who loved to drink and brawl. When he won the MVP award in '69, he went up to the dais, got this rough look on his face, and scared the hell out of everybody in the banquet hall with this angry, rousing speech about how his teammates deserved the MVP as much as he did. Kapp fit in well with the old Vikings—it was like somebody had put a defensive lineman's mentality into a quarterback.

Kapp came over to our table. I assumed from his look that he'd had a few. I figured our shared Viking history gave us some basis for camaraderie. We started talking about a backup Viking quarterback, Gary Cuozzo. I mentioned that I never though of Cuozzo as a tough guy—I often felt that as a quarterback, he unloaded the ball too quickly under pressure.

The next thing, old Joe Kapp stood up. He was leaning back a little on his heels. "Oh yeah?" he said. "Well, what if somebody kicked your ass for saying that?"

I gulped.

Fouts had a couple of bills in front of him on the table, a ten and a twenty. He pushed the smaller bill forward and said, "I'll bet ten dollars you can't kick his ass, Joe."

"Dan!" I cried. I looked around for the nearest door. I wasn't about to come back home to my wife and the show with a torn ear and a few teeth missing because I'd gotten in a barroom brawl with Joe Kapp.

Fortunately, Kapp lost interest in the proposition.

When he left, I turned to Fouts and asked him why he'd egged Joe on like that. He just laughed and said, "Listen, just thank your lucky stars I didn't push that twenty forward, because then you really would have been in trouble."

Oregon in the late 1960s, when Fouts and I were there, was a crazy place to play football. It was the only team I've ever been on that had a bunch of guys who had to put their hair in bobby pins to get their helmets on.

Yep, the Fighting Ducks of the University of Oregon—we had guys on that team who would take off from practice because they had to go to a demonstration against a recruiter from Dow Chemical who was visiting campus. We had team meetings that were rap sessions or variations on all those bogus forms of therapy. We even managed to win football games, beating people like USC and UCLA. We owned Idaho.

While I was a freshman at Oregon, Joe Namath led the AFL Jets to a shocking win over the NFL's Baltimore Colts in Super Bowl III. That same year, black students at Cornell took over a building and walked around with guns. *Easy Rider* was a hit movie. Angela Davis, a communist professor, was fired from UCLA. Lieutenant Calley was charged with the My Lai murders; Indians seized Alcatraz; the Venceremos Brigade, made up of American kids, went to Cuba to help harvest sugar cane. In the summer, Charles Manson masterminded the Tate–La Bianca murders.

The mood everywhere was outrageously liberal, and even more so on campus at Eugene. Oregon has a beautiful green campus. It seemed like everywhere you looked there were hippies moving their hands through the air, watching the trail of colors. Dogs in bandannas ran free through the streets. You would be driving through some quiet neighborhood and come upon a demonstration against the Vietnam War or this or that corporate recruiter in full swing.

By the time I got to Oregon, Ken Kesey was a professor there. The author of *One Flew over the Cuckoo's Nest* was one of the first people to experiment with LSD back in the early sixties, even before the stuff was classified as a controlled substance and made illegal. Later on, he led the Merry Pranksters, a bunch of artistic types in California, on their quest to alter consciousness. Arthur Pearl, another professor, taught a course called Can Man Survive? One of the things we did was go out in canoes and clean up a river, as if we were guys from the municipal sanitation or parks department. Can Man Survive?—impressive name for a course, huh?

Everybody was into ecology, astrology, numerology, scientology, sociology, psychology, and health foods. Nothing was weird in those days—except maybe being a straight preppy. The great centers who helped UCLA dominate college basketball for years, Kareem and Bill Walton, pretty much covered all the bases, from martial arts to macrobiotics, between them. Suddenly, the college jock was a different breed of cat, especially on the West Coast.

It was easier to find tofu than taffy in Eugene. I ate sandwiches that were made of oats between two pieces of whole-wheat bread. Grain sandwiches! If you were really lucky, there was a leaf of bitter lettuce thrown in. It was different from the cheeseburgers and chocolate cake of my childhood.

During my years at Oregon, somebody tried to blow up the registrar's office. We had a local branch of the Black Panthers— in fact, the Chicago Eight went on trial during my freshman year, and two Black Panthers were killed in the fall of 1969, my sophomore year. The neat thing about the times was that the issues were right there in front of us; we were confronted by them in a way that we hadn't been before and haven't been since. College was still a bubble, like it always is. But you had to think about all the stuff going on; you had to formulate ideas about society and its goals.

The militaristic, pseudoviolent nature of football was not too popular in those times. The Big Men on Campus were the student leaders, the activists. Some of those types lumped us football players in with the Reserve Officer Training Corps types, who had part of their way in school paid for by the army in exchange for joining up when they graduated.

Everybody hated those poor ROTC guys, when a lot of them were just taking advantage of a program that allowed them to afford school. They had to sneak into their uniforms and skulk to their meetings. But the football team had a few things going for it that made the situation better. Coach Frei and his staff ran a very liberal program, and the University of Oregon wanted to keep football in perspective as a campus activity for players and students. So we participated in campus life much more than the kids at the famous football factories, where there were separate athletic dorms, dining facilities, and sometimes even classes.

Our stadium was a funny place during games. Instead of a marching band, we had a rock band—twelve long-haired hippie dudes who played the songs of Jimi Hendrix and Paul Butterfield. They were so electric and loud that the band had to be moved away from in front of the alumni section. When we played Cal or USC, the visiting fans got all weirded out by the scene in our stadium. Half of the fans were stoned on pot, looking up at the clouds, talking philosophy, throwing a Frisbee—anything but watching the game.

I resented the rap that we were "jocks" who did nothing but play sports and lie around all day. Despite all of the drugs on and around campus, not a single guy on our team had a problem. It wasn't even an issue. In college, the dedicated athlete didn't really have time for all that stuff. Keeping up grades and playing a big-time sport fills your whole day—and night. It really does.

At the time, the NCAA still prohibited freshmen from playing varsity football. My first shock as a freshman was meeting eight or ten other guys who were high-school All-American tailbacks. Everybody ran the forty in 4.4. Those first few days guys would shake hands and say, "No, you must have made a mistake. You can't be the tailback—*I'm* the tailback." But the sorting-out process went pretty quickly. Bigger tailbacks became linebackers; smaller ones became cornerbacks.

I wasn't prepared for the intensity level of our freshman practices. We practiced for five months and played a total of four games. Life was an endless scrimmage in full pads. A few weeks into the program I just up and quit. I went back to my room and began to pack my bags. Bruce Snyder, the varsity running-back coach who had recruited me, came by and wouldn't even deal with the fact that I quit. He didn't even ask me what I was doing—probably because he'd seen it all before. He just said, "Take the day off, relax awhile, get a good night's sleep, and see if you can come back tomorrow."

The freshman team was a big, moving, tackling dummy for the varsity. The closest we got to games was scrimmaging the varsity, imitating the team they were playing that week. Ultimately, we were able to determine how we stacked up against the Big Boys, and the stone-cold truth is that we stacked up tall. I killed the varsity, playing a modified slotback-receiver position. I knew I eventually would be successful because we'd go against the varsity defense and complete just about every passing play we tried.

Leland Glass, who would play for two years with the Packers, was my best friend in college. Dan Fouts didn't arrive until a year later, but we had a bunch of other guys on that freshman team who would play in the NFL, so we really lifted each other's game.

I also played freshman basketball for Oregon, and I made national news—not because of my scoring average but because of my haircut. At the end of football season, I grew a natural again. On the first day of basketball practice, the coach, Frank Arnold, came over to me and this other guy, Bill Drake, who had a similar hairdo. Arnold said we couldn't play on the team unless we cut our hair. That evening, Drake and I went to a meeting of the Black Students' Union. I'm not even sure why we attended—maybe just to look at the girls. But when we casually mentioned that we were told to get haircuts, the BSU was outraged. They said we didn't have to do anything of the kind.

Drake and I probably would have cut our hair if push came to shove; it just wasn't that big a deal. But Arnold took a stand, and it snowballed from there, with the BSU going head-on with the athletic director. A picture of my hair made the national news, and ultimately the president of the school reinstated us. Arnold had threatened to quit if the president went over his head, and, sure enough, he did. He said he had to do some soul-searching, so he left and didn't come back until almost the end of the season. The whole affair was kind of silly, another crazy sign of the times.

Being on my own but part of a real campus scene was really neat. The first thing I did was stay up real late a bunch of nights in a row, just because I could. I enjoyed getting up early in the morning and walking to class, my own books tucked under my arm. It was a secure, positive feeling. I even made the dean's list.

I balanced that out by making a huge mistake at the start of my sophomore year: I got married.

The girl's name was Dierdre Waters. I had been seeing her on and off through my freshman year. I guess I was still looking for my niche, trying out different roles in life. At the end of freshman year, I stayed in Portland with Dierdre all summer. Just as I was about to return to school, we thought she was pregnant.

We were renting part of a teeny house. About all I remember of it was the mice, or rats, that were always scratching around inside the thin walls. Our room was a little one off the kitchen in the back. We tried to do the right thing: I was only nineteen, too young to marry under some provision or other in Oregon law. So we got a lady to forge the documents.

I went back to Tacoma soon after the marriage, and when some of my friends found out about what I'd done, they were mad. A few nights later, five of them showed up at our home in Portland, ready to kidnap me. There was a big emotional scene.

Finally, I went down to school. I knew I shouldn't be married, and to top it off, it turned out Dierdre wasn't pregnant. I told my problems to John Robinson, who was an assistant coach then, and he told me I'd made a big mistake. He went to work on arranging an annulment.

I'd just about gotten myself straightened out when Dierdre found out that she was pregnant for real. The child would be my eldest daughter, Keva. By that point, the strange relationship we had was almost over. From the start, we were overcommitted before we'd really even gotten to know each other. I mean, in college you could stay out all night, sleep in the same bed with your girlfriend, do anything you wanted. It was like what grown-ups did, and we tried to act like responsible grown-ups. It wasn't exactly playacting, but it wasn't mature behavior, either.

I wasn't too worried about the responsibility of fatherhood. It's funny, but sometimes if you come from a secure social situation, having kids seems like an awesome responsibility. I know people who have all the basic advantages but they're afraid to have kids because of the commitment. To me, having a child is a fundamental part of the human experience. The desire cuts across all social levels and standards.

At some levels of society, the fact that your unmarried sister had a child doesn't freak people out. There's been a history in black culture of strong women acting as single parents. The experience may not be ideal, but for poor people the situation has to be awfully bad before they concede that they can't make it, can't sustain the semblance of a family. People perform amazing things when they have to put bread on the table. When people talk about social norms, they mean basically the standard of a white middle-class society. But at college in the late 1960s, even these smart, beautiful hippie women were having kids out of wedlock, in defiance of the social norm.

Keeping up a strong parental image can be tough if you don't live with your kids in a traditional domestic situation. Initially, you panic—God, I'm not going to see my kid for two weeks! But you find a way to build a relationship. My kids spend a lot of time with me. Ahmad Jr., who's ten, is with me in Minnesota every summer. I often travel to the West Coast, where my daughters Maiysha and Keva live.

So the beginning of my sophomore year was tempestuous, and, to make matters worse, the very first pass thrown to me in my first varsity game hit my hands and fell off—just like a flowerpot off a windowsill. But by the end of those sixty minutes of football, I was in the Oregon record book with the first of fourteen school marks I would set: I had three touchdown catches in the game. I would end up leading the Pac-8 in scoring and pass receiving for the year, with 92 points scored on fifteen touchdowns, ten as a receiver. My fifty-four receptions for the year also set a record. I made the All-Pac-8 team as the flanker.

Over the summer, I had my first real brush with the dangers of drug abuse. I had a buddy in Tacoma who played football for another university. We were both into cars, and he suggested we visit this very slick guy who was into them, too. This guy followed local sports and knew who we were, and he was real friendly, inviting us to hang out for this little party he was having. The guy's basement was set up like a regular nightclub, with red lights, fancy couches, the whole deal. There were a few small cubicles off the main room, but we figured that's where he kept his power tools or car wax or something. Soon it was evening, and all of these women began to show up. My buddy and I were pretty naive, and these pros just swept us off our feet, they were so seductive. One of the women took out this white powder and made a little pile of it on a card table. Her friends dipped their fingernails into the powder and inhaled it, offering us some.

We figured the stuff was cocaine, and we shouldn't mess with it, but then we didn't want to be rummies in front of those pretty women. We took a playing card and scooped up a pile of the drugs, snorted the stuff right up the nostrils. We stood there looking at each other like two idiots, feeling nothing, so we each took another snoutful. Soon after that, my friend began to feel sick. He went to the bathroom.

I tried talking to one of the women, but my face was all hot and my eyes wanted to shut. I was itchy all over. Pretty soon, I followed my friend into the toilet, where he was vomiting, so I threw up in the sink. The drug wasn't cocaine but heroin. Most of the girls had habits, so they weren't sick. But my friend and I were almost unconscious.

Suddenly, the owner of the house burst into the bathroom. He collared me and flung me up against the wall. The guy just laced into me, telling me how he'd trusted us and what fools we were for fooling around with drugs. We were two guys with a great shot at becoming All-American football players and we seemed willing to throw it all away for a little dope and pussy.

The guy was so mad that I thought he was going to fly off the handle and kill us both. We sure weren't in any condition to retaliate. But he said he wasn't going to kill us—not unless he heard that we were fooling around with drugs again. Eventually, my friend and I staggered to the guy's porch and sat there, trying to figure out what had happened, waiting to be straight enough to go home.

In my junior year at Oregon, I was switched from flanker to tailback. As a flanker, I used to play basketball on any Sunday after a football game. As a tailback, I could hardly make it out of bed. Few people know how much punishment a running back absorbs, even in a routine game.

I gained 924 yards in my junior year, breaking Mel Renfro's mark of 753. I missed almost two full games, which probably would have put me in the ultraexclusive thousand-yard rushing club, a fraternity reserved for the likes of O. J. Simpson. I would be named Pac-8 Back of the Year, beating out guys like Sonny Sixkiller, the Washington quarterback, Jackie Brown of Stanford, and Jimmy Jones of USC.

The Oregon Ducks during my years were some football team, a cross between the Bad News Bears, the Wild Bunch, the Miami Dolphins, and the Rolling Stones. We had a center, Jim Figoni, who weighed only 215 pounds (but a tough 215) and a great player in guard John McKean. He took one semester off, went to South America, and came back fifty pounds lighter, with hair down to the middle of his back.

We didn't have guys who talked a lot of shit but a bunch of guys who led by performance. Dan Fouts was one of them, and so was Tom Graham, a guy who played middle linebacker for a long time in the NFL. Chuck Bradley, our tight end, played for the Chargers and the Bears. Tom Drougas was an offensive lineman in the NFL for a dozen years. Jack Stambaugh played with the Bengals.

We had a wide receiver, Greg Specht, who was so cool we dubbed him "Chatsworth," after the character in the popular TV show "Dobie Gillis." When I was with the Cardinals, Chatsworth got a tryout. He had as good a camp as anybody, but he was a free agent, and he didn't ingratiate himself with the Cardinal regulars. He was right on the cusp, where making it is sometimes just a question of whether or not the regulars like you. It was sad to see him go when he might—and should—have stayed.

Tim Stokes, an offensive tackle who missed blocks and got me killed a bunch of times, was a skinny six-five, 190 pounds when he came to school. Nobody expected him to play for long in the pros, but he just kept coming on, gaining bulk, and he ended up playing in the NFL for some ten years.

Bob Newland became a stalwart for the Saints; Tom Blanchard kicked for the Giants for a decade. I wanted to mention all these guys, plus Tim Guy and a fullback who's remained one of my best friends, Jim Anderson, because I've got a warm place in my heart for all of them. We won games together and had a hell of a time doing it. The greatest thing about this group is that we all developed a pretty good perspective. I played on a college team that didn't produce broken-down, disillusioned football players. It produced a bunch of successful people.

Last year, I was inducted into the University of Oregon Hall of Fame. I invited Jim Anderson, who has a successful plumbing-fixtures business, and he took care of the rest. A dozen of my former teammates showed up for the awards banquet and we had a blast. Nobody said anything like "Yeah, I saw old Joe Smith the other day—he's out of work again, and they repossessed his car. What the hell, I gave him a hundred bucks."

A lot of the credit for our relative success goes back to our head coach, Jerry Frei. He was a tolerant, kind, compassionate individual. He talked to you in a manly way whether you were the star quarterback or a third-string center. In his very quiet way, Coach Frei ran a liberal program that allowed us to play football without feeling like we were Meat on the Hoof or a bunch of tough supermen lost in a society of peace-loving weirdos.

Some coaches would have gone crazy if any of their players dared to go to some campus demonstration. But McKean was an activist. And Drougas was a role model for all of us. He had his own apartment; he was married to a pretty nurse; and he got involved in campus issues. With so many expressive personalities, we added up to a unique football team.

Consider our team meetings. Coach Frei would run the film, stop, and say, "See, Drougas, you missed this block right here." Drougas would lean back, take a deep breath, and answer: "Well, Coach, you see, I was trying to negotiate to get by this guard, whose orientation biomechanically was such that he cracked me in the foot. Consequently . . ."

Consequently.

One of the cardinal rules of successful football is that you

don't overanalyze and you don't intellectualize. If you're the
coach, you can't deal in excuses or the whole mission of a football
team breaks down. There just isn't any room for excuses in the
game. So when somebody started spinning the bull, it was funny
as hell to us. Frei put up with a lot from us—and from me as
much as anybody.

In my junior year, we lost to one of our main rivals, the University of Washington. I was especially pissed off because I always played my heart out against the Huskies: the school was
thirty miles from my hometown, but the coaches had made no
real effort to recruit me.

Instead of going back to Eugene with the team, I stayed on
in Washington for a few days. Then I drove to Portland with a
bunch of older guys to watch Kareem Abdul-Jabbar and the
Milwaukee Bucks play a basketball game.

After the game, my friends and I had a few beers. One of the
guys broke into a car and took a baby stroller. On a whim he
threw it over the rail of the freeway. The next thing I knew,
four guys who looked like hippies came up and arrested us.
They'd seen everything from on top of a nearby building. Everybody took off running except me. I figured, I'm Bobby Moore—
this kind of hassle doesn't happen to Bobby Moore.

Next thing I knew, I was making my single phone call to John
Robinson. I got him out of bed, but he had a guy there ten
minutes later to bail me out. The guy drove me to the house
where I had been staying, and on that short trip I must have
heard about my arrest on the car radio five times. The letters
would pour in later, from all over the country, telling me how
dumb I'd been. The charge sounded serious: breaking and en-
tering. But it had all been just a stupid prank—a stupid prank
that had a pretty stiff penalty: I didn't make the All-American
team as a junior.

Overnight, I went from being Bobby Moore the individualist
to Bobby Moore the bad dude with the big hair who was a real
thug, a guy who stole cars. That was the rap that got back to
me from up and down the coast, and for a pretty long time. It

was the first time that I realized in a big way that anybody in the public eye has to be twenty times more careful than the average Joe about what he does . . . and when he does it . . . and who he does it with . . . and why he does it.

I know the public thinks that big-time athletes have a special responsibility because they get such royal treatment, and I understand why they get down on guys who seem to bail out on the responsibility that goes with that territory. But it can be awful hard for a kid to sort all that out. When you need money for rent, you just go to see this guy you don't even know and he gives you an envelope with cash and no questions asked. You feel like you're above the rules that run life for most people.

When some guys you're with take a baby stroller as a prank and your name becomes synonymous with trouble, you pay off that rent loan and some of the other privileges too. You become the whipping boy; your mistake is blown out of proportion just as much as your achievement on the football field. You always pay for the free lunch.

In situations like that in college, I always had Coach Frei to turn to, and I can't thank him enough. He consistently stood up for me in meetings with alumni groups and hard-nosed football types who didn't like my individualistic style. After the stroller incident, he called me into the office. He turned his quandary around on me. He asked *me* to decide what to do about me. I knew the prank was harmless, but then I also knew that if he did nothing he'd get a lot of heat. So I told him he'd better suspend me for the next game. He agreed with me and told me to take the next few days off, to relax and to think about the fiasco and its impact on me and my future.

By senior year, I was wiser to the world. I understood that the world could stick to the palm of my hand just like a football, and I had to be careful not to drop it. The major pro scouting combine paid me a rare tribute: I was rated the top pro prospect as both a running back and a receiver. During that senior year, I'd gained 249 rushing yards against Utah. In the same game, I had three catches for 89 yards and tossed a 34-yard touchdown pass. I rushed for 110 against a tough Texas team, 145 against USC, and 150 against Stanford. I hoped to break the thousand-yard rushing barrier and made it with 1,211 yards.

After a game against Stanford, the press overheard and printed a conversation between me and a Stanford assistant coach, Bill Moultrie. He approached me in our dressing room and said, "You're the best back I've ever seen here."

Half-kidding, I shot back, "Better than O.J.?"

He nodded. "Yep. You can do it all and you're bigger."

That was the accolade that meant the most to me. It didn't hurt either when Coach Frei said things like "Bobby Moore is the greatest rusher in the country once he gets beyond the line of scrimmage. One-on-one he has no peer. The key is having the talent to spring him free."

The school career records I left behind included: most yards rushing, 2,306; most receptions, 131; and most points scored, 226. I made the All-American team with guys like Pat Sullivan, Jerome Barkum, Riley Odums, Reggie McKenzie, Jeff Kinney, and Ed Marinaro of Cornell, who almost won the Heisman Trophy over Sullivan.

Ed was a buddy, but I just don't think he should have been a serious Heisman candidate. Ivy League football has produced some great players like Calvin Hill and Gary Fencik, but it isn't a game played on the same level as big-time college ball. There are 180-pound tackles in the Ivys who just couldn't play anywhere else. We would watch a game on TV and see Marinaro stiff-arming these guys, but we knew he would never get away with that in the Big Ten or Pac-8. NCAA records that were set in the Ivy League ought to have an asterisk. The top guys from the league make it in spite of playing in the Ivys, not because of it. Just imagine Oklahoma playing Cornell—that would be one bloody Saturday.

I was confident that I could play in the pros, because big-time college football isn't all that different from the NFL. The intensity level rises; the game is a little faster in the pros. In college, out of twenty-two guys on the field, about a dozen of them are nervous and scared; in the pros, only about half that many guys are struggling. In some ways that makes pro football easier, because everybody is more efficient, everybody knows what he's doing, like the drivers in a Grand Prix car race. People just don't get in your way as much in the pros.

So I knew all along that I would be moving on to bigger things. Soon enough I'd learn that they weren't necessarily better things—not at all.

On Thanksgiving Day, 1987, the flu had me down and I was sick as a dog. It was a tough day in the studio, where we did a show before the game between the Detroit Lions and Kansas City Chiefs—about the only two teams in the league who could definitely be counted out of the playoff race. I found myself wishing that I had gone to watch a good high-school game. To me, that's what Thanksgiving Day football is all about.

But I was pretty lucky. Three years ago on Thanksgiving, I was alone in my apartment, eating a turkey sandwich from the local deli. Last Thanksgiving, I was going home to a nice house and a wife and family, including all my kids.

I took Ahmad Jr. to the studio on Thanksgiving. He was only ten, but he had a great time. I guess all little kids like to go to work with their daddies. Ahmad seemed really interested in broadcasting. At one point he wandered to the back of the studio, where we have a dais and a pair of armchairs set up for interviews. Ahmad sat back there, pretending to interview somebody.

Paul Maguire was back in the studio after a long stint on the road, and that's always a welcome addition. Paul is one of a handful of guys who played right through the history of the AFL. He's tough and funny. He may not be holding both a beer and a cigarette all of the time, but he's always got hold of at least one of them. Paul does our handicapping, which is a process I still don't understand. I'll probably go to my grave wondering if "Go with the Raiders, taking the three and a half points" means that you're betting for or against Los Angeles. And what's a half-point, anyway? Don't bother to write: I've had about four thousand people explain it to me and I *still* don't get it.

When Paul heard I had the flu, he cooked up some kind of a

hot toddy that had smoke coming out of it and made me feel like I should put on a hat like a traffic cone before I drank the stuff. The tea had maybe five shots of brandy in it, along with a lot of sugar, lemon, honey, and I don't know what else. I got a boost from the stuff, but by the time Ahmad Jr. and I hit the Major Deegan Expressway on the way home, the effect had worn off and I was feeling rotten.

Our house was full of people, but I went straight up to bed. I almost missed dinner, but Phylicia had worked so hard that I would have dragged myself down even if I'd had malaria. I marvel at her ability to do everything well. She was never spoiled, so she has the capacity to find happiness in little things and accomplish almost any chore without complaining or moping. It's a shock to come home and see a woman like Phylicia down on her knees, scrubbing a floor.

Don't get me wrong—there are lots of things she'd rather do than scrub floors or cook breakfast for her son every day before he goes off to school. It's just that she appreciates all the different roles real life offers, and she believes that if you're going to do something, you might as well do the best job possible with the best attitude possible.

Phylicia had orchestrated this major get-together for Thanksgiving, and to a large extent she was responsible for the feeling of warmth and well-being that filled the house. When I thought about the things I had to be thankful for, meeting Phylicia was right at the top of the list.

We got together thanks to Bill Cosby, who's been a father figure to me for ages. He took an early interest in my football career; he steered me toward broadcasting; and all along he wanted to see me settle down with a nice girl. In fact, he's like a Jewish mother when it comes to worrying about his single friends. He fixed me up a few times, after telling me how well he thought I would get along with this or that woman. Naturally, those fix-ups almost always ended in disaster.

One day when we were talking on the phone, I just blurted out that the woman I really wanted to meet was Bill's co-star,

Phylicia Ayers. She appeared to be so together, so unlike the fluffy starlet types I knew all about from having lived in Los Angeles. But Bill played it cool. He claimed there wasn't too much he could do, but if I came around to the studio in Queens on such-and-such a day, he would maybe introduce us.

I never showed up for that date, and Bill was annoyed because he'd gone to some lengths to set up the meeting. The next time I went to the studio, Bill just walked me over to her dressing room, gave me a little shove to get me through the door, and said, "Phylicia—this is Ahmad. Ahmad—Phylicia." That was it—even briefer than the coin flip in a football game.

So there I was, stuck. And Phylicia had nowhere to run, either, because she was getting some makeup done. I proceeded gently, but she wouldn't give me the time of day. Maybe it was because I had on jeans and an old sweatshirt, while most of the other guys hanging around the set were in suits and ties, walking around like big shots. On the other hand, maybe she remembered that when this was last supposed to happen, old happy-go-lucky Ahmad never showed up.

But I pushed on. I asked if she liked to go to the movies and stuff, at which point her hairdresser answered: "Oh, I love to go to the movies." I handled that little misunderstanding diplomatically. I asked the hairdresser what movie she'd seen last and how she liked it. I let the issue die on the vine, and then a few moments later I asked Phylicia if she liked to go to the theater. And the damned hairdresser piped up again: "Yeah, I really like plays a lot!"

At that point, some guy stuck his head in and told Phylicia that she had to go and shoot a scene. So out she went, and I was left with the eager and willing hairdresser. I kept my mouth shut until Phylicia came back, when the whole routine picked up where we'd left off. The hairdresser fielded every question I asked until I finally felt so frustrated that I leaned over to Phylicia and, while the hairdresser was out of earshot, whispered: "Hey, can't you get rid of this lady or something? I'm not talking to her at all."

Phylicia seemed amused by my outburst, but I think she was very skeptical of my intentions. I figured she thought I was some jive dude who had a bunch of girlfriends and was just looking for another blast down the fast lane. A few months went by without any contact between us, until one day I answered my phone and heard Phylicia on the other end. She was calling to ask if I would escort her to the People's Choice Awards in Los Angeles. I said, "Sure."

I didn't have a tuxedo, so when I arrived in L.A. I went out in Beverly Hills and bought a nice one for about $1,700—and that was the price *before* I got the shirt and all that other stuff. Then this $1,700 tuxedo didn't fit right. One leg was longer than the other, and one of the buttons for the suspenders had popped off. Plus my shirtsleeves were too long. So I put a paper clip on the cuff, a safety pin in the waistband, and rubber bands on the shirtsleeves. I was all set.

Phylicia picked me up in this huge Rolls-Royce. As soon as I got in, I blurted out, "Let me straighten this out right now so I'm not going to be embarrassed for the rest of the night." So I explained about the tuxedo, and I showed her the paper clip and rubber bands and all that, and she just laughed. She thought the whole thing was great.

I didn't exactly know where Phylicia expected me to take her for dinner, but I knew it'd better be a nice place. So I picked Chinois, a restaurant opened by Wolfgang Puck, the same man who owned Spago, which was one of the nicest and trendiest places in L.A. I'd forgotten that Puck was a great football fan whom I'd met a few times over the years.

Wolfgang was with all of these stars, but when he saw us he came right over, beaming and carrying on about how nice it was to see me again, and that made me feel good. He insisted on taking care of us without even showing us a menu, just cooking up about a dozen entrees to sample. I was thinking, "This is really cool. This is like my first date with this girl and it's all going right. I've got it made."

When I took her back to her hotel I just kissed her on the

cheek and thanked her for a great time. I knew how I felt about her because I wasn't thinking, "Is she going to ask me in, or what?" Things were just different. From the start, our relationship was on a different plane.

On Thanksgiving, I realized that more fully than ever before. I was a happy sick man.

Different things make you happy at different stages of life. When I came out of college, a great marriage and domestic security were the last things on my mind. I wanted to see the world and tear up the part of it that lay between the two end zones of a football field.

During my senior year at Oregon, I'd read a book that made headlines as an exposé of the brutality and dishonesty that existed in pro football. Dave Meggyesy's *Out of Their League* was a statement of the times by a child of the times venting all the anger he felt at an institution. He had all the jargon and attitude down pat. He wrote at one point, "After the season I broke loose like a free man. I flew out to the West Coast and visited Chuck Drulis Jr., down in Ken Kesey's old haunt at La Honda and dropped some righteous acid."

Meggyesy went through the whole catalog: he talked about the drug abuse, illegal payoffs to college players, the tendency of coaches at every level to make you play hurt. He talked about militarism and blind obedience. The main buzzword in the book was "dehumanizing." And he talked a lot about the St. Louis Cardinals, for whom he played for seven years. The Cardinals were one of the most conservative teams in the league, and Meggyesy met issues like racism and brutal authoritarianism head-on. The book made an impression on me. I didn't want to have anything to do with the kind of scene Meggyesy described. I felt I could play for anybody but the Cardinals.

The day before the pro draft, I went with some friends to a pro basketball game in Portland. We went out for dinner and drinks after the game, but at about four a.m. I decided I wanted to make the three-and-a-half-hour drive home. I was falling asleep behind the wheel, and I kept pulling over to take catnaps, fantasizing about how the headlines in the papers the next morning might read: POTENTIAL NUMBER-ONE DRAFT PICK CRASHES AND DIES ON EVE OF DRAFT.

The next morning at my parents' house, I got up early. I was all psyched up for the draft; it was the biggest moment of my life. We just sat around waiting for the phone to ring. The Cincinnati Bengals had shown some interest in me, and the idea of playing for Paul Brown, the man who coached Jimmy Brown, was my top fantasy.

Finally the phone rang.

When I picked it up, this detached voice just said, "Hello, Bobby Moore? I'm calling on behalf of the St. Louis Cardinals. We just selected you in the first round of the draft. Somebody will call you later with further details."

It was such a downer, such a flat moment. It was like at Christmas when you're really hoping for a certain present and all the clues are right: the box is the right size and shape, the paper looks good. So you go at it, tearing off the wrapping, and instead of the little tool kit or whatever, you find a pair of school shoes.

After the draft, I had to fly out to St. Louis to meet the general manager, Joe Sullivan. The Cardinals had the decency to send a man to the airport. His name was Dan, he was in charge of films, and he was from Mississippi—but I learned all that much later, because he didn't say a single, solitary word to me on the long drive to the stadium. He finally pulled into the lot, parked the car, and walked away.

I shrugged that off and went to see Sullivan. His secretary acted as if she didn't know who I was. I sat in the reception area for close to an hour. Finally, I was asked in for a session that lasted all of fifteen minutes, covering mostly dumb details. Then I was on my own.

The scene was set for disaster right from the start. St. Louis had Mr. Cardinal in Larry Wilson, a wiry, tough little safety with a crewcut and a few missing teeth. I was their first draft choice, a budding student of the Islamic faith, a guy with a freewheeling, liberal perspective on life.

I had my first taste of the Cardinal ethic during the summer, when the college All-Stars scrimmaged a handful of NFL teams. During one drill against the Cardinals, I was supposed to cut behind the linebackers, but I messed up and cut in front of Larry Stallings. This wasn't even a "live" drill in helmets and pads—just shorts and a T-shirt. But Stallings cracked me across the face, so hard that my nose bled. Then he spat and just turned away. I couldn't believe it. This guy was going to be my team-mate in a few weeks' time.

Part of the problem was that, on top of everything else, I was holding out in contract negotiations. A player has only one real, serious bargaining chip in negotiations: choosing not to play. No owner in his right mind is going to negotiate in good faith when he knows that no matter what, you're going to clock in when training camp opens. That's like going on strike, but only during nonworking hours.

The owners' response to a holdout usually boils down to scare tactics: if you're a rookie, they try to convince you that you're going to ruin your potential career in the rough, tough NFL. The other big ploy is to drag your name through the press, making you out to be an ingrate, a typical "greedy" ball player, bucking the All-American tradition of teamwork. I'm surprised that the public buys that line—it's even sold to your teammates, to create peer-group pressure.

Bob Hollway was the head coach of the Cardinals, and when I joined the team after settling our contract negotiations, he decided to show me who was boss. At the end of my first practice, Hollway made the team run sprints, or "gassers." It was a real hot day, and Hollway let the team stop after running a few of them. But he pointed at me and said, "*You*—you go, all by yourself."

I shrugged. He blew his whistle, and I ran a sprint. He blew his whistle again, and I ran. After the fourth gasser, he blew the whistle and I didn't move. "Fuck you, Hollway," I thought to myself. But I bit my tongue, because the rest of the team was hanging around, watching. I wasn't going to blow my cool to entertain them. It was a standoff. Hollway finally dismissed us without saying another word. I went out to my car after practice and found that somebody had let the air out of my tires.

So then I went to have dinner in the dining hall. I was standing in line when All-Pro Larry Wilson cut in, right in front of me. Naturally, I asked him just what he thought he was doing.

"Shut up, you fucking rookie," he snapped.

When I saw he had just a few teeth, I laughed and asked what had happened to his mouth.

"Let me tell you something, fucker. I don't care who you think you are, you're never going to be part of this team."

I was so mad by then that I almost fought Mr. Cardinal. And to top it off, as soon as I sat down the veterans tried the usual ploy, trying to make me sing my college fight song before the whole team. That's a common tradition, but this was an uncommon situation for it. I'd finally had enough. I just said, "I'm not singing nothing. You might as well go on to the next guy and try him."

That caused an uproar, and eventually all kinds of guys from the Cardinals and the media picked up the theme: who is this hippie guy with hair out to here, holding out for more money, saying he doesn't like St. Louis, arguing with Mr. Cardinal, refusing to sing for the vets? That was my welcome to the NFL, and I hated every minute of it. It got so bad at times that during my two years with the Cardinals I seriously thought of quitting the game.

Let's take another classic situation that shouldn't occur in a kindergarten, not to mention the NFL. Throughout my college career, I always had my shoes taped. I didn't do it because I wanted to look cool. I've always had sensitive feet, and when you make sharp cuts, you tend to roll your shoes—you can blow them out, like bad tires, from the power and abruptness of a cut. So I'd gotten used to taping my shoes for rigidity. But the Cardinals had some kind of rule that I didn't even know about, against taping shoes.

So I was fussing with my shoes before my first game in the NFL, against the Eagles. Jim Hart walked over and said under his breath, "Hey—cool it. Hollway's watching." Seconds later, Hollway came over and said, "You're not going to play today. I'm going to start Freddie Hyatt."

"Fine," I answered. "I'll just find a nice place along the sidelines, sit on my helmet, and watch. If you need me, I'll be right down there."

Of course, I was a highly touted draft choice, and the press was stunned that I didn't even get into the game. But instead of telling the truth, the staff announced that I "had some problems." And they wouldn't give any further explanation, which made the whole issue a mystery suggesting that I had personal problems.

The receiver coach, a former Packer called Lou Carpenter, was a good guy. He became the go-between for Hollway and me in the tape wars. Seeing that I'd taped my shoes for warm-ups before one game, Lou dropped down to his knees and began to tear away at the tape with his own hands.

Part of the problem was that I just wasn't ready to deal with a Bob Hollway after having a great coach like Jerry Frei. I couldn't believe that at the peak of your profession, in the NFL, you couldn't have an opinion that wasn't endorsed by the coach. That would get me in plenty of trouble. When somebody in a meeting asked what was wrong with the team, most of the guys would button up and mutter some clichés about desire. I'd just say what I honestly thought.

Throughout my career, I never had trouble with coaches who just wanted to win. I loved Lou Saban. I have the utmost respect for Bud Grant. It was the guys who thought they could be like Bud or Lou by playing hardass that got me. This is how Hollway would talk to grown men at halftime: "You sorryass motherfuckers, you're an embarrassment to me, you're an embarrassment to yourselves, you're an embarrassment to your families. Go out there for chrissakes and try to fucking play some fucking football."

I'd still like to know how a grown man goes home to his wife after practice and when she asks how his day went, says, "Except for the fact that the coach called me a dumbass useless motherfucker, fine."

So while the winds of change were in the air, they weren't exactly blowing up a storm in St. Louis. Joe Namath was wearing white shoes in New York and Fredd Dryer was living like a hippie out of his van in Los Angeles, but I was stuck with the most backward team in the league.

Through the years, the club had made an institution out of unspoken segregation, segregation that ate away at morale. We had electricity now and then—every team does. But there sure were weird undercurrents. There were snide remarks instead of good old-fashioned needling—all those things that drive men further apart instead of bringing them together. And there was Bob Hollway.

One time, Hollway came up to me in the locker room and started yelling at me about something. I blew my top and began yelling back. Finally, he stormed off. Jamie Rivers, one of our linebackers, came right over to me and said: "You tell that motherfucker, that's right! I hate that son of a bitch, I would have told him the same thing . . ."

While Rivers was going on, Hollway had returned. Reading my eyes, Jamie turned around. "Oh, hi, Coach! Hey, how's the wife and kids?"

But I made my share of friends on the team. Dale Hackbart was a defensive back with a great sense of humor. Hollway once got mad because so many guys were just hanging out in the trainers' room. He decided to post a chart, and you had to log in the time and duration of your visit, and the reason. So Dale made Xerox copies of the chart and posted them all over the place—including the john. Dale's favorite parlor gag—if you could call it that—was to go to a bar and bet some stranger that he could piss over the top of a car. And that was in the days before these little imports—even the Volkswagen Beetle was pretty tall.

Johnny Roland was a great player and a good guy, even though he never really got his due in St. Louis. It really was tough for black players, especially the veterans, who were just blind to the inequities from habit. I got along great with Dan Dierdorf, Bob Young, and Donny Anderson. I bought a pile of records one day and Donny gave me a unique warning: "Them records'll melt, man, but the money won't." Mel Gray, who would become such a great receiver, was also a good friend. Our lockers were next to each other, so we laughed a lot—a lot of times with hands over our faces so nobody would see us.

I got off to a crazy start with the team, but the situation improved. In any event it wasn't that big a deal, because I was a loner. Arriving in St. Louis, I had decided I didn't want to live with a bunch of football players. Driving on the freeway one day, I saw this tall apartment building. I pulled off, checked the place out, and by the next day I'd moved in. My building was right at the edge of the St. Louis University campus, so I was around other young people who were thinking about something besides football, work, and money. The friends I made there had no connection with football.

Despite all the hassles, I made the NFC all-rookie team, finishing the year with twenty-nine catches for 500 yards and a team leading three touchdowns. That was good enough to set a Cardinals rookie record. I had just 50 fewer total receiving yards than the team leader, Walker Gillette, but the same average of 17 yards per catch. I also led the team in kickoff returns and carried the ball nine times for an average of 4.9 yards per carry.

Before our final game, I packed my car right up to the roof and drove it to the stadium. I paid a man to watch over it while I gave the Cardinals the last sixty minutes I owed them for 1972. I had a good game, setting an NFL record that can never be broken when Jim Hart and I hooked up on a ninety-eight-yard completion—the longest nonscoring passing play in league history.

After the game, I was so eager to get away that my hair was still wet from the shower when I put the key in the ignition and pulled away. Somewhere in Montana two days later, I heard a sports bulletin on the car radio: the St. Louis Cardinals had fired head coach Bob Hollway and named Don Coryell to replace him.

I pulled over at the Blue Moon Saloon—Montana has a hundred Blue Moon Saloons—and had a few beers to celebrate.

Coryell, the new man in St. Louis, had made San Diego State University famous with a freewheeling passing offense that put lots of points on the scoreboard, and put them up faster than stock quotations on a ticker. But while Coryell was plotting how to make that happen in St. Louis, I was doing a lot of freewheeling of my own.

I spent most of the off-season in Los Angeles, at what turned out to be one long party, held over a few months in Beverly Hills, Santa Monica, Malibu, Brentwood, and most points in between. I was hanging out with O. J. Simpson, Bubba and Tody Smith, and Al Cowens—we were a clique of well-known athletes, with a fleet of Cadillacs that became the L.A. Party Caravan.

For about two months, the famous sunshine of L.A. was just a rumor to me. I had so many phone numbers that I could have pasted them on a roulette wheel and picked my dates like that. The one good thing about becoming a party animal is that beyond a certain point you don't get out of shape. I was burning it so hard that my weight dropped by about twenty pounds— and just in case you're snickering, I never touched cocaine.

It didn't take me long to realize that I had to leave Los Angeles. I was looking forward to a fresh start under Coryell, and I wanted to reach my potential as a receiver. I decided to spend the summer in St. Louis, getting myself into shape for football.

The only other activity I was interested in was renewing my studies in the Islamic faith. Through Kareem Abdul-Jabbar, I was in contact with a major mosque in Washington. They suggested that I might study with a learned Muslim, Rashād Khalifa. As fate would have it, Khalifa lived two blocks from me in St. Louis.

I'm not the type to go around preaching my beliefs or to come on strong trying to recruit converts to my religion. If you know anything about the Islamic faith, I don't have to explain. If you aren't familiar with the basics of Islam, you should go and find out before you make any judgments or draw conclusions. All I'll say is that I found my beliefs put into the right words and given full expression in Islam. The more I studied, the more I felt like I'd found my spiritual touchstone.

Life was pretty calm for me through the summer, and in training camp under Coryell. In the evenings, I would go to study with Khalifa. Sometimes we talked sports. He was a real fan, and his son, Sammy, would go on to play in the Pittsburgh Pirates' infield. Khalifa had organized a study group that met every Friday night at his home. There was an English guy, an Irishman, a Spaniard—a whole slew of individuals. We would study, reading the Koran in English and Arabic, until the sun came up. Then we would join in saying our morning Salat, or prayers, a Muslim tradition.

This concept of the importance of daily prayers is an integral part of Islam, but the faith doesn't require you to stop working or anything just to do your Salat. You do it when you can. Once I fully embraced Islam, I always tried to get a private room in training camp or during road games, so that I could recite my Salat without embarrassing a roommate. When I joined the Vikings and asked Bud for my own room, I expected a hassle. But as soon as I told him why I wanted it, he went along with it.

Unfortunately, the good folks of St. Louis weren't that flexible back when I was coming to grips with my beliefs. It all came to a head when I decided that I wanted to change my name, taking one that conformed to Islamic tradition. Ahmad Rashād means "Admirable One Led to Truth," and the idea behind Islamic names is that every time they're spoken, they bring praise to God. It isn't all that different from the Christian tradition of naming children after the apostles and saints, as a form of honoring their memory.

Taking a Muslim name isn't compulsory, but I liked the idea

because it made the statement: "This is what I'm all about. I'm a real person, not Bobby Moore, football player, but Ahmad Rashād, a man who believes in fairness, in truth, in life." The Cardinals' first reaction when I told them that I was going to change my name was typical. Instead of discussing it with me, I was given a simple message from the front office: "You're not going to do any such thing as long as you're playing for the St. Louis Cardinals. You'll do what we want you to do."

Of course, I went right ahead with my plans. I wasn't going to waste my time reading the front office the bill of rights they pretended to be so proud of. I gradually made my position clear to everybody: this is what I'm doing; these are the reasons why; and I only want to go through it once, because I'm not going to spend the rest of my life explaining myself to every Tom, Dick, and Harry.

I changed my name just like any other guy, in civil court. The change became official during training camp, and things came to a head a few days later, when we played a preseason game against the Bears. Right up until game time, the poor equipment guy didn't know what name to put on my jersey. The front office went back and forth on it until they grudgingly let him go with Rashad.

At game time, while we were lined up for the introductions, I wondered what kind of reception I would get. When they introduced the starting offense, the guys went running out waving and stuff, and the crowd went wild. When my turn came, the announcer said: "Ladies and gentlemen—there's been a change in your program. Number twenty-eight, Bobby Moore, has just changed his name to—"

That's as far as he got.

A cascade of boos drowned out the PA, an avalanche of bad noise aimed at me. I loped out there into this awful outpouring of disapproval, and it echoed in my helmet all the way down the field. When I got to my teammates, there were no high-fives or claps on the pads—they were all looking the other way, like they were waiting for a bus or something. They hadn't even left me a place to stand in line.

For the rest of the game, I couldn't make a move without hearing the boos. Every time a pass was thrown my way, the boos drowned out the announcer's call. At the end of the game, a pack of security personnel had to escort me out to my car. But I was saved a lot of anger and anguish because I had somewhere to go. I drove over to Khalifa's house, rejoined my study group, and found the tranquillity that was not going to be mine as long as I played football in St. Louis.

My heart might have been broken if the Cardinals were a great, winning football team: it would have confirmed all those ugly things people were saying about football and the mentality it breeds. But the fact of the matter was that we stunk, so no criticism directed at me had any real credibility. I would get on the team bus before games and the guys would file on by, nobody stopping to sit down by "weird Bobby Moore who changed his name to Armond Rasher or whatever . . ."

One of the Cardinals, trainer John Omohundro, did sit down next to me on the team bus once. He opened up by saying something incredibly patronizing, like "You know, me and my wife were talking the other night, and I think we've figured out what it is that's strange about you . . ." He went into this whole long rap on what everybody thought about me and my actions. I was simmering inside, but the last thing I wanted to do was make another enemy. To this day, I see Omohundro and he says, "You know, I remember that great talk we had on the bus that day." And I think, "What great talk? You mean that stupid lecture you gave me?"

Tom Banks, an offensive guard, became a good friend. Talk about the dangers of stereotypes: here was a southern boy, a big beefy lineman who'd gone to Auburn, yet he was the most understanding and supportive guy on the team when it came to my name change. Right off the bat, he called me by my new name and we became close friends.

Coryell and I got along well until I changed my name, and then he just seemed to forget how to deal with me. He couldn't get my name right—he was always calling me "Ramada" or "Armada" or something. One day, I took two pieces of adhesive tape and put them on the front and the back of my helmet. I wrote my name on the tape. I went up to Coryell and told him: "If you forget my name, just look here and read it off." I turned around. "And it's back here too, just in case I'm facing the other way."

In lots of ways, a coach leads by example. By not dealing with me respectfully, Coryell was giving the green light for everybody else to take me lightly. So in meetings, guys would still insist on calling me "Bobby." Assistant coaches didn't want to deal with the change, either. I was always amazed at how many guys thought it was something silly, or some kind of put-on.

But I dealt with all that and still got excited about playing football on Sunday. I kept my enthusiasm even though we were a lousy team with lousy morale. Most of the guys would go out there and try, but by the second period they'd give up hope.

There's a lot of bleeding that goes on in a losers' locker room. At St. Louis, they had buckets to hold all the blood. You think that's football until you get to a good team and realize that everybody's looking pretty clean. We had three or four bleeders on the Cardinals. You might have thought these were tough guys playing football the way God intended, but the truth is that they were bleeding so much because they were getting the dog-shit kicked out of them.

The low point occurred pretty early in the season. We were 2–1, coming off a 45–10 loss to Dallas. Our next game was against the Raiders. The night before that game, I had one of my best times in St. Louis. I took Bubba Smith, a friend from our L.A. posse, out on the town. As I drove up to Bubba's hotel on the way home, we spotted a couple of Raiders and John Madden hanging around.

I was tipsy and distracted, so I drove right up on the sidewalk. It was like blowing a trumpet to get everybody's attention. Then Bubba, who stands six foot seven, unfolded himself from the car and staggered toward the door. I thought Madden's eyes were going to pop out of his head. I had to drive back off the sidewalk with all the other Raiders watching, laughing.

Before the game the next day, Coryell gave us a gung-ho speech. Oakland was one of the best teams in the league, but by the end of this speech we were so fired up we were ready to beat anybody. We were knocking over lockers, kicking things, yelling "Kill the Raiders!" It was too bad we couldn't rush over to the Raiders' hotel and go at them right then, because Coryell made his speech two hours before the game.

Unfortunately, we hadn't killed anybody yet, and we weren't going to start with the Raiders—any sane person could see that. I was still yelling and carrying on when I glanced at Mel Gray. He was yelling, too. But all of a sudden we both realized how stupid we sounded and we broke up laughing—we laughed for about fifteen minutes. Which left us an hour and forty-five to realize that we weren't going to be killing anybody that afternoon.

By halftime in that game, we were pretty beaten up. Coryell couldn't handle it; he was really dejected. When time came to address the team, he got up in front of us and totally lost his cool. The man began to cry. He groped around and finally said, "Just go on, get out of here." Naturally, we lost the game. I still don't know what Coryell wanted to achieve with his tears. Our reaction was embarrassment at having to watch a grown man cry.

All in all, it was a tense year. Walker Gillette played the same position as me, so there was this natural rivalry between us. I thought I was a better receiver and resented having to share time with him whenever the coach or the front office wanted to play games with me. For example, I had a bonus clause guaranteeing me an extra $10,000 if I started every game or played a certain percentage of the time. The club would save money by starting Gillette or by using him to keep my playing time down.

One day during practice I refused to run a certain play, and Gillette told the coach that if I wasn't doing it, he wouldn't either. I stepped on my own heel and pretended like my shoe had come off, so Gillette had to run the play anyway. It was just one of those funny little scenes, but Walker didn't see the humor in it. In the huddle for the next play, we started to mouth on each other. We got pretty heated, and as we went to line up, all hell broke loose. We started fighting, flailing away at each other. Fights like that occur all the time, and they pass like summer thunderstorms.

But despite all the turmoil and a final record of 4–9–1, I still had a pretty good year. Our tight end Jackie Smith caught a lot of balls to lead the team. Among the wide receivers, Mel Gray and I were the big guns. I had twenty-nine catches and he had thirty; I had 409 yards and he finished with 513. His average per catch was 18 yards; mine was 14. Mel caught seven touchdown passes, and I had three.

And then there was Rod Dowhower, our receiver coach. The man was a great teacher. He opened my eyes to all kinds of nuances of the craft and taught me how to run pass routes. He's the one who turned me into an All-Pro-caliber receiver. In fact, after I left the Cardinals, I made it a point to write Rod a letter of appreciation.

Throughout that plagued season, O. J. Simpson kept calling me from Buffalo. I would tell him about my problems and he kept encouraging me to hang in there. O.J. was a megasuperstar at the time, and I knew that the Bills' front office would listen if he told them that I could really help the team. I'd made it very clear to the Cardinal management that I wanted to be traded, but football is different from baseball—there isn't nearly the same amount of horse trading that goes on between owners.

But they had to see the handwriting on the wall as clearly as I did: I wasn't about to replace Larry Wilson as Mr. Cardinal. Not in 1974, not ever.

Once again, I had the car packed and ready to go as the season ended in St. Louis. I drove back to Tacoma with Terry Metcalf, whom I'd grown up with. A few weeks later, I got a phone call at home from Sullivan. It was a pretty quick conversation.

"Hello? This is Joe Sullivan. We've just traded you to the Buffalo Bills."

I know the Cardinals must have been thinking, "We'll fix his malcontented ass—we'll trade him to Buffalo because we know he doesn't like the cold weather."

But I was thinking, "Buffalo—O.J., Reggie McKenzie, Joe Ferguson, Lou Saban—well, that's all right now . . ."

"Thanks a lot," I said, hanging up the phone. As far as I was concerned, I was out of their league, too.

8

EIGHT SETS OF EYES
AND EARS

The best feature I did in 1987 was the one with Walter Payton just a week before Christmas, before his last home game. It was hard to imagine Payton retiring: the Bears without Sweetness would be like the Lakers without Kareem or tennis without Jimmy Connors. We tied the Payton retirement feature in with a studio package, devoting a whole show to four great running backs: Payton, Jim Brown, O. J. Simpson, and Gale Sayers. We even conducted a viewer poll to pick the greatest back of all time.

"Sweetness" was the right name for Payton, all right—he was the only football player who ever gave me a kiss. Walter and I had adjacent lockers at the 1979 Pro Bowl. After the game, when the league officials came in to announce that I'd won the MVP award, Walter just poked his head around the partition and gave me a big kiss on the cheek.

The interview we did in honor of Payton's retirement moved people. He got a little choked up, and tears came to his eyes when he reflected on his career in that humble, down-home way of his. The lighting was perfect; the camera angle was just right for bringing out the dignity of the man and the majesty of his achievements. It was a powerful piece of television.

At one point, off the air, I kidded Payton about a shot he'd
taken the previous week against San Francisco. It was the only
time I could remember seeing him get knocked out cold in a
game. Like any tough pro, he jumped to his feet as soon as he
regained consciousness, pretending nothing was wrong; but in
that state he couldn't tell a football from a footstool. Walter
confessed, "Yeah, I guess my mind and body were working
different sides of the street."

That's a great running back for you: proud and tough and
unwilling to show that he's hurt. It's so bad with some guys that
when they get knocked out, the coaches hide their helmets over
on the sidelines so they don't go sneaking back into the game.
You don't want a guy in the game when his windshield is all
fogged up. He forgets the snap count, lines up on the wrong
side, runs into the quarterback.

Running back is a glamorous position that ranks right after
quarterback in most people's eyes. Smooth, silky guys like O. J.
Simpson or Eric Dickerson are like thoroughbreds. They make
running with a football look as effortless as figure skating. But
the truth is that backs get beat up something terrible. When a
guy breaks five tackles for a gain of eight yards, you admire his
ability to evade tacklers. You tend to forget that those five hits
took a toll—it's like a boxer absorbing five heavy body punches
in the course of winning a round. He's constantly being
punished.

That's why the mark of greatness in a running back is that
unglamorous quality called consistency. Every back who carries
the ball a lot gets beat up pretty badly, in almost every game.
Only the great ones line up week in, week out. A running back's
not hurt unless he's got a busted leg. If something is bruised or
pulled, the guy can play. If something's broken and it can be
taped together, the guy can play. That's what's expected of a
runner. The greatest quality a running back can have is
reliability.

Any of us can name a bunch of backs who've had a few great
years and then did a slow fade. They still play, and you wonder

why they can't perform like they did just two or three seasons ago. Usually, it's because they've been beaten up and broken down. They still have speed, they still have moves, but they don't have that explosive quality anymore. The punishment has worn them down to ordinary caliber.

I knew from playing tailback in college how much punishment a running back takes, and any illusion about the NFL being any easier on runners was laid to rest during my second year with the Cardinals.

After I changed my name, Don Coryell suddenly decided that he was going to test me as a running back. I assumed that the Cardinals were punishing me. Joe Gibbs, one of the great men in football, was the running-back coach. He told me, "I don't know what's going on or why you've been sent down to us, but if you want to put in the time and effort, I'll try to make you the best running back you can be."

We were playing the Kansas City Chiefs the following Sunday, a rough, winning bunch led by linebacker Willie Lanier and defensive tackle Buck Buchanan. Lanier looked like a big old bear. He was so bad you never looked him in the eye, because he'd scare the shit out of you—he was *that* intense. Willie was the ultimate no-neck: they had to put a piece of leather on the top of his helmet because he was knocking too many people out cold.

On game day, I put on every piece of protective equipment I could find. Compared to me in my getup, Eric Dickerson plays in a loincloth. By the time I finished putting on the pads and getting dressed, I was so heavy I could barely stand up, never mind run. I wasn't embarrassed about it, either. I figured this was a life-or-death situation.

I ran the ball three times that day. The third attempt was a simple trap play, in which we were supposed to trick six-foot-seven Buck Buchanan and send me flying past him up the middle. The guy who was going to handle Buck was my friend Tom Banks, a short dude. As the play developed, Banks plowed Buchanan to the side; the trouble was, he only reached up to

Buck's chest. Still, I saw some daylight as I got the ball. I thought, "All right, I'm gonna run right through this fucking hole right here."

My only worry was Willie Lanier, who was on the flank of the play. When you've got a guy like Lanier on the field, you tend to have eight sets of eyes and ears, and half of them are always tuned to his whereabouts. As I hit the line, I planned to cut back against the grain when I got through the hole, hoping I might fool Lanier into overrunning the play.

But meanwhile, Buck Buchanan leaned over the top of Banks. Buck was too late to make the tackle, but he did the next best thing: he just reached over Banks and swung that big old arm of his, pounding me on top of the head with a clenched fist. It was like doomsday—one moment I was planning a move past Lanier, and the next I was knocked out cold. By the time I regained consciousness, I was a wide receiver again.

That's what makes a runner like Walter Payton so extraordinary: the ability to withstand punishment. When we were divisional rivals, I got to see Walter twice a year. I should say I got to *watch* Walter twice a year. For most of that period in the late 1970s, Payton was the Bears' only weapon, and he was still unstoppable. He was that rare player whose greatness was so obvious and so overwhelming that even if you were in a different uniform on the sidelines, you couldn't help cheering for him down deep inside.

One time, Payton ran for 275 yards against us. He ran over every single guy in our defense at least once. Once in a while we gang-tackled him or drove him out of bounds, but that was about it. Before we watched the films the next day, I announced a "bounty." I said I hadn't seen the films yet, but I was going to pay a reward to anybody on the field who could actually claim that *he* had tackled Walter. I got these sullen looks from our defensive guys, but nobody could stand up and collect.

Another extraordinary aspect of Walter was the way he got his yards. A lot of the great rushers, the guys with the big career numbers, were the fluid runners who just slipped by defenders like water running through their fingers. Gale Sayers and O.J. were classic runners who had amazing finesse. Before the defense knew what was going on, those guys would go forty, fifty, or sixty yards. They broke it off in big chunks, like a hungry guy eating a loaf of bread.

Backs like O.J. and Gale don't even think about the first defender they've got to beat, because there just isn't time. Besides, beating the first guy is a given. The idea is to set up the next three defenders for the burn as you're beating the first guy. It's like three-dimensional chess, and it's a game that Eric Dickerson plays real well these days too. Eric takes a gullible defender out of a play long before they're anywhere near each other. The defender is moving with the play when—uh-oh—he realizes that he's lost the angle on Eric.

Checkmate.

At Buffalo, on third-and-anything, we would give the ball to O.J. and send him off tackle. You never knew what might happen, because O.J. could break one tackle and gain thirty yards. But Payton was different. Usually he broke seven or eight tackles and got ten yards. He specialized in *dirty* yards. He was more of a Pete Rose than a Hank Aaron. In his career, Walter gained almost sixteen thousand "dirty" yards for a team that had more losing years than winning ones. It's a phenomenal statistic.

Walter's claim to the title of greatest running back in NFL history is staked on his versatility. It's a quality that relatively few people acknowledge and nobody questions. Walter Payton did it all, the pretty parts and the ugly parts, too. He could dance through a line that showed as few holes as a solid brick wall, and he could cut down a blitzing safety like a lumberjack felling a pine tree.

The complete running back needs to do three things well: run, block, and catch passes. Walter's superiority as a runner was obvious, but he was in equally select company as a blocking back. Lots of runners don't like to block; they'd rather save their energy for carrying the ball, or maybe they've always considered blocking a secondary skill. But a versatile back transforms a whole backfield with his skills. I know that from having played with two guys who were designed along the same lines as Walter.

Chuck Foreman was every bit as good as Walter, although he was fated to fall a little bit short of his potential. He wasn't a "nervous" runner like Walter but a big, rangy guy like Marcus Allen. But at 220, he outweighed Marcus and Walter by a good fifteen to twenty pounds. Fans always linked the names "Vikings" and "Tarkenton," but in his prime Chuck was the heart and soul of the Viking offense. He had guts and he was very emotional. He may have been a little inconsistent, but when Chuck had his act together, nobody was better.

Chuck played for the Vikings from 1973 to 1979, when he was traded to New England. After one season with the Patriots, he was out of football. Chuck's career in the NFL was illustrious, but he was worn down and defeated by constant, bitter skirmishes with the front office. He never seemed to get what he was worth at contract time, and he was always outfoxed by Viking general manager Mike Lynn.

The idea that he never ended up getting what he was worth drove Chuck crazy and soured him on football. He made some mistakes, too, like trying to negotiate a better deal for himself in the pages of the newspapers. But the bottom line is that he was as important to the team as Fran Tarkenton, and he should have been paid as much as a guy like O.J. It was sad to watch a guy get torn down that way. The front office saved a few bucks on his contract every year, but in the end it cost them on the field. They got what they paid for.

Rickey Young may never make the Hall of Fame or figure on anybody's list of NFL superstars; but he was a great blocker, and he caught the ball coming out of the backfield as well as anybody I've ever seen. He stood six foot two, but he was wiry, weighing well under 200 pounds. He became one of my best friends on the Vikings. I respected him a lot, and he was always ready for a good laugh. In fact, making Rickey laugh was one of my favorite pastimes in the locker room, in the film room, even on the field.

Bud Grant liked to rotate his backs, using them to carry plays into the huddle. Sometimes Chuck Foreman would run the ball and get killed, like flipped over or something. Rickey would run into the huddle, and instead of telling us the play he'd say, "Bud liked that shit where you land on your helmet, Chuck—that's *bad*. He wants to see that one again."

I always tried to make Rickey forget the play when he brought it into the huddle. Sometimes he'd be real nervous, and as soon as he reached the huddle I'd distract him by making some joke about how hard some guy had been hit on the previous play. Or if Rickey hesitated for a second, trying to remember the play, I'd say, "Come on, tell us the goddamn play. What the fuck you waitin' on?" Sometimes he would only remember half the play. His voice trailed off as he said, "And on the rest of it, just do what you usually do. . . ."

One of the funniest moments of my career occurred during a game against the Bears. It was a typical Bears–Vikings brawl, and we were all pumped up to score, moving the ball late in the game. On one play, Rickey ran a little out, but Tommy Kramer was under a lot of pressure. He unloaded the ball to avoid the sack, throwing it about twenty yards over Rickey's head. But Rickey was so fired up that he jumped for the ball anyway.

I couldn't believe my eyes when I saw that. I came trotting up the sideline and caught up with Rickey as we headed back to the huddle. I couldn't resist sticking the needle in: "What'd you think, just 'cause this is a tough game and the ball's up, you're gonna sprout some fucking wings or something and catch that thing?"

The situation was so absurd that we both cracked up, and we couldn't stop laughing the whole time in the huddle. That's the kind of guy you appreciate having on your team. Tough guys may not dance, but they sure can laugh. And Rickey was tough, the equal of Walter Payton as a blocker and pass receiver.

The "NFL Live" viewers voted Walter the greatest back of all time, which came as no surprise to anybody. On that particular Sunday, he was everybody's sentimental favorite, and he had the great edge of being the only active player under consideration. But in the studio, Bob Costas, Bob Trumpy, and I all came up with a different choice: Jim Brown of the Cleveland Browns.

Brown led the league in rushing for eight of the nine years that he played. He averaged over 100 yards per game and a staggering 5.2 yards per carry—the best stats by far among those four giants of the rushing game. Brown's durability was remarkable in an era when the game was more elemental and the sophisticated passing attack was still an unexplored frontier in football.

Jim Marshall, the ultimate Purple People Eater, always maintained that Brown was the best he ever faced—or saw. He once told me, "Jimmy Brown was the type of dude who walked on the field and didn't care about who the Browns were playing, or what the weather was like, or any other conditions. He was going to get what he could take, and he took a lot every week. He had the speed to go around you, the power to go over you, and the elusive ability to find the weakness of your team and exploit it to the limit."

That's a pretty strong endorsement from the ultimate Viking— the same guy who walked up to Jimmy Brown before a game and predicted that Minnesota was going to hold Brown to the same yardage as the number on his jersey.

Brown wore number 32. He never broke forty yards that day.

9

KICKING SOME BOOTY UP NORTH

In December 1987, I started to think about what I could do for my second wedding anniversary. Wandering around at La Guardia Airport, I bought a souvenir—one of those clear plastic balls that you shake up, making fake snow fall around a little scene. I decided to give it to Phylicia over dinner as her anniversary present. I also bought a very expensive gold-and-diamond bracelet which I was going to hold back until later that night, in a more intimate moment at home.

I booked a table at the River Cafe in Brooklyn and invited a few close friends, including Bill and Camille Cosby, to share our anniversary. But I didn't tell that to Phylicia. Instead, I told her that I'd made plans we couldn't break with a couple we know— a couple my wife doesn't particularly like because she thinks they're phony. The trap was all set.

After two years of marriage, I still love my wife more and more every day. In previous relationships, I was the only one with the "important" job, so life revolved mostly around me and my needs. I found that stifling; it created an unhealthy atmosphere. If you're the center of attention, you take the support person for granted and even resent her—or his—dependence. If you're the support person, your self-image goes down, and you end up

163

resenting your partner for being so dominant. I've become a firm believer in having both people go for their ambitions. The only snag is when you get too wrapped up in them: it's crucial to be there when you're needed, with support and encouragement for your partner.

It isn't always easy for an athlete to form a single, lasting relationship with a woman. Kareem found that out, and so did Reggie Jackson. I did, too. As an athlete, you're measured on a performance that demands that you give your all; and the more of a star you are, the more closely you're scrutinized. The pressures an athlete faces almost daily include injury, which can end a career overnight, and a change of role from hero to goat from one day to the next. An athlete has to grab fame and fortune while they're there, and he can't easily afford distractions that threaten that pursuit.

When you reach a certain level in sports, you have a team that takes care of your professional life, and an agent or lawyer who takes care of your business life. It's hard to turn over what's left to anybody else. That's what makes an emotional commitment such a challenge. I know there are happily married athletes who perform at the peak of their craft. I know there are athletes who successfully build their lives around their families at an early age. But it's a trick some of us never master.

Wanting to be a star creates a whole pattern of behavior. There are great athletes who aren't stars, but pro sports depends on stars as much as movies or music does. If you have star potential, or perform at that high level, you want beautiful girls on your arm, just like you want that Ferrari Testarossa in the driveway. It gets old eventually, but it's a way to beat the emptiness that's sometimes there. And the adulation can make you think you're entitled to the best of everything—or at least what *looks* the best.

And finally, you've got to deal with whether a person is interested in you or your celebrity. If you're around a sport for any amount of time, you see so many rip-offs. Some rookie on your team meets a girl in a city at an away game and pretty soon he announces his engagement. The veterans look at each other and roll their eyes, because they've seen this same girl with eight or nine different guys over the years. But she's finally hit pay dirt, and everything's fine until the divorce papers are filed three years later. It happens in every sport.

I'm happy Phylicia and I came from different fields. I can't give her advice or criticism about acting any more than she can analyze a broken play. But she's such a good actress that she can watch my performance on television and make some relevant observations about it. She also knows the ins and outs of a field where image counts for so much, both to the public and to the movers and shakers of the industry. She was real helpful to me when I was struggling with a feeling of stagnation on the job, wondering if I could expand my role before I became stereotyped.

My agent's been talking to NBC executives about having me serve as a studio host during our coverage of the Summer Olympics in Seoul. It got back to me that one of the producers had said, "Ahmad can't handle that job—he doesn't even know who Jesse Owens was." That's a common reaction to my image as a "celebrity." I don't know if it's jealousy or just ignorance, but I do know that it hurts.

I've also been having trouble expanding my role on the "NFL Live" show. I've been going back and forth with John Filippelli about helping out with the highlights we show during games— you know, when the network switches to another game and gives you a quick update, showing a big scoring play. Flip didn't think I could handle highlights. I pointed out that this was Catch-22: we'll never know how I handle them until I try, and until I try I won't be able to handle the job. It was the typical case of being perceived in a certain way, without flexibility. Flip lost his temper and reminded me that as a player, I couldn't tell the coach that I wanted to make up the game plan. I reminded him that as a player, I always had the option of asking to be traded. We left it at that.

I also found out recently that I was scheduled to host the

televised Superteams competition again. I have mixed feelings about that. It's a hoot to spend time around athletes when they're relaxed, but the athletics in Superteams aren't really credible. The show is just about a bunch of great athletes fooling around in different sports. The job is a little like being the host of a game show, and the danger is that you get typecast that way—you're the guy whose specialty is goofy sports, a master of fluff, a lightweight. You're the kind of guy who never heard of Jesse Owens.

When I discussed the subject with Phylicia, she told me about a move she once made back when she was serving as an understudy for a leading role in a Broadway play. When the lead left the play, the director quietly had a new girl come in, without really explaining anything. Phylicia knew the girl was being groomed for the lead, so she just up and quit the job, even though she didn't have any other work. She knew that you can only be an understudy for so long before everybody thinks of you and sees you as nothing more than an understudy. She had a choice between pursuing what she wanted to do and accepting the signal that being an understudy was *all* she could do.

I guess I qualified as an understudy in marriage at the time when Phylicia accepted my proposal. When I got home to New York on that Thanksgiving Day in 1985, I realized what a big deal the televised proposal had become. The phone was ringing off the hook; my service was swamped with messages.

Bill Cosby was one of the first people I called back. He had an interesting take on the affair. Bill was really into the fact that it was a tender moment, something you don't see much between black people on television. Except on "The Cosby Show," you rarely see black people kiss on television. Most of the time, you see us jumping over something, beating up on somebody, or screaming about something, because that's the way the roles are written. My proposal sent a different signal, and the only thing that Bill didn't like about it was that his wife, Camille, gave him a hard time after she saw it.

She sat down right next to him after the proposal. "So," she said, giving him a nudge. "Why didn't you propose to me like that?"

Bill's approval was like parental approval to me. After all, he took me under his wing early on and introduced me to a broad view of life. Guys who told me what a great player I was were a dime a dozen—they always are, even if you stink. But Bill made me realize that football wasn't forever, and that there were important social roles for athletes and celebrities to fill.

He worked on me in a low-key way, without lecturing me. In '79, Bill asked me how much money I made.

"About two hundred grand a year," I answered proudly.

Bill smiled, looked at his fingernails, and told me that he sometimes made that much in a week. He wasn't bragging, just letting me know that there are different levels of success.

"Don't get stuck just playing that football," he would tell me. "Don't let a game run your life."

Sometimes Bill invited me out to Las Vegas for a few days when he was doing his show, just so I could see what that scene was all about. He invited me to vacation with him in the south of France, far from the beaten tourist path. He taught me the value of classic things, like the 1958 Porsche he helped me pick out last summer.

But that Porsche will be long gone before I forget something I *didn't* buy—a mobile at Sotheby's, the New York art auction house. Bill had gotten me mildly curious about art, so I went to this auction of contemporary stuff. I sat right up near the front, and I marveled at the prices the things were going for. When this mobile came up, it looked like just some little nothing to me. But the auctioneer started in, going, "Do I hear three for this—do I hear three? Three seventy-five in the front—do I hear four?"

We weren't talking about three hundred and seventy-five bucks but *three hundred and seventy-five thousand.*

Suddenly the auctioneer pointed right at me, saying, "I now have four—I have four from the gentleman in the front."

"Hey, man," I thought, "I didn't move my hand. I didn't move *anything.* I've been sitting on my hands for just this reason and I don't want that little mobile thing. This guy's gonna have to fight me to make me take that thing."

Luckily, somebody bumped up the bid.

After the sale, the auctioneer came over and explained that Bill Cosby had been bidding for the mobile over the phone. He knew that I was at the sale, so he told the auctioneer to hang me with one of his own bids. I guess it was funny—to Bill.

Bill has a tender side, too. When I lost both of my parents within months of each other in 1980, I felt a real void in my life. I was slipping into this negative feeling that I was all alone in the world. During that period, Bill sometimes introduced me as his eldest son. He did it in a lighthearted way, but it always made me proud.

It's funny how often people take shots at Bill: you read in the press that he's tough, or bitter, or money-hungry, or hard to work with. That's because people have trouble accepting his success. Maybe it all seems to come too easily to Bill.

He once told me about the time he had the grand old man of jazz piano, Eubie Blake, in his dressing room before a show. Bill was hot—he was carrying on and making everybody laugh to the point where he was actually late walking out on stage. When Bill came off the stage, Eubie, who was about ninety at the time, pulled him aside. He said, "I've got news for you, Bill. You don't have an act. You didn't do anything out there that was any more funny or entertaining than the way you were carrying on before the show in here."

I don't think you could think up a better compliment.

Bill was the first important person to steer me toward television. In fact, I first spoke with him after he saw a spot I'd done for the United Way on behalf of the NFL. He called to encourage me to pursue a career in broadcasting, and he's been there with advice and guidance ever since. We even worked together on a football feature once, and we're always throwing new ideas around.

Bill and I even work out together sometimes. He's one of those

Philadelphia guys who grew up with cinders on their shoes—track is a tradition in that town. Bill played football, ran track, and high-jumped when he was at Temple. Although he's up around fifty now, I honestly think he could *still* smoke me in a three-hundred-meter race.

Plus, Bill introduced me to Phylicia. So it was only natural that he should give away the bride when we decided to marry. The worst thing about all the publicity surrounding the proposal was that hundreds of people called to ask us the date of the wedding, so that they could plan their vacations around it. On top of that, when Phylicia and I made an appearance on the "Good Morning, America" show, the host asked us for the date of the wedding. I guess he figured that if I could propose on TV, I could announce the date of our wedding to the world, too.

But Phylicia and I hadn't yet settled on the date, so we exchanged blank looks. Besides, neither of us wanted to have a wedding with all the atmosphere of a circus. Suddenly, I had an idea. I picked a date in late January out of the blue and blurted it out, knowing all along that we could pick an earlier date and quietly fake everybody out.

Ultimately, we settled on December 14, 1985—the same day as a televised game between the Bears and Jets. We made a guest list and then pared it down as far as we could. We had a broad range of guests, including *Sports Illustrated* senior editor Frank DeFord and his wife; New York investment counselor Richard Weisman; Phylicia's dear friend Hattie Winston and Harold Wheeler, Jay and Linda Sandrich. Phylicia's sister, actress Debbie Allen, was there, along with Kathleen Turner and her husband, real-estate dealer Jay Weiss. O. J. Simpson was my best man, and my friend Mike Paulucci flew in from Miami.

We were especially strong on comedians. Besides Cosby, we had some talent from "Saturday Night Live"—Brian Doyle Murray and his brother Bill Murray. Bill had been a good friend since I arrived in New York. When I first started doing the show for NBC, Bill watched and coached me, and every Sunday he called me after the show with his reaction. Bill took me to all kinds of little underground nightclubs in Greenwich Village—in fact, he was my guide on my very first trip up to Harlem.

On the day of the wedding, Mike Paulucci and I picked up O.J. in a limousine at his hotel. We got lost en route to the Church of the Master. But the Bears–Jets game was on the TV in the limo, so we didn't mind the delay too much—in fact, we drove around the block a few times so we could watch a crucial series of downs. While we were talking about the Bears, I realized that there was no comparison between how I felt before getting married this time and how I'd felt the times before. The feeling now was entirely different.

We took our places in the church, waiting for the bride to appear. Soon she came up the aisle, on Bill's arm. Phylicia looked radiant. Somebody had poured her into this stunning silver-and-white dress that was really elegant and definitely sexy. Bill hobbled along like he was one hundred years old, cracking up the whole church. The atmosphere was festive. When they got to the front of the church, O.J. leaned over and said, "I wasn't so sure about this before, but now I see why you're marrying this lady. She's gorgeous."

Just as the bride and Bill arrived next to me, he hit me a shot in the crotch. I mean, he really nailed me, and I nearly doubled over. I stood there gasping for breath. The guests in front found *that* funny, too. At least it took my mind off being nervous. Phylicia had prepared these vows for us to recite, and O.J. had been giving me a hard time about forgetting them. I'd made myself a little cheat sheet and hid it in my cuff, just in case.

When the Reverend Eugene Calendar told me to kneel down, I complained that I couldn't because of football injuries. But the Reverend is an old-fashioned man. He looked at me sternly and said, "Boy, after tonight, you won't have any pain at all." The guests near the front cracked up, but all I could think about was those vows, and Phylicia standing there next to me in that gorgeous dress, about to become my wife. I glanced at O.J., and he cleared his throat. All I had to do anymore was get the vows right, and I'd be home free. But keeping up with Phylicia in any kind of performance is a little intimidating. She's the most intelligent, attentive woman I've ever met. When we work together on camera, she doesn't miss a beat: she gets it right the first time, without forgetting a line or blowing a cue.

Somehow, I made it through the vows, mumbling and stuttering. Suddenly, time had come to say "I do." And then I got to kiss the bride in front of all those people. Was I supposed to give her a nice peck on the lips? Was it okay to hold her shoulders? How long did you hold a proper wedding kiss? My anxiety was groundless. As soon as I got close to her, Phylicia laid a kiss on me that almost made my knees buckle.

O. J. Simpson was my best man long before I asked him to play that role at my wedding. He helped rescue my football career after two frustrating years with St. Louis. It was a reunion of sorts when I was traded to Buffalo—me and O.J. and our third amigo, that great offensive lineman Reggie McKenzie.

We'd all met right after my senior year in college, at the Hula Bowl. I'd met O.J. first, and we hit it off right away. One day we were taking a little sail when we spotted this dude ambling along the beach. He was wearing some kind of nylon shirt, regular slacks cut off at the knees, and some tall black socks, like pimp socks—transparent black ones with ribs in them. He was slogging through the sands of Waikiki in shoes—size-15 leather street shoes.

We broke up laughing. This dude was like some inner-city Robinson Crusoe, shipwrecked on Hawaii, trying to orient himself. That was our first impression of Reggie McKenzie, who was going to be playing in Buffalo, blocking for O.J. We became good friends in Hawaii, and the two of them kept a vigil for me until I got traded to the Bills.

Knowing that I'd been traded to Buffalo, I worked hard over the summer in Los Angeles. I was part of an elite group that read like a Who's Who of pro football: receivers like Bobby Chandler, Charlie Joiner, Isaac Curtis, and J. D. Hill; defensive backs like Skip Thomas; and quarterbacks including Pat Haden and

Vince Ferragamo. We played in sweats, without pads or anything
else to encumber our egos. The workouts were the ultimate test
of who was the best and the baddest in little one-on-one games
that were more competitive than anything I would ever know
in the NFL. The summer was one prolonged cockfight.

When I arrived in Buffalo in the fall of 1974, the Bills were
coming off a 9–5 season in which O.J., with the help of Reggie
and the rest of the Electric Company, had become the first back
in NFL history to gain over two thousand rushing yards. We
didn't have much of a defense, but we were a regular circus
when it came to offense. The front office had acquired me to
bring a new dimension to the aerial-display portion of the program, and in every city people flocked to see us. And I hit the
epitome in my very first regular season game, a Monday-night
meeting at home against Oakland.

We were down 13–7 when Joe Ferguson threw me an eight-
yard touchdown pass with less than two minutes on the clock.
We got the ball back right away, but then Jim Braxton fumbled
and Art Thoms scooped it up and rambled twenty-nine yards for
the touchdown. We were down again, 20–14, with twenty-six
seconds left.

We needed the touchdown, and Ferguson called my number.
I put an outrageous move on the premier cornerback in the NFL
at the time, Willie Brown. I lined up flanked left, ran down, and
faked the quick out. I unconsciously realized that there was only
one way for me to get where I wanted to go, over the middle: I
had to spin a full three hundred and sixty degrees, and do it
before Brown knew what was up.

I pulled it off, faking out Brown, the rest of the Oakland secondary, and most of the stadium and the live national audience.
In the broadcast booth, Howard Cosell went berserk. That was
my first taste of national fame, the first time that anybody said
"That guy's a star." At that point, I felt that I'd fully arrived in
the NFL. My apprenticeship, and any excuses that went with
it, were behind me. It was a sweet, sweet moment.

But the best part of the Buffalo experience was playing alongside guys who really cared about each other. The guy who best

symbolized that attitude was O.J. He's a genuine, giving person. That might sound trite, but it's true, and I don't want to find a more complicated way to say something so simple and admirable. The previous year, when O.J. met the press after gaining his two thousandth yard, the first thing he did was introduce his entire offensive line, man by man. He wasn't grandstanding, either. O.J. routinely took ten or fifteen teammates out to dinner. If he was invited to some fancy party, he'd say he sure would love to go, but only if he could bring his teammates along. When the superstar on a team behaves like that, it rubs off.

O.J. was, and is, and always will be, Mr. Superstar. Joe Namath told me that he was on the same flight as O.J. not long ago. When they arrived at the airport, Joe put on some shades and a hat so big that nobody would recognize and bother him. O.J. just got out his flag—he was waving at people, chatting with baggage handlers, stopping for everybody who wanted to shake his hand. Joe just couldn't believe what O.J. was willing not only to tolerate but to *invite*.

Some famous guys won't bother to say two words to their own kinfolk, but O.J. will spend an hour talking to some guy who doesn't even speak English. He hates Europe and makes no bones about the reason: nobody recognizes him there. O.J. once summed up his philosophy like this: "When I was a kid, I wanted to be rich and famous. Now that I am, I'm not going to let any of it go by. I didn't realize my dreams just to go all weird and sour on them. I'm going to live them to the limit, and make every minute of it count."

The caliber of athlete we had on that Bills team was awesome: guys like Jim Braxton, Joe Ferguson, Bobby Chandler, J. D. Hill, Donnie Green, Wallace Francis, and Paul Seymour. We had a cornerback, Robert James, who made All-Pro one year but had his career wrecked by a knee injury. Robert was a real Christian off the field, always ready to praise the Lord; but whenever there was a fight, he was the first guy to jump in there looking to kick himself a little ass. I'm happy I only played against him in practice, because he was the best I ever went up against.

In the evenings after practice, we put together five-on-five basketball games at a local junior college, and it was like college ball. Everybody could play but Reggie, who just wasn't designed for basketball. He got sore when we didn't let him play, but he came out anyway, just to pace the sidelines, yelling at people.

I'd arrived in Buffalo in a shell. If somebody called me Bobby Moore, even through an innocent slip of the tongue, I'd snap, "That ain't my goddamned name." O.J., Reggie, and the others helped me lift that chip off my shoulder. O.J. in particular took a special interest in explaining me to people, which I found funny and touching. The effect was that people thought, "This guy Rashad has a weird name, but he's with O.J. so he must be okay."

At the time I was a vegetarian, and O.J. got it into his head that it was for religious reasons. So as soon as we sat down in a restaurant, he would start explaining to the waiter how I wasn't allowed to eat meat because I'm a Muslim, and how we all had to respect others' religious beliefs. I'd cut him off and say I was just a plain old vegetarian.

I lived with O.J. during that first year, in a Buffalo suburb called Williamsville. Reggie lived just down the street from us. O.J. was so hyper that he was always looking to play games. I got so sick of backgammon that I refused to play unless O.J. gave me twenty-to-one odds—and when I won, I'd make him pay me.

Every day, the three of us would drive to practice together at nine in the morning. On the way home, we stopped at a gas station and bought two beers apiece for the forty-five-minute ride home. We had soup and a sandwich in the Friendly's of Williamsville, and then we hit the rack for a long nap. At nine-thirty or ten in the evening, we would go out and stay out sometimes until two or three in the morning. Buffalo loved us, and we loved Buffalo. And we loved playing football.

As a pair, O.J. and Reggie ranked right up there with the Odd Couple. Reg is a homeboy, content in almost any situation. O.J. is full of curiosity, the kind of guy who gets into something and becomes an instant expert on the subject. Once he got to worrying about trespassers at his house in L.A., so he bought some very expensive guard dogs. He gave us the whole nine yards about what killers these dogs were, how they used to hunt down tigers in India and I don't know what else; but to us they looked like two overstuffed pillows, lazy things that never barked. O.J. explained that it was because they were pups, but he's had them about six years now, and I'm *still* waiting to hear a peep out of those sleepy mutts.

In Buffalo, O.J. bought an old Rolls-Royce. At the time, I was driving a little Italian sports coupe, a Fiat. I went for a long ride with O.J., and he went on for about an hour about the quality of a Rolls. There was only one problem: it was about eight degrees outside, and *minus*-eight inside the car. O.J. brushed that off, explaining how a Rolls has this special heater and that when it finally warmed up, it *really* got warm. Meanwhile, it was so cold inside the car that our breath was turning to fog.

The next morning, we three amigos met to go to practice. Reggie wanted to ride in the Rolls, but I said, "No, man, you don't want to do that—ride with me." Of course, O.J. got mad, and so did Reggie, who thought I was jealous and didn't want him to ride in style. By the time we reached the freeway, my car was already warm. But my friends still looked out at me as if to say, "Hey, man, you're beat. We're riding in style, man. We're in the Roller."

About halfway to practice, I pulled up alongside the boys. I had my coat off and my shirt open at the neck, it was so warm in my Fiat. Reggie was wearing a scarf, and O.J.'s hands were so cold that he had a towel between them and the steering wheel. I started blowing my horn. I rolled the window and screamed out, "It's too damned hot in here—do you guys know how I turn the heat off in this car?" They just stared straight ahead, but I can tell you that O.J. had no passengers on the way home.

Reggie McKenzie was an unbelievably dedicated player, which is why he's making a coaching career for himself these days in the Seattle organization. We had a special team meeting on Thursdays, when we would discuss what we had to do to win our next game. It was kind of a brainstorming session. One Thursday morning we woke up and found ourselves snowbound. We tried to dig the car out, but we weren't too worried about the consequences if we couldn't do it. But Reggie was furious. He wasn't going to let a little snow stop him from making the big meeting. O.J. and I gave up on the car after half an hour, but Reggie stayed out there, shoveling and pushing and clearing the way.

When Reggie realized he couldn't get the car out, he stormed into the house and got on the phone. By then, it was a little after ten and the meeting was in progress. The situation was cool; everybody knew we'd been snowed in. But Reggie got on the horn and made some poor guy give him a running commentary. The guy would tell Reggie what somebody said, and Reggie would nod. He's got a real deep voice, like Barry White, and he put in his two cents and more, because it was a long-distance toll call. He said, "Now you tell them we got to get together . . ."

We imagined that poor teammate cupping his hand over the phone and yelling out, "Reggie says we've got to get together!"

Reggie continued, "And we can't drop any more balls—we dropped three last time . . ."

And so on.

Great players who have great attitudes do wonders for a team. It also helps to have a great head coach like Lou Saban. There was no bullshit about Lou. He treated you like a man and expected you to play your heart out. You didn't need a pass to go to the bathroom. If you wanted to change your name to Minnie Mouse, it was okay with Lou as long as you picked up the hem of your petticoat and kicked some booty on Sunday. We had no curfews, no crazy drills aimed at showing you who's the boss—anybody who's got to show you who's the boss isn't really a good boss anyway—and no mind games. Lou Saban was wonderful. He was the kind of guy who should have worn a gray sweatshirt that said "Coach," with a whistle lying on it.

Nobody else I know in football can hold a candle to Lou as a speechmaker. At halftime, he would go into these long, dramatic monologues that began with something like "Ever since high school, you boys have dreamed about beating the Miami Dolphins. . . ." It was convincing stuff, and by the end of his speech we would be ready to invade Canada, if that was what he asked. I'd flatten myself against the wall by the door, because when Lou said "Go," all these grown men would stampede for the door in a frenzy, sky high on Lou's oratory. The first thing I did when I got home after a game was call friends and say, "Hey, wait until you hear the speech Lou gave us *this* time!"

Weekday team meetings were just as dramatic. If we lost, Lou would let the suspense build before he walked in, five minutes late. He always had a projector and can of film handy, and when he got mad he would kick the projector over. There was one spot over by the door where the vets made rookies sit, because sometimes Lou liked to throw a can of film up against the wall in that vicinity.

We had a team meeting I'll never forget in the 1975 preseason, after we'd lost an exhibition game to Green Bay. I'd only been with the team for a year, but I was among a group of guys holding out for more money. Lou called a meeting for ten a.m., and as usual he let the suspense build before he made his entrance, five minutes late.

I was sitting next to O.J., which was never a smart move. No coach in his right mind is going to get mad and rip into a player as valuable as O.J. The tendency is to get the message across by screaming at the guy sitting *next* to the star. At least that was the way Lou got his message across on those rare occasions when O.J. had a mediocre game. As Lou got rolling in his tirade that day, O.J. began to giggle—just loud enough for me to hear. He was trying to make me laugh, and coming damned close.

Meanwhile, old Lou was giving our offensive line a cold blast. He worked himself to a crescendo and finally yelled, "Electric Company, my ass—you fuckers blew a fuse!"

We glanced at our buddy Reggie McKenzie, the mainstay of the Electric Company. There's just never been a more gung-ho football player than old Reg. He sat there like he was sitting in a theater, hanging on every word. He nodded along with Lou, looking about like he was ready to jump up and kill somebody. O.J. and I caught that at the same time and it knocked us out.

I put my hand to my face to hide the tears rolling down my cheeks when Lou hit another plateau. Switching to the money issue, he hollered, "Money, money, money. That's all some of you guys care about. When you guys die, I'm gonna stick a green flag in each of your asses and it'll say, 'This guy had money.' Will that satisfy you?"

My sides were aching, my ribs were so sore from laughing that they could have been broken.

"This is the end of my career, if Lou sees me," I thought. "If the two of us get caught, they keep O.J. because he's the superstar, and I get cut. Or, worse yet, they ship my ass back to St. Louis."

Lou could crack a whip with the best of them. His favorite line when somebody messed up was "You're killing me. God damn it, son, you're killing me."

A few days after we lost one game, we were all in the film room, with Lou working the projector. When a bad play came up on screen, Lou bellowed, "Jones, you're killing me, Jones." Lou got up and switched on the lights. "Do you hear me, Jones? Where the hell are you, Jones?"

But there was no Jones anymore. Jones had been cut two days earlier, but Lou wasn't being absentminded. He was passing us a message.

The Bills went 9–5 again in 1974, and I led the team in receptions with thirty-six for 433 yards. J. D. Hill, the other wide receiver, had thirty-two catches. J.D. was not only a great receiver, but the best blocker in his position that I've ever seen. We were so deep at receiver that a quality wideout like Bobby Chandler was a sub. Our passing numbers were pretty good for a running team that featured O.J., even though he had a sore knee for most of the year. Some people claimed that our quarterback Joe Ferguson threw "too hard," which is almost always a bum rap in football—just ask Doug Williams.

I made the All-Conference second team, and the Bills made the playoffs with a wild card. We were manhandled in the playoffs, 32–14, by a great Pittsburgh team featuring Terry Bradshaw and Franco Harris.

But my football career was finally on the right track, and the next off-season was a real pleasure. A bunch of us who played for the Bills lived in Los Angeles, and we weren't shy about strutting our stuff. It was like "Yeah, the Buffalo Boys are back in town, they'll be here for a month or two before going off, kicking some booty up North."

I had my best preseason ever in 1975. In our first few preseason games, I caught any ball that came near me. I caught balls one-handed; I caught balls behind my back. On the basketball court, I was taking people to the hoop and dunking on them. There were no major shake-ups in the Bills organization. O.J. had recovered from knee problems and he was poised for a great year. I was feeling so confident that I didn't sign a contract, choosing to play out my option if it came to that.

In the locker room before our last preseason game, against Kansas City, I was all keyed up to perform some heroics. I was so confident that I'd declared myself "the Kid"—the *Keed*—and I told anybody who'd listen that I was invulnerable. My Muslim name in my own mind could have been Muhammad Ali.

On a pass play early in the game, Ferguson threw to me. The ball was a little high, but I didn't mind that—the Keed specialized in airborne circus catches. But as I caught the ball, cornerback Jimmy Marsalis undercut me, rolling with his full body weight on my left knee.

The pain was excruciating, but the invulnerable Keed did the natural thing: I bounced up off the turf, pretending nothing was wrong. I didn't want to be hurt, and I insisted on walking it off. That provided the next real sign that something was wrong: I couldn't put my foot down. My leg was at such a crazy angle that only the inside of my foot would touch. As the trainers came out, I insisted to them, "Nah, it ain't too bad. It'll be all right. There's nothing wrong with this baby."

But something was very wrong with that baby. The ultimate

football nightmare had come to pass: I had a torn-up knee. The staff took me out of the game and told me that the team physician had to operate that very night.

I chose to stay in the locker room while Buffalo closed out the game. The atmosphere afterward was sad. O.J. offered to drive me to the hospital, but we didn't make it there right away. We just drove around aimlessly, talking. I was trying to convince him not to take me in for the operation. For one of the few times in my adult life, I found myself crying. I told him that if I just got a good night's sleep, the knee would be as good as new when I awoke in the morning.

The next thing I remember, I awoke in the hospital with my leg in a cast. O.J. and Reggie were sitting at a table by my bed, playing cards. Over the next few days, the card game in my room got to be an after-practice habit for those guys. But so many people started coming around when they heard that O. J. Simpson was holed up in that room that I had to kick everybody out. I was too depressed to deal with the situation any other way.

I felt snakebitten. Rescued from St. Louis, I'd started my career in Buffalo on a great note only to have it go way off key with a horrible injury. Maybe I wasn't meant to succeed in the NFL; maybe this was a sign that I should quit—maybe I'd *have* to quit. I went to Los Angeles to recuperate and undergo the torturous process of rehabilitation. My future seemed so insecure that I transparently reached for the easy fix. I decided to get married.

I'd known Tilly for a couple of years. We'd met at a typical L.A. high roller's party, with tons of gorgeous girls and lots of fast-track guys. We never did have a whole lot in common, but we went our separate ways often enough not to get really tired of each other—or to develop the kind of intimacy that leads to a really close relationship and marriage. Tilly was a flight attendant, so we were both on the road a lot. It was a catch-as-catch-can affair. If we both happened to be in L.A., we'd go out; but if Tilly wasn't around, I'd go out with somebody else, or to a party. The year before I got hurt, Tilly gave birth to my second daughter, Maiysha.

When I returned to L.A. after my injury, I had a chance to spend some time with Maiysha. The romance between Tilly and me was pretty much over, but she was an old friend, and I was feeling sorry for myself. When Tilly was out of town, Maiysha would stay with me or with Tilly's mom, so there was a family unit of sorts. One day we just up and went over to Las Vegas. We had a quickie marriage in one of those Wedding Bell Chapels. Ironically, I recognized the guy sweeping the floor of the place—he had been on my high-school track team but didn't remember me. What I remember most about the ceremony is that when I said "I do," what flashed through my mind was "I don't."

Tilly and I stayed together in Marina Del Rey for about two months. I thought a lot about our relationship and recognized that I'd gotten married without any real sense of commitment. In fact, we'd gotten married exactly when we probably should have acknowledged that the ultimate bond between us just never had formed. The only interest we shared was an attraction for each other, and we had confused that with abiding love.

I moved up to Seattle to think things out. The marriage was definitely over, but I would have a strange history with Tilly that lasted for a few more years. We stayed in touch. I went to visit her in 1977, after I played my first year in Minnesota. I wanted to clear things up and finalize a divorce, but she wouldn't consent to that. After the 1978 season, I made the Pro Bowl. Soon after that game, Tilly and I went out—once.

Three months later, Tilly told me she was pregnant. I couldn't imagine that I was the father—I'd only seen Tilly that one time. But when the baby was born, he looked so much like me that I knew it had to be true. Ahmad Jr. was a spitting image. Still, that big surprise didn't change my mind or my feelings. Tilly and I were finally divorced in 1979. About three years had passed between the births of our two children, and all told I'd known

Tilly for over five years. And through all that time, we pretty much remained strangers to each other.

Studio 6-A gets hectic as the struggle to make the playoffs becomes really heated. My admiration for Bob Costas went up by about ten notches after one of those frantic late-season Sundays. Because we service all of our affiliates, nationwide, we have to do "rotating" postgame reports. The early games and the late games all start at either 1:00 p.m. EST or 4:00 p.m. EST, but they don't all end in unison. So sometimes just as we finish a postgame report for one game, another is ending, and we have to go through the whole drill again after thirty or forty seconds.

I was really impressed when Bob went through a whole flurry of reports, five or six in a row, for eight or nine straight minutes, without faltering or making a single mistake as he reported scores and highlights. I was lucky to play with great quarterbacks like Dan Fouts and Fran Tarkenton, and now I'm lucky to work with a pro like Bob Costas.

In any field, certain people are so good that you sometimes forget to pay them tribute. It's like you come to expect perfection from them as a matter of course. Bob is one of those guys. He has the best mind for television of anybody I've worked with in the medium. He doesn't make many mistakes, and when he does slip up, he gets deeply upset. A lot of the time, Bob is operating under tremendous pressure because of the live nature of our show. He can pick his way through a forest of names and statistics without a glitch, and he can do it while appearing to be very loose, very casual. Like most big talents in any field, he makes the most difficult chore look simple.

Working alongside Bob has helped me out tremendously. Critics say I'm a "natural," but that's a deceptive word in any field. Most of the time, a natural turns out to be a guy or woman who's done something well for so long that it's become second nature. It's not like you just step into a foreign situation and do a bang-up job. It's not like that at all.

In fact, anybody who saw my first attempt at broadcasting would say that I was a natural, all right—a natural disaster. Once I established a name for myself with the Vikings, a local station, KSMP, hired me to work as a "star" commentator on their "Monday Night Football" pregame show. So when the station chiefs asked me to take a shot at the evening news for one weekend, I accepted without hesitation—or trepidation.

Never mind that I knew absolutely nothing about television except how to sit in a chair before an interviewer and answer questions. I didn't know that before a broadcast, a news reporter actually wrote out what he was going to say. I didn't know about TelePrompTers, those machines that had a television-type screen with your written copy displayed for you to read from. On the Saturday morning before the first show, I played a little tennis, had a few beers, and took a nice long nap. I figured I'd just get up at dinnertime, eat, and go knock off this show.

I got to the studio at about eight o'clock for the eleven o'clock news show. My first surprise was learning that I had to write the show myself. I got this experienced reporter to help me hammer something out, and when we got something up on the TelePrompTer I felt less nervous.

At showtime, I was still convinced that when my turn came, I'd just whip some cool stuff out and that would be that. The anchorman gave me this elaborate introduction, and just a few seconds before I went on the air, it hit me: I didn't know what I was doing—not really. I had the TelePrompTer and this bunch of written pages in front of me, and a monitor that would show me the image people at home would be seeing, but I didn't even know how long it would take me to read the bits I'd written out.

As I began to broadcast, I did remember that most newsmen had this slick move, where they looked down and shuffled some papers, taking a peek at the TelePrompTer. But when I tried the ploy, I lost my place on the TelePrompTer. I started reading again, and realized a few seconds later that I'd already read that bit. Of course, that threw off the whole timing of the show.

I looked at the camera and got this real empty feeling in the pit of my stomach. Sweat broke out on my forehead like huge drops of rain on a window. And all this time the TelePrompTer was moving. I was hopelessly lost, so I just started babbling about the Twins: "Today, Joe Blow hit a three-run homer." But when I glanced at the monitor, the image was from a golf tournament. Without missing a beat I shifted to, "And this guy in the plaid pants teed off and hit one about four hundred yards, a monster shot on any course."

I couldn't fool the audience, and I couldn't fool myself. The sweat was just pouring down my face, and I felt totally self-conscious. To make matters worse, out of the corner of my eye I could see that the news anchorman was gaping at me, slack-jawed. I might have grown another head, with horns coming out of it, the way he stared. I was dying before him, and he just shielded his eyes, swiveled in his chair, and turned the other way. I realized that two of the great things about football are that your face is hidden in a helmet, and there are other guys on the field to help you out. Here, I was naked and alone.

I never did find my place. I kept screwing up, over and over, until I actually wanted to do one of those Marx Brothers routines—you know, slide down in my chair and just crawl out of the room. When my time was up, I realized that I'd covered only about an eighth of the news; I'd taken up most of the time with my floundering. It may rank as the most embarrassing moment of my entire life.

I drove home that night with a cardboard panel between my face and the car window; I was afraid someone would recognize me. For weeks, when people said they'd seen me on the news, I wanted to curl up and blow away.

"That wasn't me," I told one guy. "That was just some guy who looked like me. I'd never do any crap like that television stuff."

I've learned a lot since those early days, and I've had a lot of help. How many apprentice broadcasters had guys like Bill Cosby and Bill Murray in their corner? I also go back a long way with a man whose personality once dominated sports broadcast journalism, Howard Cosell.

I know Howard grates on some people. At first, his distinctive nasal voice was a novelty, and everybody tried to imitate it. Later, a lot of people thought he was just overbearing. But I always thought he brought a new dimension to sports journalism. For one thing, he was a brilliant commentator on boxing. And in other sports, too, he had a way of making you think—either with some perceptive observation or because what he said sounded so off-base. He injected ideas and social commentary into sports events, and he certainly always told it like it was—or at least like *he* thought it was.

Howard's fallen from grace in the past few years, but to my generation he'll probably always be the ranking sports commentator. He tended to get a little sloppy late in his career, but then the freewheeling, let's-all-have-another-round atmosphere was well established on "Monday Night Football" back in the days when Howard worked with Dandy Don Meredith.

Then, on one telecast, while watching a black running back make a great play, Howard cried out, "Look at that little monkey go!" That was interpreted by some as a racist remark, and Howard took a lot of heat over it. It was one of those strange spontaneous outbursts, when all kinds of people jump up to vent their anger or guilt, like believers at a prayer meeting. There's a lot of finger-pointing and the atmosphere of a public lynching. The Howard-haters out there had been hiding in the hedges for a long time, and this gave them a chance to jump out and nail him.

In dealing with the subject of racism, people don't always pay attention to the important, concrete issues.

I'm a great tennis fan and try to play as often as I can. I've gotten to know a lot of the guys who play on the circuit through my long friendship with John McEnroe. One of the qualities the public never sees is John's tendency to act on principle. For instance, he has refused to play tennis in South Africa because of its social system of apartheid. Meanwhile, all kinds of other players, from Vitas Gerulaitis to Ivan Lendl to Chris Evert, have taken the huge purses that the resorts there offer to attract the top tennis talent.

One of the pros I know played in Johannesburg in 1987 because he needed the points offered by the tournament there to qualify for the Masters. This guy is a football fan and I always liked him well enough, but I feel a little rift between us now. I'm hurt by his basic insensitivity to the controversy in South Africa.

Don't get me wrong. I know that whatever my convictions are, dealing with a nation that has institutionalized the most flagrant kind of racism is a tricky proposition. Societies, like adults, often become what they are without fully realizing where they're headed. Who's to blame? Who pays the price? How do you help justice and fairness to come about without destroying any of the good things a society has built? Those are the real issues, because any person in his right mind finds apartheid abhorrent.

You can fool some people into thinking you care by getting up on a soapbox and denouncing apartheid—that's especially easy when you've got nothing at stake. I don't expect anybody to do that. But at the very least you owe it to yourself and to your society to have an opinion on the subject, to take a stand.

What gets under my skin is when someone claims he's "just" an athlete, and that playing in South Africa has nothing whatsoever to do with the social policies there. It's that old argument that sports and politics don't mix, that an athlete can go to South Africa for the points, or the money, or the glory, with no political significance to his actions.

I don't know if the guys who play in South Africa truly believe that, but I do know that sports and politics are always mixed. Politics exists in every area of life, at both a personal and an institutional level. Now that almost all athletics is a professional proposition, there's no real difference between the tennis player and the guy who sells computer software. Do you buy the argument that Joe Blow isn't into politics, he's just selling software in Johannesburg? Does Joe Blow deserve a special exemption from judgment because he's a software salesman, like some athletes claim they deserve?

Believe what you want, but believe something. Don't break

the world's heart by saying that you're not "into" politics—it's like saying you're not "into" being a human being. A person of integrity ought to explain why he went to South Africa, and whether or not his actions were consistent with or contrary to his convictions. I'd rather deal with a guy who supports apartheid, or supports the rights of people to play and sing and dance there, than come up against the cop-out "I'm not into politics. I'm just an athlete."

Kevin Curren is a native of South Africa who moved to the U.S. I've hit tennis balls with him and never gave his background a second thought. I've questioned those black athletes who believe that performing in South Africa paves the way for social change. I don't agree with their argument, because sports is an elite spectacle, with little genuine interaction between athletes and the people in the street. It usually comes down to a question of who's using who, and sometimes only history answers that question.

But everybody can hold himself accountable. Everyone can acknowledge that he or she is part of the world and acts in a way that ultimately influences it. Everybody can at least think about the issues. John McEnroe thought about the issues and decided that he wouldn't play in South Africa, and yet he hasn't tried to capitalize on his stand. That's admirable.

Howard Cosell is a controversial figure, just like McEnroe. But I know Cosell is no racist. He was an ally of Muhammad Ali when he became a Black Muslim and changed his name from Cassius Clay and all of America was in an uproar. And he's been a close friend and supporter of mine since the evening we met during my rookie year, before a Monday-night game between the Cardinals and the Dolphins.

At the time, Monday-night games were the ultimate television spectacle. I was hanging around the hotel lobby, dressed to the nines. I was really into clothes, but I tried to tone down the Superfly image on team trips. I left behind the square-toed shoes with the nine-inch heels, but I was wearing an immaculate white suit and a hat as big as a flying saucer.

Howard saw me and called out, "Bobby Moore, the best-dressed man in the NFL!"

We sat together for about twenty minutes and talked about lots of different things, striking up a friendship that's lasted over the years. Howard followed my career, and he tried to recruit me for ABC when I made my most important career move in 1982. I'd been working for WCCO, a CBS affiliate in Minneapolis, when I got a call from Brent Musberger. He invited me to New York, to be a guest co-host on his "CBS Sports Sunday" show. Brent was generous and helpful, and I got to interview Sugar Ray Leonard, and Frank Shorter at the New York Marathon.

It was great exposure, and because I was still playing with the Vikings, my name had high recognition value. Suddenly, all three networks had some interest in me. A few days later, I got a call from the Vikings' owner, Max Winter. He and Howard were friends, and they invited me out to lunch with them at Winter's club in downtown Minneapolis. Howard made a pitch on behalf of ABC, but when I ultimately decided on NBC, he remained a friend.

When I moved to New York to plunge full-time into broadcasting, I felt as lonely as any other new arrival. No matter how many times you've been to New York, or how many friends you have there, living in the City is a different and sometimes wrenching experience. Everybody seems to have a million things to do, a million people to see. In New York, half the time you're trying to figure out how to fit your close friends into your schedule and the other half you're trying to figure out how to get a little time alone or with your loved ones.

When I was new to the city, Howard and his wife, Emmy, had me over for dinner and a football game on TV, and we talked about everything under the sun. It was a warm, thoughtful gesture. That evening for the first time, I really felt at home in New York.

Some of the cutthroat elements in broadcasting are hard to get used to, especially when you're coming out of a simple put-up-or-shut-up situation like pro football. I'm still surprised how often TV personalities put their faith in critics instead of in their own sense of the craft. It's like they don't know if they did a good show or not until they read the TV column in the newspaper the next day. That mentality puzzles me.

When I first came to the network, I was prone to confusion. A lot of people were coming up to me and telling me how I should or shouldn't be, what I should or shouldn't project. One day Bill Cosby would call and joke around with me, accuse me of stealing his best lines. The same day, Howard would call to say I was really coming along, except he wished I'd stop "horsing around."

The most important thing sports experience can give you is confidence that you can make it in life when the games are over. You know you can deal with pressure; you know you can make something happen when the need arises. That confidence got me through when I was getting lots of conflicting messages from people.

There's prejudice on television against "jock broadcasters." Professional journalists or critics sometimes resent the access and power former athletes have because of their past, while producers might write them off as amateurs, or celebrities who can fulfill only specific supporting roles.

I'll tell you what really hurts: when a critic nails you unfairly because of your insight into the game. In Boston once, I was covering a playoff game. On the air, I said that the most impressive quality of the game to me was the intensity level of the players, the quality of the hitting. The next day, a critic wrote that I hadn't said anything at all—that everybody knows that the intensity level in football doesn't change from week to week or from the regular season to the playoffs.

Believe me, the physicality of the game rises to another level in postseason play. At halftime, there's a lot of locker punching and all kinds of oratory, from the coach down to the guy standing behind you before you go back onto the field. This player is a grown man who hasn't opened his mouth all year, and now he's all emotional, yelling, "Take no prisoners!" or "There's no to-morrow!" That's the intensity of the playoffs. How can a critic challenge that—especially a critic who's never been inside a locker room right before a game or at halftime?

Former players also take criticism for not asking "tough" questions. There's a big difference between a tough question and a provocative, stupid one. Athletes don't like to be put down; it undermines their ego too much in a situation where ego is a man's best friend. Sugar Ray Leonard's boxing win over Marvelous Marvin Hagler was a great feat, but the really remarkable feat was Leonard's ability to ignore the overwhelming chorus of voices who said he'd never win the fight. That was a triumph of a man's will and ego—and the same loudmouths who said he couldn't win were ready to canonize him the morning after the fight.

I don't think there's ever been a sports feat that turned on so many professional athletes. Leonard's triumph was the ultimate statement of the "Yes I can" mentality that sports demands. For a few weeks afterward, whenever you picked up the sports page you read how this golfer or that basketball player was inspired by Sugar Ray's win.

I don't shy away from asking a "tough" question. If I miss a question, it's because I didn't think of asking it. Besides, players see the game in much simpler terms than a lot of analysts and fans. If I say on the air that one team is kicking another's butt because they have better talent, some people will be disappointed. Maybe they want to hear something complicated about the nickel-back defense, or about the drug problem of this or that guy on the losing team. But we overlook how often football is about fundamentals—the team that blocks better, runs faster, and tackles harder almost always wins.

It isn't just broadcasters and self-styled experts who run away from reality sometimes. Coaches are great ones for ignoring the ugly truth that another team is just plain better than theirs. When Don Coryell told us we could beat the Raiders, I knew that was a crock—were our halfbacks magically going to gain a second of speed? Were our defensive ends suddenly going to put on twenty pounds of muscle? All that rah-rah stuff sounds good on paper, but remember: a football player studies the team he's going up against. When you watch films all week, it's hard to ignore reality. If a journeyman cornerback watches Jerry Rice on film, all he can do when the lights go up is ask for help.

Sometimes you face a conflict of emotion, if not interest. In 1987, I was really happy for the Chargers. It looked like my old buddy Dan Fouts might get into a Super Bowl in the twilight of his career. Chip Banks, a linebacker acquired from Cleveland, was bringing some credibility to the San Diego defense. The team had good morale, but somehow it all slipped away as the Chargers folded about three-quarters of the way into the season. Denver came charging from behind to take the divisional title.

On camera, I had to say that the Chargers blew it—they choked. I even gave them the Collapse of the Year award on our show, with some footage of a huge old building being demolished. It wasn't really fun; but then if the truth hurts, you'd better start toughening up your skin. That's why guys rip each other in the locker room or in practice. They goad each other into facing reality, into performing better. They remind each other that nobody is going to get away with anything.

In the long run, players are more inclined to take that kind of criticism from a guy who's been in those same shoes. If anything, there should be more of that locker-room honesty out there in the world at large. In one game against Tampa Bay, Lee Roy Selmon was beating up pretty good on Steve Riley, a Viking tackle. Riles would come back to the huddle after a play and just stand there, eyes fixed on his shoes, saying nothing. He knew, I knew, we all knew that Lee Roy was just too much for him to handle that day. I finally said, "Don't worry, Riles—he may kill you, but he can't eat you." That kind of thing is commonplace in football, but I wonder how many lawyers nail their partners that way for messing up and losing a case?

Football is a more direct challenge than many other professions because it's all hanging out there for everybody to see and judge. I get a big kick out of self-important businessmen who talk about "competition" like they're cavemen vying for the carcass of some dead lion. If their world is a jungle, I'd hate to see what would happen to them if they ever lined up opposite Mean Joe Greene. Sitting around and thinking up "tough" questions in the heated press box with a couple of empty beers in front of you isn't exactly a courageous act. The only good questions are *intelligent* questions.

I have an advantage as a commentator because a former player has credibility in the locker room. But that isn't a permanent condition—in sports, you're sometimes forgotten as fast as you get famous. In a few years, none of the players will know who I was or what I did on the field—in fact, I think most of the younger guys in the NFL already think of me as Phylicia's husband instead of a four-time Pro Bowl choice who played for the Vikings. When Irv Cross started working in television, I didn't know anything about him except that he'd played, but that automatically gave him credibility.

Journalist friends of mine who never played sports sometimes confess that it's hard for them to ask a guy how he managed to drop a certain pass or fumble on a big play. I never have trouble asking those questions, because for most of my career I had to answer them. The reporters may have been too diplomatic or too timid to ask, but on Monday the coaches sure weren't, and neither were my teammates.

Most players get defensive for one of two reasons: you actually touch on a flaw in their execution or style, and that makes them feel vulnerable; or they feel that instead of asking a question, you're passing judgment on their ability to do something you were never good enough to get to mess up in the first place. It's easy to see how having played the game is an asset in either of those delicate scenarios.

I was intent on playing out my option and getting a better salary deal, when the knee injury destroyed the 1975 season for me. Overnight, I went from being a guy on the threshold of an

All-Pro year to a seriously injured receiver with no commitment to any team. My original NFL contract with the Cardinals set my base salary at thirty–thirty-five–forty thousand dollars over the three-year period, plus my signing bonus and incentive clauses.

My hope before my injury was to get $100,000 a year from Buffalo, and that was still my target figure for 1976. The Bills offered me $90,000; the Seattle Seahawks expansion team offered me $125,000. The negotiations went down to the wire until I had a Seattle contract sitting on a desk before me, waiting for a signature. I called the Buffalo people and told them I was ready to sign with the Seahawks, even though I would much rather have played in Buffalo—even for $25,000 less. Not only did the Bills refuse to pony up the extra ten grand, they told me they were withdrawing their final offer of $90,000.

I signed with Seattle, only to have the Bills' front office call me back a few minutes later, saying they wanted me at $100,000. They told me not to worry, I could get out of the Seattle contract.

I couldn't get out of the Seattle contract.

When training camps opened, I was a Seahawk. I was a good property for an expansion team—the local boy coming back to be the star of the new team in the league. It made for good press and local relations. I was young enough to endure the building years of a new franchise and still hope to play for a championship.

Being a new club, Seattle had no chemistry and no reputation around the league. As it turned out, the atmosphere soon reminded me a lot of St. Louis, and I felt like I'd been thrown out of heaven, back into hell again. Jack Patera, the head coach, was a disciplinarian. One day he told us to walk from one field to another during practice. Patera decided he didn't like our slow pace, so he told us to run laps until he blew his whistle, when we could stop.

So we started running laps. At one point, the track went by a highway. Here were all these nice people driving home, watching this group of adults doing punishment laps like some junior-high-school team. Man, that was embarrassing. I must have been lapped by the gung-ho guys about ten times. And the situation gradually got worse.

I had a big problem right off the bat with the receiver coach, Jerry Rhome. I know he doubted my ability and I felt he didn't like the color of my skin. Rhome wore a toupee that looked like a dead cat lying on his head. That created a problem when we argued.

"Mah-mod"—that's what Rhome called me, in this syrupy southern drawl. He'd say stupid things like "I don't care what your name is, I just want you to be an All-American."

"This is the NFL," I answered. I avoided eye contact, because it was hard to keep a straight face arguing with a guy who appeared to have a dead cat on his head. "Those All-American days with the band playing and the color guard marching around with the flags are behind us now."

Once Rhome made us take a written test, with questions like "What do you do on a fifty-two play?" All these other guys were writing long essays for every answer, loading them up with all kinds of technical mumbo jumbo and pure bullshit. I just wrote, "A fifty-two—sure, that's a little ten-yard out." I finished the test in record time, let it flutter down on Rhome's desk, and walked out—with Rhome following, two inches behind me.

We had it out in the hallway. He accused me of pulling airs, walking around like some hotshot guy. A couple of guys through my career got it in their heads that they wanted to cut me down to size. I may not be the best judge for whether it was their problem or mine, but I know for sure that it made for some unpleasant conversations. Coaches are funny that way: when good ones get fired up, their emotional speeches and diatribes get the players motivated. The bad ones get all emotional and they lose control—you never know what kind of crazy shit is going to come flying out of their mouths.

My confrontation with Rhome quickly became a shouting match. The entire team must have walked by us in that hall before we finished hollering at each other. Finally, Rhome threatened to leave me behind when the Seahawks played their very first exhibition game.

Later that day, Patera called me into his office. He said he'd decided to leave me behind for the game. Furthermore, I had a ten p.m. curfew while the team was away. I had to laugh. Who was going to check on me if everybody was off in Seattle at the game? Patera said he was leaving me on the "honor system"— I was going to check on myself! That was the atmosphere in the Seahawks camp, an experience most adolescents would have outgrown in a week or two, never mind college-educated adults.

Meanwhile, local merchants were capitalizing on my presence. There were a number of billboards around town featuring me. A local sports magazine on the newsstands featured my picture on the front cover. But one day Patera called me into his office.

"I hate to tell you this," he said. "I know this is your hometown and you're real eager to play with the Seahawks, but we've just traded you to Minnesota."

Like the Cardinals two years earlier, Patera probably thought I would hate shipping out to a team that played in a cold northern climate.

Without missing a beat, I said, "You mean the Minnesota *Vikings*? The team that has Fran Tarkenton? The team that's been to the Super Bowl three times?"

"That's right. Their coach, Bud Grant, wants you to call him right away."

Patera pushed the telephone toward me.

"That's okay, Coach." I jumped out of my seat. "I'll call him just as soon as I get home. I'll see you around."

I flew out of Seattle that very afternoon, with mixed feelings. My parents were really looking forward to having me close to home. I'd gotten back in the groove with some of my childhood friends. On the other hand, the Seahawks looked pretty hopeless to me. A few of my friends had fallen on hard times and decided they were going to hang out at my house. I was feeling pessi-

mistic about football and claustrophobic after the initial thrill of
the homecoming wore off.

The Seahawks would finish at the bottom of the NFC West,
with a 2–12 record. The Vikings would go 11–2–1 and reach
the Super Bowl. I hope Patera hasn't had any sleepless nights
worrying about how he ruined my career by trading me to the
Vikings.

When I joined the Vikings, I stepped into a different world—
in every sense of the word. My first practice at Minnesota
shocked me. The team worked out at Midway Stadium over in
St. Paul, and it was one of the raggediest facilities ever. It was
the kind of place you read about in those colorful articles about
life in the semipro leagues. The Vikings had a reputation for
being a bunch of rough, earthy guys, but this was stretching it.
High-school teams had better practice facilities than the perennial Super Bowl contenders.

The locker room was tiny, and every morning the rookies had
to bring doughnuts for the veterans, who weren't the only ones
eating the stuff. One day Chuck Foreman reached into his locker
and a big fat rat scampered out. I swear the thing had some
vanilla cream on its whiskers.

They had rock concerts at Midway Stadium, which freaked
out Jerry Burns, the offensive coordinator and the current Viking
head coach. When we practiced on the day after a show, Burnsie
didn't want anybody to fall down: he thought the kids at the
concert had all been sniffing cocaine, and he was afraid that if
we hit the turf, some of the coke would accidentally fall into our
noses, or that we'd roll around, snorting up some leftovers.

I made a good first impression—a *great* first impression. In
fact, I had an all-time day in my first Viking practice. I caught
every ball that came near me. On one play, Fran underthrew
me, with Bobby Bryant covering. I slowed down, lucky that
Bryant didn't know where the ball was. I pinned the ball against
his back with one hand, and as he spun around I pulled the ball
free and tucked it away. Nobody said anything, but I could hear

this collective "Aaahhhhhh" from the sideline, rising like a fog. It was like an audition, and I knew I'd passed with flying colors.

Right after practice, Coach Grant asked me to see the trainer, Fred Zamberletti. He examined my leg, trying to determine if I had the proper extension after my injury.

Fran Tarkenton walked in on us. He asked, "What the hell are you doing?"

"Beats me," I said.

A few minutes after I left Zamberletti, Coach Grant called me into his office. He told me that he was very sorry, but the trainer had determined that my leg wasn't 100 percent. The Vikings were going to exercise their option to send me back to Seattle. It was a devastating blow for me. Back to Rhome and Patera? No way . . . I could still smell the bridges burning. I had the sobering realization that this time I might be out of football for good.

I was packing my kit bag, mulling all this over, when Tarkenton walked into the locker room. When I explained to him what had happened, he told me not to leave. He rushed off to see Coach Grant. A few minutes later Fran came back, all smiles. He said Coach Grant wanted to see me.

When I went to his office, Coach Grant told me the team was willing to give me a second chance. I knew it was baloney, that Fran had gone in and all but demanded that Coach Grant keep me. But I didn't say anything. The Vikings shipped Bob Lurtsema, a second-string defensive lineman, to Seattle. For the second time in my brief career, I wound up being "the deal of the century."

I learned something—or had my convictions reaffirmed—about winning football teams at my second Viking practice. I had a rental car and made my way to Midway Stadium all alone. I got terribly lost and arrived forty-five minutes late. I realized that was no way to break into the Vikings, especially not after they almost shipped me back to Seattle just twenty-four hours earlier, so I flew into the locker room and started putting my stuff on, trying to read the extent of my crime in the attitude of the equipment man, Stubby Eason. But Stubby was a friendly old dude, and he just launched into the story of how he'd lost his leg in the war—a story I would hear in infinite variations throughout the years. The way Stubby told it, he must have started out in life with more limbs than a daddy longlegs.

I walked through the bowels of the stadium, worrying about Coach Grant. I'd seen him on television plenty of times—some sports writers joked that he was a monument instead of a man, a craggy, stone-faced presence on the sidelines. He scared you in the same way that Tom Landry could, with his eternally cool, dispassionate look.

When I reached my practice group, nobody said anything about being late. After a while, Coach Grant moseyed on over.

"What did you do," he asked, "get lost?"

"Yes, sir," I said. "I couldn't figure out where I was."

Coach Grant chuckled and walked away. At that moment, he became Bud to me. And also at that moment, I realized that this football team was working to win games, not to manufacture bullshit. As it turned out, the Vikings had a special way of winning games, too. Jim Marshall, the closest thing the team had to a spiritual leader, summed it all up when he said the attitude of the Vikings who belonged to the Purple People Eaters generation was simple: Whatever It Takes. That was the motto. The Vikings did whatever had to be done to get the job done.

Whatever It Takes.

That point was driven home for me by Fran Tarkenton a few days later, when we started to establish the special relationship that exists in any successful quarterback-receiver combination. Fran had invited me to ride to and from practice with him, suggesting that we have a beer together after the session. When we left practice, I toted the precious Viking playbook under my arm.

Fran stopped in the parking lot and unlocked his trunk. He said, "Ahmad, do me a favor. Put the playbook in there."

Fran closed the trunk. I shrugged and got into the car.

Soon my curiosity got the better of me. I asked him why the

playbook was riding in the trunk. He explained that we wouldn't be needing it—he never called plays from it anyway. I did take the playbook home with me that night—I mean, I was worried about what would happen to me if Fran ever got hurt—but he had made his point. And soon enough I knew exactly what Fran meant.

10

A LITTLE SOMETHING
ON THE BACKSIDE

In one game between the Vikings and the Lions, our offensive line was taking a beating and Fran Tarkenton was feeling the heat. During a measurement for a first down, Fran sidled up to the Lions' big old defensive end, Dave Pureifory. "Man, it's tough out here today, ain't it, Dave?" Fran said. "Say, how's the wife? Them two little kids of yours doing okay?"

Pureifory's chest puffed out and he smiled broadly. You could almost hear the other Lions thinking, "Hey, this Tarkenton must be a pretty good guy—a big star like him talking to us . . ."

The fire went right out of the Lions' eyes. Pureifory was neutralized just as effectively as if he'd been hit with a tranquilizer dart. The rest of his posse started to play "civilized" football. Slowly but surely, Fran just picked them apart. *Whatever It Takes*.

Fran Tarkenton was a great, great quarterback. It wasn't because he threw the ball hard or far. It wasn't because of his fiery leadership. He wasn't the most impressive theoretician in the game. He was lots of different things; but most of all he was *resourceful.* If you ever got shipwrecked and had to scratch out a living on a desert island, he'd be the guy to have along.

The quarterback position has changed in two ways over the

years, because of the growth of the game and the elimination
of the old "anything goes" defense. Up until the 1970s, quarterbacks had a lot more in common with the other guys on the
team than they do now. A quarterback got tackled a bunch of
times in a game. He wasn't "sacked," and the guy who nailed
him didn't do a special dance. The quarterback was the leader
on the field; he called the plays or changed the plays that were
sent in from the bench. *He* was the one who interpreted the
defensive alignments and tendencies, not some guy with a video
camera and telephone on top of the press-box roof.

All of that changed as the NFL grew and teams began to
operate like high-tech industrial firms. Electronic technology
had a big impact on football, and the fantastic television revenues
allowed the owners to indulge in any extravagance they wanted,
from hiring assistant punting coaches to developing comput-
erized scouting systems.

The technological and technical blitz shifted the decision-
making to the coaching staff, who sifted through all the data
and came up with a game plan. The quarterback became a
communications center, the link between the sidelines and the
offensive unit. And just like in a war, knocking out the enemy's
communications center became a prime objective. That's the
great value of those quarterback sacks—the disruption of
communications.

At the same time, rewriting the rules to bring more passing
offense into the game increased the value of the finesse quarterbacks—the classic drop-back passers like Joe Namath or Dan
Marino. But it also made them special targets for the defense,
to the extent that the league had to write special laws like the
"in-the-grasp" rule. Unfortunately, every bit of extra consideration a quarterback gets from the rules has had a reverse effect:
it's made him that much more of a target.

To some extent, the name of the game has always been Get
the Quarterback. Whenever there's an interception, the cry goes
up, "Hit the quarterback!" Every defensive guy on the field is
looking to lay a lick on the poor guy. The tendency has escalated.

These days it sometimes seems like the game isn't football anymore but Kill the Quarterback—bring me the head of John Elway.

It grates on my sensibilities as a player that the quarterback gets special treatment. I can't help thinking rules were rewritten partly because the quarterbacks represent a bigger cash investment to the franchise. Quarterbacks who can't play are pulling down million-dollar salaries these days, and the starters get flagrant star treatment—in the locker room along with every other place. Those are the reasons why Pittsburgh linebacker Jack Ham bitterly said that the next thing was for quarterbacks to wear skirts. He was right: some quarterbacks just aren't one of the guys anymore.

A team is hurt when the quarterback is regarded with cynicism or isn't fully trusted. Jim McMahon is an outstanding exception. He knows how to win and is willing to do whatever it takes to see that winning happens. One of his complaints is that when he calls an audible, or decides in the huddle to call something other than the play sent in from the sideline, some of the guys balk. They're afraid they're going to get in trouble with the coaches if they go along with Jim's call.

All of these tendencies make me appreciate Fran Tarkenton that much more. Fran couldn't outthrow, outjump, or outrun anybody. During warm-ups, you see lots of quarterbacks limbering up with forty-, fifty-, sixty-yard moonshots. Tark got loose by throwing quick outs, which were his trademark. But if we were in a dome, one of us receivers would say, "Give me a deep one." Fran would make this mighty effort and heave the ball forty yards or so and he would get this ear-to-ear grin on his face. He became like a little kid: "Did you see that? Who said I can't throw deep?"

Nobody was better than Fran at reading the tendencies of a defense and picking up small details that he could file away for later use in a critical situation. He was a very watchful quarterback, who would say in the huddle: "Watch that outside linebacker now—every time we run this type of play, his first two steps are into the line. See what you could run on him."

For the next few plays, I'd watch and probe, figuring out the best way to take advantage of that linebacker. I'd tell Fran how I could beat the guy, and Fran would file it away. Then, when we needed a big first down in a drive ten minutes later, Fran would say, "Okay, let's do that thing now." I would run this quick pattern where I cut in and across the area vacated by the linebacker. The ball would be there, thrown long before I made my cut. Whenever we were in a hole, Fran would pull an ace.

Often, pulling that card meant playing with a different deck than the one held by the coaches on the sidelines. In a standard play like an X-and-Y Double Swing, I might be required to run a delay pattern over the middle. But Fran would call the play in the huddle like this: "Okay, an X-and-Y Double Swing. Ahmad, you give me a post this time."

It didn't matter to Fran what the playbook outlined: his observations and instincts told him that on that particular play against that particular team, I should run a post pattern.

Jim Marshall told me that Johnny Unitas was the same way. Jim felt that whenever the Vikings did anything wrong, or betrayed a soft spot in the defense, Unitas would pick it up. He was keeping a book on the entire team, through the whole game. The Vikings once led the Colts by some twenty points, with just a few minutes left, before Unitas went to his book. "Unitas led his team down the field three times," Marshall said, "like a man walking his dog—*boom, boom, boom.* He was using a little of this and a little of that. He exploited some weakness in every guy on the team. He was the ultimate field general. The Colts beat us by two."

Tarkenton and I hit it off from the moment he threw his first pass to me in practice. No matter what the situation, we seemed to be reading from the same page. Every Thursday through the whole season we'd get together at Fran's house, maybe with one or two other guys, and sip scotch, just talking and touching on little things we might do to help us win on Sunday. Fran pretty much ran the team. He would even tell us who was going to be cut before it was announced.

Fran knew how to take care of his receivers. When a guy drops an easy pass, some quarterbacks give him a long, hard stare—the kind of thing that looks so dramatic when the zoom lens from the TV camera on the sideline closes in. I guess the viewer's supposed to think that the quarterback is a real competitor, a no-bullshit guy. Fran never did that kind of thing, and I respected him for it. I always thought that giving away your emotions, especially when they make the receiver look worse than necessary, was grandstanding. How many receivers stand around glaring at the quarterback when he overthrows them by twenty feet?

Fran kept all of his receivers' attention, too. He was good about spreading around the action. That's a great asset when you have more than one clutch receiver on the team. One of the reasons that Sammy White and I got along so well, with so little competition between us, was that we never felt we had to vie for Fran's attention. Some receivers lose interest when the ball isn't thrown to them early in the game. They tend to lose concentration; then, in a crucial situation, they're not mentally ready to do the job. As a psychologist, Fran was superb.

A great quarterback has a lot of power on a team, and he should exercise it *for* the team. When we went over the films during our Monday meetings, Fran always protected his receivers. Sometimes, when Burnsie saw one of our free-lance specials unfold, he'd yell at the receiver for running the wrong route. Fran would pipe up: "Sorry, Burnsie. I told him to give me a post." That was great for morale—we felt that Fran was one of the guys. We laughed when Burnsie eventually saw through the ploy and growled, "I don't care what the fuck you told him to do, how about you guys both getting the fucking thing right?"

Fran knew that a quarterback has to fit in with the team. Some guys are so well spoken that it's funny to hear them cut loose and curse up a blue streak. It was doubly funny with Fran, because here was the son of a Georgia preacher man, a guy with an immaculate, clean-cut image, fuming and cussing with the best of them. It was always a little bit of a shock, but it brought him closer to the team.

The way football is today, I'm not sure any quarterback could hold the kind of control over an offense that Fran did. It started right in the huddle. One time, our tight end Stu Voigt came running in with a play from Bud. As soon as he arrived, Fran sent him back, saying we already had the play we were going to run. We were down at one end of the field, so Stu had to sprint like a hundred-meter man to get back to the sideline before time ran out.

We rarely had dissension in the huddle. If Fran had an idea, he would consult the guys who would be responsible for making it work: he might turn to his offensive guard and tackle and ask, "We need three yards on this one. Can we go over on your side with Chuck [Foreman]?" Fran motivated people by asking their opinion; he helped them take special pride in what they were doing.

The result of all this communication and group involvement was that we rarely ran a play according to the blueprint. Fran was forever working on the defense, probing and trying to find some weakness to exploit, and the coaches respected him enough to let him do it his way. We were a "free-lance" offense in the best sense: tight but flexible, disciplined but innovative.

Sometimes Fran would call a routine play and break the huddle. On the way to scrimmage, he would ask, "What've you got, what've you got?" I'd say under my breath, "Post, post." He would nod. We were the only two people in the stadium who knew I was going to run a post pattern.

If Fran picked up something in the defense, he might say to me, "If anytime during this game you can give me a deep break-in, just do it. I'll be looking for it."

Or Fran would call a play designed to go right and he'd say, "Ahmad, you give me something on the backside."

"Okay," I'd answer. "I'll run a post-corner-post."

Well, there isn't a team in the NFL that has such a play in its book. But I'd go down, fake to the post, fake to the corner, and cut back for the post. The amazing thing was that when I looked up, the ball would be coming right for me. Fran had uncanny senses of timing and touch, which are worth a whole lot more than having a gun for an arm and a perfect spiral.

Tarkenton's resourcefulness freed me to run any pattern I wanted, which let me exploit any weakness I detected in a cornerback. If he was a better defender when you took him outside, I wasn't locked into playing to his strength because that's how the playbook said I had to run my pattern. I'd just mention to Fran that I could take him inside, and we'd work off that.

It was never anarchic on the field—we did have a basic plan, with primary and secondary receivers, and most of the time we ran the fundamental, correct routes. But if Fran thought you were a superior player, or that you could beat the man on you, he was willing and eager to improvise. One reason he got away with it was that he had amazingly quick eyes and, it seemed, the equivalent of 360-degree vision. Those gifts of perception made him tremendously effective either scrambling or throwing.

Most quarterbacks pan across a field like a camera might, checking off one receiver after another, across the field, closing off the options. Fran absorbed it all. His perception was selective; his eyes darted from one target to another and back again in a split second. Only the great quarterbacks can absorb and process that much visual information in the time they have to throw a pass. Most of them have to use the pan technique, going by the book. Fran never went by the book on anything.

I know John Elway has a better arm than Fran ever did, but in some ways he's a similar quarterback, an opportunist. In fact, it seems that the trend in the NFL now may be toward the versatile quarterback, after a period when it seemed like every coach wanted a guy who was like a windup toy, dropping back into the pocket and firing away—sometimes whether or not anybody was open.

That's one of the more interesting dimensions of a big story in 1987, the emergence of black quarterbacks like Doug Williams, Warren Moon, and Randall Cunningham. Three things particularly impressed me when I did a feature for the show on the subject. First, there's a new frankness about racial subjects these days—fewer people are weighing what they should or shouldn't say. Discussing racial problems no longer threatens to destroy a team. The issues are out in the open, to be openly discussed.

Secondly, I was struck by how relaxed the black quarterbacks are about their leadership roles. One of the more insidious examples of bigoted thinking was the ancient saw that black quarterbacks weren't "leaders." That went hand in hand with the theory that blacks didn't have the intelligence to run a team—on the field or, for that matter, in the front office. The attitude was gospel: scouts and coaches went out looking to reinforce the prejudice rather than to challenge it.

The black quarterbacks in the NFL today are intelligent, poised, and well-spoken. They conform at every level to the stereotype of the successful quarterback. They wear loafers and coats and ties; they have very businesslike attitudes; they use language that might lead you to confuse them with lawyers. The rough edges that most players had not very long ago have been filed off in the last decade or so. In general, the football player is a more sophisticated breed.

Thirdly, the very thing that used to be held against blacks in their desire to play quarterback is suddenly becoming an advantage—namely, their great athletic skills. The great athletes in the past tended to be converted into halfbacks or wide receivers, but the stakes in the game have gone up in recent years. For many blacks, the minuses have suddenly become pluses. Front-office types now see that it makes sense to have your best athlete playing your most demanding, vital position. The prototype for the quarterback of tomorrow seems to be an Elway or a Cunningham, and guys like Fouts and Marino look a little dated.

One of the few guys who had it all in almost equal measure was Roger Staubach. He often got painted with the same brush as Tom Landry—as a conventional, ultraconservative guy who stood for outdated, corny values. Nothing could be further from the truth. Staubach certainly was an upstanding guy, but he was wild and funny, as competitive and open-minded as anybody I've ever met. We became good friends at the Pro Bowl in 1979. He took me to a luau with a bunch of his navy friends; we raced in the swimming pool; we developed a lasting friendship. I regret that I never had the chance to play on the same team with him.

I won the MVP in my first Pro Bowl because Roger threw every ball my way. In our second trip to Hawaii the following year, Roger came into the game and threw a few balls my way, all of them high. After the third or fourth attempt, I said to him in the huddle: "Are you trying to get me killed or what? Even if I do jump high enough to catch one of them suckers, I'm going to get nailed."

"I thought you liked them high," Roger said.

Sure enough, he threw me another high ball, in the middle of a crowd. When I returned to the huddle I said, "Rog—this is an all-star game. An all-star ought to be able to bring the ball down to a catchable level."

Without missing a beat, Roger answered, "Hey, all-star—did you win the Heisman Trophy in your *junior* year?"

We looked at each other and cracked up. For the first time in that game, I guess, Roger was right on target.

11

THE BADDEST DUDE
IN THE VALLEY

f you ever want to really get away from it all, you can book a
summer camping trip to the Gobi Desert—or spend Christmas in a hotel. I'm no Ranger Rick, but I can sure tell you
all about hotels on Christmas. When I was a player, the rallying
cry was "Don't be home for Christmas!" We wanted to be in the
playoffs instead. As a broadcaster, the rallying cry at playoff time
is "Hit the road, Jack!"

My job gets hectic and complicated as the NFL's second season begins. Instead of flying out for two or three days to shoot
a midweek feature and then working on the studio show, I
become more like a traveling newsman looking for playoff angles. On game day, Bob Costas mans the studio with a guest or
two while Paul Maguire and I do reports or analysis before the
game, at halftime, and in the locker room afterward. It's more
challenging than a canned feature sometimes, because it's immediate and relevant. But there's less craft to it, and nothing is
older twenty-four hours later than yesterday's hot news.

In our last studio show before Christmas of 1987, I did my
annual awards, a kind of tongue-in-cheek feature on the best—
and worst—the NFL had to offer. My choice for disappointment
of the year was the New York Giants, the defending Super Bowl

champs, who were never really in the hunt for the playoffs. Because they're from the media center of the world, their problems were discussed, analyzed, and written about day after day, week after week, until maybe the press, the fans, and even the Giants themselves lost sight of the fact that in the end, football is a pretty simple game.

Early in the season, I facetiously suggested that the Giants were suffering from "writers' cramp" because so many of the players wrote books after they won the Super Bowl. Others said the team went into some kind of psychological shock when Karl Nelson, one of their veterans, came down with Hodgkin's disease. That caused a mild cancer scare centered on the environmental conditions at the Giants' home stadium in the wetlands of northern New Jersey. Eventually, that was put forth as a reason for the Giants' problems, too.

Give me a break. Nobody was writing any books on the sidelines or in team meetings. And the Nelson factor is hard to accept, because one of the cruelties of the sport is that once a guy is gone from the locker room, he's pretty much forgotten. The ship sails on. The players may put on that black arm band, but halfway through the season they've often forgotten who it was for in the first place. It's inevitable. It's pretty hard to swallow the theory that Karl Nelson took the wind out of the Giants, yet even the great Giant linebacker Harry Carson suggested that in a column.

Phil Simms probably made the most accurate diagnosis when he told *The New York Times*, "This game feeds on itself. You make one play and then you make another. Last year, we ran the simple play—Packer Sweep Right—and everyone else fed off it. Last year, we were so simple it was funny. We'd say, 'Let's sweep right and go five,' or 'Let's fake a sweep and throw to Mark Bavaro and get twenty.' This year, we just can't do simple things we were doing. And we're working harder."

That sounds more like it. The Giants were frustrated because they couldn't do what they'd done easily a year earlier. As Simms said, they were a little "spoiled," unprepared for the reaction of other teams to their success. But being in New York, the Giants became a continuous melodrama; and it was probably impossible for the team not to get caught up in it, the way they were exposed to the armchair psychologists every day. It rubs off.

Meanwhile, all of the tough teams from less glamorous cities than New York made the Giants a special target. If you're from a lesser city, you take special pride in beating a team from New York or Los Angeles. It's like saying: *"We're* the ones living up to *your* press clippings."

My choice for greatest play of the year was Bo Jackson's ninety-one-yard touchdown run against Seattle, which was the highlight of the most exciting story of the year. But the thing that got me about the Bo Jackson saga was the amount of criticism Bo took for becoming a potential superstar in two sports. Nobody had even come close to doing that since Dave DeBusschere, who played basketball and baseball from 1962 to '74. But DeBusschere was a big star only in basketball.

So here comes Bo, a potential modern-day Jim Thorpe, a guy who hits twenty-two home runs as a rookie for the Kansas City Royals and has the best numbers as a rookie NFL running back since Eric Dickerson, and what do you read? This expert says that joining the team once the season is under way is bad for team morale; that expert says that Bo can't hit a curveball.

The news media were uniformly skeptical of Bo's plan to succeed in both sports. Most of the people who were busy asking whether or not Bo could play both sports had never played either in the first place. As far as I was concerned, he'd *already shown* that he could do it.

A lot of people out there are telling Bo what he can't do, so don't be surprised if you find a little arrogance creeping into his manner. You've got to have a colossal ego to undertake such a challenge with so many critics saying you can't do it. Sure, Bo speaks in the regal third person; but if everybody else is talking about "Bo," *he* might as well talk about "Bo" too.

Once again, Al Davis was a guy with a clear fix on the subject. He told me that if Bo could give the Raiders ten games a year and also succeed in pro baseball, he would be the happiest guy on earth. The idea of working with a guy who's a latter-day Jim Thorpe blows Al's mind; besides, he's always taken pride in the great players who've worn the Raider uniform.

Which brings us back around to the Giants. The Raiders had a rough year, too. When I saw Al after the Seattle game in which Bo went ninety-one yards, I mentioned that winning that game might have boosted the Raiders' morale. Al said, "You know I don't care about shit like that. I want to win, and the fact is we didn't get the job done before."

Al never even bothered to point out that in a dozen weeks he used as many combinations of offensive linemen. What did it matter? In his mind, the Raiders just didn't get the job done—the flip side of doing Whatever It Takes.

On Christmas night, our NBC staff pretty much had the Pittsburgh Greentree Marriott to ourselves. The next day, the Steelers and the Cleveland Browns would meet to decide the AFC Central Division championship. A hotel is such an eerie, empty place on Christmas that it's almost fun—it would be a great location for a mystery novel.

I had dinner with Paul and assistant producer Cary Glotzer. Only three other tables were occupied, so we had waiters hovering like seagulls over us. I felt sorry for the little band in the bar as they belted out lounge-lizard standards like "Flashdance: What a Feeling" and "Say You, Say Me." The dance floor was empty except for the little colored dots thrown around by the crystal on the ceiling. I left Paul and the others early, before the bullshit began to fly thick and heavy, and went upstairs.

We didn't make a big deal out of Christmas at home, partly because Phylicia and I had so many work commitments. Our celebration consisted of making a nice little pile of presents for Phylea. But when our daughter's a little older, I'm definitely going to make Christmas a more festive occasion; I want to put up a tree and colored lights and the whole bit. I may stop short of the big cardboard Santa on the roof, but you never know. Parents get into that stuff.

Christmas was always my dad's favorite holiday, and when I think of the trouble my folks went through to make sure that Christmas was magical for the kids—well, I realize then how much I miss them. I got to thinking that night about Mom, who'd succumbed to cancer in 1980. I last saw her during the '79 football season, on a West Coast trip with the Vikings. My brother Dennis brought her over to the hotel where I was staying, but she was too weak to come inside. So I went and sat in Dennis's car with her. We talked, rambling on about lots of things from the past. Her time on earth was almost up. I never realized how fast it goes by.

In that hotel room Christmas night, I understood that one of the nice things about being married is that I don't feel that void left by the loss of my parents as often as before. But I felt it in that big empty hotel on Christmas night. It was cold and windy, with sleet lashing at the window. I read a little, and then I called Phylicia like I do every day when I'm on the road.

She'd given me an antique watch for Christmas, a gold tank job, one of the first self-winding models ever sold. The watch reminded me of the first self-winder I had, when I was in junior high school and the feature was still pretty new. I remember how proudly I walked around, holding up my wrist and shaking it for friends: "Yep—this here one winds itself!" We've got an unconscious knack in our family for presents that, fancy or not, bring back simple memories. A self-winding watch, a crystal ball full of fake snow—all the things we grew up with and maybe never left behind. I kept Phylicia on the phone for a long time, and then turned out the reading light early.

The next morning, Paul was waiting beside the NBC van in front of the hotel, cigarette in one bare hand, shifting from foot to foot because of the cold. "All the post-Christmas sales start today," he grumbled. "My wife and daughter back home in Buffalo are already down in their track stance, waiting for the stores to open."

Paul is a very funny man whose humor often borders on the outrageous. It's a quality left over from his playing days. Picking up on my penchant for wearing a different hat on the air each week, he began to borrow the most outlandish headgear he could lay his hands on from the fans. So in Pittsburgh, he was looking for a dog mask with snout and whiskers, because the Browns' defense, the best in the AFC, had come to be known as the Dawg Defense. Their fans threw dog biscuits into the end zone and got up in all kinds of canine costumes.

Driving over to Three Rivers Stadium, we couldn't help getting a little nostalgic. It's funny, the things you remember about playing—they're mostly the weird little things. Paul started in about some guy Roverson. His pregame meal every Sunday was, according to Paul, "a big-ass old bowl of ice cream, vanilla ice cream that Roverson would chew like it was taffy." On the morning of an away game, I myself leaned toward raisin-bran cereal with banana and an English muffin with plenty of butter.

We pulled into the parking lot, passing all the diehard Steeler fans who arrived early for tailgate cookouts on the asphalt lots. For the next few hours, we would just prep for each of our pregame spots. Sometimes it's still hard for me to adjust to the fact that for all the time, money, and equipment that the network expends, we go on the air for just ninety seconds, or maybe two minutes. On the job, the broadcaster counts seconds the way an auto worker counts hours.

I don't like to hide away to work out my pregame comments, or write them down and memorize them. I prefer to hang around and absorb the scene, think of the character and history of each team. Eventually, an idea will jell. I'll toy with it for a while, and then shortly before I go on the air I'll wander off down the hall or to an empty room to pull my delivery together. Then I'll go on camera and half-recite, half-improvise my comments.

That particular week I decided to talk about Pittsburgh quarterback Mark Malone and the Browns' All-Pro cornerbacks, Hanford Dixon and Frank Minnifield. The Steeler fans were merciless on Malone, who had thrown seventeen interceptions up to that point. Dixon and Minnifield were looking for a field day against a guy who was getting harassed from all quarters. And I would say something about the Browns coming to a peak after losing back-to-back games about midway through the season—an experience that shocked them back to reality.

While Paul and I were hanging around in the hall, shooting it with players as they wandered by, a Browns assistant coach stopped and introduced us to a guy who had been named Pennsylvania's High School Coach of the Year.

Paul comes from Ohio, a state that's a real hotbed of scholastic football. Without missing a beat, he said to the coach, "Oh yeah, you've got some good teams down here. We used to book games with Pennsylvania teams all the time, just to kick their ass."

The poor guy looked like he'd been clubbed. I tried not to laugh.

"Just kidding, Coach," Paul said, winking at me, and he talked to the coach for a little while about some schools they both knew about.

We finally got my bit done, and then it was down to Paul. He was doing an interview with Mean Joe Greene, the great defensive tackle who anchored the Steel Curtain defense of the late 1970s. Just a week earlier, the Steelers had gotten into a gang war with the Houston Oilers. There were fights and whatnot on the field.

Joe got on an interesting subject when Paul asked about the controversial Houston game. He said that football was a tough game, a physical game, so the Houston encounter was his kind of football. But he pointed out that while today's players were bigger, faster, and probably stronger than in his own heyday, he didn't feel that they were as committed. They weren't as willing and eager to do whatever it took to win.

But some technical glitch messed up the interview.

When you have to reshoot, it's often better to go with a fresh question—the idea is to keep the subject's mind busy so he doesn't think about being on camera and get all nervous and stiff. Paul asked how the Steelers were going to contain Browns quarterback Bernie Kosar. Mean Joe said some routine stuff about the Steelers designing a few special defenses for Kosar, a few new looks. . . .

We lost the best part of the interview, but I guess you can't win them all.

You can't win them all, but you couldn't tell that to Jim Marshall. He was a Viking among men, and a giant among Vikings. He was thrilled by danger, and he loved to test himself. Jim was, among other things, a skydiver. One winter, he went on a snow-mobiling expedition in the Rockies. His party got caught in an unexpected blizzard; the group was split up and utterly lost. One man died, but Jim survived.

Marshall described himself perfectly when he explained the goal that each of the Purple People Eaters had lodged in his mind and never forgot. "Every one of us wanted to be the baddest dude in the valley. That's what it was all about—winning football games and proving yourself, individually."

Rickey Young still remembers his first day with the Vikings, after he was traded from San Diego in 1978. In the locker room, some of the guys were limping. Alan Page was sitting in a corner, reading a book for his law course. Jim Marshall had climbed up on top of the lockers, where he was sleeping like a big Cheshire cat. Rickey had expected to walk in and find the guys doing calisthenics, studying playbooks, or poring over game films.

Rickey went out and did his best in practice that day, eager to impress Bud Grant. But at one point Marshall told him, "You can go a little easy, man—this is practice. You can play, we see that. Don't you worry about Bud. He's not really watching. No-body's watching. Nobody watches until Sunday. That's when you've got to go out and do your fucking job."

That was Marshall, the defensive end who began his career in Canada in 1959, played the next season with the Browns, and then moved to Minnesota, where he played in 282 consec-utive games, the NFL record, between 1961 and 1979. Jim Marshall: the baddest dude in the valley.

"You might go out to party with these guys," Rickey said to me once, "but then on Sunday you're out there in the thick of it, and suddenly Marshall or Eller looks at you and it's like, 'Hey, partner, this is the *game*. Fuck this sleeping and shit, we've got to kick some ass."

That's exactly how it was. On Sunday, Marshall and company became giants. And if you weren't ready to stand with them, you couldn't even be around. They put pressure on you just by being who they were and doing what they did—the baddest dudes in the valley.

Joe Senser called me over in the locker room one day and pointed to a sheet posted on the wall. If you were going to miss practice, the trainer signed your name and listed the reason. Marshall's name was down for three days in a row. The reason: "tired."

Nobody questioned Jim; you don't second-guess the baddest dude in the valley. Jim's room in training camp was called Murder City—somebody even made a little sign and hung it on the door.

Every newcomer to the Vikings had to go through an obligatory car ride with Marshall; it was a better gauge of what kind of stomach a guy had than any amount of time he spent knocking his head against a blocking sled. The trip from Minneapolis to our training camp in Mankato took about two hours, but Jim routinely made it in about forty-five minutes. When Jim and his passenger arrived for practice, the guy was not ready to play. He was ready to puke.

Nate Allen was a tough guy. But after riding to practice with Jim one day, he came into the dining hall late, in a state of shock. They had been driving along a secondary road in the sticks when Nate saw a sign saying the road had been washed out. Instead of slowing down, Jim speeded up and tried to jump the ditch. The car made it halfway across before it crashed to the ground, stuck.

That time, he literally was the baddest dude in the valley— or at least in the ditch.

I see Jim frequently when I'm back in Minneapolis. He always reminds me of what football should be all about. It isn't only the rough physical stuff, blood and guts and kicking ass and all that.

It's about pride, too—quiet, individual pride. And Jim, like Mean Joe Greene, isn't sure that the players today have that pride.

"I had so much respect for the game back then," he told me last summer. "It was truly an honor to go out and play. We considered it a privilege to go out and play for free, never mind getting paid. Football gave us a chance to display our talents and our love for the game. We played offense and defense and came off only at halftime and at the end of the game. Now they pick guys for the Pro Bowl as special-team players. Back then, there was no such thing as special teams. If you were on the team, you played everything."

Today, specialization rules. The tendency is to turn players into robots. I know I sound like an old-timer, but I also know that the game has definitely changed. Some of today's players— guys like Cornelius Bennett, Steve Largent, or Reggie White— would have been great at any point in history. The problem is that a lot of the other guys today aren't expected to do as much as in the past. And they're not expected to be *individuals* anymore. "Responsibility" has become a strange, corporate-type word in football, with its gangs of coaches, high-tech devices, and complicated game plans.

The big difference between Jim's generation and a lot of the guys today is that the current players know how to do their jobs but not necessarily how to play the game. The NFL is full of quarterbacks who haven't ever called their own plays. Defensive ends who play only in passing situations and counterparts who come in to guard against the run. Linebackers who run off on a third-and-short situation but stay when it's third-and-six.

If you had told any of the Purple People Eaters that they had to come out because it was a passing down for the offense, they might have torn your head off your shoulders. It doesn't make sense to blame today's players. They're just the raw material in a changing game. But the situation sure doesn't diminish my appreciation for the guys whose simple philosophy was Whatever It Takes.

Granted, the game was wilder then—and wilder still when

you went back to the days of Marshall cronies like Lonnie Warwick, Joe Dean Anthony, Joe Kapp, and Gary Larsen. What Jim most remembers about those teams was the sense of "family," summed up by the early Viking motto "Forty for Sixty," translating to forty men for sixty minutes—a total team effort. And all of them were committed to doing Whatever It Takes.

The mentality originated in the 1960s with Norm Van Brocklin, the notorious "Dutchman." He instilled in the Vikings the attitude that even if they were destined to lose, they were going to beat up the other team. If they had to lose the game, they'd at least win the fight. During that time, any Viking who knocked out an opponent—with a punch or a clean hit—received a little trophy, a bronze-plated jockstrap.

Van Brocklin had created a monster, the only problem being that he couldn't control or coach it. That's where Bud Grant, who took over in 1967, came into the picture. He brought with him the last pieces to the puzzle in the form of his football intelligence, and he put the thing together.

Those Vikings had amazing pride. The Front Four of the Purple People Eaters weren't really playing against the offensive line but against each other. They ran a private foot race to get to the quarterback, and if Marshall and company didn't get to the quarterback in three and a half seconds, they blamed themselves for whatever happened.

Sometimes, the tendency to play against each other got out of hand. After one close game that the Vikings lost, a big fan of the club invited the entire squad to a pig roast. It was an elegant setup, with a great spit on the lawn. The players then took their food inside, where great windows opened onto the grounds. Quarterback Joe Kapp walked into the house, cursing and mumbling to himself about how he lost the game for the team.

Lonnie Warwick said, "Naw, hey—*I* lost that game for us."

"What do you mean?" Joe said. "*I* lost the game."

Kapp got so mad that he invited Lonnie to step outside to settle the issue. The team crowded around a picture window as the two men went at it, falling over hedges, crashing into flower beds, busting each other in the head. It was a big-time fight: Joe Kapp was nothing if not a big-time fighter.

Marshall and a few others ran out to break up the fight, which was always a dangerous thing to do when Kapp was involved. Kapp really was a crazy dude; he fought for real. His opponent could grab a Louisville Slugger and bust him in the head and he'd go, "*Arrraagggghhhh. That was a good shot, boy. Come on—see if you can do it again.*" But Marshall found the courage to step in, trying to sound as humble and reasonable as he could. He convinced both men that it was inappropriate to settle a "family" matter in front of strangers and generous hosts at that.

Kapp had to be the toughest quarterback ever, doing things that nobody in that position before or since ever dared. He'd go after a defensive end and smash him in the head with his forearm. He wasn't a great passer or strategist, but Joe always found a way to get the ball where he wanted it. The awards banquet when he won the league MVP award was a real Viking moment. Joe got up there, and when he took the trophy Marshall thought he was going to throw it in the audience's face. He growled, "I don't want this, there ain't no one MVP on the Vikings."

The character of the team was formed by the individuals who played defense. Sometimes they decided among themselves that since the offense wasn't producing points, they would have to take care of the scoring, too. The defense became a power unto itself. In a meeting, coaching harangues were tolerated only for so long before one of the guys got up and said, "Hey, man, that's enough. You ain't one of us. Shut up and get the hell out of this room." The coach would back out and the defense would run its own meeting.

By taking matters into their own hands and accepting full responsibility for them, the Vikings developed leadership. If a guy wanted to keep the team's respect, he had to produce. At different times, sparks of leadership would come flying out of the eyes of a guy who hadn't shown them before, and might not show them subsequently until his own moment of truth came again.

The only thing the early version of the great Viking teams needed was better organization, which was what Bud provided. When he first came in, the Vikings panicked like a bunch of unbroken horses. But Bud made his message clear: We want that fire, we just don't want mistakes. We don't want penalties that are going to cost us football games. If you want to get a guy, don't lay into him with a fist—throw a great block on him. The Vikings responded, because even though they always won the fights, they didn't always win the football games. They were sick of being hardassed losers.

Bud analyzed the squad with a cold, accurate eye, and he put together a team with parts that meshed. He let Alan Page do whatever he wanted, because the other three down linemen were good enough to cover any flank Page left exposed. The Vikings became disciplined without having to suppress their individual skills and talents. Marshall put it this way: "It was like that Warhol dude once said, everybody had a chance to be famous for fifteen minutes. When the chance came our way, we grabbed it. It was infectious."

Marshall believes that the Vikings of 1975, the year before I joined the team, were the best Minnesota team ever. The Vikings won their first ten games that year, but they lost to a wildcard Dallas team by 17–14 in the NFC Championship game when, with twenty-three seconds left to play, Roger Staubach hit Drew Pearson with a fifty-yard scoring bomb. Still, the Viking offense produced the most points in the NFC that year; Tarkenton led the conference in touchdown passes; and Chuck Foreman tied Gale Sayers's scoring record of twenty-two touchdowns in one season.

I'd seen the Viking system at work way back when I was still with the Cardinals. I scored two touchdowns against them, beating Bobby Bryant for one and Nate Wright for the other. But they were a deceptive team, and most other clubs never could figure them out. The Vikings were good at overlapping and helping each other out. They looked gimpy and slow, but each guy knew that if he could do the job for three or four seconds, he'd have help. Or that great defensive line would have buried the quarterback by then.

The mystique was still intact when I arrived in Minnesota, and we went right to the Super Bowl in Pasadena. Playing in that game is supposed to be the highlight of a guy's career, and I guess it is—at least for the ones who walk off as winners. Unfortunately, we got hammered by a great Oakland Raiders club.

I don't believe that we lost that game because the left side of our defensive line was weak, as some critics suggested, or because Chuck Foreman was held to forty-four rushing yards in seventeen attempts. Those were certainly factors, but to me we lost that Super Bowl—the last one the Vikings would play in to this very day—because we didn't think that being the 13–2–1 Minnesota Vikings was good enough on Super Bowl Sunday. And Oakland didn't have that kind of self-doubt. Make no mistake—the Raiders had a hell of a team, a great team. But we didn't help our own cause any with our approach.

Basically, we coached ourselves right out of contention. One of the problems with the two-week span between the conference title game and the Super Bowl is that it lets the coaches sit around for a long time thinking up new ideas. When you add them all up, you run two risks. First, you may have come up with a weird game plan that's like one of those Rube Goldberg drawings where a ball rolls through a hoop, down a drain, falls on a mousetrap, shoots into a cup. . . . You get the point. If the ball gets knocked off course once, the whole plan falls apart. Second, a new game plan gives the players lots of new things to think about, and under the pressures of a big game it's easy to get confused and forget what you're supposed to be doing. I always believed that you can win the Super Bowl only by doing what got you to the game in the first place. In other words, if it ain't broke, don't fix it.

So through those two weeks leading to the game in Pasadena, we installed about fifty new plays. We were going to trick them with a new look, but we only tricked ourselves. You never play your best football when you have to do too much thinking about what you're supposed to be doing on any given down. All of that stuff should be second nature, so you're free to operate on instinct, with confidence.

The task of radically changing a game plan poses other pitfalls. It takes a lot of work, study, and meetings—meetings on top of meetings. We had meetings to announce when the next meeting would be—all of which worked together to build the game up into something on the scale of the invasion of Normandy. The strangest thing was that Bud Grant was not the type of guy who panicked in the face of a tough job. It was uncharacteristic of him to take the approach we tried in 1976—maybe the three past failures in the Super Bowl haunted Bud and made him believe that he had to do something drastic.

When I look back, it's obvious that we were the uptight team, the underdog in our own minds no matter what the bookmakers or columnists said. An underdog can do one of two things: he can play it loose, saying in effect, "The hell with it, I've got nothing to lose"; or he can work like crazy to come up with some special plan to beat the favorite. We picked Plan B, and it proved to be the wrong choice.

While we were having these endless meetings and drydocked with a ten p.m. curfew, the Raiders were playing it loose and living it up. That was typical of an Al Davis team, coached by a good psychologist, John Madden. The Raiders have always epitomized the attitude I admire most: you go out and do the job with maximum talent and minimum bullshit. Leave the theories and rationalizations to the pundits.

The Raiders were famous for taking cast-offs and "problem" players and giving new life to their troubled careers. Their approach was conducive to that process. This is how Madden defined discipline on the Raiders: "Discipline in football occurs on the field, not off it. Discipline is knowing what you're supposed to do and doing it as best you can. On the field, the Raiders were a disciplined team. On third down and short yardage, the Raiders don't jump offsides. That's discipline—not a coat and a tie, not a clean shave. I had only three rules on the Raiders: be on time, pay attention, and play like hell when I tell you to."

In Super Bowl XI, we were the clean-shaven guys in the coats and ties, jumping offsides.

Because of our new game plan the chaos on the Vikings' side of scrimmage was startling. Nobody had all the new plays down pat. On almost every down, I left the huddle trying to figure out if I was supposed to line up on the left or the right. We had to give each other hand signals to get that right.

The climax occurred in the huddle when Fran said, "Okay, guys . . ." He hesitated. "Let's run . . . let's run that one we tried in practice on Thursday. Do you guys remember that one?"

Everybody murmured "Yeah." Everybody thought "No."

The Raiders jumped to a 16–0 halftime lead; and I felt that once we got behind, a lot of the guys who had been in the Big Game before developed a case of déjà vu. When I looked around the locker room at halftime, I didn't feel that the guys' eyes were saying, "Hey, relax, we can still get back in it and pull the game out." It was more like "Uh-oh, here we go again."

The Raiders' Clarence Davis ran for 137 yards. Fred Biletnikoff caught four passes for 79 yards, setting up three touchdowns. (He won the MVP award.) My rival Willie Brown intercepted a ball and ran it back 75 yards for a touchdown, giving Oakland a 32–7 lead midway through the fourth period. It was that bad.

Maybe I'd feel differently if we'd won the game, but I'll always remember the whole Super Bowl drill as a big letdown. By the time we got to playing the game, I just wanted to get it over with. All the elaborate plans and meetings had a Mickey Mouse quality. I felt empty, without emotion.

My best memory of the Super Bowl was a drive I took with Fran Tarkenton, down Rodeo Drive in Beverly Hills. We were Vikings, we were the toast of America, on the eve of the Super Bowl. As we looked at all the expensive shops and knockout women walking around, Fran said, "You know, the trick is for us to be able to drive down this street feeling the same as we do now in five or ten years, when we don't have football anymore."

I had another disappointment at the end of the '76 season: I didn't win the Comeback Player of the Year award. After all, I led the Vikings in receptions and the team went to the Super Bowl. I'll always believe that I might have won that award if I hadn't changed my name. In the long run, the change hurt me in lots of unexpected areas. I wasn't like an actor who changes his name at eighteen, before he gets his first big part. My change wiped out in one stroke my whole history in football.

Everything ever done by Bobby Moore, the guy that people knew as a football player, was buried with his name. Starting over, I had to build on a whole new foundation. And I met with a lot of resistance. I was "that guy with the weird name," a guy without a past or a real identity. People were cautious and skeptical, even when it was only manifested subconsciously.

In '77, we won our ninth consecutive divisional title, but we lost to Dallas in the NFC title game. We won our division again in '78, losing to the Rams in the playoffs. In '79, we finished third in our division, but we bounced back to win it again in 1980. We fell to fourth in 1981 but still landed a wild-card playoff berth in '82, the year I retired. By then, the Vikings were running on memories. But we'd been doing that for a few years, which was a great tribute to the nucleus of the great Viking teams of the early 1970s.

Being around the great Viking players taught me never to make excuses, win or lose. It was never too cold, too wet, too windy, or too harsh out there. I was comfortable with the standard established by my teammates; I'd always tried and usually succeeded in playing at my highest level as a matter of course. When a guy like Jim or Carl or Fran turned to you and said the team needed you to do something, you found a way to do it. That's what being a Viking was all about.

The challenge suited me fine. I was never afraid of failing, and I was always ready to make the big play. I had that mentality since high school, and it became my trademark in Minnesota. The example most people remember is the Miracle Catch against Cleveland, the one that won the game and the division title in 1980 with no time on the clock. To me, it was just the crowning touch on the right occasion on the right stage. But I made an even better catch against Green Bay in '79.

We got into a war with the Packers that day, and we didn't want to lose it. Our record was 1–2, identical to the Pack's. The loser would have dug himself a pretty big hole for so early in the season. I'd made a one-handed touchdown catch early in the game, but the Packers stormed back and the game ended tied, 21–21. We got the ball first in overtime and moved into Green Bay territory. But a couple of dud running plays and an offensive pass interference call against me moved the ball way back to around our own 40, for third-and-22.

Tommy Kramer called my number, looking for first-down yardage. I was double-teamed by Mike McCoy and Steve Luke. The ball was thrown a little high and away, beyond the reach of the defenders. I managed to get up high enough to get one outstretched hand on the ball. The thing just stuck to my hand like it had Velcro on it. I was as stunned as anybody, but I didn't forget to run. I beat two other guys and broke one tackle to take the ball all the way in for the TD.

When the hubbub died down, Rickey Young walked over to me and said, "Come on over here, man. Let me cut that ball away for you now."

That day, it was just my turn to be the baddest dude in the valley.

On the day after Christmas in 1987, Cleveland beat Pittsburgh on a steely, wintry afternoon in Three Rivers Stadium, solidifying the playoff picture. The highlight of the trip was that I actually caught my 7:10 p.m. flight back to New York, while Paul went on to Houston. I had a chance to spend a few days at home before I flew out to Seattle to do a playoff preview of the Sea-hawks–Oilers game.

Then, things got really hectic. From Seattle, I had to go straight to Tampa, where Bob Costas, Paul, and I were going to do something a little different—cover the Hall of Fame Bowl game between Michigan and Alabama on January 2. Meanwhile,

Phylicia and Phylea were going west, where my wife was going to host the Rose Bowl Parade on New Year's Day. We'd miss each other on New Year's Eve, but she was flying out to join me in Tampa as soon as the parade was over. We'd have that one day together anyway, even though Phylicia was singing the national anthem and I was commentating.

I had a few of the Alabama players over to my room on New Year's Day to watch a tape of one of their games and the Auburn–Syracuse Sugar Bowl game. They seemed shy and self-effacing at first, but once they loosened up they admitted that they were a little intimidated. They expected that I would be pompous or stuck-up or something. I wondered if I was *that* old, but I realized that they were *that* young.

I picked up Phylicia and Phylea at the airport that evening. At three in the morning, Phylea got sick. Phylicia was bushed, so I got up and gave the baby a nice hot bath, dressed her up in fresh nighties, and put her back to sleep. It was a strange and peaceful experience, the kind of simple, intimate happening that forms a family bond that nothing in later years can break. I didn't worry about the job I had to do the next day, and I wasn't in any hurry to get back into bed. I guess I was like any other parent, operating on automatic pilot.

Phylicia sang the anthem beautifully before the game. And I was satisfied with our telecast. We laughed a lot, called the game pretty incisively without overanalyzing it. I knew we'd done a good job when some guy came up at the airport after the game and said, "I hope you guys didn't get paid for that. It looked like you were having too much fun." Isn't "fun" what football's supposed to be all about—especially at the college level, on a holiday?

That evening we all headed back to the Tampa airport. Phylicia was hauling a suitcase, a baby bag, and her shoulder bag. I had my suit bag and pushed Phylea in the bulky baby stroller. It was time to say good-bye again.

I got into Houston and covered the game the next day. At ten-thirty that same Sunday night, I touched down in Denver. Upon

arriving, I found out that I had no reservation. That's the ultimate bummer when you've been lugging around bags and brief-
cases, standing in line for taxicabs, and all that. Fortunately,
there were so many NBC people booked that the hotel made
room for me.

The next day, I shot a feature with the Denver receivers, the
Three Amigos. All the roadwork was beginning to catch up to
me, so I had an early dinner and watched some college basketball. I called Phylicia and got up early to fly to Cleveland, where
it was minus three degrees. I met my friend Jim Twig, with
whom I'd arranged a tennis date in advance—that's my way of
putting away all the traveling, the taping schedules, and other
pressures. A few hours of tennis blows out a lot of stress, and
I'm ready to go again.

I stayed in Cleveland for the game between the Browns and
the Colts. The Dawgs won, 38–21, putting them in the AFC
Championship game against the Broncos in Denver. We decided
to move our whole "NFL Live" studio show out to Mile-High
Stadium and broadcast our last show of the season from there.

In the summer of '82, a bunch of us Vikings went over to the
Hall of Fame in Canton, Ohio, the day before we played the
Colts in the traditional preseason opener. I was surprised and
happy to find my picture in the hall, right near the jerseys of
idols of mine like Raymond Berry and Charley Taylor. Near my
picture was a list of the top receivers in NFL history, and there,
next to the number 17, was my name. I had 474 catches at that
point, 177 catches behind Taylor.

Bud Grant came walking up and he stood alongside me without saying anything for a few seconds. Then he pointed at Taylor's name. He asked, "See that number one?"

I nodded.

"You can do it," he said. Then he turned and walked away.
Just like that. Typical of the man.

Right from the start, Bud and I had a special relationship. I
think he first showed interest in me because I was a little dif-

ferent, a little more of an individual than some guys. Maybe he wanted to figure out how to handle me. Whatever the case, I think Bud came to look at me as somebody he could talk to, and even a stoical football coach needs that.

If I were a coach, I'd try to be like Bud, especially when it came to oratory. His basic speech went like this: "Either win or I'll get other guys who can."

When I was with the hapless St. Louis Cardinals, Don Coryell gave us a big gung-ho speech about how we could take the Raiders, and then he broke down crying when the truth caught up with his fantasy. When the Vikings played the Raiders, Bud just said, "There's not very much I can say to you. If you guys don't play well, the Raiders are going to kick your asses."

After his All-Pro year, our tight end Joe Senser was at a banquet, talking to Hank Stram. Bud walked up to the group and shook hands with Stram. Joe extended his hand to his coach. Bud looked at Joe and said, "Do I have to shake your hand every time I see you?"

Toward the end of my career, I tried to save my body. I practiced only two or three times a week. Somebody must have complained to the press about it, because one reporter walked up to Bud one day and asked what was wrong with me. Bud looked him straight in the eye and said, "Bad escargot."

In 1982, I wanted very much to be the Viking offensive captain. I was an elder statesman, one of the very few guys who went back to the glory years of Marshall and Eller and Tarkenton and Hilgenberg and Tingelhoff. I got dressed for the preseason opener against the Colts and was getting ready to go onto the field to warm up when I felt a tap on my shoulder. I turned around and there stood Bud. He said just three words: "You're the captain."

My heart was fluttering and my stomach churned with pride and excitement, but I just raised my head slightly. I tried to sound like Bud would, or like Jim Marshall would. I said, "Okay."

One of Bud's pet drills was our annual national anthem practice. We did it before every opening game over the years, because

Bud wanted everybody to learn how to stand at attention, whether they were inclined to sing along or not. The Vikings always looked sharper than any other NFL team on the sidelines before a game. While the anthem was played, I'd stand alongside Rickey Young and imitate a particularly soulful version that Lou Rawls sang at the time. Rickey would struggle not to laugh while I sang this horrible imitation and whispered, "Lou Rawls, man. Listen. . . ." And when the crowd began to cheer at the end, I'd take my bows.

The players didn't mind the anthem drill at all, because Bud had very few petty rules. If he asked you to do something, you knew that it was important to him, not some silly whim or brainstorm that would vanish the next day. Given Bud's image, most people can see how the anthem drill was important to him.

Bud's other pet cause was the cold weather, and he tried to psych us out of any dislike for the harsh Minnesota winter. When I went to bed the night before a home game, my last wish always was that it would be at least 20 degrees the next day. Usually, it was about 8 or 10. The only thing worse was coming to Minnesota as the visiting team. Then you could hardly get to sleep at all, worrying about how cold it would be in the morning.

The Vikings always ran out for the warm-ups with this big façade, acting like we weren't cold. Of course, we were freezing. But the other team didn't know that, not for sure. They would be looking at us out of the corners of their eyes, thinking, "How come those guys look so warm? They must be some bad dudes."

We might have been freezing our asses off, but at least we knew we wouldn't die. We knew you could play with numb fingers and frozen feet, which gave us an edge. And we couldn't make excuses, because the cold was a fundamental condition, as permanent as your own time for the forty-yard dash. The other team could fumble or drop passes and blame it on the cold, but not the Vikings. A lot of times I caught passes without ever feeling the ball—just this heavy thump against my frozen hands.

If I dropped the ball, I couldn't run up to Bud saying, "Hey, sorry, my hands were real cold—you know how it is." That wasn't winning football. When I first got to Minnesota, I used to go looking for somebody to talk to about the cold, but everybody turned his back on me. It was like "We've got to go on, man. We can't talk about this shit."

Our equipment guy, Stubby Eason, wasn't allowed to pass out the turtlenecks until the temperature was down near zero. We weren't allowed to have heaters on the sidelines, but other teams brought along regular furnaces. Long johns under the uniform were strictly prohibited, and heaven forbid you dare to wear gloves. At halftime, my feet were so cold that instead of drinking bouillon in the locker room, I poured it on my shoes.

Bud's philosophy was that the more equipment you had for dealing with the cold, the more you thought about the cold and let it become a factor. That seemed to be true when we looked at the other team (in Metropolitan Stadium, both teams were on the same sideline). They were so busy huddling around the heaters that they hardly paid attention to the game. And the guys on the field were wondering how long it would be before they could get off and over to the heaters.

When the Ice Age part of the season arrived, Bud would trot out his infamous Eskimo story. We got to know it so well that we developed a ritual. As soon as the weather started to chill, the veterans began clamoring for the tale.

Finally Bud would trot out his famous parable. During World War II, the Americans feared a Japanese invasion from across the Bering Strait. Our men were up there guarding the Alaskan shore, along with some Eskimos we'd recruited. The weather was so cold that we changed guards every twenty minutes, while the Eskimos stayed out all day. The government decided to run some tests on the Eskimos, thinking we could learn something about the differences in human metabolism and apply it to making our own men more resistant to the cold.

At that stage Bud would pause, his eyes getting narrow. He finished up by asking, "Do you know what the metabolic difference was between the Eskimos and the American soldiers?"

The rookies would be wide-eyed; they'd shake their heads, waiting for the answer.

"Nothing," Bud finally said. "There is no difference."

The veterans would cheer.

Given Bud Grant's image, most people can understand his attitude toward the cold.

But then, most people didn't see the man on the far side of Bud Grant's image: the incurable practical joker, the dreamy outdoorsman who fantasized about duck hunting during practice, the guy who treated his players like adults, cutting them a lot more slack than they would ever get from guys who couldn't hold Bud's clipboard as a coach.

If we were having a team meal of roast beef, I'd often go to the kitchen and ask for an end cut, because I didn't like rare meat. Usually, the staff would accommodate me, bringing my plate out first, creating only one problem: it looked like I was getting special treatment. One time, some guys started grumbling about favoritism. So I laid it on pretty thick, telling them how in Buffalo, O.J. *always* got fed first, and that's just the way it was for superstars—in Minneapolis as well as Buffalo.

Later, when the waitress was ready to serve the vanilla ice cream, I called to her as she passed me by and reminded her that I was supposed to be served first. She kept right on going, but soon came back and apologized, saying she didn't realize I was *the* Mr. Rashad.

I was putting on the airs so convincingly that I just lifted my spoon, snapped back my cuffs, and shoved a huge spoonful in my mouth. At the same time, I glanced over at the coaches' table, presided over by Bud. They were about to burst out laughing, and I realized why as soon as I tasted the warm, overpoweringly rich wad of pure butter in my mouth.

Over the years, Bud and I developed a routine of sorts. He got into the daily habit of coming over during practice and having a few words with me. Sometimes Bud would pull me out of a drill for one of our discussions, and I could almost see the smoke coming out of the earholes in some guys' helmets.

The topics of our little chats were always different. He might tell me about a little duck that could fly at sixty miles an hour, or about a bird that flew from Mexico to the North Pole every year. He might quiz me about basketball: in his salad years, he'd played with the Lakers, and he was proud of it. He talked about his football career in Canada, or he'd talk about Lou Saban, pointing out what good things Saban had said about me.

Sometimes I pulled a name out of a hat, an old-time basketball or football player, and asked Bud if he ever played against the guy. Bud liked that. He would blow his whistle to start a new drill, but he'd grab me as I started back to the field: "Let me tell you about that guy . . . stay right here."

Most guys wouldn't dare to tease or act chummy with a man as aloof, stoical, and terse as Bud. But he seemed a little lonely to me. He intimidated so many guys that he must have missed the banter and teasing of the locker room. After all, he'd known those things as a player, and there was no question that he had a sense of humor and loved to play pranks. So I tried to get a little action going when I was around him. It brought us closer.

Bud once sent for me to go to his office. When I turned the corner and walked in, I found myself face to face with a full-grown lion. The big guy licked his chops and I booked it back down the hall. During practice once, Bud slipped a pair of duck heads into my dress shoes. Another time, he gave me a ride someplace and asked me to get the map out of his glove box. When I told him I knew the way, Bud insisted I get the map. At that point, I figured something was up, and I was right— he'd emptied out the glove box and put a live snake into it.

Sometimes I tested the boundaries with Bud. Once, in the middle of a drill on an unseasonably hot day, I just announced to the team that I couldn't practice in that shit—I was going to talk to Bud about it. Some of the guys snickered. I trotted over to Bud and told him that we all were too tired and we wanted to go in. When Bud blew his whistle and waved us off the field, nobody could bring himself to move from disbelief. It eventually got to the point where my teammates tried to zing me by calling me "Bud Jr."

I guess the relationship between Bud and me evolved out of

mutual respect and trust. I performed at a high level that never dipped, which is what I've been proudest of from my high-school days right through the pros. I didn't really have many bad days or periods, so it didn't really matter if I spent the entire week talking to Bud. But if I'd started to mess up, you can bet those sideline chats would have been cut short.

We took care of business on the field, but we had fun there, too. It would start in the locker room, where I was a big instigator, a loose cannon. I liked to take shots at guys who talked a lot of shit or invited a rip because they were so flamboyant and full of themselves.

The locker room got busy about two hours before a game, when most of the players started to arrive. Everyone had his own routine, his own quirks. Bobby Bryant was a guy whom nothing ever seemed to fit. You knew things were all right when you'd hear Bryant cussing and hollering at Stubby Eason, "God damn it, Stubby! Who's got my pants? These pants are too small. I can't fit in these pants."

Most of the guys allowed Stubby to repair their pads and equipment, which was a real sign of confidence. Usually, guys don't like to turn their stuff in to be fixed; they prefer to jury-rig something that feels comfortable. When somebody else fixes your pads, you've got to break them in all over. Stubby was different; he never got too fancy in his repairs. It was more of the shoestring-and-spit routine.

"Stubby," Bryant would bellow, "where are my pads?" and he'd start slamming his shit against the wall, and the guys would all think to themselves, "Okay, we're ready now."

Fran Tarkenton and I were similar in the locker room. We were always checking out the action or sneaking looks at each other when some craziness started to happen—when a guy would start punching the wall, or another guy would be heaving up his lunch in the john. I often moved from one group to another, making cracks, zinging guys, turning up the music on some beat box.

If we were playing Houston and two guys had the flu, I'd yell,

"Hey, how come when we have to play against Earl Campbell every goddamned lineman suddenly comes down with the flu? Sounds like you guys are afraid he's gonna be kicking your asses on television again."

Naturally, our guys would think, "Yeah, that's right. Oh, man, everybody's going to be watching. We've gotta find a way to stop Earl."

There were worried guys, scared guys, excited guys, loose guys. Alan Page was the most composed of them all. You just never saw a trace of pressure on his calm face. He was the most professional ass-kicker in the business. One year, Bud let him miss the entire training camp because Alan was enrolled in law school. He could have been in divinity school and still come out as bad as ever.

My good buddy Joe Senser had the locker between me and Ron Yary. It was a good thing, too, because Yary was my opposite; he was all intense and serious. But Joe and I would carry on something awful before games. Before a huge game with Cleveland—in fact, it was the time I made the Miracle Catch—Yary was so uptight that Joe and I just couldn't stop laughing about it. Yary jumped up and in this high, strangulated voice of his complained, "God damn it, Ahmad, get serious! Let's go."

Of course, we laughed even harder.

I was always serious. I just wasn't very uptight.

My quirk was shoes. I never wore metal cleats, only rubber. The metal studs just tore up my feet when I made sharp cuts at full speed and power. So Nike made me special shoes based on their soccer model, and I went through them fast because they were made of glove-soft deerskin. The other guys were jealous, so they always gave me heat, saying I got more shoes than the whole rest of the team combined. I'd wear a pair for one or two games, until I felt I'd blown them out. Then I'd donate them to a worthy cause like some local high-school team.

Rickey Young had the same size-EE foot as me, so he was always looking to steal my shoes. Every time I got a shipment, I'd give Rickey two or three pair. After I trampled mine out, I'd get the shoes back from Rickey, nicely broken in. When he caught on, Rickey started to pinch a few extra pair when a shipment came in. He'd hide them somewhere and I wouldn't notice until we were standing in the huddle during a game. I'd say, "Hey, wait a minute—that's a new pair of *my* shoes."

"No they're not," Rickey would hiss. "They're mine."

We'd argue about that for ten minutes; then I'd drag him over on the sidelines and make him take the shoes off. I had one guy, Sam Harrell, who was my designated shoe breaker-in. I let him wear my shoes for half of practice; then I made him give them back.

After my back injury, the guys figured I wasn't coming back. They went after my stuff like rats: they got my meeting shoes, my drinking mug, my special film-room hat that I could sleep under—they scavenged everything.

I did return a few days later, surprising everybody. When I assessed the situation, I actually wrote out a will. Sam, who had scooped up all my shoes, didn't recognize the will; like some fancy lawyer, he claimed that I couldn't make out a will after I was already dead. He hid the shoes in different places to keep me from finding them over the next few months.

Once our owner, Max Winter, was giving some of his big-shot civic-leader friends a tour of our locker room. He stopped in front of my locker, which was full of new shoes at the time. He swept his hand over the scene and said, "Yeah, I buy Rashad all these shoes." I just happened to be coming back from across the room as he said that. I cleared my throat, and when old Max turned around he just went white, knowing I'd heard that line of bullshit.

My loose attitude carried out to the field. A lot of coaches don't want you talking to the other team, before or after a game. Bud would watch us after the final gun, to see who went around shaking hands and slapping backs. But I was a gregarious guy, so I just did my talking on the field. I was like an ambassador-at-large.

Sometimes I carried messages between these big old linemen.

Some defensive lineman from the other team would say, "Hey, tell that fucking Riley guy to stop holding me." I'd give the message to Steve Riley, adding, "Oh, he also said he's been kicking your ass all day anyway. . . . Now, I don't know if *that's* true, but . . ." You could see our guy get all fired up when he heard something like that.

Walking back to the huddle was the ideal time to talk, either to your own team or to the other guys. But so many of the guys out there are wired shut. It's such an emotional game that most guys figure they can't afford to be loose. They stay permanently fired up and intense. They've got those game faces spray-painted on.

We had a little time to talk when we were standing in the huddle, but when we bent over to hear the call we had to concentrate. Still, even that wasn't necessarily a call to order. Rickey Young could never get over the way we carried on in pressure situations. The Vikings would be down by four points with two minutes to go, with possession on the other team's twenty-five-yard line. Francis would wait until everybody was real quiet, leaning in to hear the play, and he'd say, "Hey, did you guys check out those cheerleaders over there at the first-down marker?"

Fran never lost his sense of humor, which is really a sign of composure. Other guys would get tense about nothing at all and had trouble handling the most basic assignments. The greatest example of that is the problem so many guys have bringing in plays from the sideline. Let's say the messenger is supposed to tell the quarterback to call Flanker Right 62X and Flanker Fly, which is a pass. If the guy bringing in the play is a running back, he's often so busy figuring out what he's supposed to do on the play that when he gets to the huddle, he knows what he's going to do but he's forgotten the actual play.

Or the messenger comes trotting in, repeating the play over and over in his mind. He's so wound up that he gets to the huddle and fires off this unintelligible stream: "Flankerrightsixtytwoxandflankerfly."

"What?" the quarterback asks.

"Oh . . . ah, yeah . . . do that one we tried two downs ago."

The worst thing is that the messenger knows that the guys in the huddle are just waiting for him to screw up. Not only is it funny, but it relieves everybody else of any responsibility whatsoever. It's a variation on the old "Kill the messenger" theme.

Bud tried to make Sammy White a messenger once, but Sammy had some trouble with the job. As he came dashing into the huddle, Joe Senser whispered to me, "Sammy forgot this play the moment he ran onto the field. I can tell by looking at him."

Sure enough, Sammy mumbled something like "Flanker right, put the rest together."

"No, no, no, no, man," I interrupted. "That ain't what Bud said. You forgot the damned play."

"I did not," Sammy shot back. "That's it."

Suddenly our quarterback Tommy Kramer started laughing, too. He was always one of the guys, continuing the tradition established by Fran Tarkenton. Very few things ever got by Tarkenton, and the petty, funny ones never bothered him a whit.

One of my favorite pastimes was wandering into the *defensive* huddle. The trick was to make my way upfield slowly while they were forming up. Then I'd plow through, clearing my throat, going, "Sorry, boys, sorry . . . excuse me."

"Get out of here, man, before I kick your ass," some linebacker would growl. After a move like that, the defensive team would all join hands in the huddle to keep me out. It was comical. But it all goes to show that football is at heart a game of territory—if you go prancing around on the wrong piece of real estate, you're asking for trouble.

I never felt like it was a complete day unless I mixed with everybody. I was fascinated by defensive linemen, the way those huge guys would either bust ahead like wildmen or resort to elaborate pirouettes to get around the offensive line. Some of those linemen depended on moves no less than running backs. When I saw a guy make a good move, I congratulated him and made a friend. When I first played against the Raiders, I caught a short ball and got nailed. Bubba Smith, who was a friend from our Los Angeles crew, was there to haul me up, saying, "Nice catch." I could sense all of these Raiders thinking, "Hey, man, this guy's a friend of Bubba's. He must be okay."

So many of the funny things that occur on the field go unseen by the spectators in the stands or on TV. Tony Galbreath was traded to the Vikings in 1981, joining us for the same Monday-night game in which Duck White tripped on his way to the huddle and bowled over a bunch of our guys. We were playing the Bills, whose stands were real close to the field. One of the sideline cameras was trained on our bench, so naturally Tony goes walking over to wave and say, "Hi, Mom."

Poor Tony didn't know that one of Bud's strictest rules was against hamming it up for the cameras.

Rickey Young spotted Tony and sprinted over to save him, but it was too late. Rickey got there just as Bud grabbed Tony by the collar and yanked him off national television. For the rest of the game, the boisterous Buffalo fans were all over poor Tony, daring him to wave to Mama again.

Some of the guys who came down from playing Canadian ball were funny. They had superstar attitudes and talked a lot of shit, probably to compensate for the stigma of having played in a pale imitation of the NFL. We had one guy in 1979, Jimmy Edwards, a little guy who became a kick-return specialist for the Vikings. Bubba Baker, a big defensive lineman who played for Cleveland in 1987, was with Detroit in '79. Edwards started to mouth off to Baker during one of our home games, and we immediately warned him: Baker was a tough guy, and with both teams on the same sideline, Edwards was playing with fire.

But Edwards didn't listen. He kept talking shit until Bubba just reached over and grabbed him. He pulled Edwards to the Lions' side, held him up, and punched him in the head a few times, right in full view of the Vikings. All we could do was laugh, partly because Edwards was getting just what he asked for. When Bubba was finished beating up on Edwards, he literally threw him back on our side, like a fisherman throwing back a small fish.

Edwards was mad that we hadn't jumped in to help him. Somebody finally said, "This isn't Canada, Jimmy. You leave Bubba alone next time."

The transition from the old Vikings, personified by Marshall and company, to the new team that would move indoors and lose its air of domination was a pretty slow one. When Tarkenton left, we found the right replacement in Tommy Kramer. A fun-loving, tough Texan, he wasn't intimidated by having to follow the Tarkenton legend.

But our draft choices and trades never quite filled the shoes worn by the great Vikings. And we had some bad luck. Joe Senser had Hall of Fame potential as a tight end; he made All-Pro in 1981 with over seventy catches for over a thousand yards, and he was a punishing blocker, too. But a degenerative knee injury drastically reduced his effectiveness. A number of the old Vikings hung in there and would try to do so as long as Bud was around. But the handwriting was on the wall.

For Marshall, the message on the wall was spelled "Hollway"—the same Bob Hollway who had been my first NFL coach in St. Louis. He was hired by Minnesota as a defensive coach, and I had to admit that he had mellowed some over the years. We made a separate peace. But Hollway managed to drive Jim out of the game. At that stage, in '79, Jim was a forty-three-year-old *grandfather*. One day in the film room, he was dozing in the back row when Hollway stopped the projector and singled Jim out as an example to the younger players—for sleeping.

The irony was amazing. Hollway was going to nail the baddest dude in the valley. He was about two sentences into his speech when Jim barked, "You asshole. I been doing this for thirteen years and it's worked out fine. Don't say another word to me or I'll put your head through the wall."

But eventually, Hollway broke Jim down, bit by bit. He asserted his authority and challenged Jim to defy it. It came to a vivid head in one game, when Hollway benched Jim, telling him that he couldn't go back in until he "looked" like he wanted to play.

After brooding for a while, Jim went over to Hollway and humbly asked if he could go back in. He later explained it to me: "I didn't care—I was willing to do anything to get back in there. I figure the man who's got the most inside him can give up a little. So I put on the face. I played his game."

But a real Viking died that day. Jim retired at the end of the season.

Funny, the thing I remember the most is the guys and the antics, not the glory or the statistics. Football may leave you broken down or toughened up, penniless or rich, confident or unprepared for the "real" world. But if it hasn't given you a lifetime of memories, you've missed something along the way. Because there's nothing like life in the foxhole, no stories better than the basic war stories you take from football.

Eddie Payton played for us. Whenever somebody asked him what it was like to be the brother of an All-Pro, he'd grin and answer, "Go ask Walter." Eddie's nickname was "Nuisance" because he always seemed to be in the way. Even Bud called him that. Eddie loved to yell at refs, and Bud would always be screaming at Eddie to back off, because he was afraid we'd get a bad call in spite.

Eddie loved jewelry, so he had all these gold chains and charms with his number, 32. We'd always tease him, asking what he was going to do when Bud finally found a team that would take him in a trade and make him wear a different number.

Not long ago, Joe Senser played in some kind of celebrity golf tournament. When he asked who won, he was told Eddie Payton. "It figured," Joe told me, laughing. "I mean, I saw Eddie walking on one green, kicking his ball along." In the locker room once, Eddie and Rick Danmeier got into a fight. Eddie swung, Rick ducked, and our punter Greg Coleman got a fist right in the face.

Most kickers are content to do their jobs and keep their mouths shut. Ray Guy was a noteworthy exception, but most kickers just aren't football players—especially in the era of the soccer-style place kicker. But Touch Coleman always wanted to be at the heart of the team. I walked into the locker room before one game and he was marching around giving a speech about how we had to get tough, how we had to *hit*. I ripped into him: "Shut the fuck up and sit down! Who the hell are you ever going to hit? You shouldn't even be in uniform—you could do *your* job in one of them nice expensive sweatsuits."

Another time, I was in the shower with Touch when I saw Bud by the door. We had a curfew the previous night, so I said, "Touch, man, I heard that when you snuck out last night you did some bad boogieing. You had that one step when you went way down to the ground. . . ."

Bud's ears perked up. He stuck his head in the shower room and Touch went crazy, calling me a liar and swearing that he'd been in his room all night.

"Ahmad's never lied to me before," Bud said, walking away.

Like most guys, Touch was terrified of Bud. He was so mad that he challenged me to fight.

Fran Tarkenton had worked hard behind the scenes to get Bob Tucker, a tight end he played with in New York, over to the Vikings. Tucker was in the Viking mold, all right. Les Steckel, the receiver coach, once got it into his mind that nine a.m. meetings would be good for team discipline. One morning Les was up at the blackboard, and he'd written three sets of figures: $5,000, $10,000, and $20,000. He was telling some stupid story about how if you invest twenty grand, you put more effort into getting a return or something.

Tucker walked in late, hair mussed, holding a cup of coffee. "What the fuck is that shit up there?" he said.

Les got all defensive and said he was trying to make an analogy to football.

"Shit, Les, I made more than all of that playing backgammon at Maximillian's last night."

Kevin Miller was a running back who used to put all kinds of chemicals in his hair, so we called him "Do" Miller, for hairdo. He was a naturally funny, cool guy who never departed from his street jargon, whether he was talking to some hanger-on or to Bud. He barely made the team as a rookie, but he thought he was better than me and he said so. I liked his exuberance—he was real enthusiastic, and he had a lot of natural talent, but he never realized the importance of doing things the right way.

Time and again Burnsie yelled at him in a meeting for running the wrong pattern.

"Yeah," Do said. "But I was *open*."

You could see Burnsie's veins swell with blood as he hollered, "You were fucking open all right, but nobody fucking knew where the fuck you were because you were on the wrong fucking side of the fucking field!"

During films, Burnsie once hollered at Do for dropping a ball. Do shot back, "Yeah, but I caught the *next* one."

Burnsie gave up. "Yeah," he muttered, "and you're going to catch the next fucking bus out of here, too."

At the height of the cocaine plague in the NFL, a Viking tapped Do Miller on the shoulder and said, "Coach wants to see you, Do. It's about chemical abuse."

Do's jaw dropped.

"They're going to check your hair, Do."

Our backup quarterback, Steve Dils, was the butt of the best locker-room prank ever. It all started with our trainer, Fred Zamberletti. Whenever players have a physical problem, from a social disease to a broken leg, they go to the trainers' room. One day I noticed some pills sitting on Fred Zamberletti's desk, and asked what they were for. Fred told me that they were the greatest pills, that they would turn me into a "tiger" as a man. They were a real aphrodisiac.

I asked Fred how many I should take and he recommended that I swallow the whole packet. So I wolfed down these pills and went off to a banquet, where I was to speak along with Alan King. It was about two degrees outside, but as I got into my car in the Viking lot I noticed that I was really hot. I even cranked down the windows for the ride home. Soon my heart was racing so fast that I was worried about having a heart attack. At the same time, I was itching like crazy.

When I got to the banquet, I power-drank a couple of beers and somehow made it through the night, even though my whole body felt like an itching flame. I noticed the next day that Fred was looking at me funny. When I demanded to know what he'd given me, he admitted that the pills were niacin vitamin tablets. You were only supposed to take one per day. The effect of an overdose was to open the capillaries and really make you itchy and hot.

I wasn't about to be the only sucker on the team, so I went up to the guy I figured as the perfect fall guy, Dilsey. He was a preppy-type guy who went to Stanford and liked to remind you of it. Dilsey was going prematurely bald, and the word around the locker room was that his wife ran the show at home, ruling with an iron fist.

I recommended the pills to Dilsey, saying that after their effects his wife would worship the ground he walked on. He assured me that he had no problems at home, he didn't need any pills to impress his wife. He put the pills down, pretending he wanted nothing to do with them.

Then I noticed Rickey Young talking with Sammy White. I gave those guys the same line about the pills, showing them the last two packets. They both wanted them, but I said they were too valuable to give away. But a few minutes later I pulled Rickey aside and told him that as a special favor I'd let him have some of the pills.

At that point, Dilsey was leaving the locker room. Once again, he denied the need for any pills. But I noticed that the packet I'd shown him was gone. Fred told me that Dilsey had taken the pills on the sly. The locker room was almost empty by then, and I could hear Rickey's voice from the shower room, "Oh, I can feel it in my bones now." He stood in front of the mirror, combing his hair. "When I walk into that club, the ladies are going to fall over backwards over me, I can feel it in my bones."

Moments later, Rickey started to itch. He looked at the can of talcum in his hand, and accused me of putting itching powder into it. He still didn't connect the pills and the itch. I retreated to the trainers' room just in time to hear the phone ring. Dilsey was calling Fred to ask about the pills. He was burning up so badly that he admitted to Fred that he'd taken a whole handful.

A few minutes later, the phone rang again, and Dilsey's wife was on the other end, demanding to know what we'd done to her Steve. Dils spent the evening in bed, tormented by the itches. It turned out that I'd told him the truth, all right—the pills did make Dilsey jump into bed, and his wife sure got hot about it.

The guys who topped everybody when it came to talking shit and keeping everybody entertained were our very own SWAT team—make that SWAC team. For some reason, guys from the Southwest Athletic Conference were some funny dudes. Texas guys in general are a little larger than life, and their stories are even bigger than that. Show me a football player who went to school in Texas and I'll show you a guy with tales to tell.

One of those Texas homeboys came down to us from Canada. He proclaimed himself "all-world" and kept telling us he was so bad that he wore blue shoes, blue shoes with tassels on them— tassels! He played in one exhibition game for us, fumbling every punt that came his way. Something was wrong, but we didn't figure it out until we went back to training camp. We found out that he'd been smoking pot right before the kickoff that night. When one of us confronted him about it, Tassels just said, "Sure, I smoked up before the game. It helped to relax me."

During camp, a whole bunch of us used to congregate in the room where those SWAC guys hung out. The crew included David Shaw, Sammy White, Chuck Goodrun, Nate Allen, Jimmy Edwards. This was a real country football throwdown. Fran Tarkenton was the only white guy on the team who used to come around, and he was fascinated.

I remember the legend of Peachhead, the fastest guy in the South. He was fast, but he had tender feet, so he never wore track shoes, just sneakers. It was all he needed, anyway. Peachhead got a football tryout with the Jets, but he refused to wear spikes on his feet. The Jets were adamant but so was Peachhead, so he quit and never played pro football.

The funny thing was, as the story was being told, three or four different guys would suddenly remember that they'd heard of Peachhead, and they'd start adding details. In the end you had four or five guys trying to top each other with tales of Peachhead's exploits.

Another one of these Eddie Lee Somebodys was supposed to have been so good that he was nicknamed "the Lord's Prayer," because whenever he came into a game the other team started to pray. This guy was a cornerback from West Texas who had never been timed in the forty- or hundred-yard dash. He got into an exhibition game against the Dallas Cowboys, and when Bob Hayes caught a little out ball on the other side of the field, our boy Eddie Lee lit out after the World's Fastest Human.

The whisper raced along the sidelines, on both sides of the field: "Check it out—this guy's going to catch Bob Hayes." Eddie Lee kept gaining, and gaining, and he was just about to grab Hayes when he stopped short and just watched Hayes cover the last ten yards into the end zone.

Back on the sideline, the coach asked Eddie Lee why he'd stopped. "Hey," Eddie said, "I saw the name on the jersey— that was Bob Hayes. I can't catch Bob Hayes."

These guys would just talk shit, one story topping another, and out of the corner of my eye I could see that Fran was loving every minute of it, lapping it up. They called everybody "Homes," for homeboy, and turned every story into something like a football revival meeting. Talking about some Texas sprinters, they would remember some track meet like this: "These guys were so fast, Homes, that when they took a picture for the photo finish it came out blurry. They were too fast for the shutter of the camera!"

Without missing a beat, Nate Allen said, "Oh yeah, how about this one, Homes." Nate, who'd gone to Texas Southern, launched into a story about a Texas track meet where the guys in the hundred-yard dash were so fast that at twenty-five yards they became a blur; at fifty, there was barely an outline; at seventy-five yards, all you could see was a little disturbance in the air; and by the time they crossed the finish line, they'd all disappeared—the photo finish showed an empty track!

The room was silent. After a moment, somebody piped up: "Yeah, yeah, I remember that—I was there too."

Finally, I got my chance at one-upmanship with those guys. We were playing an away game at Oakland, and the SWAC team was up in my room, shooting it. At the time, the word "intimidation" was synonymous with the name Jack Tatum, the Raider free safety known for the stupendous licks he laid on people. Although we were natural enemies in the football scheme, Jack and I got along. He was tough but he was clean. I thought that the Raider strong safety, George Atkinson, was more inclined to take a cheap shot at you.

So there we were, spinning some Texas bullshit, when there was a knock on the door. I opened up and in walked Jack Tatum and Clarence Davis. They were all dressed up for a night out, wearing these little round dark glasses that hid their eyes.

Suddenly, the SWAC team fell silent. Jack and I began to talk, but you could feel the tension in the room.

A few minutes later, the clock struck eleven and there was a knock on the door. It was Bob Hollway, making sure we were all in for curfew. He stepped inside, saw Tatum, and without saying a word he did one of those 360-degree turns on his heels and left the room.

Jack and I burst out laughing, but the SWAC team remained quiet. Besides, Tatum and Davis were going on to some nightclub, because the Raiders didn't have a curfew. The rest of us felt like a bunch of nerds who had to be in at eleven.

The Raiders said good-bye. But Tatum was still wearing his dark glasses, so he made a mistake and grabbed the wrong doorknob and walked into the closet. I mean, he walked in so far that Clarence actually followed him all the way in before they figured out what they'd done.

It was the funniest thing I ever saw, but nobody in that room was going to laugh when Jack Tatum made a mistake. You couldn't tell what that dude would do if you laughed at him. So everybody pretended like nothing unusual had happened as Tatum and Davis got pointed the right way and said, "Okay, catch you later, man."

It stayed quiet in the room until Jack and Clarence were out of the hotel, in the car, and on the freeway. Finally, somebody broke the ice and began to laugh. Within seconds, all the guys were holding their sides or rolling on the floor.

What the hell—Jack Tatum had to be in the next county by then.

12

A SUNDAY FRAME OF MIND

f you got to the stadium early before a game and saw my pregame "warm-up," you might have thought I was some kind of panhandler looking for loose change. The only thing missing was one of those weird metal-detector devices, like you see people walking around with on Venice Beach in L.A.

I would take a careful tour of an away field, pushing down with my toe here, twisting my foot there. I might get down on my hands and knees in a certain place and sight down the length of the field. The ritual was every bit as much a part of being a good wide receiver as quickness drills or the ability to make a catch in traffic. I scouted fields as carefully as most players scout opponents, because no two natural-turf fields were alike, and their personalities varied as much as those of the cornerbacks I'd go up against.

My favorite place on the Vikings' former home field, Metropolitan Stadium, was down around the six-yard line at the south end of the field. That was exactly where the third-base coaching box for the Twins baseball team was situated, and for some reason there was a small hump in it. Nine times out of ten, if I could back my man in there, he'd slip and go down. Once I even used the hump as a springboard to make a leaping catch against the Eagles. Fran threw me a fade, and I caught the ball for the winning score.

At the far end of the field, near the end zone, there was a little bog, a mild depression that always retained moisture and stayed slippery. I would time my post pattern to make my cut across that patch and—literally—give my man the slip. Good old Metropolitan Stadium—the field had as many peculiarities as an old car, and the better I understood them, the more it helped me as a receiver.

I also found that some fields had dead spots where the turf was spongy and "slow," and areas where you could really burn, making sharp cuts without kicking out the turf. Sometimes the very best footing was where they painted the lines on the field— the gooey paint and grass created a flypaper effect.

I used to comb over every field we played on; it was all a part of the education of a receiver. Of course, it was a much more important element before the proliferation of artificial turf made most fields about as different from each other as shopping-mall parking lots. That's one more subtlety gone from the game, one more equalizing factor that works against the craftsman and puts that much more of a premium on being a bigger, faster, and stronger guy. I miss those old fields with their distinct personalities.

The University of Oregon was one of the first colleges to put down artificial turf—we even held our spring practices on the carpet. One of the major reasons for laying a rug in a place as lush and green as Eugene was that you could play on the stuff during or immediately after rain without ruining it. And it rained a lot in Oregon—which is why everything *except* the football field was naturally lush and green. I'm still trying to figure it out.

At first I thought artificial turf was great: it made you faster, it allowed you to cut more sharply. Different kinds of players excel on different kinds of fields. Like horses, some guys were "mudders"—Gale Sayers was the most prominent of them. Other guys were particularly good, showing quick feet on spongy turf.

If the Vikings had continued to play outdoors on turf, they might have drafted sure-footed, rangy Marcus Allen on the first round in 1982 instead of Darrin Nelson. But when they moved to the Metrodome, they began to look for smaller, quicker guys to exploit the rug. Joe Morris of the Giants is a prime example of a carpet runner.

Unfortunately, carpet isn't ideal for longevity. For one thing, getting tackled on artificial turf is like going down on asphalt. The down side of the fabulous traction you get from carpet is that you tend to tear things up as you explode into a move. In that sense, the traction is almost too good. Artificial turf ruined my feet—I could barely walk after most games on the stuff. But I learned my craft on artificial turf, at Oregon, St. Louis, and Buffalo. The turf helped me develop precision, and that's of paramount importance to a wide receiver.

I guess the wide-receiver position suited my temperament. It's the ideal place for a guy who's a little bit of a loner. Split out to the side, you're usually removed from the hurly-burly. You're more of an observer, and being observant is vital to perfecting your craft. On the other hand, you're definitely expected to make the big play, to emerge on a moment's notice as the most important guy on the field.

Your presence has to represent that game-breaking threat. Making the big play, especially if it involves a spectacular catch in addition to running a great pattern, is a highly individualistic act with a big payoff for the team. So the wide receiver is an individualist who has a tremendous impact on the group. That was always the relationship I wanted to have with football.

To the casual eye, being able to catch the ball probably looks like the chief skill a wide receiver needs. But the fact is that literally thousands of high-school kids have great hands, and hundreds of college players do, too. There are no wide receivers in the NFL who have bad hands, period. The ability to catch the ball is a prerequisite for the job, not the epitome of the craft.

As a veteran, I always got a kick out of how eagerly our defensive backs would cover me in practice, and how much it meant for them to feel like they shut me down. They never realized that I wasn't in a Sunday frame of mind—I wasn't out to beat them and haul in a scoring pass. On any given day, I might have been tinkering with my footwork or experimenting with a new combination of moves. But I was happy that they played me so aggressively, because it created great lab conditions for me.

The real difference between ordinary receivers and great ones lies in what they can do *besides* catch the ball, because those are the things that determine whether or not you're going to be open in the first place. I'll take a guy with average hands who knows how to beat a cornerback over a guy with great hands who can't get open, any day. I'll take a slow guy who understands the defense and his own quarterback over a guy with blazing speed who runs sloppy patterns, any day. I'll take a diligent receiver who knows how to work the seams in a zone over a gazelle who can leap higher than any defensive back, any day.

But from the start, I tried to be the fast guy with great hands who could beat a cornerback, exploit the seam in a zone, run a precise pattern, and jump like a gazelle to make a one-handed catch—not just any day but *every* day. Because that's what it takes to be a great receiver in the NFL. I felt I'd reached that plateau in my first year at Buffalo, but the knee injury threw me back. In my second year with Minnesota, I led the NFC in catches with fifty-one. I was back on the plateau, and I stayed there for the rest of my career. I posted my best numbers in '80, when I led the league with eighty receptions for 1,156 yards.

The groundwork for those kinds of numbers is set by the ability to run disciplined, precise patterns. Rod Dowhower taught me how to do that when he was an assistant coach with the Cardinals. I didn't even realize the value of his teaching until the following year in Buffalo, when I saw how few of the Bills' receivers had that kind of training.

Dowhower tried to instill in his receivers the sense of rhythm that ought to exist in every pass route. It's like a dancer getting locked into a piece of music. I worked on those rhythms in those summer workout sessions we had in Los Angeles. After those sessions, Bobby Chandler and I used to sit around and get into these elaborate discussions of defensive philosophies and how to exploit them.

You can almost hear a perfect pattern being run: *tick, tock, tick, tock—BAM!*—completion. Steve Largent is the consummate pattern runner in the NFL today, while Jerry Rice has the best tools and talents. His ability to find an extra step, an extra eight inches of reach at the very last moment is mind-boggling. Rice always seems to have something in reserve, while the guy he's up against is at the end of his ability. How many times have we seen Rice, apparently covered, get that extra last step or that little move to the flight of the ball. Part of this is body position, part of it is physical talent; but the most important part is a natural marshaling of resources.

The perfectly run pattern isn't a cut-and-dried routine that you lay over a field like one of those transparent pages in a biology textbook. That's fine for a quick out where you're looking to make a catch at the first-down marker, but most of the time you have to be more flexible. Run a pattern the same way twice and the cornerback will be locked in on you as surely as a heat-seeking missile.

The patterns you run change in one game, with the defenders and defense you're up against, with field position and the game situation. Receivers and cornerbacks study each other on film all week. In fact, at the Pittsburgh–Cleveland game, Frank Minnifield had a portable videocassette player—he was checking out Louis Lipps and John Stallworth right up until game time. He even took the device into the john.

A good quarterback knows that you can't run your patterns with the same predictability you bring to daily rituals like your morning shower. Running a good pattern means working on the weaknesses of a specific defensive back and a specific defensive strategy. Mostly, it means taking a cornerback to his point of vulnerability. You take him right to the edge of the territory where his responsibility ends. There, he experiences a moment of doubt—are you his responsibility or the other guy's? Then you take him to the edge of his territory on the other side. After that, you might take him up the middle. You have to keep him off balance, because everybody knows what to do in the safety of his zone. The trick is to draw him out of his area of comfort.

You always hear people talking about seams in a defense, but they're not as clear-cut as the seams in a piece of cloth. The idea is to stretch a defense and create a seam, then make your cut in that borderline area. Stretching that defense also gives your other receivers greater room to work—it invariably opens up the middle for the tight end. The single most difficult thing for a young wide receiver to learn is that when he's cutting across the middle and *feels* wide open, he's being sucked into double coverage. The idea is to prevent a defense from setting those traps and collapsing around you by stretching it out.

But your chief concern is almost always an individual, the cornerback. You work him like a pitcher works on a batter. We don't tend to think of football as a one-on-one game, but that's the best description of the matchup between a wideout and a cornerback. On a typical sweep left, the television viewer doesn't even see that the wideout on the right has had yet another in a series of confrontations with the cornerback. The receiver becomes the center of attention only when he's the target of a pass—*after* he's spent eleven or fifteen downs setting up the cornerback.

The tools for setting up a defensive back are your moves and your speed. You have to be careful not to fall into a pattern— say, throwing a little head fake every time you're about to cut to the outside. An alert defensive back will pick up on that right away. Habits always betray you.

The thing every receiver should remember, no matter what his speed is when he gets into the league, is that time, unforeseen injuries, and even changeable playing conditions can wreak havoc with your natural ability. The sooner you begin to rely on intelligence and craftsmanship instead of raw ability, the better off you are.

Never let a defensive back know just how fast—or slow—you are. I used to change pace fifteen or twenty times a game. Just when a cornerback thought I was at full speed, I'd turn on the afterburners. I wasn't the fastest receiver in the NFL, but I had a good knack for creating *impressions* of speed.

The ability to control your side of the field is worth full seconds of speed. The difference between a guy with good speed and one with blazing speed is negligible when you take the other factors into consideration. If you've beaten a cornerback with a neat fake or move, you may have as much as a two-second jump on him, either to the ball or with the ball. In terms of speed, two seconds is a lifetime. It amounts to a ten-to-twenty-yard head start in a game where a thirty- or forty-yard play is a big gainer.

There are two kinds of speed—clock speed and practical speed. If you can't have both, you're better off with the practical variety, like a Fred Biletnikoff.

I always leaned toward an effortless, artistic style of play. I was much more concerned with developing finesse and lulling defenders with it than going head on, helmet to helmet, with a cornerback. My object was to get a defender off balance—to introduce that element of doubt, to make him think. For me, the most satisfying compliments were the ones I got from guys like Willie Brown, who said that my strength was in combining athletic skills with intelligence and experience.

Over the years, I developed techniques for reading a defense. I would look at the triangle formed by the cornerback, the safety, and the outside linebacker. The cornerback told me the least, because he was a given—his job always was to cover me. But if the safety took off deep at the snap, I knew it was a zone. If the linebacker moved inside, I knew I had man-to-man with the cornerback. After a while, I could tell what the other eight men on the field were doing by the movements of my triangle.

One of my chief assets as a player was the ability to stay cool, no matter how much fur was flying around me. That enabled me to concentrate on strategy—to survey the field with a cool eye instead of following the whims of a hot temper. That's what being a finesse player is all about. Tarkenton and I got along so well because fundamentally we were both tacticians who tried to accomplish our goals with skill and intelligence rather than brute power and speed.

Sometimes I manifested my philosophy in unexpected ways. Unlike guys who got into verbal wars with cornerbacks, I always tried to be reasonable. If I was lined up left and the play was a sweep right, I'd say to the cornerback, "Hey, they're going over there, why don't you and I just go down this way a little and stay out of trouble." That would blow a cornerback's mind. A lot of times, he thought I was trying to set him up, so he'd lope along with me suspiciously, checking things out as we ran, as if I were going to break for the post at any second.

I once told Bernard Jackson of the Bengals that a sweep was coming our way, and he could either let me block him or face Jackie Smith instead. He didn't believe me, and on that play Smith broke his nose.

Fran had a lot to do with my success, because most of the time I was free to do anything that would get me open, without worrying about whether or not he would understand what I was up to. We were in sync, which gave me carte blanche to look for the Achilles' heel of any cornerback.

When you run a deep route, the cornerback can play you to run either the post or the corner pattern; he can't effectively play you to run both. So I would take off with no predetermined route, and if the cornerback played me outside, I'd go post, and vice versa. The amazing thing was that when I looked up, the ball was right there, on the money, almost every time. That was Tarkenton—psychic.

I developed the same kind of relationship with Tommy Kramer too, but to a lesser extent. We had a tougher row to hoe, because by that time I was facing double coverage on almost every play. The only teams that didn't double me were the ones that stuck to the man-to-man defense, like Green Bay and Oakland—and I had my best games against those clubs. No matter how you slice it, a good wide receiver should *always* win in a man-to-man confrontation. Only a great pass rush nullifies that condition.

The real problem with double coverage isn't that it's twice as hard to get free; it's that you automatically have too much value as a decoy. When they throw double coverage on you, most quarterbacks tend to look elsewhere, even though the very best ones can still find you.

The consolation in facing double coverage is knowing that you're helping the team by making somebody else's job easier. The defense tries to get around that by disguising their intentions, leaving the offense uncertain of just who is going to get doubled up on any given play. Two years after I caught eighty balls, I caught only fifty-eight, but I never felt it was a sign of decline. I'm really proud of those numbers, considering the kind of coverage our opponents put on me. Plus I provided Sammy White with a lot of opportunities.

But when a team's intent on shutting you down, there's little you can do to prevent it without a concerted effort from your teammates. Joe Senser told me that he all but saw my back injury coming as far back as '81, because of the way teams used to converge on me. Throughout my career I'd avoided getting creamed on crossing routes over the middle, because I knew where to go; I knew how to work the seams without attracting attention. I could pussyfoot my way through a mine field and get away with it—at least until everybody and his brother had my number.

But to this day, Joe's convinced that somebody missed an assignment on the play that busted my back. Somebody messed up and forgot to run through there to clear the middle the way we usually did. In fact, Joe's sure that the mixup had something to do with some of the turmoil and dissension that had started to eat away at the Vikings by that time, as the era of the "real Vikings" came to an end. But let's save that for the last chapter.

13

HOME AT LAST

Well, the long and winding road finally came to an end in Denver, in the shadow of the snow-capped Rockies. Looking out of the window at the Hyatt Regency at those towering peaks, I felt very serene. But down in the lobby of the hotel, grown men were walking around barking. They wore dog masks, Browns jerseys, and windbreakers with dog biscuits tied to them. The next day, the Browns would play the Broncos for the AFC Championship—and a trip to the Super Bowl.

I liked the Browns. They were a team with great balance, a tough, rugged bunch of guys who reminded me a little of the old Vikings. The Dawg Defense was proud and effective, and the offense had great balance with Kevin Mack and Earnest Byner in the backfield. Bernie Kosar, who left college to fulfill his boyhood dream of playing for Cleveland, was having a great year, throwing to receivers like Webster Slaughter, Reggie Langhorne, Brian Brennan, and the venerable tight end, Ozzie Newsome.

Kosar and everybody else on the club was eager to get revenge against Elway and the Broncos. For a year, the Browns had to live with the nightmarish memory of the previous year's AFC title game, when Elway produced the Drive. With under two

minutes left in that 1987 game at Municipal Stadium in Cleveland, Elway led his team ninety-eight yards, scoring on a pass
to Mark Jackson to tie the game with just seconds left. Denver
won the game in overtime with a field goal. Cleveland had been
waiting for an entire year, and their moment of reckoning was
at hand, in Denver, on Sunday, January 17, 1988, in another
AFC Championship game.

On the eve of the game, Bob Costas and I had dinner in the
hotel. We were going on to the NFL party afterward, and then
we hoped to catch some of the basketball game between the
Nuggets and the Golden State Warriors at the Denver Arena.
Costas is always good for some funny stories. He's a shrewd
judge of human nature, and he's got a good eye for the quirks
and mannerisms of others.

Early in his broadcasting career, Costas was the voice of the
St. Louis Spirits of the American Basketball Association. You
couldn't imagine stranger partners than Costas, an articulate,
sophisticated guy who stands about five and a half feet tall, and
Marvin "Bad News" Barnes, the towering problem child of pro
ball who had the street in his blood.

One time, Costas told me, he was with Barnes and some other
players in an elevator with an elderly operator. Costas was nicely
dressed in a coat and tie, carrying a briefcase filled with stats
and program directions. One by one the basketball players got
off, until finally it was just Costas and the operator, who turned
to him and said, "Don't tell me, let me guess. You play guard."

We got to talking about drug problems and the way an athlete
never shakes the label of "abuser." An entertainer may overcome
a drug problem and the issue is forgotten; but even when an
athlete frees himself of drugs, the past trails him around. It's
always "Charles White, who has had drug problems in the past,
gained ninety-two yards . . ."

The athlete who really played it smart in sports was the Mets'
first baseman, Keith Hernandez. He refused to talk about his
alleged cocaine problem, and he refused to apologize for anything. He took some flak for holding out; but when the story

blew over, he came out clean. After all, nobody could tag him with any kind of neat label. An athlete with a drug problem has a right to privacy just as much as a guy with marital problems or financial difficulties.

Early in the 1987 NFL season, Lawrence Taylor did a halftime interview with Frank Gifford on "Monday Night Football." It was one of those deals in which LT agreed to talk about his drug problems in exchange for a plug for the book he'd written in the off-season. It was a dumb idea because the interview was boring. What could Taylor really say besides "Yeah, I did them, they're bad, don't do them"? He wasn't about to go into details or start telling stories about his experiences on network TV— everybody from the producer to the viewers would have freaked out about that. Interviews with drug-rehab cases are as dull as interviews with guys who just found religion. There's a time and place for those things, but prime-time TV isn't it.

I know the idea of the LT piece was to warn young viewers against drug abuse, but sometimes those interviews work the other way. There's an element of the self-fulfilling prophecy about all the drug stories of the past few years. We don't have to ignore or hush up drug problems, but we don't have to make them a staple of every telecast or news story, either. By concentrating on drugs, they give drugs an inflated value. Devoting that much time to a vague discussion of drugs may glorify the problem.

The press or the public, maybe both, seem particularly fascinated by drug issues in sports, to the detriment of sports. Maybe it's because the party line says that sports and drugs don't mix. So when an athlete gets busted, this ripple of real or pretended shock races through the sports pages and over the airwaves.

So let's get realistic about this issue.

Sports and drugs have always been linked. That's the cold, hard reality of it based on the past few decades of evidence. Drug abuse is a danger that comes with the territory of pro sports, whether you're talking about performance-enhancing drugs or recreational abuse. Every promising athlete must be ready to deal with the temptations and consequences of dabbling in drugs.

Pro sports is a big-time, big-money, big-ego aspect of society. Pro athletes are glamorous figures, pampered and worshiped and tempted by all kinds of hangers-on, from groupies to drug dealers. Tons of people are always looking for ways to ingratiate themselves with a superstar; and offering him something that makes his body feel good and blows his mind is one quick way to do it. A lot of athletes have confessed that only drugs gave them a high comparable to that of sacking a quarterback or scoring a touchdown. It's sad but true.

People who say that sports and drugs don't mix are whistling in the dark, ignoring logic and common sense. An athlete hooked on drugs isn't a unique, accidental occurrence. He's the reflection of a way of life and an easy-come, easy-go life-style. But that's no reason to single out athletes, either. Because the truth is that drug abuse is pervasive, and drug victims exist at both ends of the social spectrum and on all levels of the economic scale.

It's an open secret that a lot of the old guard NFL players liked to pop amphetamines before a game. At one time, the standing joke was that if ever there was an amphetamine shortage, all you had to do was round up all the old football players and drain the stuff out of their blood.

But that was a different type of drug abuse. It had more in common with other, "officially" accepted practices like shooting up an injured player with an anaesthetic made of xylocaine and cortisone, risking permanent damage just so the guy could play on. The use of amphetamines fell under the heading of Whatever It Takes; but then everybody at the time knew much less about the long-term affects of drug abuse.

I'm sure amphetamine abuse ruined the lives of some guys in the NFL, but you rarely heard or read about it. The harmful side effects of amphetamine abuse came as news to some people, just like the discovery that steroids caused hormonal imbalances. The big change occurred when drug abuse ceased to be a problem related to the desire for enhanced performance. The turning point was the birth of a large-scale drug culture in America in the 1960s, starting with the pot, speed, and LSD popularized by the hippies. In the 1980s, cocaine emerged as the "designer" drug. It was expensive, so having it gave you social clout.

As football became more liberal and made more room for individualists like myself, it became harder and harder to control the habits of the players. Starting with my generation, you couldn't tell players *not* to do things. You couldn't just take the bad apples and kick them off the team like they once did. It became easier to mess up for guys who were looking for a fast-lane life-style to go along with their football celebrity.

Toward the end of my career, the Vikings acquired a cagey veteran defensive back. In training camp, a draft choice made the mistake of asking this vet for advice on how to make the team—at the same position the vet played! This wily old guy gave the kid a handful of pills, claiming they were amphetamines that would really get him going. But the pills were Quaaludes—powerful muscle relaxants that turn you into drowsy jelly. The rookie fell asleep on the bench, and he was cut the next day.

That same year, I drifted into the hotel room of a young player a few hours before a game. He and his roommate were sitting around with a bunch of visitors, with lines of cocaine all cut and ready to go on top of the television set. Sensing my shock, these young guys tried to tell me everything was "cool." The really shocking thing for me was the blasé attitude of these guys—their natural belief that there was absolutely nothing unusual or wrong in getting coked up before a football game.

In fact, if it had come to a confrontation they might have turned the tables on me—didn't my generation invent chronic abuse and the whole "rehabilitation" process? Everyone knew that respected Vikings, including stars like Tommy Kramer and Scott Studwell, had an excessive fondness for the sauce. Hard-drinking ball players were a Viking tradition. Until very recently, there's been a universal mystique about the type.

On the other hand—and I'm not rationalizing here—drinking

is more sociable than drug abuse. One of the signs of good team
morale is when the guys go out together to have a few. Drinking
is in the social mainstream; it's a ritual that brings people together when it's done the way most people drink—in modera-
tion. You just can't equate it with a couple of guys holing up in
a hotel room and snorting coke. The drug abuser has a secretive
mentality, and his vice is more like an act of hostility and re-
bellion than a social ritual.

Our Viking carousers, like most carousers in football history,
were major figures on the team. Kramer, like Bobby Layne,
would go out with a monstrous hangover and play the game of
a lifetime. That's why he got away with some of his more outrageous off-duty activities. Tommy liked to sing country-and-
western songs. He once had a few drinks and got up to sing
with the band at one of the biggest hangouts in Minneapolis.
You can imagine the publicity generated by that stunt. It was
almost enough in and of itself to force Tommy into a rehabilitation program in March 1981.

At about that time, we had a group that met on Thursday
nights, the Fellowship of Pagan Athletes, as a response to certain
pressures to conform we felt from the guys in the Fellowship of
Christian Athletes. We had a regular drinking song and certain
rituals—like if you were the eighth guy to arrive, you had to
drink eight beers to join the group. Joe Senser and Rickey Young
were members, along with most of the linemen. We had real
camaraderie; the FPA bonded us together.

One evening during the dead of winter we met in a Minneapolis steak house, where a group of ladies happened to be
having dinner. They were out on the town, because their hus-
bands were away deer hunting. We got to talking and soon we
were buying each other's table drinks. Then the ladies decided
they wanted autographs. We couldn't find any paper or dry nap-
kins, so one of the women just up and popped her breast out of
her blouse and asked us to sign there.

Rickey Young had decided to go home about then, but one of
us went running after him as the ladies exposed their breasts

one by one, to collect signatures. Naturally, Rickey came sprinting back. There was a big picture window facing the parking lot in this joint, and just as Rickey got to the window he hit a sheet of ice. His legs went flying out from under him and he flew higher in the air than he ever had on the field. He hung suspended for a second, the look of surprise on his face clear to all of us. After a long second he crashed to his back. It took two guys to trundle him into his car.

But the existence of the FPA highlighted a rift in the club, one that went back to around 1978, when the nucleus of the great Viking teams began to come apart. The clearest image of the end of an era formed before my eyes during a game against Green Bay at the Met. It was a freezing-cold day, and there was a high-school band right behind our bench, with a heater trained on the musicians. Alan Page came off the field on a change of possession and went and sat down in front of the heater, all by himself, in defiance of Bud's rules. This was a guy who at one time played with bare arms, without gloves or long johns or a turtleneck. I knew it was the end for Alan; I knew he no longer had a taste for the game the way it used to be played in Minnesota. A few days later he was traded to Green Bay.

The changing of the guard was prolonged and stretched out over two or three years; but by 1981, some words Fran Tarkenton said once echoed in my memory: "The day when you look around you in training camp and decide that you can't win with the guys you see, that's the time to get out."

In 1981, we were a 7–6 team with three games to go. We'd won a handful of games and lost a handful by just a few points—it was that kind of year, a year of hanging by our fingernails. We still had a shot at making the playoffs, but we had trouble getting our talent together, and the signs of dissension were becoming evident. At the lowest point during the next few weeks, we had a team meeting, called by veteran linebacker Matt Blair.

Blair had been with the team since '74, and he considered himself one of the old guard; but some of us thought he played up the All-Pro image too thoroughly. Matt was the defensive captain, and he had every right to call the meeting. But in my experience, the gesture was like reaching up for the handle so you can flush yourself down the toilet. I just thought it was a stupid idea, and I told him so. Matt went to Bud and got his backing, and the meeting was called.

Matt stood in front of the team and began his harangue, about how none of us cared about football the way he did, about how we just wanted to get drunk after practice while he would go home to study his playbook. He told us how dedicated he was, even though he had so much more experience in the game than most of us.

I was about ready to puke.

And in the middle of his speech, Matt Blair, All-Pro, turned on me. I was sitting in the back, steaming, when he began to say that there was one guy in the room who wasn't one of "us." That guy, he said, didn't even want to attend the team meeting. He looked at me and said, "Yes, Ahmad, I'm talking about you."

At that point, I blew up. I began to see red, because I remembered the great Viking tradition and all those Purple People Eaters. I saw the whole thing going down the tubes. So I raised my voice and shouted Matt down. I said we didn't need any stupid soul-searching meetings; we didn't need to hunt up lame excuses. All we had to do was play harder, play better.

My outburst created chaos, and the meeting became a heated debate. Scott Studwell got up and supported me. The worst blow for Matt was when his main man, fellow linebacker Fred McNeil, got up and spoke. Fred was a vet too, and he said he agreed with me.

At about that point, Matt Blair, All-Pro, broke down.

I thought, "This never would have happened in the old days. This is a six-foot-five, 250-pound linebacker coming apart before our eyes." I just couldn't imagine captain Jim Marshall standing up in front of the Vikings, losing it like that.

We lost our last three games and finished 7–9. The next July, I looked around training camp and saw that we couldn't win. It was time to get out.

. . .

All hell was breaking loose around me on the morning of the AFC Championship game, but I didn't know it. After coming back from the Denver–Golden State basketball game with Bob Costas the previous night, I had a call from a friend who told me about some remarks made by Jimmy "the Greek" Snyder, the CBS-TV commentator and gambling specialist.

When I heard that the Greek, a friend, had said some things about blacks having been "bred" to be great athletes by plantation owners in the days of slavery, I laughed. Then my friend told me that the Greek also had said that if it wasn't for coaching jobs, whites would be driven out of football. The remarks were absurd. I had no idea of the kind of publicity they were generating until my friend said that the situation was serious—deadly serious.

I called the Greek, whom I've known for a long time. He wasn't at his hotel, so I left a message asking him to call me. I didn't want him to get paranoid, so I signed the message, "Love, Ahmad."

When Jimmy called back, he said, "I really fucked up this time." He filled me in on the aftermath of the interview, and I realized the extent of the damage. The Greek was going to lose his job as a CBS analyst, and since he's up there in his sixties, there was an excellent chance that he'd never work in television again.

The shame of it all was that the Greek was going to have a national reputation as an idiot at best, a racist and a bigot at worst. I don't know where those stupid remarks he made came from, but they sure didn't sound anything like what I expected from Jimmy the Greek. The closest I could figure was that he had just erupted, with this weird stuff coming up out of his subconscious. It was the kind of thing that a lot of people either thought or said in privacy, or in their worst moments. The Greek just succumbed to lazy, sloppy, and *really* stupid thinking at the worst of times.

The situation was ludicrous in the first place. Who made Jimmy the Greek an authority on race and the Civil War era?

He's just a professional gambler, a kind of uncle figure for all the shmoozers in TV land. The Greek addressing those issues was like me getting up and telling an arms-control conference about nuclear warheads, explaining how they're those things on the ends of missiles that hit the ground and blow up. Who in his right mind is going to listen?

The Greek felt a little better after we talked, because I tried to understand. Although I found everything he said ugly and ignorant, I still supported the man, because I'd known him for years. My advice to Jimmy was to apologize if he felt that was in order and to let the controversy run its course. It could only hurt him to rehash and explain, over and over.

Jesse Jackson met with the Greek and came away saying that the Greek shouldn't be made a scapegoat. Jackson's point was that the Greek just said what a lot of people secretly believed. Jackson was moderate and reasonable. I know that some people thought he was just making a pitch to white voters in an election year. But his take was fundamentally accurate. When Gene Stallings, the head coach of the St. Louis Cardinals, had been the coach of Texas A & M, he told a reporter from *Sports Illustrated* that there was no room for blacks in his program. He was quoted in the magazine, and nobody ever made a big deal about it.

In television, shades of tokenism still exist. When a black director or commentator gets acknowledgment, it's often because of his race. Every successful black person has to deal with that kind of backhanded compliment, all the time. Jackson and Bill Cosby, who issued a statement similar to Jackson's, had a valid point. Punishing the Greek for his remarks didn't give society a clean bill or prove that racism didn't exist. I'm sure that a lot of folks with skeletons in their closets made the Greek their fall guy. They were right up front, leading the chorus of criticism.

A lot of people in our NBC production meeting were taking potshots at the Greek. At one point, Paul Maguire made a reference to some silly thing the Greek had said about the thickness of black athletes' thighs: "I want Ahmad to wear boxer shorts so we can see how thick his thigh muscles are."

"I've got a better idea," I said. "Why don't I wear some boxer shorts and kick your ass on TV."

Paul laughed louder than anybody else, but I think I stopped that vein of humor. I probably came off as being hostile, but I just didn't find the situation funny. After all, the Greek's entire career went down the tubes, and what he said was so derogatory that it preempted humor. We don't tell crude Polish jokes in production meetings, and we don't tell Jewish jokes, either. So I'd be damned if we were going to tell plantation jokes.

On the phone later, I tried to explain to Phylicia how wearing and sad it was to have racism thrown up in your face as an issue time and time again. Her reaction was comforting. She didn't even entertain the remarks of Jimmy the Greek. After all, it wasn't as if he were a scholar, or a man esteemed by society for his intellect. Nothing he said about anything except the point spread in a football game had any real credibility in Phylicia's eyes, and she isn't exactly the type who bets on football games. As far as she was concerned, he was just some professional gambler.

We had a nice set constructed for us in one corner of the end zone at Mile-High Stadium: a veritable glass cube, from which we'd throw the "NFL Live" show across the TV screens of America with special guest analyst Don Shula and our own commentator Gayle Gardner sitting in with Bob Costas.

Down on the field, Paul and I were trying to figure out what tack to take in our pregame remarks and at halftime. Usually, at halftime, we select two or three plays that represent some trend in the game and make remarks about them. But we knew that it was going to be awfully hard to come up with anything original. After all, besides the usual play-by-play and color commentator, we had Shula and Costas weighing in with their opinions.

"Let's show one of those one-yard gainers, some straight-ahead, off-tackle play," Paul suggested. "Let's put that up on the monitor, and after they show it, we can say, 'Yep, that's *football.*' "

I laughed. " 'That's right. They're playing football is what they're doing. Hit-'em-high, hit-'em-low football, folks.' "

"Imagine all the TV critics trying to figure out what we're doing."

"We can say, 'We've got game people, and we've got Shula, but me and Paul, we did something different. We showed you some *football.* Life in the trenches.' "

Paul rubbed his hands together. "And I can say, 'Yeah, but you know, I always wondered about those trenches. Where is that trench everybody talks about?' "

" 'I don't know. I was never near that stuff. I was flanked wide and I still am. I'm about as far away from that trench as I've always been—about fifteen yards. Except now I can't run into the huddle and say, "Good job, boys." ' "

"Do you think it might work?"

That's one thing I like about Paul: he's willing to try anything.

We went walking around the field. It was still two hours before game time on a sunny, gorgeous day for football. The halftime band was a crack outfit from some local high school. While they were practicing, I climbed up on the bandleader's podium and waved my arms around for a while.

Sometimes some of these young kids will recognize me, probably because they're fans of Phylicia and "The Cosby Show." Their eyes will get real big, and their mouthpieces might fall out for a second. I get a kick out of those cute kids, but I'll never understand how they sit there through the game wearing just those skimpy kilts and modest uniforms. They've got more discipline than half the players on the field.

Gayle Gardner was doing an interview with Cleveland's All-Pro noseguard, Bob Golic, at midfield. I hadn't seen Bob since the Pittsburgh–Cleveland game, when he'd busted his arm. I'd walked into the Cleveland locker room about midway through the second half in that game and Bob just sat there, looking disconsolate, knowing he was going to miss the playoffs. He said, "I keep thinking that it'll be all right if I just rub a little dirt on it."

That's a noseguard for you.

I walked by Bob and Gayle, who were talking about the job facing Bob's backup, Dave Puzzuoli. I said something under my breath, like "Cut the bullshit, Bob." Without missing a beat, he said, "Yeah, I guess there really *isn't* anything we can do to stop John Elway." ✗

Big games make me think of big games, and I guess my biggest game in some people's eyes was on December 14, 1980, Vikings against Cleveland, Metropolitan Stadium. It was the day of the Miracle Catch, the Hail Mary Pass, whatever you want to call it. To me, it was just the old Squadron Right, wing-and-a-prayer deal. In fact, I might never have made the Miracle Catch if I hadn't been so damned tired that I just trotted down that field like an old bloodhound on one last, vague scent after a long, long day in the field.

Let me back up.

The Vikings were playing for the NFC Central Division title, against the AFC Eastern Division Browns. We sure had our hands full—the Browns led by 13–0 when Kramer really came into his own, leading us ninety-eight yards and throwing a thirty-one-yard touchdown pass to Joe Senser. But we fell behind and trailed 23–9 with just five minutes left. Then the Texas came out in Kramer: he threw a seven-yard scoring pass to Ted Brown and then a twelve-yarder to me to tie the game. With fourteen seconds to go, the Vikings got the ball on our own twenty, with no time-outs left.

Kramer called a play, "Squadron Lateral," which left me baffled. Most "Squadron" calls mean that everybody goes deep and hopes to latch on to a prayer pass, and this sure was the right time for it. I lined up right and sprinted straight down the sideline at the snap. When I got about thirty yards downfield, I heard a massive roar of hope and figured the ball was in the air.

I turned it on, but at the same time I realized that there was no way Tommy could throw the ball from our twenty down to the other end zone, so I looked over my shoulder.

I was surprised to see Ted Brown getting run out of bounds up at the Cleveland forty-six. Kramer had thrown a ten-yard pass to Joe Senser, who broke a tackle by Charlie Hall and lateraled the ball to Brown. So that was the Squadron Lateral. Why didn't I know the play?

Let me back up even further.

On December 6, just a little more than a week before the Cleveland game, my father was driving my sister Mary and my twelve-year-old niece, Dhevin, home when his car skidded on the wet pavement, smashed through the guardrail, and flew off a bridge into Tacoma's Commencement Bay. Jerry Gibson, a shipyard worker, waded and swam through the frigid water to the car. Gibson's co-worker Bob Noel hooked a chain to the leaf spring of the car, and they hauled the vehicle up out of the bay.

They gave Dhevin mouth-to-mouth resuscitation and brought her around, and my sister was all right. But my seventy-three-year-old dad was rushed to St. Joseph's Hospital in critical condition.

When the local authorities called the Vikings with news of the accident, I flew out immediately to be with Dad. I missed a couple days' practice, but while I was in Tacoma, Dad started to come around. I left him to join the team for our important divisional game against Tampa Bay.

I made a good catch against the Bucs, but I got hit in the leg so hard that the shot actually knocked the wind out of me. I went home that night with swelling that went from the thigh to the knee and called my sister Clare in Tacoma. She told me that Dad had been revived by my visit. He was so proud of the fact that I had come home that he just kept telling her, "My Bobby, my Bobby came home. He was here . . . I knew he'd come."

That night, Dad had a relapse and his heart gave out.

The following week, I couldn't practice because of my injury.

I went into the Cleveland game hurt, and I didn't know any of the handful of special plays Bud had installed for the game. One of them was Squadron Lateral, which was how we ended up on the Cleveland forty-six with four seconds to play.

I was exhausted when I got back to the huddle and heard Kramer call, "Squadron Right." Our rookie guard, Brent Boyd, looked at me through his lineman's bird cage. "Now's the time to do something good," he said.

On the Squadron Right play, three of us—me and Sammy White and Terry LeCount—would sprint down the right sideline, and Kramer would throw the bomb, hoping that one of us could catch it.

I was dead tired, thinking there was no way I could run to the end zone, never mind catch a ball. But I took off at the snap, and just as I began to run out of steam I heard that telltale cheer. A little surge of adrenaline drove me on. But I was slowing up as I approached the end zone, and I was a hair late as Sammy, Terry, and a couple of Cleveland defenders jumped.

Thom Darden of the Browns tipped the ball.

Sammy made a grab at it but missed.

Another hand in that mess of bodies touched the ball.

I could hardly believe it. The ball came down, seams down, into my waiting hands. I took one backward step into the end zone, and the Vikings won their eleventh divisional title in thirteen years.

In one of the major newspapers the next day, the picture showed Matt Blair, All-Pro, with his arm around a grinning Bud Grant.

"Matt ran over to Bud right away, to get in the picture," Senser said later. "You can almost see that Bud's actually pulling away from him in the shot."

The Browns–Broncos game for the AFC Championship was a shoot-out that surpassed everybody's expectations. Two great quarterbacks, Kosar and Elway, went head-on and produced these numbers: Kosar was 26–41–1 for 356 yards, and Elway went 14–26–1 for 281 yards. In our Miracle Catch game against Cleveland, Kramer passed for 455 yards and completed 38 of 49 attempts.

Denver led by 21–3 at halftime, but the Browns produced four touchdowns in just over fifteen minutes to get back into the game. With the score tied at 31, and 5:14 left on the clock, Elway led his team seventy-five yards, culminating with a dump-off screen to Sammy Winder, who took the ball twenty yards for the go-ahead touchdown.

When Kosar brought the Browns up to scrimmage at their own twenty-five, with 3:53 left in the game, the stage was set for his answer to the Drive of '87. Kosar took the Browns all the way down to the Denver eight. He then called Earnest Byner's number, partly because the versatile Cleveland running back was having a great game, leading both clubs with seven receptions and sixty-seven rushing yards.

Byner took a hand-off, saw the middle congested, and broke for the outside to his left. He cut back inside, against the grain, and put a move on Jeremiah Castille. Byner was past Castille when the defensive back reached in and stripped the ball. It happened so fast that Byner just stood for a second, looking down at the ground, like a guy who'd just dropped a dime in the grass.

Castille pounced on the ball, and the Broncos held on to win. Earnest Byner, who had done so much to help bring the Broncos to the Championship game, slowly went to the sideline, where he sat alone, in shock. Now and then, a teammate walked by him with a comforting word or a pat on the shoulder in that last, agonizing minute of play.

I really felt for Byner, and I wish I could have told him how unreliable the game can be sometimes—how often things don't go exactly like you expected when you were a kid, fantasizing about last-minute touchdown runs or heroics before the home crowd. He might not have understood it then, but he would certainly understand it later in life.

After I made my Miracle Catch, a lot of people noticed that I didn't jump up and down, I didn't go hog wild in the celebration afterward. Wasn't I excited? they wondered. Didn't I feel the ultimate in emotion? they asked.

No, all I'd done was catch a football that won a game among the thousands of games that have been played and are going to be played in the NFL.

Sure I was happy, but I was dealing with a lot of other things.

I'd caught a ball, but I'd lost both of my parents in the span of a year. Was that supposed to be a good deal? Even with the national attention and a divisional title thrown in?

I remember sitting with my dad, how hopeless it was, because even as I found myself telling him things I'd never said before, I knew he was dying and that was why I was talking that way. I sensed that he didn't even want to go on—he'd lost my mother, after fifty years together. Why would anyone want to go on?

There was a view of downtown Tacoma from Dad's hospital window. I could see the harbor where the ships came and went. I saw the train station where I took my first ride to Seattle—a whole big new world for a little kid! I saw the complete route of the annual Daffodil Parade, and I remembered how proud Dad had been the year I was named grand marshal.

I held Dad's hand, for the first time since I was a little boy.

I could even see the field at Stadium High School, where I'd played so many games for Mt. Tahoma. I remembered how I used to be able to pick Dad out of the crowd during the second half, a dignified, erect man in a proper hat.

I wanted to tell Earnest Byner what I'd learned that cold day in Minneapolis, when I made the Miracle Catch against the Browns: the balls you catch, just like the ones you drop, they're only drops in a bucket, a big, big bucket.

With the Denver game I was finished for the year. A few weeks later, Doug Williams would play a sensational game to lead the Washington Redskins to a Super Bowl victory, and I felt his performance justified a lot of my opinions about football, about the ever-changing face of the game. Who knows—maybe the day will come when the NFL will have a black head coach, too.

But I was tired of football. As I pulled into the driveway of my home, I saw the figures through the kitchen window: Phylicia was standing there, holding Phylea. The soft lamplight fell on Phylicia's shoulders and hair. I had a surge of incredible happiness, a feeling of deep, deep security. I just love them both so much. I could think of only one problem in life—which one of those two was I going to hug and kiss first when I walked in the door?

And all the rest—all the rest is just football.

WARLORD OF MARS

based on the stories of

EDGAR RICE BURROUGHS

written by

ARVID NELSON

illustrated by

EVERTON SOUSA
LEANDRO OLIVEIRA
RAFAEL LANHELLAS
MARCIO ABREU
WAGNER REIS

colored by

THIAGO RIBEIRO
MAXFLAN ARAUJO
INLIGHT STUDIOS

lettered by

MARSHALL DILLON

collection cover by

JOE JUSKO

collection design by

KATIE HIDALGO

This volume collects issues 26-35 of Warlord of Mars by Dynamite Entertainment

 Visit us online at **www.DYNAMITE.com**
Follow us on Twitter **@dynamitecomics**
Like us on Facebook **/Dynamitecomics**
Watch us on YouTube **/Dynamitecomics**

This book is not authorized by Edgar Rice Burroughs, Inc.

 ®

Nick Barrucci, CEO / Publisher
Juan Collado, President / COO
Rich Young, Director Business Development
Keith Davidsen, Marketing Manager

Joe Rybandt, Senior Editor
Hannah Gorfinkel, Associate Editor
Josh Green, Traffic Coordinator
Molly Mahan, Assistant Editor

Josh Johnson, Art Director
Jason Ullmeyer, Senior Graphic Designer
Katie Hidalgo, Graphic Designer
Chris Caniano, Production Assistant

ISBN-10: 1-60690-500-7   ISBN-13: 978-1-60690-500-5   First Printing   10 9 8 7 6 5 4 3 2 1

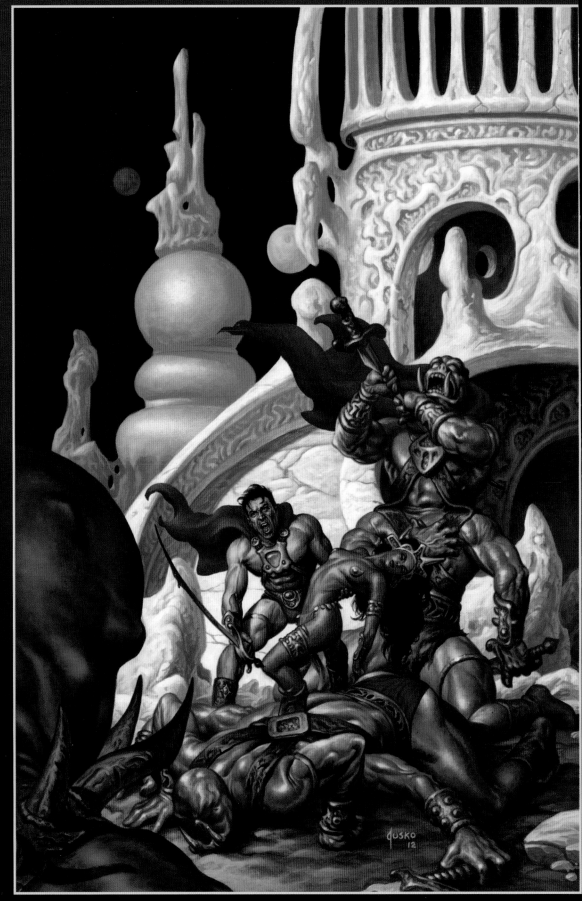

SAVAGES OF MARS PART ONE
THE GREEN MENACE • Issue #26 cover by JOE JUSKO

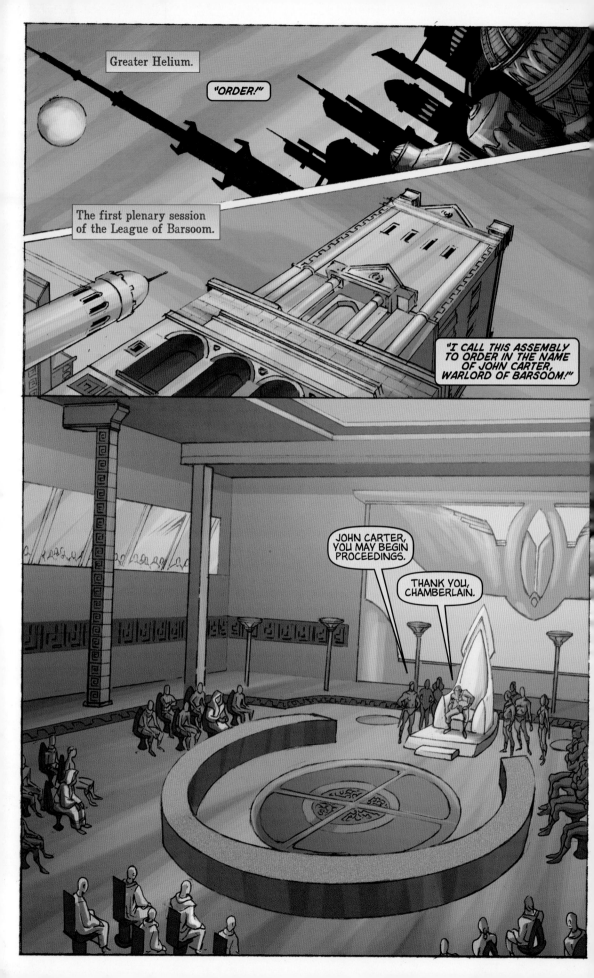

*The capital of the yellow people, located in Mars's arctic north. --E.R.B.

TARS TARKAS!

WHAT ON BARSOOM DO YOU THINK YOU'RE DOING?

DO NOT TRY TO STOP ME, JAWN KAR-TURR!

I DISGRACED MYSELF IN COUNCIL TODAY. I FAILED YOU, MY GREATEST FRIEND.

ALL THAT IS LEFT FOR ME NOW IS AN HONORABLE DEATH.

TARS, THIS IS COMPLETELY INSANE!

LISTEN TO ME, YOU THARK.

THERE MIGHT BE A REASON FOR ALL OF THIS.

THERE MIGHT BE SOMETHING GOING ON COMPLETELY OUT OF YOUR CONTROL MAKING YOU AND YOUR PEOPLE ACT THIS WAY.

THE YELLOW AMBASSADOR WAS RIGHT. WE GREENS ARE NOT CAPABLE OF BEING CIVILIZED.

MORE AND MORE, I FIND MYSELF CAUGHT UP IN FITS OF BLIND RAGE. AND IT'S ONLY GETTING WORSE.

I'M LOSING CONTROL OVER MY PEOPLE, OVER MYSELF, OVER EVERYTHING!

WHAT DO YOU MEAN?

I DON'T KNOW. BUT I HAVE A LEAD. A REAL THIN ONE, BUT IT'S WORTH FOLLOWING.

AS YOUR WARLORD--AS YOUR FRIEND, TARS TARKAS--I'M ORDERING YOU TO COMPOSE YOURSELF AND HELP ME GET TO THE BOTTOM OF THIS.

SAVAGES OF MARS PART TWO
WHITE LIES AND ALIBIS • Issue #27 cover by JOE JUSKO

Kadabra, capital
of Okar.

*The Barsoomian term for a pack of apts. --E.R.B.

SHE ACTED AS A COURIER BETWEEN THE PALACE AND THE CARRION CAVES, THE FORMER BREEDING GROUNDS OF THE APTS.

OH, I REMEMBER THE CAVES.

INDEED, WARLORD...

"ON ONE OCCASION, I MANAGED TO OPEN THE CHEST SHE ALWAYS BROUGHT BACK FROM THE CAVES."

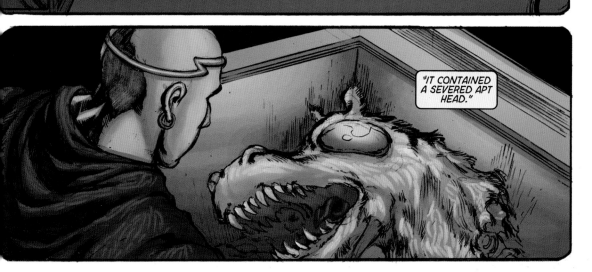

"IT CONTAINED A SEVERED APT HEAD."

SAVAGES OF MARS PART THREE
BLACK DAWN ▪ Issue #28 cover by JOE JUSKO

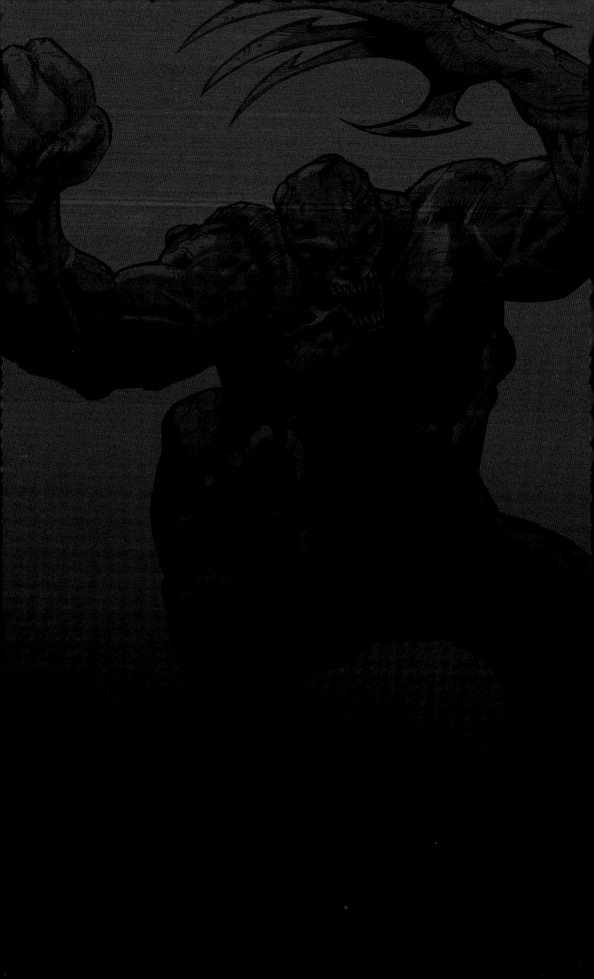

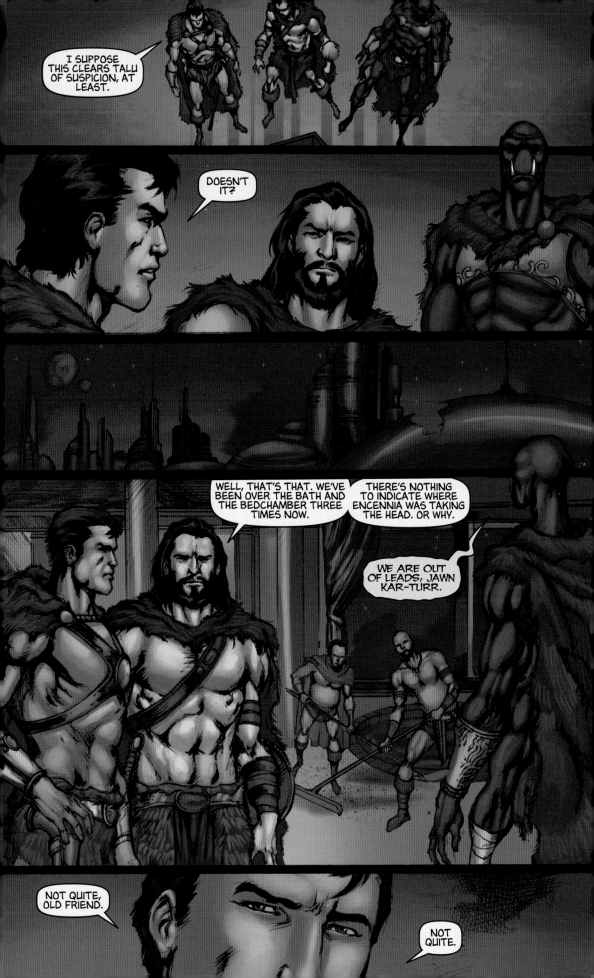

JOHN CARTER, MY HUSBAND, I'VE BEEN WORRIED TO DEATH! WHERE ARE YOU?

I'M IN OKAR, DEJAH THORIS.

OKAR! YOU'RE IN THE ARCTIC CIRCLE?

I'M SORRY I LEFT SO SUDDENLY, BUT I DON'T HAVE TIME TO EXPLAIN RIGHT NOW.

PLEASE, DID YOU HAPPEN TO COME ACROSS A WOMAN NAMED *ENCENNIA* WHILE YOU WERE A CAPTIVE OF SALENSUS OLL?*

*Warlord of Mars, vol. 3. --E.R.B.

YES, OF COURSE. OF ALL THE WOMEN IN HIS HAREM, SHE WAS THE WORST. AND THAT'S SAYING SOMETHING, BELIEVE ME.

DID YOU NOTICE ANYTHING STRANGE ABOUT HER, ABOUT HER DAILY ACTIVITIES? ANYTHING AT ALL?

WELL... YES, COME TO THINK OF IT. SALENSUS OLL HAD A PRIVATE ELEVATOR HE ALWAYS TOOK TO HIS CHAMBERS.

NO ONE ELSE WAS ALLOWED TO USE IT, BUT ONE TIME I SAW ENCENNIA ENTER WITHOUT HIM. TWO OF OLL'S GUARDS WENT WITH HER.

WERE THEY CARRYING A METAL CHEST?

YES, HOW DID YOU KNOW?

THIS IS VERY HELPFUL, DEJAH THORIS-- PLEASE GO ON!

I HAD FORGOTTEN ABOUT THIS, IN LIGHT OF EVERYTHING ELSE THAT HAPPENED. BUT AT THE TIME I DID THINK IT WAS ODD.

AND HERE'S THE ODDEST PART-- ENCENNIA ENTERED ON THE GROUND FLOOR, THE LOWEST LEVEL THE ELEVATOR REACHED. OR SO I THOUGHT.

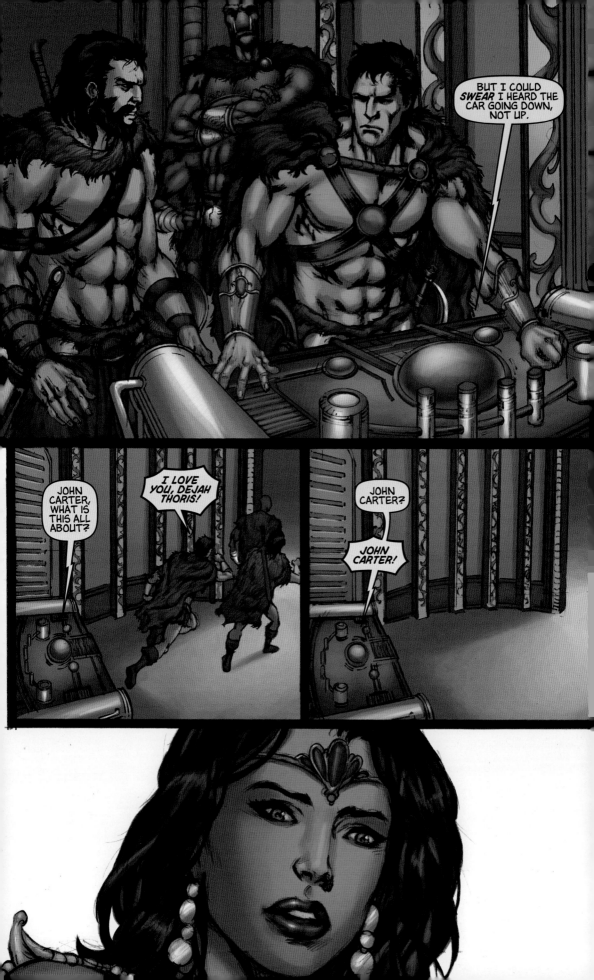

LOOK HERE--OTHER THAN SIZE, THE BRAINS OF GREEN BARSOOMIANS ARE IDENTICAL IN NEARLY EVERY RESPECT TO THE OTHER RACES.

Text: "Green specimen". --E.R.B.

GREENS HAVE AN ENLARGED MOTOR CONTROL AREA, BUT THAT'S NOT SURPRISING CONSIDERING THEIR EXTRA SET OF ARMS.

BUT GREEN BRAINS *ALSO* HAVE AN APPARENTLY VESTIGIAL GANGLION OF NERVES LOCATED BENEATH THE FRONTAL LOBE. WE HAVE NO IDEA WHAT PURPOSE IT SERVES.

WHAT OF IT?

LOOK AT THIS APT BRAIN-- IT'S THE EXACT SAME THING!

APTS HAVE THE EXACT SAME GANGLION AS GREEN PEOPLE!

Text: "Apt specimen". --E.R.B.

SO WHAT DOES IT MEAN?

MARIK, I HAVE NO IDEA.

BUT I'LL BET THE ANSWER TIES IN TO THE WAVE OF UNREST AMONG THE GREEN PEOPLE, TO WHATEVER SECRET OUR CONSPIRATORS ARE TRYING TO COVER UP.

KEEP LOOKING, THE ANSWERS HAVE TO BE--

WRASHH

SLASH!

RAH!

IT IS... NOT NATURAL, JAWN KAR-TURR. A LIFELESS, VAT-GROWN ABOMINATION.

NO ARGUMENT FROM ME.

SAVAGES OF MARS PART FOUR
YELLOW SUPREMACY ∎ Issue #29 cover by JOE JUSKO

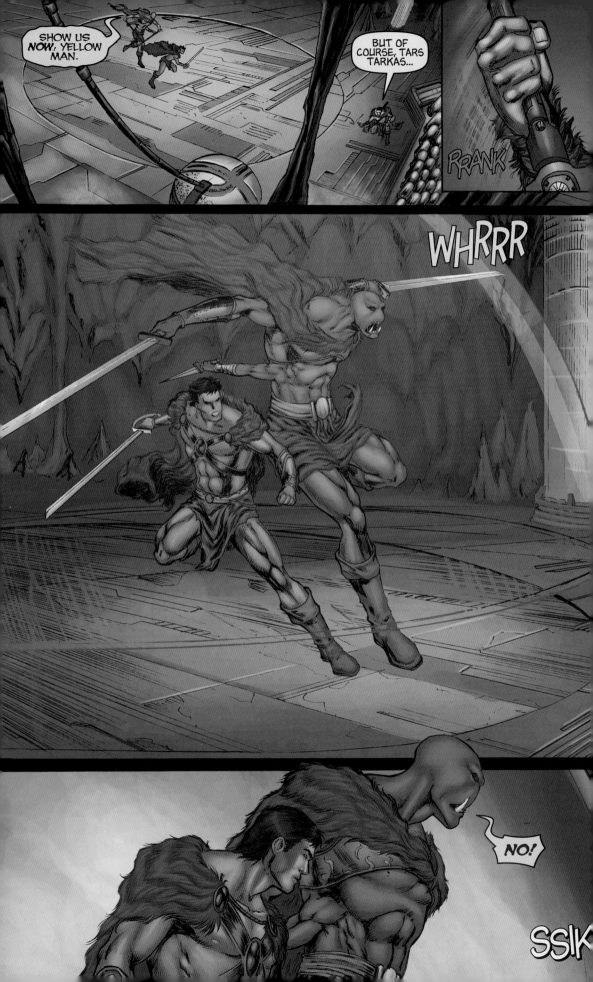

SAVAGES OF MARS PART FIVE
REDEMPTION IN RED ■ Issue #30 cover by JOE JUSKO

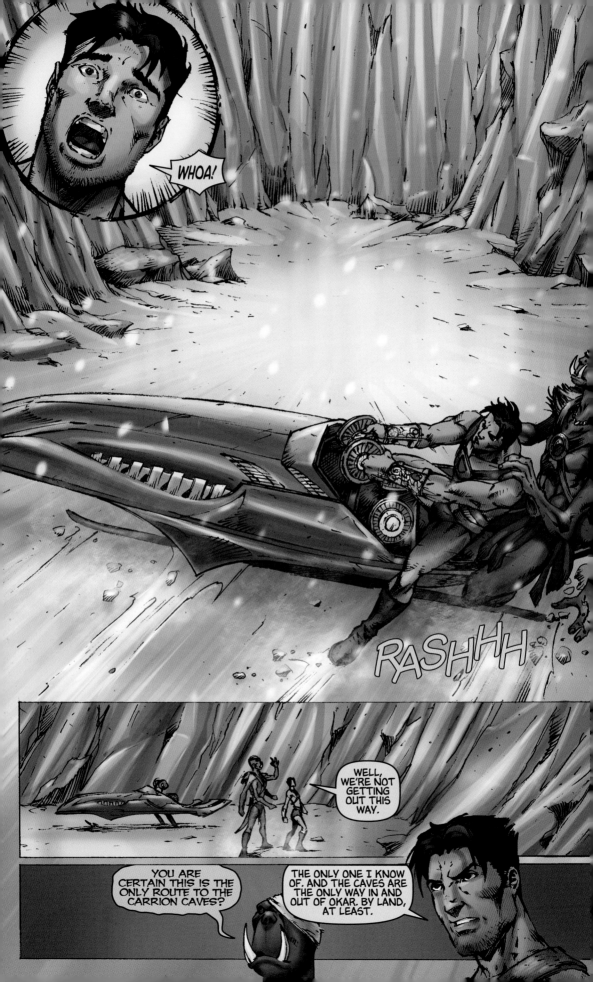

Greater Helium.
Several days later.

The Embassy of
the Allied Hordes.

CONGRATULATIONS,
SOLA!

IF NOT FOR HER, THE CONSPIRACY WOULD NEVER HAVE COME TO LIGHT. I'M JUST GLAD SHE DIDN'T DIE FOR NOTHING.

WELL. I HAVE SOME GOOD NEWS--TALU LEFT BEHIND A WEALTH OF DATA FROM HIS EXPERIMENTS. WE'RE GOING THROUGH IT NOW.

THE MIND-CONTROL GANGLION IN YOU GREENS DOESN'T DEVELOP UNTIL EARLY ADOLESCENCE.

WITH THE RIGHT THERAPY, WE MIGHT BE ABLE TO PREVENT IT FROM FORMING IN GOZAVA ALTOGETHER.

HER AND EVERY OTHER GREEN PERSON BORN FROM NOW ON.

GOOD NEWS INDEED, JAWN KAR-TURR.

JAWN KAR-TURR?

I... AM DEEPLY ASHAMED OF MY CONDUCT. WHEN WE WERE CAPTURED BY MARIK.

I HOPE YOU'RE NOT APOLOGIZING FOR ATTACKING ME, TARS. IT WASN'T YOUR FAULT.

NO. I MEAN BEFORE THAT, RIGHT AFTER I RECEIVED THE APT SERUM INJECTION.

I BROKE DOWN, JAWN KAR-TURR.

I... WEPT.

YOU MUST UNDERSTAND, ANY DISPLAY OF EMOTION IS *PROFOUNDLY* DISGRACEFUL FOR A THARK.

I TRUST MY UNSEEMLY LAPSE OF COMPOSURE WILL REMAIN BETWEEN US.

TARS. LISTEN TO ME.

BY WEEPING, YOU PROVED YOU GREENS ARE *PEOPLE*, THE SAME AS ANY OF THE OTHER RACES OF BARSOOM, CAPABLE OF ALL THE SAME EMOTIONS.

TYRANT OF MARS PART ONE
THE GUARDIAN TWINS ▪ Issue #31 cover by JOE JUSKO

Mars.

Barsoom.

The Red Planet.

For untold millennia, the Twin Spires of Greater and Lesser Helium have stood watch over the sprawling metropolises beneath them.

The Red Spire of Greater Helium...

...and the Yellow Spire of her sister city, Lesser Helium.

Together, they are known as the Guardian Twins.

John Carter now rules all Barsoom from the two Heliums, after a long and bloody war to unite the troubled races of the dying planet.

But no one, not even Helium's wisest scholars, knows who built the Guardian Twins, or why.

Their origin, like so much else on Barsoom, is shrouded in mystery.

A mystery John Carter is determined to uncover.

Greater Helium. The foot of the Red Spire.

JOHN CARTER!

YES. YOU'RE RIGHT, OF COURSE. JUST-- BE CAREFUL.

*Warlord of Mars, Book Two. --E.R.B.

OH, GRAND-FATHER. I THOUGHT I'D LOST YOU FOREVER...

THERE, THERE, DEJAH!

THERE THERE.

DO YOU REMEMBER THE LAST TIME I SAW YOU CRY? YOU WERE JUST A LITTLE GIRL...

YOU WERE OUT RIDING ON A THOAT, YOUR FAVORITE.

I HAD ALMOST FORGOTTEN! THE... THE ACCIDENT...

DID I EVER TELL YOU HOW TERRIFIED I WAS WHEN I FOUND YOU, ALL ALONE IN THAT CANYON? BUT *YOU* WERE FINE.

THE THOAT, ON THE OTHER HAND...

ITS LEG WAS BROKEN. IT WAS IN PAIN. YOU... HAD TO PUT IT DOWN, RIGHT THERE...

AH, DEJAH! YOU WERE INCONSOLABLE, YOU KEPT BAWLING *"I WISH IT WERE MY LEG! I WISH IT WERE MINE!"*

ALWAYS SO GENTLE, MY GRANDDAUGHTER. ALWAYS SO KIND.

"WELL
SAID."

TYRANT OF MARS PART TWO
THE LOST JEDDAK ▪ Issue #32 cover by JOE JUSKO

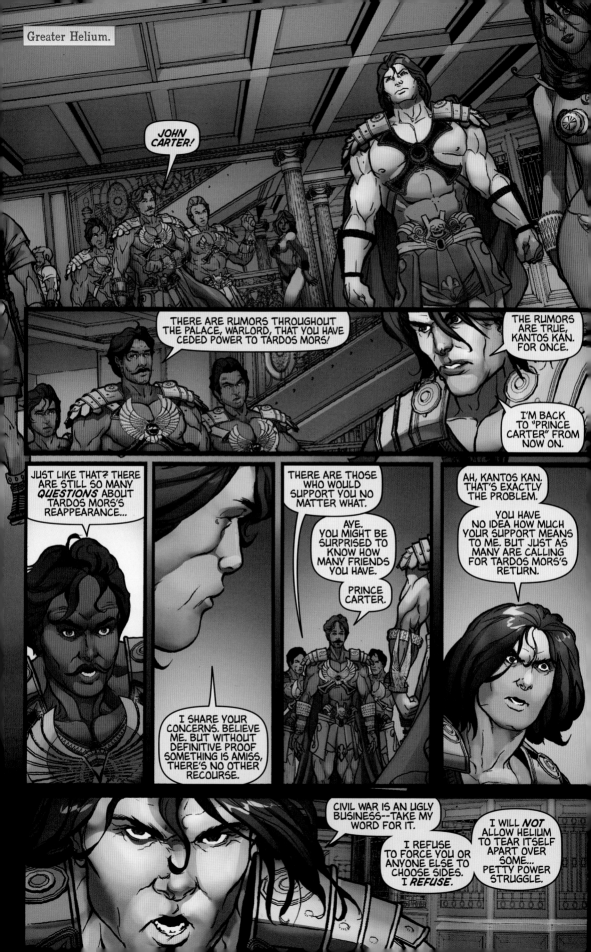

Greater Helium.

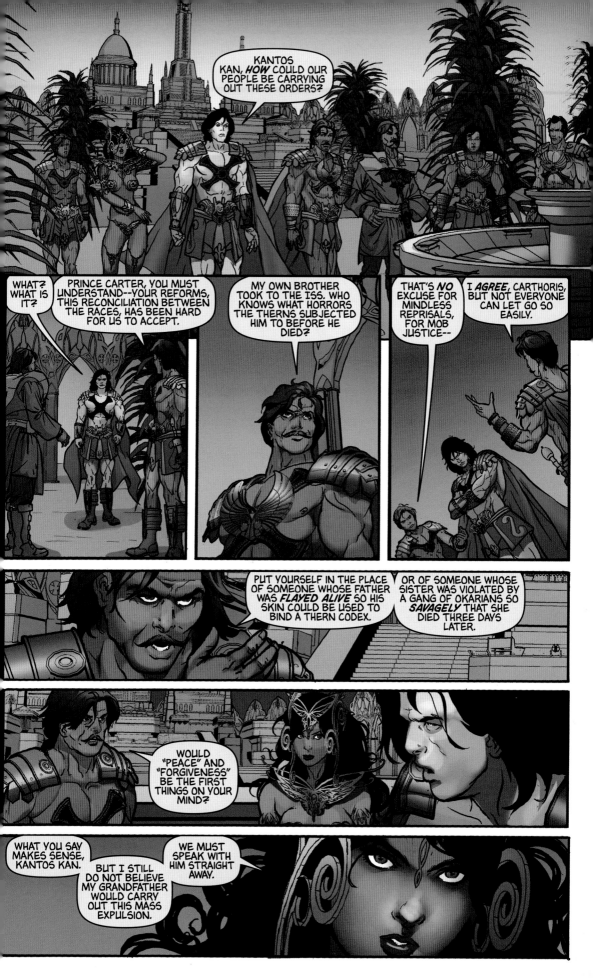

WHAT ABOUT THEM?

THE GREEN PEOPLE BEAR NO FAULT FOR THEIR CONDITION.

RRR.

YOU WERE THE ONE WHO DISCOVERED THEY WERE CREATED BY THE OKARIANS, AS BATTLE DRONES.*

BUT THEIR NATURAL PROCLIVITY FOR BLOODSHED AND RAPINE ARE GOING TO PROVE VERY USEFUL FOR WHAT'S TO COME.

AND WHAT'S TO COME, TARDOS MORS?

IN THE FULLNESS OF TIME, JOHN CARTER. IN THE FULLNESS OF TIME.

I DON'T KNOW *WHAT* TOOK PLACE IN THE TIME YOU DISAPPEARED, BUT MY GRANDFATHER WOULD *NEVER* CARRY ON LIKE THIS.

WHATEVER MADNESS YOU'RE PLANNING ENDS HERE AND NOW.

BE *VERY* CAREFUL, DEJAH.

YOU ARE MY GRANDDAUGHTER, BUT THERE IS A LIMIT TO MY PATIENCE.

Okar.
The Barsoomian North.

One week after his re-ascension, Tardos Mors assumes direct control of the Arctic wastes, using the savage Warhoon tribe as his enforcers.

MOVE FASTER, YOU TWO!

OR I'LL BREAK YOUR ARMS AND LEGS.

NOT SO HIGH AND MIGHTY NOW, ARE YOU?

WHY ARE WE DRAGGING THESE CRYSTAL-THINGS OUT OF THE RED SPIRE ANYWAY?

ALL I KNOW IS, THE SOONER WE'RE DONE, THE BETTER.

THE CRYSTALS FROM THE RED SPIRE WILL BE INSTALLED ON THE BATTLESHIPS BY THE END OF THE DAY, TARDOS MORS.

LIQUIDATED? FOR WHAT REASON?

INDOLENCE. CONTUMACY. PURE WHIM--WHATEVER YOU LIKE.

WE HAVE ABSOLUTE POWER NOW, ADMIRAL.

THAT IS WHAT MATTERS. THAT IS THE MESSAGE TO OUR SLAVES.

WE HAVE A SAYING ON EARTH, AFTER ALL--"AN ENEMY OF AN ENEMY IS A FRIEND."

HAH! I SHALL REMEMBER THAT.

VERY WELL, JOHN CARTER.

THE DARK LIBRARY IS LOCATED IN THE CRYPTS OF THIS PALACE. QUITE EASY TO REACH.

TAKE THEM NOW, WITHOUT DELAY.

I SUGGEST YOU BE QUICK ABOUT THIS. I CANNOT STALL FOREVER.

DO YOUR BEST.

AND WATCH YOUR BACK, HOLY ONE.

Okar.

"THIS IS IT, KANTOS KAN!"

The Dark Library
of the Holy Therns.

"BOTH DIED IN THE COURSE OF THE BATTLE, BUT THEIR VICTORY ENSURED THE SURVIVAL OF THEIR PEOPLE.

AND LISTEN TO THIS!

TO IMMORTALIZE THEIR TRIUMPH, THE OROVARS BUILT MONUMENTS ON THE SITES WHERE THEY LOST THEIR TWIN SAVIORS.

HUGE SPIRES--ONE RED AND ONE YELLOW.

THE RED AND YELLOW SPIRES OF HELIUM!

"THEY WERE HEROES."

SO IT WOULD SEEM, CARTHORIS.

THAT WOULD EXPLAIN THE STATUE IN THE YELLOW SPIRE--IT'S A MEMORIAL TO THIS "XARAYA" WOMAN.

BUT WHAT ABOUT THE RED SPIRE? THE CRYSTALS, THE SPIDER THINGS, THAT WEIRD SAC YOUR GRANDFATHER EMERGED FROM?

SOMETHING TELLS ME THE ANSWER IS IN HERE, JOHN CARTER.

THE RED VOLUME, THE ONE WE STILL HAVEN'T--

TYRANT OF MARS PART FOUR
PRIMAL SEED ▪ Issue #34 cover by JOE JUSKO

The catacombs of Xodar's palace.

"WITH MY PSYCHIC POWERS, THERE IS."

WE'VE ONLY GOT ONE SHOT AT THIS.

The Chamber of Issus.

ISSUS WILL PUT UP DEFENSES AS SOON AS SHE REALIZES I'M POKING AROUND IN HER HEAD.

Xodar's palace.

GAH!

The Chamber of Issus.

JOHN CARTER, ARE YOU ALL RIGHT?

ISSUS MIGHT HAVE BEEN NASTY, BUT SHE WAS CREATIVE.

I'LL GIVE HER THAT.

SHE TRAPPED ME IN A MENTAL RECONSTRUCTION OF THE TEMPLE OF THE SUN. WHERE SHE IMPRISONED *YOU*, DEJAH THORIS.*

AND SHE LOCKED THE INFORMATION WE'RE AFTER IN YOUR CELL.

JUST TO TAUNT ME.

*Warlord of Mars, Books 2 and 3. --E.R.B.

BUT *YOU* DISCOVERED SECRET ENTRANCE TO MY CELL! AND IT WAS *AFTER* ISSUS DIED, MEANING--

--MEANING THE JOKE WAS ON HER.

I WALTZED RIGHT ON IN.

SO YOU HAVE IT, THEN?

I'VE GOT *SOMETHING*...

"Xerius could still communicate telepathically, from his crystal matrix in the Red Spire.

"He advised the Orovars to press on and **annihilate** the black and yellow people.

"Some agreed with him, others did not. A bloody civil war followed, with the moderates winning out.

"The winners couldn't simply destroy the consciousness of Xerius, their savior...

"...but there had to be justice for the strife he had caused.

"In the end they sealed up the Red Spire and guarded it with those robotic spider-things."

TYRANT OF MARS PART FIVE
MARIONETTE ▪ Issue #35 cover by CLINT LANGLEY

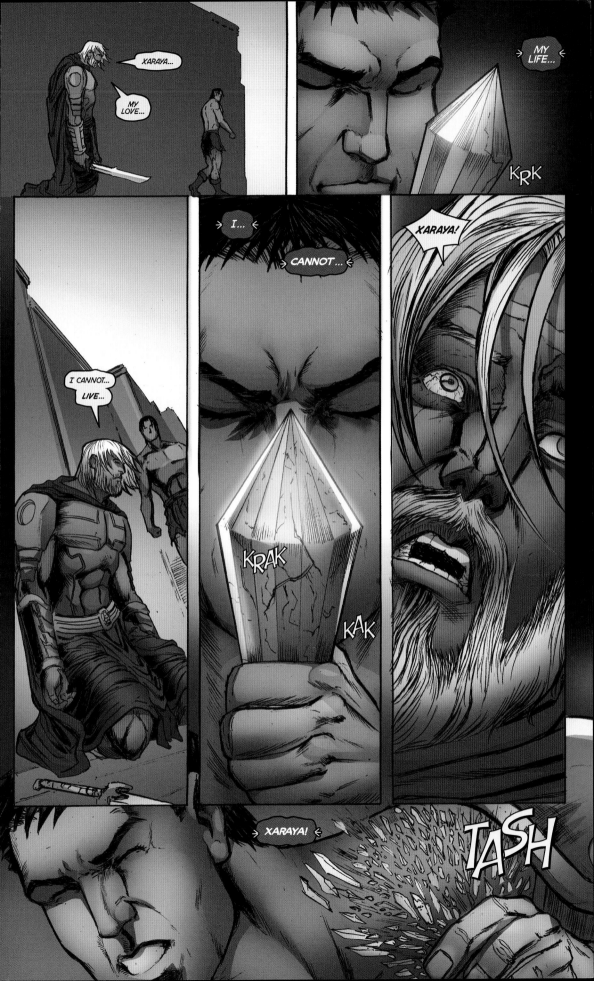

ALTERNATE
COVER
GALLERY

Issue #26 cover by LUCIO PARRILLO

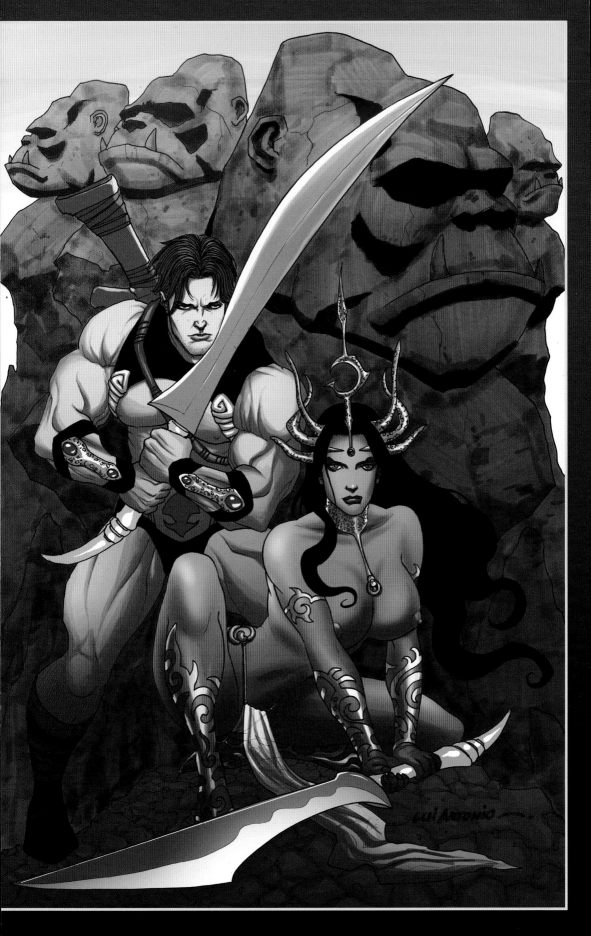

Issue #26 risqué cover by LUI ANTONIO   colors by ADRIANO LUCAS

Issue #27 cover by LUCIO PARRILLO

Issue #27 risqué cover by JOSÉ MALAGA   colors by ADRIANO LUCAS

Issue #28 cover by LUCIO PARRILLO

Issue #28 risqué cover by LUI ANTONIO   colors by ADRIANO LUCAS

Issue #28 risqué cover by WAGNER REIS   colors by ADRIANO LUCAS

Issue #29 cover by LUCIO PARRILLO

Issue #29 risqué cover by LUI ANTONIO   colors by VINICIUS ANDRADE

Issue #29 risqué cover by CEZAR RAZEK   colors by ADRIANO LUCAS

Issue #30 cover by LUCIO PARRILLO

Issue #30 risqué cover by JOSÉ MALAGA   colors by ADRIANO LUCAS

Issue #30 risqué cover by CEZAR RAZEK   colors by ADRIANO LUCAS

Issue #31 risqué cover by CARLOS RAFAEL   colors by ADRIANO LUCAS

Issue #31 risqué cover by WAGNER REIS   colors by ADRIANO LUCAS

Issue #32 cover by LUCIO PARRILLO

Issue #32 risqué cover by CARLOS RAFAEL   colors by ADRIANO LUCAS

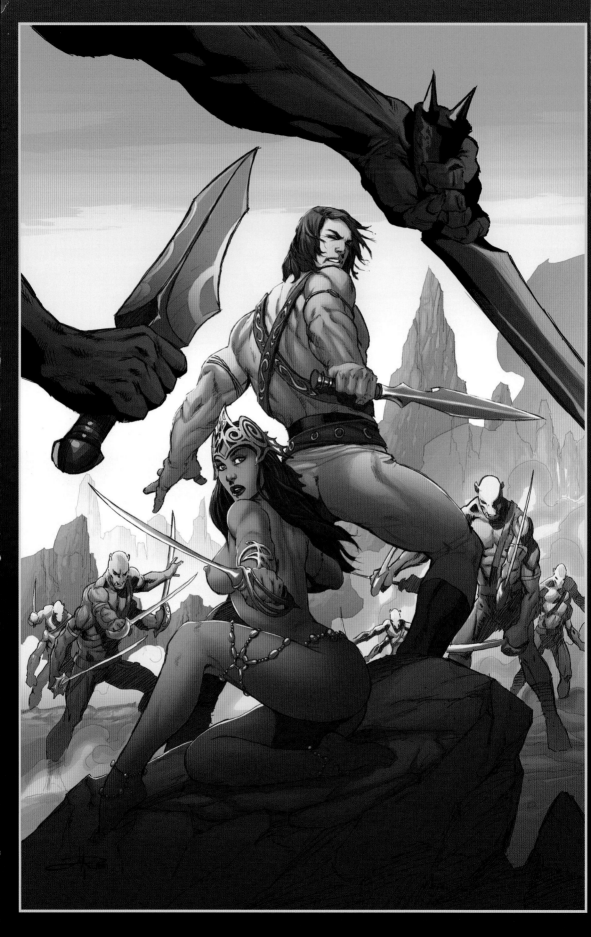

Issue #33 cover by LUCIO PARRILLO

Issue #33 risqué cover by CARLOS RAFAEL   colors by ADRIANO LUCAS

Issue #34 cover by LUCIO PARRILLO

Issue #34 risqué cover by CARLOS RAFAEL   colors by ADRIANO LUCAS

Issue #35 risqué cover by CARLOS RAFAEL   colors by ADRIANO LUCAS

EXPLORE DYNAMITE'S WORLDS OF MARS!
WARLORD OF MARS COLLECTIONS

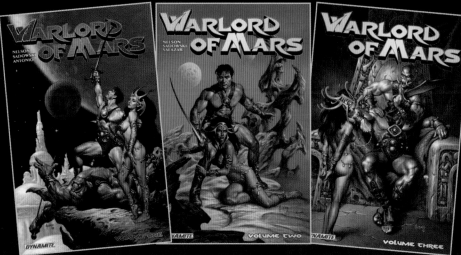

DEJAH THORIS COLLECTIONS

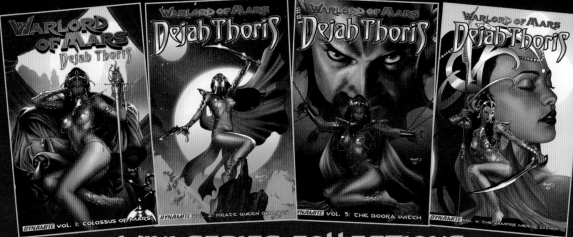

MINI-SERIES COLLECTIONS

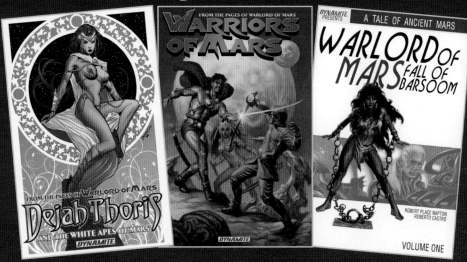

DYNAMITE. WWW.DYNAMITE.COM   TWITTER: @DYNAMITECOMICS   FACEBOOK: /DYNAMITECOMICS

DYNAMITE ENTERTAINMENT PRESENTS

Dejah Thoris
AND THE GREEN MEN OF MARS
VOLUME ONE: RED MEAT TRADE PAPERBACK

"Tells a wonderful yarn."
– Unleash The Fanboy

"Definitely pick it up for old-school, sword and planet adventure."
– Weekly Comic Book Review

"I want to see what's next!" – SciFi Pulse

The peace John Carter brought to Helium and Thark is new and fragile. On the eve of a Red & Green festival to balm age-old hatreds, Dejah Thoris is kidnapped. The ordeal triggers her lingering nightmares of abuse and helplessness at the hands of brutal Tharks. And the kidnapper is nightmare personified: Voro. He caters to a taste some green men never lost: the red meat of Helium women!

Collects issues 1-4 of the hit-series by MARK RAHNER and LUI ANTONIO, and features all of the beautiful covers by JAY ANACLETO as well as a risqué art cover gallery!

DYNAMITE.

Twitter f You Tube

Visit us online at www.DYNAMITE.com
Follow us on Twitter @dynamitecomics
Like us on Facebook /Dynamitecomics
Watch us on YouTube /Dynamitecomics